VENGEANCE FOR ALL THINGS

ANTHONY FLACCO

SEVERN RIVER

PUBLISHING

Severn River Publishing
www.SevernRiverBooks.com

ISBN: 978-1-64875-551-4 (Paperback)

ALSO BY ANTHONY FLACCO

The Nightingale Detective Series

The Last Nightingale

The Hidden Man

Vengeance For All Things

Gold in Peace, Iron in War

To find out more about Anthony Flacco and his books, visit

severnriverbooks.com/authors/anthony-flacco

Knock at his study, where they say he keeps
To ruminate strange plots of dire revenge;
Tell him Revenge is come to join with him,
And work confusion on his enemies.

—William Shakespeare

Before you embark on a journey of revenge, dig two graves.

—Confucius

1

BELOW THE STREETS OF SAN FRANCISCO

* July 17th, 1916 *

IT WAS DEATHLY SILENT in the old bank vault, save the forlorn plink of water dripping from a nearby pipe. Amber light from two fat candles threw shadows in pairs across the steel walls. The vault's sole occupant kept the silence, a thin slip of a man producing no more sound than scratches and scrapes from the bolts, washers, and bits of barbed wire he carefully dropped into a short steel pipe standing on the table before him. To ensure a thorough mix, he dropped in precisely a dozen pieces of each type of shrapnel before topping them with a layer of gun cotton and black powder before returning for the next go-round. Layer after layer, the mixture rose to the end of the pipe, the last one protruding just a bit at the end. Buda considered patience to be the most powerful tool any elite soldier could possess. It was as vital as his backbone.

Next step: gently, gently, press it all down to compact the contents. Time to stare into the face of Death once again. Of course, the art of "packing the pipe" began with the avoidance of accidental ignition, but properly packed, a bomb's moment of glory boiled down to one's skill at guaranteeing the blast sent its full array of red-hot shrapnel evenly in all directions. A democratic wave of death. He was comforted to know, in this regard, a good bomb was nothing if not perfectly fair.

His foldable worktable was set with four more nearly completed bombs. They would all function as designed, but they were not as powerful as the new one. His newest creation was in the hands of another, now, scheduled to debut next week.

No. There before him were not merely powerful pipe bombs, they were little makers of death and blood-curdling screams built for associates from Chicago who hungered to deliver important messages. To achieve this, the Chicago brothers required his expertise above all others. His chest swelled with pride, even in these humble conditions. Yes, him: Mario Buda—Bomb Maker Nonpareil.

For the love of symbolism, Buda had cut each bomb's pipe to the length of an Egyptian royal cubit, meaning just over twenty and one-half inches by Western standards. But Buda held Western standards in contempt and found it ridiculous that the closest that inferior system could come to expressing the length of the royal cubit—successfully used for many centuries—was an ungainly *twenty-point-sixty-one inches.*

Thus his work was perfect on the face of it: to bring ancient Egyptian wisdom and knowledge down on the heads of the same societies now destroying the ruins of that great civilization. Bomb them with royal cubits.

Gifts from the worldwide anarchist movement.

On the rare occasions when Buda drank enough and was in the company of trusted fellow anarchists, he held forth on bomb making as a happy meditation upon instant destruction. Done right, the enemy is eliminated and you move to the next problem; done wrong, your problems are over.

Of course, alcohol was anathema down here. He permitted himself nothing to dull his concentration. He maintained tight focus despite air gone stale after hours of exacting labor. His body heat had warmed the tiny room to the point of sending sweat beads into his eyes. Every drop was potentially lethal if it blurred his vision enough to make him connect the wrong wires. He wiped his forehead with the damp cloth again and then bore down on the task.

Mario Buda was not cautious out of fear, rather out of pride. The thirty-two-year-old bomb maker valued his reputation among the worldwide anarchist cause, where he was known as a highly effective manufacturer of innovative explosive devices. In truth, he valued this reputation more than his life.

He had read somewhere, "Death comes to everyone, but a legacy of respect will endure." Buda had struggled for years in his potentially lethal endeavors to earn the respect paid to him. He so valued his place among other exalted anarchists that his standard line, "I'd rather die than fail," was used as a joke but was true, nonetheless.

And because Buda was a professor of caution, he had selected this assembly site for the vault's thick steel walls. The entire bank had been buried back in 1906 when a ten-foot fissure opened beneath it during the Great Earthquake. Later, when the vault door was uncovered and the vault emptied, authorities determined the damage around it too great to risk digging it up. Within months of the quake, new dirt was trucked in and filled over, soon followed by new buildings atop the wreckage, and the old bank vault was forgotten.

But Buda had workmen on loan from the great Luigi Galleani, the firebrand Italian anarchist. Galleani required the help of Buda's specific skills, and in payment, a group of Galleani's men came off whatever job they were working nearby and used old city maps to scour the quake zone and locate this vault. The experienced digging teams then hand-dug a tunnel from the inside of a standup sewer pipe straight to the vault itself. The first time he entered, he measured the tunnel's precise length and was thrilled to find the miners unknowingly made their tunnel twenty cubits long.

The thick walls were more than enough to conceal the explosion if his work went wrong. After all, just because it never had before... As a lab or as his tomb, the place would preserve his status among his comrades by concealing the failure. If his road came to an end here, his shredded remains would congeal against the walls while the vault continued its forgotten existence.

A martyr is not dead if his comrades cheer his name. Buda practically sang it under his breath.

The pipe sections were extra thick, designed to bear up under great pressures. As bomb skins, they also added fractions of a second to the time required to blow through them, helping to concentrate the blast. The resulting pressure wave would be so intense, solid metal would react as a crystal—shattering into fragments, then joining the murderous shrapnel cloud.

And now after his long night of dangerous labor, Buda's wiry frame slumped with fatigue. His thin fingers had grown shaky with the hours of precision work. He sat back and regarded the table's contents. Of course his labors had been grueling, but hardly for nothing. Hardly for nothing.

Each of these sweet *bambinos* would wake up an entire neighborhood. A very large neighborhood indeed. The thought of it made Buda feel like he had instantly gained ten kilos of solid muscle and half of a royal cubit in height. He felt himself standing tall among fearsome men.

It was a grand feeling. Oh, it was good indeed.

The home of San Francisco luminaries Harold and Felicity Saunders was empty of Mr. Saunders on this morning. He invented an early meeting at his men's club to dodge the monthly breakfast meeting of his wife's suffragette group. Felicity Saunders was the group's organizer and had been since forming it a few years before. She filled the lower half of the house every month with local suffragette women, some prominent citizens and others who were just workers with low-level jobs. She routinely maintained seating for twenty in the dining room, and this morning all the seats were filled while a few more women stood back against the walls where they could listen in.

Just as Mrs. Saunders stood up to tap her glass and bring the room to order, one last attendee hurried in, a young woman wearing a leather outfit such as a bicyclist might wear to protect herself from falls on the cobblestone streets. Her hair was flattened by the leather helmet she carried, and her cheeks were bright with windburn.

"Sorry, everyone!" she called over the buzz of conversation. "Apologies to all." Nobody but the hostess seemed to notice.

Felicity Saunders went ahead and tapped her glass again, a bit harder this time. Everyone quieted down half a notch.

"All right, ladies, with the arrival of our *almost* tardy sister here, I think we can begin." She smiled to take the strength out of the rebuke. "Let's bring the San Francisco branch of the American Suffragette Movement to order."

The young female spoke up, "My apologies again for being late, but if it's all right, I'd like to begin this morning by talking about the Women's Club of Palo Alto. The *Chronicle* has reported the women there completed their fundraising, and after years of work, they're ready to build a dedicated clubhouse! San Francisco is so much bigger, why can't we do that?"

"We have plenty of places to meet in this city," Saunders replied, using a smile and tone of voice indicating her intention to be patient with idiots.

"Yes, but meeting in a home is a bit informal, isn't it? Wouldn't we have greater credibility and visibility if we had our own offices?"

Felicity glared at the young woman, name of Vinny or Vinegar or something. She rarely showed up at the meetings unless she had an argument to start. "Do you have any other order of business this morning?"

"Well, yes, in fact I do," persisted the young woman. "Why is this group moving so slowly in general, and not just on a meeting house, either? Do we all hold the opinion that women's issues are somehow less important in California?"

Saunders hammered on her glass with the teaspoon again, harder this time. "Not again! You are not going to take over another meeting! You are not the only person with concerns!"

"Plenty of us have concerns!" one woman chimed in.

"All sorts of them, and we got here on time," added another. The rest of the women generally nodded in agreement.

Saunders repressed the urge to sneer at the impertinent visitor and ran her tongue over the roof of her mouth as if to savor a lozenge made of smugness. "We all know you skip half our meetings. Still, whenever you deign to appear, you attempt to make the event your own."

A mutter of resentful agreement went through the room.

The woman in leather stood still. "I just think we could do a lot more. Other cities in other states, women have the vote. They have it all over the country now. Aren't we all embarrassed for our city to be shown up that way?"

"That's enough!" shouted Mrs. Saunders, all decorum gone. "We are up against a thousand-foot wall of male supremacy here. Every gain we can make is meaningful!"

"Good enough. Except what gains would that be? Here in San Francisco, I mean?"

This was too much for the room. The entire group rose as one and shouted protests over this insult to their sincerity. Saunders shouted over the din, "If you want credibility with a group of women, why don't you dress like one?"

The entire group burst into laughter at that, trying to turn the verbal barb into a group weapon and force it into the young woman's brain. But the young woman appeared to have a ready response. She gave the entire room a cheery wave and walked out.

Saunders called after her, "Don't leave your bicycle on our porch!"

The rest of the room burst into the sort of laughter so often employed by the righteously vindicated. But the impertinent visitor was already gone, so nobody could tell if she heard the rebuke or not.

Buda's work was nearly done. Exhaustion gripped him. Still, he couldn't help noticing an increase in the sound of dripping water. The pleasant *poik...poik...poik...*of droplets was now replaced by a louder sound, far louder in fact, more like a curbside horse relieving itself on the bricks. Within seconds, that sound expanded again and became a stable full of draft animals urinating in unison.

A thin stream of water or something liquid ran into the vault, gathering on the dirty steel floor as brash as an unwelcome in-law. The puddle rapidly grew.

Water, dynamite. Frustration and rage filled bomb maker Buda. Bile backed up into his throat. The diggers were competent enough to get him here but never really finished off their work. They just stopped. What for?

Laziness? Sheer incompetence? Experience had taught him even passionate supporters of the cause could be stupid beyond belief.

Or was it sabotage? The deadline for the San Francisco mission was fast approaching, and it was beginning to seem as if the secret organizers might have failed to allow for possible leaks, for failures such as this. Maybe no act of sabotage was present at all? Nothing beyond the workers' casual disregard for the consequences of their work upon him, the guy getting a favor from their boss.

Or maybe just an unintentional aggregate of tiny mistakes, mostly unnoticed, errors made by people with good intentions and no training. In this case, riding in on the foul water pouring into the vault door.

He unfolded a large canvas bag and quickly loaded the bombs into it, carefully adding all the loose parts. Rage filled him while he imagined himself trying to explain this to his Chicago clients. Nobody was allowed to have problems when it came to deadlines. It was considered disrespectful to even mention any sort of excuse. To fail to meet a deadline and plead difficulties was to call the others fools for trusting you, since your primary obligation was to find ways around obstacles, no matter what they were. *Your failure is an affront to them.*

His chest ached for retaliation. Perhaps in the form of something the size of a lunch pail waiting outside the proper doorway, as a reminder: *Shoddy work is not permitted.*

But no. His hands were tied. He owed the man too much, even though Galleani only provided the labor and tools for the tunnel after Buda constructed and delivered Galleani's so-called "Very Special Bomb." A brand-new type of explosive device with a blast wave that could be focused in *one direction*. It was a piece of magician's work pulled from stolen military schematics, and it could only exist in that gray zone between the scientific method and flights of fancy. Buda was captivated within moments of first seeing the plans...

And so for now he would just have to make this all work and move on. The final act of connecting the detonators could be done later, maybe on-site, by him or any of his fellow fighters. Of course, none of that mattered unless he got everything out on time.

He tied off the loaded bag and gave a last look around. All done here.

Safe to depart. The air had gone foul, anyway. He took the last breathable gulp and hefted the bag onto his back to keep the contents dry. He made his way down the tunnel and back to the sewer, up the ladder, and to the manhole cover. Desperation gave him strength to slide it aside enough to squeeze through.

He emerged from the manhole like a gasping swimmer coming up for air into bright morning light. He was in an alley just off of the heavily trafficked Market Street, pulling his bag up with him like the farthest thing from Santa Claus there could ever be. A few people stared at the wiry fellow while he emerged from below the street with his heavy bag of objects, but each witness was absorbed in personal concerns. They remained polite, continued in their own directions, and did nothing about the strange behavior.

Buda took in a deep breath. The air up topside blended with engine fumes and suspended particles of horse manure, but at least it contained oxygen. *Mother of God, even this rotten city air is better than what I ended up breathing back in that vault...*

He wondered, could anyone ever doubt his sincerity if they ever learned of his dedication on this night? Surely not. His head swam under an overdose of oxygen.

In the next moment, in spite of Buda's lack of respect for all things Divine, he was smiled upon by the Dark Angel of Timing, the secret of comedy and some say of life, when he heard the water pipe rupture with a terrible metallic shriek down below street level.

This was followed by the unmistakable sound of gushing water, as if a flash flood was crashing through the tunnel. He knew his bank vault-slash-bomb lab was being lost to the cause at that moment. He had made it out at the last instant.

He stood in the early morning light and took another deep breath with a mixture of relief and a rush of shame. The Bomb Maker Nonpareil was a man of action, not words. He certainly hadn't broken the pipe, but nevertheless responsibility for the tunnellers' incompetence rested on his shoulders. If something like a ruined assembly room caused his competence to be called into question by the Chicago money men and their bosses, or worse, by Galleani and his unbelievably wealthy supporters, Buda's reputation would be permanently stained.

And who would Mario Buda be without that reputation? Nothing more than a boring working man pissing his life away while he endured every working hour for the sake of quitting time. Maybe a glass of wine after work, maybe a warm companion, female in his case, thank you very much. But also, maybe a cold companion who resents you because you are a boring working man pissing his life away.

His full strength returned after several deep breaths of clean air, and now his brain felt like it was revolving in his skull while a realization began to form. It arrived complete. In it, he saw the folly of having set out to do his bomb construction in a buried vault in the first place. The safety reasons for a vault were obvious enough, but the way he saw it, Life or Fate or the nonexistent God had just sent him a warning: it was unwise to declare his lack of faith in himself by using a vault, because the idea that he needed a vault in the first place was self-defeating.

Caution is one thing; self-doubt is another.

And with that thought, his decision was made. For next week's larger creations, he resolved to break with tradition and risk working in the comfort of his hotel room.

True, a few years ago, he would have roundly condemned the ethics of such a thing. Back when he was still an idealistic punk. But in the days since then, he had come to feel history coursing through his veins, and more so with every new device. He could only hope Mr. Big-Deal Galleani had the overall mission under control despite the million small devils of bad luck.

His intention at the moment was to blend in with the pedestrians and cross over from the alley, then head up Market Street and make his way out of the neighborhood. But just as he stepped off the tall curb, a shiny new Harley-Davidson motorbike flashed past him and nearly ran over his foot.

Buda gasped in shock and instinctively recoiled, clutching the bag to his body with too much force and jostling the bombs. He heard them clank hard against one another.

He held his breath, flexing for death. And yet, in the next moment...he was still there.

He gasped in relief like a man saved from drowning. A strong enough impact could have detonated any one of the bombs, thus all of them, leaving Buda in the wrong time and place, opportunity wasted, friends from Chicago seriously disappointed.

A sterling bomb maker's reputation ruined. That most of all.

His blood turned to lava. *Who was on that motorbike?* The audacious rider wore an aviator's leather helmet, with a full leather riding suit and thick boots. The bike looked new, still painted in the factory standard of battleship gray. There was nothing more to identify it than a brick-red license plate bolted to the front fork. He had caught a flash of double digits painted in white, but it was gone before he could read them.

And on most any other day, he would have loved to find out who owned that motorbike and wire a special surprise to the gas tank that would flatten the fool and wake up the snakes.

But no. Everything had to go right if the plan was to have any effect at disrupting America's entry into the great war in Europe. No distractions. Buda's correspondence sources assured him Washington was secretly buzzing with talk of mobilizing and shipping out. The task before him and his fellows was no less than that of moving a mountain.

He felt haunted by the knowledge of the horrors occurring in the battlefields of Verdun at that moment. Creating thousands of casualties with every passing day. The phenomenon of poison gas was rolling over the trenches on both sides, boiling skin and frying lungs.

For Mario Buda, that fact alone was more than enough to justify every bomb he built. *Make the civilians see the mayhem they pay for overseas when it visits them at home.* Let them decide if they want more.

Homegrown attacks were going to give the arrogant and soft Americans a taste of what they would cultivate if they joined in on the idiocy of this war. That urgent message would be brought to them on this occasion by Mario Buda, Bomb Maker Nonpareil, deliverer of death and blood-curdling screams.

2

ON THE SAN FRANCISCO STREETS

* Immediately Following *

THE GRAY HARLEY-DAVIDSON shot westbound on Market Street and took a hard right turn north onto Leavenworth. The rear tire hit a pile of horse flop and skidded, sending the bike and its rider into a full spinout and stalling the engine. A nearby surrey rocked back on its wheels and nearly dumped the driver when its draft horse panicked and reared, whipping the air with its hooves.

The leather-clad rider instantly stomped the kick starter, refired the engine, and peeled away. The powerful motorbike left a dark rubber streak on the cobblestones. The reason for the motorcyclist's speed now appeared when a motor truck came barreling in pursuit, tires squealing while it rounded the corner and pressed hard after the big bike.

Both vehicles cheated death at every second while they roared up Leavenworth and threaded through traffic, but the motorcycle was far more adept at quick maneuvers. The truck repeatedly forced pedestrians to leap out of the way.

Motorcycles were still a new sight on city streets, and a lot of people saw them as little more than noisy devices for scaring draft animals and causing traffic nightmares. This time, everybody was lucky. Horns honked, horses screamed in protest, drivers shouted, pedestrians gawked, but the traveling show was too swift for observers to do more than watch. Nobody showed much interest, anyway. Pedestrians already had to contend with the chaos and stench of animal traffic along with powered vehicles and their clouds of unbreathable fumes. Abandoned recklessness such as this was merely another strange display in the proud flesh of an expanding city.

Inside the pursuing truck, three young men crowded on the front bench seat. "There she is!" shouted the one in the middle. "She just passed that garbage wagon!"

"Step on it!" added the one on the passenger side.

"What if it's a man?"

"What kinda man? I tell you, that's a girl on that damned motorbike!"

"I never seen a girl ride anything that big."

"You just did! Handles it like she thinks she's hot shit, too!"

"Come on, she's way too light to stay on top of it if the tires lose their grip!"

"So put her in the dust. Maybe change her mind about riding the thing."

But the motorcycle and its rider continued to elude them. After seven long blocks, the Harley reached Sutter Street with the pursuers two blocks behind. The rider leaned into a hard left turn, which enabled her to dart into a service alley for the Carlyle Hotel and shut the engine down.

Two seconds later, the truck sped by without slowing before it disappeared into the chaotic street traffic. The rider waited a few more moments, then fired up the big bike's engine and held it to a quiet, deep idle, slowly moving several more doors down the alley and pulling behind a low wall.

Vignette Nightingale, age twenty, decided it was safe to put a bootheel to the Harley's kickstand and climb off. As if the failed suffragette meeting hadn't gone badly enough, she had also managed to pick up a pack of angry fools on her way home.

Vignette was not the type to ask, "Is it me?" She already knew it was.

She carefully removed her leather pilot's helmet, just in case she needed to blend into a crowd of what she thought of as "normals." Vignette kept her hair short, so once she had the helmet off, all she had to do was part her locks with her fingers to look more or less like one of them.

She ran a rueful gaze over the new Harley. The motorbike was proving to be a mixed blessing. It was supposed to be a last-ditch effort to escape the cold depression that gripped her the day Shane was killed. He had been her senior by two years, and years ago he transferred his love of motorcycles to her. All he ever seemed to want was to ride his bike and serve on the same police force where their adoptive father once served. He had to take the exam three times before he passed. Luckily for him, motorized escapes had recently become a problem for the city's mounted officers; he gained acceptance based on his impressive motorbike skills.

And it was his motorcycle that got him killed for the unspeakably stupid reason that a truck driver made a sudden turn in front of him. Shane was one of the first motorcycle patrolmen in the city, until a drunken driver turned directly in his path.

If you believed the official story.

Of course, Vignette did not, but as Randall warned her, with a drunk driver there was nothing to investigate. People drink, and some of them cause tragedies. Nobody seemed to know what to do about it.

The only cautionary message she took from the wrenching loss was to get her own bike and watch out for trucks. Shane had already taught her to ride, so she survived the day of his funeral by changing clothes as soon as they got back home and then going back out to blow her savings on the Harley.

She loved the feeling of power and freedom that rode with her even though the big bike was dragging problems behind it like a cloud of fumes. This was the third time in a week male drivers noticed her and took umbrage at the sight of a female on a powerful motorcycle.

Modern society accepted the swirling skirts of a Gibson Girl as a symbol of "emerging young female independence," but somehow an actual young female zipping in and out of traffic was an affront to men everywhere. The first few times men on the street took objection to her, they reacted with mere catcalls. But today's attackers raised the ante when they tried to run her off the road.

Face it, she told herself, *you're too easy to spot*. The leather helmet didn't cover her face, and her features were delicate and feminine even without adornment. It was not helpful that she also refused to use goggles. She could get used to having watery eyes while she rode, but she couldn't stand the feeling of having anything over her eyes. Too many things had been used to cover her eyes before she escaped St. Adrian's.

Nothing goes over the eyes.

She knew there were men who felt no need to attack a woman over her choice of transportation or her personal style. But not only were there never enough of such men around, she knew no way to tell which would take offense to her and which would not.

As much as possible, she avoided males altogether.

She sat quietly for nearly an hour, a hidden set of eyes and ears in the clang of an urban morning. The truck passed by out on the street several more times to recheck the chase route before the men gave up and retired from the hunt. At last she judged enough time had passed to prove her escape successful. Time to go look for problems of a more interesting sort. For this operation, she would be avoiding everybody: men, women, children, dogs. Anything with eyeballs.

She donned the helmet, then refired the engine and headed off toward Russian Hill, one of the crookedest streets in the country. Her destination was close enough to be there in minutes, and this time she traveled the whole distance without interference. She parked the bike on Leavenworth and made her way uphill on foot to her target for this mission, the same brownstone castle she departed under censure earlier that morning.

One glance confirmed her plan had worked. Nobody was around at all. She had made the meeting unpleasant enough for the women to want to get it over with and go home. By now, all the motorcars and carriages belonging to the suffragettes were absent from the street. The front was still fenced and gated, however, and this time, Vignette's visit didn't involve permission to enter.

In the past, she entered the Saunders home by invitation and always through the front door. She had never seen the back of the house, so she slipped around to see what the rear entrance looked like. She shook her head at the sight greeting her.

The back door was metal clad and looked ready to deflect a cannon blast.

Vignette pulled two metal barrettes, barely visible in her short hair, and opened them to expose their thin clips. She bent forward until she was level with the backdoor keyhole, moving her fingertips like those of a surgeon. She defeated the lock almost as quickly as someone with a key could turn the tumblers. The hair clips were replaced atop her head with a dainty pat.

Moving easily, she made her way inside and kept herself light on her feet. She knew Felicity Saunders employed a large staff and some of her butlers were large men. But her pulse was already so high with the moment's excitement that unlike anyone else she might encounter, she could reverse direction and be at a full sprint in half a second. The element of surprise would allow her to outdistance them. The butlers were unlikely to recognize her, but Felicity Saunders certainly would. Under no circumstances could she allow the woman to spot her.

Intuition assured her she could outrun almost anybody, and she knew her endurance was high. So let some tough guy chase her, then. He would need a ton of luck. And of course once she made it to her bike, well, she'd just feel sorry for the jerk.

Today's costuming was perfect for the job; her leather riding suit was nearly a man's outfit, but the function of the suit made its form acceptable and allowed her to ignore feminine attire. When she first bought the Harley, she quickly noticed that people were more accepting of masculine clothing if she carried her helmet along. Something about the helmet assured people she had to dress this way. It put a little frame of acceptance around her.

"Ah, not to worry. A messenger person of some sort. The attire isn't a personal fashion choice. Nothing to see here."

The outfit itself was glorious. It allowed her to move without forcing her to fight her own garments. She gently closed the door behind her but left it on the latch as a possible emergency exit.

Her eyes needed a moment to adjust before she found herself looking into a space outfitted for household storage, along with a coal-fired heater and a black pile of fuel. The area was a maze of deep shadows and very little light.

She floated in and across the dim basement. Vignette didn't know anything about Japanese ninjas, but she moved like one anyway: a perfect combination of instinct and desire, honed by experience. She barely rippled the air while she climbed up the stairs to the first-floor living area. Although she had been in and out of the house for suffragette meetings, the house itself was never open to anyone. She had only seen the front entrance and the large dining room.

As always, the décor inside oozed quiet wealth and smelled like money: clean woolen carpeting, opulently ornate furnishings, freshly washed stone walls and wooden paneling. No trace of dust anywhere.

Fortunately for Vignette's sense of adventure and need for stimulation, this little errand wasn't just a go-see. It was finally time to start Moving Things Around, her favorite part of detective work, maybe favorite thing period. Frequently effective and yes-yes, usually illegal.

She liked it better than making money. She liked it better than sex, which in fairness to sex itself, she only knew from her childhood experience at the hands of the phony monks at St. Adrian's. And as much as her adoptive father resisted her use of this special skill, even he had to agree sometimes nothing else worked.

She padded across the main floor and proceeded through the mission as a pale-skinned young man, unless you looked closely, and in that case, young woman, dressed mostly in leather and carrying nothing but a pilot's helmet.

If confronted, she planned to pull an envelope from her pocket and pretend to be a lost messenger. She had never actually tried that.

And so the hunt was on for a trove of priceless personal artifacts taken from a falsely arrested immigrant who failed to pay his head tax. Miniature paintings, was all they were. But supposedly done by a master painter and portraying the victim's family.

The police took the art objects from him instead of accepting a cash bail. They had reasoned: Who could know how much spare cash these new arrivals saved up ahead of time? A mere cash fine, no matter how large, might be little more than an inconvenience to him. The head tax had to be respected or nobody would pay it, and the government was starving for funds. The confiscated items would guarantee his appearance at trial.

However, before the man's court date, the "bail" mysteriously disappeared from the evidence locker at City Hall. Police concluded it was a mystery. They announced their intention to look into conducting an internal investigation over the mystery. The case would be added to their overwhelming caseload and addressed with action at some point. They kindly agreed not to demand more bail, but left his trial date on the books.

So when he showed up at the home office of Blackburn & Nightingales – Private Investigation, the distraught man's pain was evident even through his broken English. "I pay tax! They say no, but I pay tax. What they take is beyond jewels! More than gold! For my family, children!" He dropped a small wad of cash, then augmented a few more isolated words with dramatic gestures to promise a bonus if they retrieved his precious paintings.

And since the new detective agency had only managed to pay the bills so far by following married men on behalf of suspicious wives, the opportunity to rise to a higher challenge elated Vignette. What a relief to mount an investigation with citywide consequences such as this one, and to work with Randall on it as a team.

But from the start, from that very first round of door-knocking and polite inquiries around City Hall, she watched Randall discovering that respect from the men on the force had mysteriously dissolved. She joined him in attempting to get others to talk, but nobody spoke up, and the art thieves seemed to enjoy the Devil's luck.

She and Randall tried splitting up to double their coverage, but both hit roadblocks in every direction: coincidental breaks in the line of custody, lost paperwork, the failure to report, witnesses who suddenly recanted their stories.

And yet the evidence locker was run directly by City Hall in order to simplify the whole system and thus guarantee clean evidence handling and safe storage. Every exhibit for every prosecution was held there without incident, making it the logical place to hold the seized artworks until the court heard the case. The evidence system existed specifically to avoid "loss of custody" situations.

She and Randall found themselves stonewalled so effectively, they were only able to make one major discovery—everyone in the short chain of custody had already produced valid receipts for handling the artworks and alibis for their whereabouts. All except one.

One man would have no such receipt or alibi: the mayor's adjutant, Harold Saunders, husband of the suffragette leader Felicity Saunders. However, he sneered at the request for an alibi and apparently trusted his corrupt compatriots to protect him. The law stood powerless.

Now Vignette floated on the pads of her feet and made the boots perform like slippers. It was a fine thing to be the means for bridging the distance between something you can't prove in court and something you know to be true.

Knowing was good enough for her. Fortunately, the Saunders home had no children, meaning a lower surprise risk. She knew the top floor of most homes was the most personal area, so she made a beeline for the main staircase, skirting the oversized grandfather clock at its base. She moved in fluid motions when she flicked her way up the carpeted stairs.

As soon as she hit the top floor, she was surprised by a solid wooden door. It completely blocked the hallway and all access to the bedroom area. She tried to recall ever seeing a hallway blocked by a door, much less one so heavy. This one was mounted on posts suitable for railroad ties, leaving half of this upper floor locked away. It looked as if it could only be breached with a sledgehammer. Maybe a small explosive.

The hair clips again. The defeated locks again. The clips neatly replaced. Vignette planted her heel at the base of the open door, did a little spin into the sealed-off section, then pushed the heavy door closed once more, soft as a powder puff.

She was in and alone.

The sensation enveloped her in the first moment—an atmosphere of heaviness, as if the air had already been inhaled two or three times. A delicate memory hovered in the blended essences of expensive cigars, fine perfumes, armpits, halitosis, and a faint top note of malfunctioning water closet.

Her eyes searched for threats in every direction and found none. But the sight of the place hit her like a gong strike. Opulence here was amplified to ridiculous proportion. Each piece of fancified furniture boasted adornments of scrolled woodwork by master carvers. Unpleasant faces glowered from dimly lighted portraits. Silk wallpaper on wainscoted walls flashed with ornate gilding.

A large living area adjoined the bedrooms. There every tabletop, cabinet top, and even the fireplace mantel were all sparkled with large single jewels and rich pieces of jewelry. Here a fat ruby, there a tiny Swiss watch made of gold, a diamond ring, a necklace of emeralds, a set of minia-ture Japanese sculptures done in exquisite porcelain. The stuff was every-where, and it was a fortune, ransom for some great king.

If either Felicity Saunders or her husband inherited such great wealth as this, why would they bother to get into petty local politics? Such wealth would allow far more efficient means of effecting change without the need for mixing with the contagious hoi polloi.

Vignette's ability to enter that part of the house proved the false security of the reinforced door; the couple was taking a far higher risk of detection and public exposure with this indulgent display. What rational explanation could cover it?

She felt certain Felicity Saunders would never permit this display if she could prevent it, and could not imagine the doyenne accepting a risk such as this. There had to be a compelling reason. Something bone deep. Even if the thick hallway door was made of steel, vaults get opened for one reason or another. Discoveries get made.

She walked around the room, studying the scene. At best, it might pass muster as a random aggregation of finery by an eccentric collector. But once she moved on to the master bedroom, eccentricity no longer explained things. She found herself looking at a display more strange than anything she had ever seen.

There, items of gold and jewelry covered every flat surface like a glit-tering cancer. The tiny fineries also lay spread across a five-drawer chif-fonier of cherry wood with a matching set of three-drawer dressers. The chiffonier and the dressers were each affixed with beveled mirrors mounted on swivels to move up or down, magnifying the effect of the scattered sparklers.

Vignette pushed her concentration around the room, taking in every tiny detail. Why was everything laid out like this? The expensive items were packed much too closely together to be individually appreciated. The overall display more closely resembled pirate booty.

At last, the point of her visit revealed itself on one top corner of the chiffonier: a collection of a dozen tiny oil paintings, the miniatures purloined from City Hall custody. Making it a fair call that the rest of this stuff was stolen as well. Her heart rate jumped. She allowed herself a rare on-the-job smile. But she put her elation in park and considered her next move. If this were an official police investigation, anything she took from that place would be tainted evidence and unusable in court.

And yet... Vignette appreciated a well-aimed barb and a well-timed joke. She was also a proponent of effective workarounds when it came to dealing with obstacles. Now those traits fit together to form her response to the situation, meaning it was time to start Moving Things Around. She pulled a silk pillowcase from the bed and carefully lay the tiny paintings within it, then wadded a second pillowcase over it for padding. They would be back in their owner's hands within hours, delivered directly to the man and completely outside the knowledge of the police. Other parts of the loot she was about to purloin would go to a more interesting form of custody than a leaky evidence locker.

But Moving Things Around wasn't about retrieving stolen goods. Big men with guns were good at that.

In today's case, it consisted of using a person's own familiar environment to send a message, accomplished through the theft of a good portion of the collection, which she piled into a third pillowcase. She tied the two bags together and strung them over her shoulders to carry home.

She checked to be certain she was taking every trace of her presence with her aside from the missing loot, then smooth-ran back toward the heavy second-floor door. She locked it from behind, eased it closed, and kept her footsteps fast and light on the stairway.

She was back on the ground floor in seconds, through the living area, down to the basement's occasional kitchen, and finally to the well-picked rear door. There was not so much as a scratch left on the lock when she slipped outside and pushed the heavy door closed.

She had left nearly half the booty in place, begging the question from the owners, *Why would anyone do that?*

Why indeed. Unless for the purpose of letting Mr. Mayor's Adjutant attempt to figure that out while he paced the floor in the middle of the night instead of getting any sleep. It would be so much better if he reflected on things long enough that he finally decided to go to City Hall and talk on his own.

All things considered, she figured he might do just that. People didn't like it when things seemed to move around for no reason. It scared them down to their bones, whether they would admit it or not. It was instinctive. And the more they might try to reason their way out of it, the more the fear would drill its way down into them. It would burrow deep and commence to feed, like so many tiny screwworms.

That being Vignette's weapon.

3

BLACKBURN & NIGHTINGALES – PRIVATE INVESTIGATION

* That Evening, July 17th *

RANDALL BLACKBURN COULD ONLY shake his head while Vignette explained with great delight how she not only returned the stolen items and fulfilled their contract, but the grateful client insisted on a hundred-dollar tip for the agency.

"Fifty bucks for each of us!" She folded her arms and smiled. "Duck soup."

Randall smiled, started to laugh, then checked himself. "Maybe. Vignette, I'm glad this one was easy for you, but you're pushing things harder than you used to. I have to think about what happens if you get caught, whether you want to think about it or not."

She plopped the bills of tip money onto the dinner table, right between the plates of Randall's nicely prepared meal. "I didn't. It all turned out jake. And since this guy made a game of using his authority to steal valuable evidence, the only iffy part was how to get justice on a protected crook."

Randall sat up straighter. "All right, don't tell me you went wild on this…"

Vignette exhaled hard. "Randall. It wouldn't do any good to have him arrested. Even if we could, he's back on the street the same day."

"And that's a perfect example of why I switched to private work. But if we end up on the wrong side of the law, that excuse won't get us off."

She let out a laugh that came out as more of a snort. "Okay, I'm with you so far on that. I will *absolutely* not get caught." Then she added, "If he's connected up with someone in a high position, that would sure explain keeping evidence on display like that. He believed the justice system was rigged on his behalf, and maybe it was. So, you agree I needed to Move Things Around and do some actual good?"

"First, maybe you could be so kind as to tell me exactly what you moved, here?"

"Fine. First, after I dropped off the client's belongings, I took half the sack of the other recovered items to the offices of the *Chronicle* and the other half to the *Examiner*, as anonymous gifts to their crime reporters."

Randall kept his eyes on the floor, but he couldn't help grinning. He took up the story, "Who will instantly begin to compete in the hunt for the original owners to do a story on them."

"Yep. And to make sure, I wrote 'Harold Saunders, the Mayor's Adjutant' on a piece of paper inside each bag, along with a note saying all of it came from his home and there's a lot more of this stuff there. All stolen from custody at City Hall.

"I wrote, '*Why* is he getting away with this?' And told them they had three days to uncover the story before I go to all the other papers in the region and they lose a chance at a scoop. Neither paper knows the other is on it yet."

"That's not bad," Randall said. "Once they get whiff of a great scandal story, there won't be any protection from their questions." He nodded, but his expression wasn't any lighter. "The chief has to distance himself from this, whether he was in on it or not. Express his surprise that his trusted adjutant would do such a thing. All that horse flop. He's gonna scramble to make himself hoosegow-proof and sacrifice anybody, whoever he has to. Another fine day for me to not work there anymore."

"So it all worked out!"

"Thing is, Vignette, you were supposed to *just* go do some surveillance on the man. If you had gotten caught, stabbed, shot, killed—"

"It worked out. Didn't it?"

Randall held up his hand. "Hold on. We're not going over 'moving things around' again tonight." He took a deep breath. "Fact is, all the right people won and lost here, so maybe this time we should just—"

A powerful thump hit the front door of the house, striking the wooden porch like a giant drum. It sounded as if someone threw a bale of hay at the door.

Randall jumped to his feet and hurried to the front of the house, pulling his handgun from the holster on the hat rack by the door. He held the pistol tight to his side with the barrel pointed at the floor while he inched the door open. There was no sound. He peered out.

A boy of about twelve lay sprawled across the threshold. His face was purple, eyes open and staring. A deep red line around his neck showed where he had been throttled with something, and there was no doubting he was dead.

Randall recognized him as a sidewalk newsboy and occasional messenger around the neighborhood. If the boy had a family, somewhere that family had just been dealt a terrible blow. He craned his neck up and down Lincoln Way. Not a soul moving out there.

Vignette stepped to the door and gasped in shock. A yelp escaped her before she slapped her hand over her mouth. She bent to the boy and felt his neck for a pulse. Nothing.

"Randall...Who is this poor boy?"

"Don't stand in the doorframe, you're backlit. Stay back inside." He waited until she backed up a few feet, then said, "This boy's name is, ah, Will, Will something. You see him around. Doing odd jobs."

He caught the sound of commotion coming from the brush just inside the trees across the street. Randall strained his eyes, trying to pierce the darkness. Their three-story brownstone house stood facing Golden Gate Park, and somebody was beating a retreat into the cultivated forest. His impulse was to go bounding after the source of the noise, but twenty years as a beat cop made him pause to consider the idea of starting a running gunfight in the deep darkness of the park, in pursuit of a quarry he couldn't identify by sight.

All right, then. Not a moment for heroics. He stayed put on the porch.

He called out, "I'm coming back in, Vignette. The boy has to stay where he is for now."

The next thing that caught his eye was enough to guarantee he stayed home; the dead boy's right hand held a sealed envelope with "Randall Blackburn" printed across the front. He blinked in surprise. For a moment he could only stare.

Randall knew without having to think about it that the envelope and its contents were *ipso facto* evidence in a murder. Meaning it was all supposed to be left in place, untouched.

However, the envelope had his name on it and the flap was loose, leaving no way to tell if anyone had already opened it. Someone besides the writer could have already read whatever was in that envelope. They would have left no trace.

By the same logic, there would be no way, later, to tell if he opened it right now. *Careful, careful...*

He carried the note back into the house and caught Vignette's attention with a loaded glance. That was all it took. She hurried to him and read over his shoulder.

Detective Blackburn –

I have discovered in the course of my work at City Hall incidents of anarchists in our country who are quietly bribing and intimidating their way into power in this city. They have already infiltrated City Hall itself. I tell you this because a private hawkshaw like you can do what nobody can do on the official record—find out why this is happening. I will send this by private messenger. No one knows who to trust here.

That was all. Plain white paper. No address. No signature.

Randall's blood ran cold. Somebody had not only found out about the note, they knew when the messenger was coming.

Vignette stared at him and spoke in a choked whisper, "They waylaid this boy and killed him, Randall."

"Whoever it is, no doubt they read the message. And yet they not only permitted it to go through, they used the boy's dead body to deliver it. They were delivering a message of their own, in the strongest possible way."

By now Vignette was breathing like she had just run up a few flights of stairs. "Wait a minute, now. Are they actually daring you to go after them? Who would do that?"

"The way to find the answer is figure out what would be in it for the perpetrators."

"You believe all that about the police getting infiltrated and corrupted?"

Randall just looked at her.

"Oh. All right."

"Under no circumstances can we allow the police to know we have this. As long as we keep it hidden, it never happened. Sure as hell the killers have no reason to make it known. Maybe we can keep this contained."

"Damn, Randall, if these accusations are true and they know we have this note..."

"And if the corrupt police are the killers here, bad things will absolutely take place in our lives. First thing we have to do is report the boy. Same as anyone else would."

He tucked the note back into the envelope and slid it onto the top shelf of the coat closet. His next order of business was to step into the living room, where the household's newfangled telephone device was fastened to the wall. He began the process of calling the police to report a murder.

The uniforms were there for several hours and took statements from both of them. Their little agency was well known to the police, and Randall Blackburn's reputation was still good enough that it kept the tone of the investigation neutral and without any particular suspicion.

But there was the inconvenient reality of a dead boy on their porch. Certain things had to be established. The boy was known for minor run-ins with the cops in the past couple of years, but he also came from a derelict family who did little to support him.

To Randall's disgust, it was clear the authorities were going to give this crime a low priority. It was all they could do to keep up with crimes against people who mattered. And so it was well after sunrise when the coroner's horse-drawn body wagon arrived and the victim was finally taken away.

As soon as the police were gone and the house grew quiet, Vignette shook her head. "That poor boy, Randall."

"I know. At least Shane had people to mourn him. I hope this boy does."

"He's got us, if that matters." She exhaled a heavy sigh. "Well, that's it for me. Bedtime." She started for her room atop the stairs.

Randall's voice stopped her. "Not yet."

"What?"

"We both need to be on this."

"Randall, I'm beat."

"Yeah, me too. I'll bring the car around and pick you up. We have to go to City Hall."

"What, now? Why?"

"Whoever wrote that note wanted to remain anonymous. That was well and good, but the game changed when the boy died. We're going to sniff around until we figure out who sent it."

She knew better than to protest. "I'll get my shoes."

Randall started off down the street to retrieve the car at the electric stable. The two-passenger Waverley was conveniently housed only two blocks away, where it was kept charged along with five other local electrics. He had celebrated opening their detective agency by replacing his Model T with a much more expensive electric Waverley, one of the last produced before the company closed its doors. The electric car boasted solid rubber tires, ideal for wear and tear from fractured cobblestones.

Inside the stable, the cars lined up nose to the wall like horses at a trough. Each one stood at a power box mounted on the wall with its own set of charging cables. The body of Randall's Waverley came with interchangeable tops, but he usually kept the hard shell installed in surrender to local weather, while the soft top hung from the ceiling on a pulley system.

He pulled the charging wires free, then hopped in and activated the magneto to wake up the motor. He engaged reverse gear and backed out of the stable while the attendant closed the big doors. In the street, he changed gears to forward and turned toward the house to pick up Vignette.

He loved driving the vehicle, moving as if by magic and creating no noise, no exhaust.

It was also a great car for making a silent approach when circumstances called for it. He had no doubt that in ten years or so, the entire automotive industry would be electric, since no matter how people might disagree on other things, everybody likes to breathe. For the present, the silent electric vehicle traveled the common roads by gliding through clouds of pulverized dung and diesel exhaust.

Vignette hurried out of the house and hopped in, and along the way they flogged their tired brains for a plan while Randall maneuvered between potholes and horse piles. "All right, Vignette, you've had some time to think about it. What did the note tell you?"

"The note. Well, the handwriting was too good for an unschooled person. The writer has an education. More important, though, he works in some capacity that allows him to get this information in the first place."

"Right. If we take whoever wrote this at their word, either everyone else who knows about this is in on the fix or they're intimidated enough to turn a blind eye. That would make for a big secret, hard for a large group of people to keep. But lucky for us, the range of responsibility is narrow in this city because the Prosecutor's Office is the sole agency holding evidence."

"And so if the Prosecutor's Office is compromised, say, blackmailed or bought off..."

"That would leave the mayor himself actually running things in the city. Meaning only he and his adjutant would control everyone else's access to evidence."

Vignette caught on. "So they're the only ones who could make valuable evidence disappear *and* simultaneously derail any investigation into it. Don't you wish we could ask Shane about it? He always had so much insight."

Randall gave a tired smile and let out a sigh. "Yeah, that he did." He had decided shortly after Shane was killed to avoid bringing it up to Vignette unless she mentioned it herself. That was for her. But lately he treated an offhand reference like this as something to simply be acknowledged and dropped. That part was for him. Everything was still raw. It had only been four weeks.

He reached over and placed his hand on her shoulder. "Proud of you, though. I'm too tired to have figured that out by myself."

Ten minutes later, the pair completed the relatively short drive to City Hall. He pulled their silent ride to the curb in front. "Let's just hope Adjutant Saunders keeps regular office hours so we don't have to wait around. I'll never stay awake."

Vignette pointed to a small stand with a sign reading, *Ice Cold Coca-Cola* on a red-and-blue enamel sign. "That new drink's been around awhile, and I haven't tried it yet. Maybe it's what we need. It's supposed to give you energy."

"I tried it," Randall replied. "The stuff will give you energy, all right."

They walked over to the street stand and paid for a bottle apiece, but just as they turned back toward City Hall, a wave of excited voices and commotion rolled out the front door. Something had riled people past the boiling point.

Randall recognized two grim-faced cops among the wave of uniformed men exiting the building. "Whitfield! Jackson!" He left Vignette and hurried over to them.

The men turned. "Oh. Hey there, Blackburn," Whitfield replied without smiling.

"Nice day to be a private citizen," Jackson added.

Both men kept walking away. Randall fell in with them for a few steps. "Funny, I just said that. What happened?"

"Mayor's adjutant. Saunders. This is gonna stain the whole department, mark my words."

"I never liked him, anyway."

"What the hell happened?"

"So, reporters started fishing around first thing this morning, asking questions."

"Yeah, and they've got samples of stolen evidence from here. Our evidence lockup. Gold and jewels."

"So there's that, bad enough, what with the department getting stolen evidence charges and all, but from that he decides the best thing to do is blow his brains out?"

"Nice of him, though, he left a note said the mayor wasn't part of it.

Coward tells his wife he's going to some sort of meeting, then retreats to his office and takes a bite out of his service revolver."

"When was this?"

"Sometime early this morning before everybody came in! My guy got a look inside the scene, says Saunders painted the walls with his brains."

"And he was always such a tough guy, you know? A real bruiser."

"Just like that! Just like that! What the hell kind of man would do that? Over what? Some stolen money or something? I never liked that sonofabitch."

By now Vignette had already downed her drink. She drifted over to listen in, just in time for Randall to turn to her and quietly announce, "Mayor's adjutant killed himself."

Vignette frowned. "What? Why? I thought he had a fix in."

"You can bet he had a fix in," Randall agreed. "About the stolen evidence, anyway."

Vignette caught on. "So...if he had enough favors to call in at City Hall that he could sweep problems under the rug, then the suicide motive disappears. Meaning..." Her eyes widened. She turned to stare at Randall.

He smiled at her and nodded. "He did it over something else. His death wasn't about stolen evidence."

"So what did he know that we don't?"

"Assuming he pulled the trigger himself?"

"There's that."

Mario Buda sat in his comfortable hotel room inside a narrow "shotgun" building down off of Battery Street not far from the waterfront. It was too far from the shoreline to see the water but close enough to smell the ocean. The tiny hotel was sandwiched between a dozen others like it. He actually liked the place. It reminded him of his old life in Europe. The sexy crowding of all those bodies, and the earthy smells of cooking and sweating humanity marbled together to form a sustained olfactory blanket. It was just right.

He made a little vow to himself to always work from his residence from now on, wherever it might be. No more bunkers and basements. Instead he would seek out a tiny hotel near a waterfront, if there was a waterfront, and if there was no waterfront, then a tiny hotel on the back end of town. Find a place submerged in the oddly comforting stench of life-forms whose closeness he craved until he pulverized them with shock waves and shrapnel. And in a way, made them one with him.

Because he loved the powerful and utterly distinctive smell to the air after one of his detonations. Knowing all odors are particulate in nature, he frequently made it a point to stroll the scene in the immediate aftermath and deeply inhale while he walked, thus taking bits of his own explosives into his lungs as well as bits of his victims. There was almost a sexual component to the intimate sensations of the recent dead lining his nostrils in their newly powdered form, tickling his sinuses and coating the back of his throat.

Once the Chicago bombs were successfully handed off to the brothers from that city, there was still enough time left to wire safety switches into this new set of five sitting on the table before him. That task was now done.

Thus the riskiest part was over and he was safe from accidental detonation. There would be no flash of light followed by a boom he would never hear from his place in oblivion.

Now it was safe to allow the giddy glow of success to fill him. The confidence it bore left him to ask what the hell he had been afraid of, huddling as he had in that underground vault? He shuddered at the thought of going down into another one. From now on, such risks and discomforts were better suited to younger men.

He could keep secrets without artificial constraints. Buda assured himself he was not at all like the fiery orator, Galleani. That man's public verbal outpourings and displays of emotion were much too flagrant. They grated on his bones. He lived a life mostly conducted in silence. That silence was always the overture to his great solo act.

In Mario Buda's eyes, the man's extreme reaction showed him to be a complete fool. Getting caught with jail booty was a crime, but hardly any reason for a self-destructive reaction. All he had to do was let himself be arrested; the anarchists already had people in place who could have gotten him out.

But no. Instead the Yankee idiot panicked like a child at the thought of being exposed as a thief who allowed his guilt to be exploited and a man who ended up funding the anarchists' need for parts and explosives. But while that might be considered nothing to brag about in the late adjutant's world, still he would have been all right. A little public shaming, a few professional setbacks, perhaps even nominal jail time. Nothing more.

Public outrage would fade as it always did. New sources of outrage would be decried by all the bustle-rumped biddies and high-collared humps. Anger at him would be covered over by unending waves of judgment directed at others by the ones who loved to cluck and hiss over everything that wasn't them.

And then, once things got quiet, the coward could have discreetly slipped out to freedom. Maybe a medal and a nice job with a friendly government somewhere. Instead, he lost all self-control and swallowed a bullet *ten minutes* before Buda arrived to collect his next payment.

This not only deprived Buda of the monthly payment, it left him in forced silence in the aftermath. The man's only real accomplishment in this life was to disappear into history as a mere thief, a devotee of greed. The truth would remain hidden; Saunders's brains painted the walls behind him because he feared having his connection to the Parade mission revealed.

He should have been proud instead of swallowing useless shame. Pissant.

That was it, then. With the loss of Harold Saunders as Buda's primary funding source, his work would end in this city on the day his comrades made their explosive public announcements. Which, he thought with great pride, would take place there in San Francisco but would be heard by the entire government-enslaved world. He was more than an essential mechanic in the public attack system; he was a devotee of the cause.

It galled Buda to think of this civic travesty, this so-called "Preparedness Day Parade," taking place strictly for the purpose of propagandizing the hapless public into accepting the lunacy of this European war. The newspapers bragged about floats being constructed to rival anything paraded before the emperors of Ancient Rome. It was going to be a multi-faceted circus of patriotism.

Meanwhile, the war was turning much of Europe to rubble. It wasn't going to bother Buda to move on from San Francisco. There were plenty of other cities in the United States where brothers of the movement were already in place. The difference would be that in the aftermath of great success here, they would gladly pay for his work. Decent wages for reliable work. Like good capitalists.

Meanwhile, any local anarchists who shared his passion but lacked his skills with explosives could nevertheless continue worming their way into the halls of power using the time-honored means of blackmail and bribes.

Because America had to fall.

4

SAN FRANCISCO CITY HALL

* Late Morning, July 18th *

RANDALL NOTICED A BALD MAN in horn-rimmed glasses urgently waving in his direction amid the buzzing hallways of the City Hall building. The atmosphere was so noisy and confused there was no way to tell if the man called out to him or not. He looked back over his shoulder to see if the gestures were meant for someone standing behind him. Nope.

With no better leads at the moment, he stepped over to the stranger on the off chance that this might be something. The eager man stood at the door to an office labeled *US Customs Collection, S.F. Field Office*. Randall recalled there had been a Customs office housed in City Hall since the Great Earthquake. But it was a federal office. He never had contact with anyone who worked in it.

Vignette followed him over to see what was up.

The man bowed slightly in lieu of a handshake and spoke in worried tones. "Mr. Blackburn! I'm Jacob Prohaska. So glad to see you! I had planned to visit you today! Right to your office. It's in your home, correct? That's the address I have, over there on Lincoln Way?"

"It is. I worked out of the City Hall police station for a long time. Now I prefer a home office."

"Home office! Ah, those words, sir. A home office. Do you have any idea how good they sound to someone like myself, Mr. Blackburn? Please come in. Right this way, sir, and your companion, please. Perhaps I can't work where I live, but at least I don't have to live here, ha-ha! Yes indeed. This way."

He ushered them in, glancing around the hallway before closing the door. "My secretary is out gathering office gossip about the suicide, so let's take advantage of some rare privacy."

He led them to his office and closed the door. Prohaska turned to Randall as if Vignette had disappeared. "I know your reputation, sir. You were a terror for justice when you were on the force, and I don't doubt you are the same as a private investigator."

"I'm not much for flattery, Mr. Prohaska."

"Nothing of the kind. Look here now, I imagine there are certain things a private detective can do that others cannot. I mean others such as a city detective bound to the system. Yes?"

"Mr. Prohaska," Vignette interrupted. "Do you have something specific to tell us?"

Prohaska turned to her, then back to Randall. He nodded to himself and spoke to the floor. "I sent the note you received overnight."

The next moment lasted long enough for a trained horse to stomp the ground three times.

"Ah," Randall responded. There was another awkward pause while he and Vignette waited for more.

At last Prohaska shook his head and cleared his throat. "I told you why I reached out to you, but today everything is changing. They're moving much faster than I realized. The luxury of anonymity disappeared with the murder of my messenger. Now this suicide today. I heard the gunshot upstairs, did I mention? Nobody is safe anymore." He paused, panting with something resembling exertion.

"Where were you at the time, sir?" Vignette asked.

Prohaska's eyes went wide. "Where was I?"

"Mr. Prohaska, this is my adopted daughter, Vignette Nightingale. She is also my partner at the agency."

"Nightingale?"

Vignette reddened and replied in a loud, flat voice. "Mr. Blackburn adopted me. And my older brother. Our family name was Nightingale."

Prohaska turned to Blackburn. "You were a friend of the Nightingale family, then?"

"Never met them."

"...Oh."

Vignette cleared her throat. "Yes. As to where you were, of course I only ask because we try to be as thorough as possible. No reason for offense. I'm sure you have someone here who can vouch for your whereabouts?"

Another awkward pause took its time passing.

It was Randall's turn to break it. "She's right about there being no need to take offense. Us being thorough. All that."

"I was here in the office, ran upstairs, and was the first one to find him. Most everyone else hadn't even come in yet. My secretary can confirm it for you later."

Vignette smiled. "Mystery solved, then."

"Yes, well. There we have it." He turned away to address Randall.

In that instant, Vignette saw a flicker of expression cross his face: rat cunning. It was a face she had often seen on the monks back at St. Adrian's. But with no opportunity to see more in this moment, she had to let it go. "Would you mind telling us more about what you described in your note?"

Prohaska glanced around as if the walls really did have ears. "I can do that. This office is rented from City Hall by the federal government. That's important, because I'm not part of the City Hall system. My responsibility is just to keep track of the head tax collected from immigrants when they pass through."

"We don't know anything about the Customs Department, sir."

"All you need to know is this: I also ask our collections officers to flag suspicious arrivals. A few weeks ago, they landed a whale. His name is Luigi Galleani, and I've built a file on him."

Prohaska stepped to a file cabinet and produced a thick manila folder.

"Luigi Galleani has followers, and they will commit theft, arson, or murder for him. We know this from their work on his behalf in Europe."

He pulled copies of numerous editions of *The Subversive Chronicle*, showing fiery anti-capital and anti-business headlines. He also took out a detailed pencil drawing of Galleani's face. It showed the subject straining with emotion while he shouted.

"We allow people of every stripe into this country, but we do tend to notice when they come here for the express purpose of destroying us."

Randall took a deep breath and spoke in a soft voice, "Yeah, I know. I know. So. You think this Galleani fellow not only wants to do us harm, but he's got enough followers to accomplish it?"

"Oh, no doubt. Human lemmings. They even call themselves 'Galleanists,' and if they're not a surefire cult, then they're cutting it so close the difference doesn't matter."

"Cults are not a crime."

"*Major* crime has been coming from their ranks, Mister Blackburn. Theft, assault, murders rigged to look like accidents. But this is the thing: there's been a complete failure of our system to prosecute them after they get arrested. Not one has gone to trial. No jail time, anywhere."

"Sounds like you're paying attention," Randall said.

"Working here, what choice is there? I have personally recommended two of them for arrest over grievous assaults and robberies, but nothing happens. Even coming from me, nobody in city government or law enforcement responds. Why is that, Mr. Blackburn?"

"I can't tell you."

"Perhaps not yet, you can't. But I trust you can see I'll never get an honest investigation going here; who would I approach? If I ask the wrong person, I might join the late Mr. Saunders."

"In suicide?" Blackburn asked.

Prohaska flinched. "There's no way to know who can be trusted. I took the risk of coming to you because of your reputation here."

"And because Randall lives outside the system now," Vignette added in a sarcastic tone.

"Well. Yes." Prohaska pulled a stack of fliers from the file and spread them on a table in front of them: wanted posters, dozens of them. Many were in English, but there were languages from all around Europe.

Prohaska pointed at the display. "Most of these in English are from cities on the East Coast where they've had this problem longer than we have, I believe. The anarchists like to operate in secret, and every one of the men you see here is a Galleanist. Of course, the crimes they're wanted for are just the ones we know about. Tip of the iceberg and all that."

"And which problem on the East Coast do you mean?"

"The problem of people coming to the United States for no other reason than to commit murder and kill as many Americans as they can, regardless of who the individuals are. There has been a noticeable rise in the number of known anarchists showing up on our shores. The ones we can break down and get talking to us tell us anarchists regard American capitalism as the root of all evil."

"Another root of all evil?" Vignette asked with mock innocence.

"I hope you don't find humor in this," Prohaska sniffed.

"No, Mr. Prohaska," Randall intervened with a warning glance at Vignette. "Not at all. We're just functioning without sleep since the boy's murder. Will something. What was his last name, by the way?"

"I don't know. He hung around looking for odd jobs. I'd go down to the street corner and call out, 'You, boy!' and one of them came running over. Sometimes another one, sometimes him. Guttersnipes, mostly. They stay reliable so you'll use 'em again."

"I understand he didn't get much from his family."

"Who knows? Enough about him. Perhaps you heard we've had a spate of accidental deaths in City Hall and the police department?"

"Any chance these deaths really are accidental?"

"Depends who you want to believe. But I'm not the only one who understands about these invisible people. Whoever they are. They are either evil or insane."

"So, if people find out about this cult or this conspiracy or whatever it is, they get eliminated?"

"Yes. And I'm also convinced the only reason I'm still alive is that I haven't told anybody but the two of you about my concerns. Nobody else in the building knows."

"None of them? You're certain?"

"Well, what, *certain*? Hell no! This is a federal government office not particularly well liked by the city government in the City Hall where it resides, and the whole kit 'n' kaboodle is run by politicians. But I have never breathed a word of this to anyone here, and at home I'm a confirmed bachelor. No domestic pillow talk."

"Mr. Prohaska, what do you want us to do?"

Prohaska looked surprised by the question. "Good Lord, I'm sure I don't know. You're the expert here." He reached over and took up the drawing of Galleani. "But if I were in your position, I would start with Mr. Galleani."

"Without forgetting Galleani's men," added Randall, "since they won't hesitate to kill for him, they already killed a messenger boy, and they would likely kill Miss Nightingale or myself."

"Well. Yes." He balled his hands into fists. "But you choose to be detectives, don't you? I've spent my career working at this. We collect taxes, but it's supposed to come from people who come here to see what they can *build*. Now I'm forced to watch the whole process get poisoned by people who came here to see what they can destroy."

Prohaska handed Randall a small card. "This number will connect to my office telephone. These days, I'm here most of the time." He looked directly at each of them in turn. "I risked my life to contact you. I'm risking it again to give you this. You see that, yes?"

He handed over the drawing of Galleani. Randall scowled while he accepted it and then stood silent for a moment and studied the featured face: Luigi Galleani, age fifty-five. The man's scraggly beard did little to conceal the damage done to his face by years in prison and still more years being hounded and deported all over Europe.

After taking in the drawing, Vignette said, "This Luigi Galleani can't accomplish much with a bunch of guys fresh off the boat. If he's going to do anything big, he's got to have inside help."

Blackburn nodded. "A lot of it."

5

CABLE CAR TURNABOUT AT MARKET AND POWELL

* July 18th, 8:00 p.m. *

THE FACE FROM THE SKETCH was live now. Despite his fifty-five years of rough living, the real thing was in top form. Galleani balanced atop a tall wooden crate while he boomed his voice to a cluster of dockworkers.

Sunset was still half an hour away. A crowd of perhaps a hundred working men had stayed around the job site long enough to catch Galleani and hear his attack on their bosses. His people had spent the past two days passing out freshly printed fliers, calling out to these particular workers, pointing out one flagrant labor outrage after another. Using words to throw lit matches and start up random fires of resentment.

Even workers who had no idea what most of the references meant felt attracted to this free opportunity to hear their greedy bosses get lampooned. That alone made it worth their time.

Galleani began softly. He used a warm, cordial tone, calling out the names of the various dockside unions represented in the crowd. Each group name was greeted with a loyal whoop.

Meanwhile, with the speech just beginning, Randall and Vignette stood in the back and kept a discreet profile. They exchanged amused glances over the way Galleani was manipulating the crowd, pulling the men together with competitive "worker pride" and the chance to applaud themselves as competing teams who were nonetheless in the same league.

The sinking sun began to cast shadows in longer forms. The shaped patches of darkness fell from tall buildings and crawled over the crowd. To Vignette, the creeping shapes added a trace of menace to the streets.

Both detectives held near-empty bottles of the new "Coca-Cola" beverage. In spite of having no rest since they lost their night of sleep to the murder, Vignette leaned close to Randall and announced, "Still not tired."

"Me either. But I stopped after two bottles, and you've had three. Size difference here, also. You should slow down."

"I should find a privy." She studied the bottle. It didn't tell her much. "Guy over there saw me with this a minute ago. He said he heard they make this stuff with cocaine."

"I guess that's what the 'Coca' part stands for."

"Cocaine, plus water that's been colored and flavored."

"Not anymore. They quit. They're sorry."

"What I heard, is all."

"It was a different time."

"Carbonated to give it a fizz… You suppose they're selling stock?"

"Seems like a fad. Let's stay on the subject."

"Right-o."

Now Galleani's voice shifted into power mode while he launched into the main body of his address. His voice reverberated from his perch atop the soapbox, rolling around the turnabout area. He paused every few sentences to give his audience time to cheer. They did with reliable gusto.

"Everywhere I go," he called out, "I am harassed by the authorities. Why? Gentlemen, I publish a small magazine called *The Subversive Chronicle*. They call it 'propaganda.' But my friends, what is propaganda? Words! Does your country *not* have a First Amendment to protect your words? Why be afraid of news columns, pamphlets, speeches? What has anyone got to fear from the exchange of ideas? Words are not the issue!"

Galleani was rolling now, projecting at full voice in pulsing tones. "I say words are a waste of time unless they are backed by *action*! Propaganda of the *deed*, my fellow workers!" (Pause for cheers.) "*Propaganda of the deed! We make our statements with work stoppages, with sabotage, with arson if need be.*" (Pause for cheers.) "The *deed*, my friends! While your bosses squeeze every ounce of life out of you, day by day, hour by hour. We know it isn't 'propaganda' they fear. Only the *deed* prods their fears of losing control over you!

"The worldwide anarchist movement wants to revoke the power of *all* governments, so political hacks will have nowhere to hide!"

Galleani raised both fists high and shouted at the top of his voice: "*No nations! No borders! No nations! No borders!*"

The crowd immediately took up the chant and repeated it at top volume, over and over, blurring it a bit more each time until it dissolved into a throb of angry male voices. The words no longer mattered since the anger got expressed without them.

Randall and Vignette shared a glance while the din reverberated from the cobblestones and ricocheted off the nearby buildings. The sounds of male voices chanting in unison somehow landed red hot in Vignette's ears.

It reached back into her past, before she and Shane had met Randall. It dropped her back into the orphanage and the chanting of the friars. She kept control over her behavior, but with skin thinner than an eyelash. Anything could break her.

When she was fourteen, a bunch of men took up a street preacher's forceful chant. Randall had to pull her hands from around the nearest man's throat and extract her from the crowd with copious apologies and man-to-man-style reminders that boys don't fight girls. When Vignette heard that, she turned to pummel Randall, which at least allowed him to drag her away from the crowd and get her back home.

Tonight he had to admire the way she forced herself to endure the voices. They didn't sound that much like a group of monks, but he knew the sounds of men chanting, chanting, chanting, made her flesh crawl. To her credit, she stood and took it until it was over.

Once the energy of the chanting began to deflate and men started moving away from the scene, Randall and Vignette headed over to Galleani's platform. They were immediately waylaid by two large body-guards with sour dispositions.

Randall asked the lesser psychotic-looking of the two whether he and his companion might have a word with Mr. Galleani. The bodyguard sniffed. "*Signore* Galleani doesn't talk to just anybody. If you look around, you'll notice half the people here tonight want to stay and speak with him."

A large crowd had already formed a sloppy line. To Randall, they appeared to be in a vague hypnotic daze over Galleani's persuasions. These hardened dockside laborers had just been converted to eager fans through the combination of the kernels of truth in Galleani's words and his power of delivery. They eagerly jockeyed for position to be among the first to speak with the Great One.

Vignette spoke to the bodyguard using her fake coquette smile. "This crowd puts away the rumor that he doesn't talk to just anyone, though, doesn't it?"

"You gettin' smart?"

"Already did. But I believe *Signore* Galleani would want you to tell him two reporters from the *Chronicle* are here to see him. After all, he desires publicity. Yes?"

The bodyguard glared at her in resentment. Reporters? He was boxed in.

Randall grinned. "Ain't she somethin'?"

"Yeah, yeah. Wait here." The man slipped away and headed toward a cluster of men who presumably had Galleani in their midst.

"Nice touch with the newspaper angle."

"Taught by a master. Hey, look over there. Recognize that guy?"

Randall looked over at a thin, scraggly looking man in his thirties, dressed as a laborer. He wasn't engaged in any banter with the other men. He appeared a bit nervous and self-conscious.

"Wasn't he on one of the wanted posters?"

"That's it. Buda. Mario Buda."

"Buda! Right, right. Bombs are his specialty."

"Yes indeed. Leaving us to wonder what Mr. Bombs has to say to *Signore* Galleani."

Two minutes later, the guard returned looking sheepish. "Mister Galleani said to show you right back to see him."

"Mister?" Vignette asked, opening her eyes too wide for sincerity.

"You some kinda smartass?"

"No, it's just that you made a big deal about calling him *Signore*, so I thought—"

"Hey, maybe you guys want to turn around and leave right now?"

"Come on, Vignette. Maybe *Mister* Galleani doesn't want any help from the press."

"Wait! Wait. No need to run off. Sorry about all that. I didn't realize you two are from the press."

"We told you we were."

"No, I mean at first. Not now. I didn't realize Mister, *Signore* Galleani would want to—" He abruptly paused. "Hey. Before we go, you wouldn't happen to have your press credentials handy, would you?" He gazed at them like a bomber holding a dead man's switch.

Randall spoke forcefully without raising his voice, merely by adding steel to his tone. "Your boss has already asked...to see...us."

This confused the guard, who did not appear to like the sensation. Without another word, he guided them to their quarry. Then he stepped slightly to the side, folded his hands over his crotch, and adopted a silence reeking of contempt.

Luigi Galleani was seated in a comfortable chair amid the crowd of standing men. He glanced up at Randall and Vignette while they approached, looked them each up and down, then motioned them over. He flashed a smile too warm for the occasion, although his first comment was directed at the men fawning around him.

"Ah, here they are! Two members of the capitalist press!"

The men around him chuckled appreciatively at the arrival of the capitalist press.

"So! How do you do, reporters?" he said while Randall and Vignette stepped up closer.

"Sir, my name is Randall Blackburn, and this is my partner, Vignette Nightingale. We were hoping—"

"What is wrong with the interview I gave to your paper yesterday?"

"...Yesterday." Uh-oh. Vignette threw a warning glance at Randall.

He picked up the slack without a pause. "That was the basic interview. We were sent to follow up on a few questions."

Vignette nodded and chimed right in. "Little things, though. A few small things."

"Ah!" Galleani cried like an opera star. "You hear, my brothers? The *Chronicle* sent these reporters to *clear up a few things* from my interview yesterday! I wonder if that *actually* means my interview did not give the press enough to hang me, so another team was sent to try again!" He laughed at his joke, and the men around him guffawed in agreement.

Randall forced a smile. "I was not told your English was so fluent, sir. My compliments."

"How many languages do you have?"

"Just this one, I'm afraid."

Galleani made a little smile of regret. "I see. Well. Perhaps if you will attend my next rally later this evening over in Lafayette Square, I can further impress you."

"You are certainly staying busy."

"It's no sacrifice. The place where I'm staying is not far from the park, over on Russian Hill. It's the home of one of the gentlemen on the City Council."

"What city is that?"

"Ha! You joke!" He yelled to the men. "He jokes! What is the name of this city, again? Oh, yes: San Francisco." The men behind him laughed like a group of boys sharing a dirty joke.

To this, Galleani added, "A member of the board of supervisors of the City of San Francisco, Mr. Reporter!" He bellowed with laughter like a gambler who just brought home a long shot. The men were happy to join in with him.

Randall and Vignette waited for things to die down, then Vignette calmly said, "Indeed. We heard all that. At the paper."

Randall spoke in a flat voice. "Didn't think we'd find many anarchists around the castles on Russian Hill, though."

Galleani beamed. "I am certain you would be surprised by what can be found all *around* you, my friend!" He laughed at himself, and the men joined in again.

Randall spoke up. "*Signore* Galleani, our real question today is that we understand there has been a sharp increase in the number of people who openly claim to be members of the anarchist movement. Can you—"

"I answered this before."

"Ah...yes. But we were asked to get clarification on the purpose. Or I guess I should say, *is* there a purpose?"

Vignette added, "Because it seems to us, at the paper, that you must be—"

"Yes," said Galleani in a pleasant tone.

"...What?"

"Yes, there is a purpose. Yes, they are here for a reason. I would have told your other reporters if they had asked me. These are advance fighters in an unstoppable cause: freedom and dignity for the working man!" He directed the last lines at the men around him, who angrily agreed with freedom and dignity for the working man.

"And yet," Galleani went on, "unlike your powerful publication, my *Subversive Chronicle* has a subscriber list of only five thousand. It never runs more than eight pages."

"Well, I don't see how—"

"He doesn't see how!" Galleani shouted with glee to the men around him. "I don't see how either!" The men laughed along in speculation of understanding why later.

Galleani pointed back and forth at Randall and Vignette. "Your paper can sway whole populations, but you do it for the powerful bankers who own you! *My* small publication acknowledges the simple fact that we can never fight back against those bankers with mere words. We must create change with *deeds*!" He offered a fatherly smile. "An opponent will refuse to listen to words. But nobody can drown out the explosion of a well-constructed bomb."

Randall kept his face neutral. "So you know something about making bombs?"

"Poor research on your part!" Galleani cried out with even more joy than before, looking up from his seat at the other men standing around him. They laughed along, sharing their mockery of poor research.

"I publicly celebrate anarchist assassins and bombers for what they are: martyrs and heroes! Your government can't stand that. And yet your government is stupid enough to let me come here. To let all my brothers and sisters come here." He turned to the other men and resumed his public speaking tones. "Twelve years ago I published 'Health Is In You,' and I explained how to be healthy by blowing up your enemies. I laid out the formula for making *your own nitroglycerin*! No one stopped me! Ha-ha! This is how you use the free press!"

Vignette spoke up. "You know, I recall reading about that. Didn't you misprint the formula?"

"I corrected it later."

"Several *years* later, though. If I'm not mistaken?"

"Three years. What did you say your name was?"

Vignette pressed the point. "It's just that I recall there were people who got blown up by following your incorrect recipe. Your own followers. Right?"

For one long, soured moment, his face was a death mask. "I...*corrected*... the misprint."

"I know, *Signore*. I know you did," she said as if she sympathized. She shrugged. "Dead followers, though."

Galleani leaped to his feet. "What newspaper reporter talks like this? What paper sends reporters to mock me?"

The men around him dropped all appearance of having a good time and assumed the look of a hit squad. Now all they needed was a call to action.

The security guard who had already decided he didn't like Randall and Vignette stepped over and whispered in Galleani's ear. Galleani's expression took on the cunning of a pawnshop broker. "Well! I think you two will now show us all your big, important newspaper identification cards!" He turned to the men for agreement. "Eh?"

The men began to babble like wild chimps at the mouth of a cave.

Blackburn's two decades on the force taught him to recognize the moment just before crowd violence was to break out. As soon as any crowd could turn away from their individual distrust of one another by focusing on a greater source of irritation, anything could set them off. They were there now. Randall decided it was time to go balls-out on a full bluff.

"Your disrespect is *offensive*, Mr. Galleani! We only came to clear up a few details. So I think we will just end this interview right here!" He grabbed Vignette by the arm and walked backward away from Galleani and his cluster of admirers, then turned them both around and kept on going.

She knew enough to play along and allowed him to handle her without objecting.

Galleani stood glaring after them. But when the men around him began to move in that direction, he waved them back.

Vignette threw a glance back at the crowd while she and Randall walked away. "Hey, isn't that the bomb maker still hanging around over there?"

Randall looked back to see Mario Buda shuffling around, apparently determined to have a moment with Galleani. "It is. And I think we need to go work other angles besides wasting time at his rally."

"Right. We could, though. Still not tired. A bit thirsty. I could use a bottle of that cocaine drink."

"Get one. You'll have the energy to drive us home without falling asleep."

"No chance. I like driving. Still not tired. Hey! They've got some privies over there. Let's go."

They stepped over to a few temporary outhouses equipped with Harper and Reynolds Aqueduct Toilets that emptied into a sewer manhole. Definitely not legal. She emerged a minute later wearing an expression of relief. Randall stopped in his tracks and turned back toward the crowd. "You know, I can't just let it go like this." He pulled out his PI badge and held it up, waving it around so nobody could actually read it.

"Gentlemen! The City of San Francisco is here to check union organizing tactics. We will be reporting this unlicensed anti-employer gathering...to your employers! I need to interview everyone here! Let's form an orderly line, right over there! Come on! Let's go!"

It was like the arrival of the feds at an illegal brewery. Only Randall's size and strength kept the stampeding crowd from trampling both of them.

Once things grew quiet again, the place was mostly deserted. Mario Buda had disappeared with the rest. Only Galleani and a few of his most loyal sycophants remained. They looked as if a different sort of bomb had just exploded.

Vignette gave a low whistle. "Well, that put a quick end to the party."

Randall kept his voice as soft as possible. "Listen, Vignette, maybe you should change your plan for tonight, in case he decides to quit early and retire to his accommodations up on Russian Hill."

"You joking? We just confirmed he won't be home this evening. A man like that lives and breathes on crowd approval. There should be plenty of time before he calls it a night."

"So how do you want to do this?"

"I'm parked right behind you, and my bag's in your car. I'll change right there. Then I'll head for Russian Hill and later we meet at home."

"Mm-hm. We can agree, though, can't we, that this is on an entirely different level of challenge than following illicit lovers around, yes? I'm letting you reach out with this, Vignette. If you were this green on the force, they would make you wait in the car."

"They would *tell* me to wait in the car."

He just looked at her for a moment. Several appropriate responses ran through his mind. Instead he smiled and shook his head. "Meet you back at home, then."

The pair headed back to their car and her motorcycle, parked up on Powell. But on the other end of the distance between them, Luigi Galleani stared. He leveled his icy gaze from a face dead of expression.

6

ON RUSSIAN HILL

VIGNETTE KNEW THERE WERE three members of the City Council with homes among the luxury castles up there on Russian Hill. If Galleani was truly being hosted on that pricey hilltop, it was in one of that select group. Today her simple mission was to learn by covert observation, if possible from a distance, where Galleani was staying.

Her sense of impatience had no room for passive stakeouts. Not that she had done many, but she understood herself well enough to be confident that sitting on her hands and waiting for somebody else to do something was likely to cause her legs to move, of their own volition, toward wherever she had parked the bike.

So for now, she concluded it was far better to break the question of Galleani's location into one, two, or three pieces. She would simply break into one, two, or three homes. Gently, of course, no damage intended.

She approached the Russian Hill targets by parking her motorbike at the bottom of the hill, then switched to foot travel for a silent approach. She had replaced her leather riding outfit with a blue velour walking suit pulled from Randall's trunk. Its baggy trousers were designed to look vaguely like a skirt.

In her eyes, the velour looked ridiculous, but she needed a costume for this one, and it would have to do. Better than attracting random attention with her motorcycle togs.

She hiked up the steep wooden sidewalk with long strides and was soon breathing hard from the bottom of her lungs. She endured the pain of exertion without slowing her pace, feeling more than ready for this little outing. She was energized by the prospect of getting into it and Moving Things Around, all the while remembering Randall's admonishment, "Only if it proves necessary."

To Vignette, the pendulum of interpretation swung back and forth on the word "necessary." She smiled at the memory and at the freeing nature of it.

Despite her feelings of glee, the hill she was on had a steep angle to it, and the effects of gravity were fighting her at a bone-deep level. She slowed her pace. The decreased stride allowed her to observe more detail; she was already in her stealth investigator mode and alert to the surroundings.

Each house appeared extraordinary in its own way. As usual, she had memorized her research, so she already knew many of the same architects who designed the grand stone castles in downtown San Francisco also put their talents to work in this district, creating these smaller homes of wood. Each one was a creative inspiration, custom designed to fit the incline of the hillside.

To Vignette, it was as if every unique and creative house had at least one person sitting on the front porch calling out mockery at the world's colorless lemmings for living in less interesting accommodations.

It made her want to light one on fire. Still, she wasn't here for that. And if she did, Randall would be so mad she didn't even want to think about it.

Because she never forgot and would never forget that Randall was her Fat Break in this life. Her Fat Break. She may have been forced to learn too much about brutality during her first ten years, but the idea of a Fat Break was one positive area of life she had figured out for herself. She experienced it as true.

Years ago, she came to the conclusion that Satan ran the universe, but somewhere in all that fire and agony there were these idiots running around with buckets of cold water and thick wet blankets to shield you from the heat. And if one of them came toward you, then you got yourself a Fat Break. Fat Breaks were here in this life, and they were just as real as the cruelty woven throughout the days.

A Fat Break could take guaranteed disaster and transform it to victory. The enduring problem was that nobody could ever explain how they happened to get selected for their Fat Break, why they didn't get one sooner, or whether they would ever see another.

Therefore, Fat Breaks were far too rare to be wasted. To Vignette's way of thinking, anyone with half a brain took full advantage of their Fat Break if they were lucky enough to receive one. She took several more deliberate deep breaths and resolved not to do anything that could ruin things with Randall this time.

She was halfway up the hill by that point. The only thing she liked about the neighborhood was the lovely irony of the fact that so many politicians and wealthy bankers lived up here on Russian Hill, home to Lombard Street with all its crooked switchbacks. On top of that, the bordering neighborhood was called "Cow Hollow," but it was just as affluent and as creative-looking as Russian Hill, making San Francisco the only place in the country where someone could mention living "over in Cow Hollow" and actually impress people with the information.

The first of her three potential target houses was an attractive Spanish Colonial Mission Revival, designed by the legendary Charles McCall after the Great Earthquake. In her eyes, it reflected the sort of modern taste a person in local government might want to use to make a statement to the world, delivered through an appropriately charming smile: *I'm richer than you. See? I live in a more interesting and creative-looking home. Envy is allowed.*

So house number one, then. She climbed the steps to the front door and listened for a moment: sounds from inside. A woman's voice, apparently lecturing a servant about something.

Ignoring the risk, Vignette pulled the barrettes from her hair, opened the clips, picked the lock, replaced the barrettes, and stepped inside.

The woman's voice was louder now. "I don't know why you give me such trouble about cleaning windows when you obviously need more practice! Streaks everywhere. Smudges. Dead flies? In the windowsills? Dead flies?"

Vignette quietly peeked around a doorframe between the foyer and the front room. A middle-aged woman was pacing back and forth, lecturing an overweight older woman in a housemaid's uniform. The maid stood with her head down and kept her hands folded in front of her.

"A lot of domestic help out there would love to have a position like yours. Don't you ever consider that?"

Vignette turned the other direction and glided up the stairs to the next floor, leaving the voice to mercifully fade behind thick walls and heavy carpets. Three bedrooms lined the hallway, but in the first one she checked, her inner gong struck.

The use of the guest accommodation was obvious. Several suitcases stood on the floor.

Vignette moved into the room, turning in a quick circle, memorizing details. Standard Edwardian furnishings, each one a master sculpting done in fine wood. The colors of every item in the room were selected to match with one another.

But the swanky uniformity of the accommodations made the visitor's foreign items stand out; well-worn travel bags stood at the foot of the bed, paired with nothing else in the room. The giveaway was obvious. She had found it already.

Holy stumbling monkeys! This is the place, all right. First try!

Stacks of *The Subversive Chronicle* stood on the dresser. She had never seen one before, but she grasped the significance. Here were the man's thoughts. She was inside Galleani's "safe house." But since evidence had to be legally obtained, what she had just discovered would never get into a California court. The process of the law needed more proof of wrongdoing than this.

She didn't. But she had pulled off this little meet-and-don't-greet on the first try. Randall would like the efficiency of that.

With a hint of grudging admiration, she realized it was pretty smart of Galleani to stay in a place owned by someone whose duty was to have him arrested for sedition. Leaving the question of why anyone on the City Council would host such a visitor.

Vignette imagined Randall saying the answer to that question was their new top priority, because these Galleanists struck back at the people who oppressed them by attacking the easiest available targets. Innocent people suffered and died.

That lack of concern for innocent victims was a hard stopping point for Vignette. Now when she considered the emerging enemy, she felt the same force at play she had learned to recognize as a helpless child. She could identify it because the ache from all of that invisible scar tissue still reverberated, throbbing along with her pulse. Back before the Great Earthquake and Fires gave Vignette the chance to flee St. Adrian's, life had already taught her to be suspicious of anybody who holds power over someone else. Especially if they have doors they can close and lock.

She learned the hard way, the lack of concern over the harm one does to others is the worst form of power abuse. It established her definition of Evil: a featureless thing that takes the form of anyone willing to host it.

Her experience enabled her to perceive the same rotted soul in different sets of eyes. From those days until this moment, she frequently perceived that demon behind an array of masks.

The threat of the nasty thing was first waved at her by the monks who were supposed to protect her and the other children. She only survived following her escape because a beat cop named Randall Blackburn stepped up and volunteered to take care of Shane, and Shane backed up her story about her being his sister. So Randall took them both in. Shane's quiet heroism in saving her made it all the more painful to lose him.

Now each day was another vignette in the greater story of her life of revenge against the Thing, which was always the same demon, no matter the face. All these years later, she was still collecting on a debt long owed to her for being forced to stare into the Thing's eyes while it grunted between her legs and gloated in its power.

Today in her full adult strength, she cowered in a corner for no one. She loved to battle the Thing in secret and especially loved winning through subterfuge and trickery. She realized, however, that the moment she defeated the person hosting the Thing, it merely fled and found another home. Then once again, through new eyes, the same rotted soul would stare out into the world.

She was seldom fooled by new eyes, new voices, new turns of phrase. She hunted the Thing and knew the look of its tracks. Vignette was nobody's hesitant foe.

Now this Galleani fellow was in her country to advocate for the random murder of innocent people, claiming nobody in the country was innocent, so therefore everyone was fair game. The idea galled her, murderous arrogance coming from people who posed as decent members of society.

"Fair game it is, mister," she muttered under her breath. "I don't play by the rules any more than you do." She was not merely talking to herself; she spoke as though her lips were two inches from his ear, addressing him in confidence. Passing on a little secret.

And that's when she noticed the small suitcase under the bed. Too small to hold much in the way of clothing, it called out to her eyes. Without another thought, she was on her knees, pulling it out onto the floor. The handle was padded in leather but the case was hard, probably wood beneath the same leather covering. It wasn't locked.

She opened it to see a metal box embedded inside it with several dials and knobs on the front. It took a few moments for her to put it together, but she realized she was looking at a portable radio. It had a heavy battery inside the case. A needled gauge was there, marked to indicate frequency. A paper sheet of frequency codes was fastened to the inside of the lid, along with a small white envelope with "Signore Galleani" scrawled on it.

She opened the envelope and removed a small note card.

Signore – Confirming half dozen bugs hired for as many locations along the parade route. Everything coming together.

Burn this note. – Hemo

Bugs. Firebugs? So it was to be arsonists on the parade route, along with bombs? Apparently propaganda sheets weren't enough for Mr. Galleani anymore. This Galleani fellow was turning out to be more than a mere political pamphleteer. Cheering from the background, he was threatening his way ever closer to gaining civic power over an international seaport.

And yet the note was a highly dangerous piece of communication, so why was it never burned? Galleani was saving it as what, a souvenir? A trophy? She had heard of such dark plots with the gathering storms of war but had never seen one. Now this. Portable radio communication? Such a device permitted individuals and groups to coordinate their movements. Probably great for soldiers and policemen, but a prescription for tragedy in the hands of criminals.

She knew far too much about the dark side of human nature to feel anything more than a sinking sensation at the prospect of instant communication between organized outlaws. She considered the level of mischief a criminal mind could do with this communication power. It put a lump of dread in her stomach.

Her first impulse was to steal the radio, but a better idea struck her. Why not leave it for Galleani to use, and instead ask Randall to get his hands on a radio receiver? Maybe it would be of some value if they got a chance to listen in on Galleani's plans without his knowledge.

She smiled and nodded. This was most likely going to call for some serious episodes of Moving Things Around.

She tucked the note in her pocket and packed up every copy of *The Subversive Chronicle* in the room, along with a copy of the June issue of *Electrical Experimenter* magazine, because it was open to an article explaining how to build the same completed radio sitting there before her. Perfect, then. She left everything else, careful to leave the room otherwise pristine. It was improvisation, to be sure, but with a purpose: a pleasant introductory thrust to the base of the skull with a jolt of electric fear. *Hello, Big Boy... So you're in my town to play, eh?*

Sure thing, pal, she thought with a satisfied grin. Why not get on the radio and complain to your friends?

Her leather messenger bag could be converted into a backpack by repositioning the straps. She packed the stash inside, swung the bag onto her shoulders, and light-footed her way back downstairs. Upon reaching the ground floor, she reacquired the voice of the same woman, now emanating from somewhere at the rear of the house while she hollered back to her servant. The unhappy woman stood in the same spot at the front of the parlor, head bowed, hands folded together.

"...loggers use those belts to hang a hundred feet in the air, and all I ask is that you use it to get outside the upper-floor windows and get those windows clean! We have hooks on either side of the window frame, and it seems to me someone who appreciates how easily she can be replaced would want to find some backbone and just climb on out there..."

Just as Vignette turned the front latch and eased the front door open, the servant looked up. She put her gaze straight on Vignette. They locked eyes.

Vignette had no other ideas, so she smiled and raised a finger to her lips while she pantomimed saying, "*Shh!*"

The maid glanced back over her shoulder in the direction of her employer, who was still hollering away. Then she turned back to Vignette, gave her a mischievous look and a sexy little shrug. Then this woman, who clearly needed her job enough to endure the shaming she received, simply raised her gaze to the ceiling. She kept it there, a contented little smile on her face.

Not a peep.

Seconds later, Vignette hopped over the front doorsill onto the porch and silently pulled the door shut behind her. She paused just long enough to wonder what the hell had just happened while she adjusted the weight of her bag and skipped back down the steps. She ran downhill without serious effort despite the demands of the heavy load. She moved like a young greyhound, feet flicking over the ground just long enough to contact and push off again, each step providing another thrust forward.

At moments like this, exercising her running ability made her feel as if she were in the right place doing precisely the right thing. It mattered not at all if anyone else would agree; it was true for her. A truth she could feel in her freedom of motion with every step.

7

AMBASSADOR SUITE AT THE FAIRMONT HOTEL

* July 18th, 10:30 p.m. *

CONFIDENCE WAS HIGH FOR THE FACELESS initiators behind the planned Preparedness Day Parade attacks. However, of the five attendees summoned by those same initiators, four were only present because of individual threats of blackmail. The sole female was a planted spy who had been unhappily in place for years. Her ruse was unbroken because who would suspect something so obvious as to plant a female spy among a panel of men?

As always, they were meeting at a hotel room anonymously rented for the purpose. But this time there was no hiding in a run-down flophouse hidden in some dark armpit of town.

Oh, no. On this auspicious evening, they were in a top-tier suite selected for its opulence, for its extruded message that if you dance with the forces who make this world what it is, then you are on the side of the ones who actually run things, regardless of what they say about City Hall or even the state capital itself over there in Sacramento.

The luxury accommodation was practically a palace, with no pretense toward interest in the common people, achieving its atmosphere through the perfect balance of contemporary fashion and individual flair. Average working stiffs who gave up enough rent money for a month or two might snag the place for a night, but they would have to be gone by the following noon.

The suite was a perfect exhibition of wealth and taste. Fresh-cut flowers adorned every cabinet and table. The furnishings were so ornate, they shocked a person into wondering what such things must have cost while simultaneously shaming them for needing to ask.

On this evening, a blue-gray haze of cigar smoke dominated the air, stoked by four of the suite's five occupants. The fifth sat holding a handkerchief to her nose and glaring at the others. The aura she exuded was in tune with the rest of the room, where the sour atmosphere of caged hostility was thicker than the smoke. The sole female spoke in a voice almost as pleasant as a metal file rasping rusty iron. "If we can move past the chitchat and get down to business, I believe my lungs will be grateful to you all."

The group leader, known to the others only as "Hemo," responded. "Rogue has a point. We have important ground to cover. Perhaps you notice the difference in accommodations this time?"

"Oh, Jesus."

"Was that a yes?"

"Put out your cigar, I'll agree with whatever you want," she snapped. "Start with these ridiculous nicknames. What is the purpose of continuing with them at this late date? I feel foolish every time I hear mine. Really, 'Rogue'?"

"Nicknames are easier to remember if they refer to something about the person. In your case, while your contemporaries are busy arranging social events and looking after their households, you're here working for the anarchist cause. 'Rogue' fits you."

He turned to a man seated next to Rogue and continued, "Just as the name Shadow fits you."

"Because I work in the shadows?"

"Because your shadow was on the wall behind you when I thought of it."

"Oh. Swell."

"I am Hemo because 'Hemo' is Greek for blood. And since I fully expect to die in this operation, I believe the name suits. Does Fox or Fire want to complain about their code names?"

Two youngish men with features so similar they could have been brothers, although they were not, shook off the question with a bored look. "Let's just get to it," said Fox. Fire nodded and said nothing.

"Good," replied Hemo. "These names could end up being the last safeguard between capture or freedom. We use them now, when we meet, so we get used to using them in moments of crisis. That way when the heat is on, nobody gets called by their real name."

"Except you know our names good and well," objected the one called Shadow. "You've been in town for six months and I still don't know yours." He glanced around at the others. "Do any of you know Hemo's real name?"

The question landed with a thud. They all sat without motion. The only movement in the room was the swirling of thick cigar smoke.

Shadow tried again. "And this is the first time you've said anything about dying, by the way. What's going on?"

Hemo ignored him and took another puff. "Today this is a celebration because our road ahead is finally clear to us. At last, at last, at last, we are done with the endless frustration of trying to infiltrate far enough into their system to have any real control.

"Four days from now, the morning of the twenty-second, we are setting off events so shocking they will embolden every one of our anarchist brothers and sisters throughout your country, inspiring them all forward."

Hemo turned to Rogue and smiled. "Offer us insight into your state of readiness, will you?"

She snorted in derision. "Yes, yes, even though Harry and I were in place for three years before you showed up and started us all in with your orders and your code names."

"You and your husband were put here by the people who are paying us, *Rogue*."

She blew a deep exhale. "All right, then. As of tonight, I can report that I have three women secretly cooperating. No coercion, either. They're true volunteers."

"Yes. No less expendable, you understand."

Rogue faltered a bit but managed to continue. "All three are married to men who work in City Hall. Low positions. They're either sold on the cause or they're just having fun with a secret, but they will be supplying fresh changes of clothing and a few items for personal comfort to any fighter who survives and needs to get away. We just need to decide on the best location to have everything made available for them. Until then, the escape kits, as you call them, are currently hidden in the basement level of my home."

"So our firebugs could just get them from you, then?"

Rogue's next answer was well rehearsed. "No. My home is a landmark house. A train of single young men traveling in and out will be seen and noted. Surely you agree."

Hemo pressed ahead. "Perhaps. For now, please tell the rest of us how you recruited three women in the short time since our plans were finalized. After all, since you're not authorized to tell them anything—"

"I never tell them anything that matters. What I do is, I talk about the families of these men who are so unfairly called 'anarchists.' Their children."

"Good. What else?"

"Each escape kit will include food to suit one escaping man for three days, plus extra clothing, since they surely won't want to make any more stops than they have to."

"And you're certain we can rely on these women to produce the goods?"

Rogue nodded. "Their level of enthusiasm is extraordinary. You ought to see them. As long as they're not part of the attacks, they'll go along with whatever we need."

"As with the one hosting Galleani?"

"In the same fashion, yes."

"Perfect. Because that brings us to our purpose tonight. Fox and Fire have that for us."

Fox sat up straighter and allowed a small smile, but he didn't stand before speaking. He nodded to Fire. "I'll take this one." Then he turned to Hemo and Rogue.

"Funny you should mention the City Council, but we've analyzed the new city charter, and everything about it is bad for us."

"You were certain there would be loopholes."

"There are not. It's too simple for loopholes. The new structure uses a 'strong mayor' who has all the decision-making power. That's it. No wiggle room for us at all."

Fire spoke up without breaking the rhythm. "This means the City Council has no real power at all when it comes to the nuts and bolts of governing. The mayor can run the city off a cliff and there isn't a thing anyone can do."

Hemo's pause was long this time. Certainly deliberate. He held it for another moment, then turned to Shadow and inquired, cool as moss, "And there we have the reason for tonight's meeting. Shadow, do you understand what this means for all of us?"

"I believe so, yes."

"Okay... What?"

"Oh. Well. Every avenue is now closed to us, except for direct action."

"He wins the cigar! What Signore Galleani calls 'propaganda of the deed,' my friend."

"Yes. Propaganda of the, ah...deed."

"We didn't want this. But the United States is about to join in a war of such madness that the American people would never support it if they knew what was waiting for them."

"Odd that you have such concern over it, however," snarked Rogue, "given your contempt for this country. By the way, if we have to keep up the names, I want to be known as 'The Rogue' from now on instead of just 'Rogue,' okay?"

Hemo drilled his gaze into her and held it a few moments too long. It was enough to shut her up for now.

He finally went on. "We might have trapped each of you into helping us by playing on your various points of personal guilt, but once you see we are the next new wave, you will no longer regard yourselves as hijacked for a foreign cause. Instead you will rightfully see yourselves as pioneers who blazed a trail. You see it now, don't you? What you just heard about your own city government? Democracy? Why call him a 'mayor' at all anymore? He's royalty now. Let's crown him king and call him 'Your Lordship'!"

Hemo knocked on the table like a man knocking on a heavy wooden door. "And so attention, please! Yes, this is a huge change of plan, a big surprise, blah blah blah, but these are the conditions that prevail: we can't get far enough into the government to steer the US away from Europe's great war, so now we have to deliver our message directly to the People. Down in the streets, just as we have prepared with our alternate plans. So. Shadow, how deep is your group as of now? Today?"

"Out of the list of firebugs the police provided, and I still don't know how you got it, I have six of the longshoreman who can and will do the work for us. It's just like you predicted. They're pawing the ground, ready to go."

"Still only six?"

"Problem is once you weed out the drinkers, the field is small. Tiny. But we need sober men."

"Understood. Keep them tight-lipped. A group that's small and effective can do as much as a larger force."

Shadow looked troubled. "I think we told them too much by trying to use politics to motivate them. It backfired. Several in my group have raised a question about how smart it is to use this for political gain. They told me, 'The photographs you showed us were of hungry families, to make it clear who you are fighting for. But now you want us to kill a random number of innocent people?'"

"Why would they care?"

"I don't know. But they're suspicious."

Hemo stood to his full impressive height and leaned forward to knock on the table again, much harder this time. "Tell them what you have to tell them and not one word more! Be certain they understand what will happen to them if they betray you!

"This country is going to become part of the greatest mass slaughter in history! Who can believe that the People of America—the actual working people who pay the taxes and make the country run—actually see what is happening in Europe and yet still want to get involved? This war is nothing more than your titans of capitalism pushing for profit. I suppose the smart thing to do is open a few casket factories!"

He made it a point to take in each of them through the eyes, one at a time. "You're lucky to have the job of helping this rotten country to end."

Shadow took a puff on his cigar, blew a smoke ring, and dared an impertinent question. His tone of voice made his intent clear from the first word. "Hemo, your sponsors are trying to start a popular revolution using people you had to coerce into helping you."

Hemo just stared. Somebody in the room had a loud pocket watch. *Tick...tick...tick...* Nobody else wanted to chime in, so the silence hung in the air. Finally, Hemo managed a tired smile and addressed them all in a psychotically gentle voice. "All right, I'll entertain that topic with you."

He turned to Shadow. "I'll add my appreciation that you, a known bigamist who is only here because of his desire to keep this out of the court system, is unhappy about our methods. He finds them unfair while he allows his bastard child to grow up in poverty. Excuse me, his bastard *children.*"

Shadow leaped to his feet looking like he was going to unwind with his fists. Instead he stood frozen, avoiding eye contact with all of them. He took several deep breaths, turned away, and stepped over to the bar. In silence, he poured himself another drink, keeping his back to them.

Hemo went on, "The decadence of this nation is its Achilles' heel. It's how I got each of you, and it's how we will make millions of worthless Americans pay."

"By killing them," taunted Fox.

"No, by filling them with fear. You scare people bad enough, they will rationalize anything at all to get away from danger. You will then own them. Call it what you want."

He turned to Fox and Fire. "You two don't want your embezzling of city funds exposed."

Fire interrupted, "And maybe you're overconfident! I still say there is nothing anyone can prove about either of us!"

"But we can prove your personal relationship with witnesses who will attest to it." He leaned forward and spoke in a mocking whisper. "And because this country is run by narrow-minded moralists, you can kiss your political careers goodbye."

Silence returned to the room. But it was a rotten form of quiet. More like a freshly opened tomb. Both Fox and Fire looked like they would love to take turns throttling Hemo, but they pinned their eyes to the floor.

"The four of you just need to make sure your people are in place and nobody talks ahead of time. After it happens, we don't care who finds out what."

He clapped his hands in happy summation. "So! That's it! This evening's message reads: 'No More Polite Political Change.'"

Shadow snorted in derision. "You said the language of explosions would be your absolute last resort."

"Yes. True. And here we are. Last resort."

"One step after the beginning? The last resort? Was this your plan all along? Was all the talk of infiltrating the system so you could create political change just, what, a bunch of malarkey?"

"It certainly was for me. So what?"

The air temperature plummeted.

Now it was everyone else's turn to stare at Hemo. He chuckled, even though he detected their whiff of opposition, as if to wonder if these fools thought they had a way out of their duties.

"Listen to me. This movement is too powerful to be stopped. Period. The rest of you just be ready to do your jobs. Get aboard or dig your graves." He lit another cigar and glared back at them.

Rogue broke the pause. "So at least now you can finally tell us what the signal to start will be?"

Hemo beamed at that one. "Yes! Yes, I can! No signal from us at all! They will give you the signal themselves! Ha!"

"What's that supposed to mean?"

"It means that later on, this will sound like prophecy: The parade will begin with a cannon blast and sirens, all done by the authorities themselves! When our devices go off at the same moment, and our fires begin to rage, at first people will think it's all part of the action!"

Hemo laughed in a manner that suggested they join in. They did not.

"Why so glum? Once people realize what has happened, every fire team and police squad in the city will be called into action—and be overwhelmed! Nothing could be more perfect!"

He turned to Shadow. "Your firebugs, can we trust them?"

Shadow snorted. "Trust them? God, no. Trust? They're firebugs. But what we *can* trust is they will crawl over broken glass to get a chance at a free ticket to set major fires in this city and have a shield against any prose-cution. Every one of them will be ready when the parade starts. You could set your watch by them. We can *trust* things to begin burning within minutes after that."

"Good. And you still have six? Even if a couple of them fail, we estimate that four strong fires can completely overwhelm the fire department."

Fox nodded. "The public remembers the Great Fire. Plenty of us lived through it."

Fire added, "Meaning panic will set in. The streets will completely jam up."

Hemo was warming to the idea of goading them with little bits of truth. Not enough to threaten the overall plan, naturally, but enough to keep the unknowing servants reminded who was in charge.

Of course he had moral clarity on the idea of his lie about dying for the cause, or any other lie. All justified by the game in play. The end result could shift the world's balance of power.

Hemo leaned forward and offered his unhappy stooges a fatherly smile, gesturing toward the exotic spread on the sideboard next to the table. "So, good-good, then. Here we go! Try some of the *foie gras* over there as you leave. The little biscuits are perfect for it. I'm afraid there isn't going to be much importing done for quite a while."

He made the icky face. "War and all."

8

BLACKBURN & NIGHTINGALES – PRIVATE INVESTIGATION

* July 19th, 12:30 a.m. *

AT THEIR HOME ON LINCOLN WAY, Randall Blackburn sat before his second-floor bedroom window overlooking Golden Gate Park. The arch-framed windows were open and thrown back wide against the July heat, allowing the faint sounds of a cable car bell to reach him. Double-dings rolled out in a set of three, receding as if falling into a deep well while the car traced its route through the park. He liked the sounds of cable cars and never felt distracted by them, but now a diesel-powered heavy truck rumbled by, turning into the park at the Ninth Avenue entrance just down the road. He could feel the reverberation in his stomach and chest. He much preferred the quiet clip-clop of passing horse wagons, but progress had its prices.

Inside the room with him, no candles or lanterns. The darkness matched his mood while the question tormenting him circled in his mind: *Where are we going with this?* He had done his best to raise his two young charges with plenty of personal support, but in most things he had adopted a hands-off approach in a humble nod to his own ignorance of raising children. Shane made it to young adulthood before his life was taken by something as stupid as a drunk driver, for God's sake. As for Vignette, she had always been determined to raise herself. For the most part, he didn't blame her.

And while he knew only the basic outline of their dual pasts, even in those early days he realized neither of them had any prospect of anything close to a normal life. The extraordinary trauma radiating from each one was at levels he seldom saw anywhere, even after a career in the streets.

Vignette's childhood, whatever it was, remained largely closed. She had never been willing to tell him anything at all about that part of her life. In spite of her lack of shyness about speaking up for herself, she avoided all talk of her past.

Randall didn't know what else to do but respect her need to choose the time and place to reveal more to him, if ever. Any of it, or all of it, he would love her either way.

He didn't really need to be told specifics. He had a clear idea how bad it must have been for her at St. Adrian's. The dark side of human nature as Randall knew it gave him the general outlines of her story. To this day, she woke up with a scream or a panicked gasp every night, without fail. It was such a regular occurrence that he had learned to take a cold form of comfort from the noises, knowing at least she was both home and safe in her bed, not out on her strange wanderings. The most he had been able to do for her was to provide a welcome place and try to keep it safe. More and more these days, the "safe" part was a real challenge.

When he first took Shane and Vignette in, all they seemed to need was a hand in getting ready to jump out into the world. Eventually their mutual pasts showed up in the fact that neither of them showed any interest in making friends. That part went well enough, as far as their little family was concerned. Randall had spent his life as an introvert, anyway.

Shane excelled at their PI work but remained determined to make it through the police academy and follow in Randall's footsteps. He could not be convinced otherwise, and he was so proud when he got his uniform. The idea that he died trying to be like Randall twisted a dagger in his chest.

As for Vignette, regardless of the boredom they felt at the prospect of making a living on the usual domestic surveillance cases, the work was relatively safe. It was as close as he could come to an answer: building a workable life for a young woman whose back-breaking burden of experience was such that she lacked all patience when it came to suffering fools.

Especially if they were male. Randall snorted a laugh and shook his head.

And so this new City Hall case started out as an interesting variation on their workload. At first blush, it appeared to be about familiar forms of civic corruption, the sort of thing he encountered with the department off and on over the years. It looked like the usual backroom garbage perennial to politics.

The bad guys in this case were hardly above using murder as a scare tactic, but he had seen plenty of other criminals who killed without hesitation. No. This thing, this group, this conspiracy, this whatever it was, seemed familiar but felt completely different. It had been swirling inside City Hall for a long time. Now it was running out the windows and spilling into the metropolis itself.

It was bigger than the hijinks of local politics. He knew that much now. And whatever this thing was, calling it "politics as usual" failed to capture the truth of it. At least with ordinary politics, there were acceptable ways to combat power.

Another diesel truck rumbled down the road. Like the one before it, its engine noise reverberated in his chest, in his stomach.

They had stumbled into something, or more accurately, they got pulled in because of Blackburn's reputation, and Vignette got herself dragged along with him. It was as unfair for her to be harmed because of him as it was to lose Shane for the same reason. The crimefighter load was his to carry. Not hers. Law enforcement was not the agency's job.

Now he had to consider what else he might bring down on her head. Ten years earlier, he had only been able to keep her with him because nobody else wanted her or her brother. Kids their age only got adopted if there was labor they could perform. He did the adoptions legally, but it was a flurry of stamped pages. Nobody had any interest in a custody challenge.

He never doubted their little home was a vast improvement on any other place the pair might have ended up without him. Now, though, how much of that was still true?

Shane had always concealed his feelings much more than his sister. Perhaps that stalwart quality was how he managed to hide, keep silent for many hours, and survive the murders of his adoptive family. That was all he knew about Shane's ordeal. Even though he had only been a source of cheap labor to them, it left a deep scar to witness their cruel murders.

When Vignette arrived in Blackburn's life, the hurt radiating from her somehow soaked into his heart. When she began to blossom under his steady supply of strong male support, he got a glimpse of how important he became to her. That was when he realized he would gladly give up his life for her if it ever came down to that.

He would have done the same for Shane, given the chance. The enduring problem was never one of a lack of love and warmth in their home. With Shane gone, it was that the verdict had not yet come in on whether or not this young woman, who eschewed all friendships in school and who never accepted attentions from a suitor, could ever manage to find enduring kindness toward herself.

Randall knew it was easy to forget how much he knew in his bones, taught by rough experience. Surely any predator out there would have a much harder time dealing with Randall than with Vignette. She might make fundamental errors in judgment for no other reason than she lacked his twenty-year police career of surviving encounters with criminal thinking.

Naturally she was a free adult by all rights, twenty years old now. Many young women that age had married and begun families of their own. But he still got nightly reassurance that she was safer in their home when he heard her screaming in her sleep.

First my death, he said to himself, *before any harm comes to her because of me.*

The sun was already up by the time his thoughts finished painting him into a corner. They forced him to the conclusion that got him up and started him walking. He made his way downstairs and headed out through the early morning light to the electric stable. It was an easy morning walk, maybe a few hundred strides.

9

CITY HALL

WHEN BLACKBURN WALKED INTO CITY HALL, morning activity was at beehive level. Foot traffic crowded the halls to the point that he nearly missed Jacob Prohaska when the Customs man surprised him by threading his way past, moving in the opposite direction, heading for the main exit. He looked harried. No, Randall corrected the impression. He looked scared. Like a man late for something terrible.

Randall started to call out to Prohaska, but intuition told him to remain quiet and tag along. Logically, it could add up to nothing, but it didn't have that old "nothing" feel to it.

He would know soon enough. Otherwise, if he needed direct contact, he could always pretend to just be out there coincidentally running into Mr. Jacob Prohaska, the man from the US Customs field office, the note writer whose messenger was mysteriously killed.

Once they were outside the building, it took barely ten minutes of fast walking until they came to a warehouse converted into a temporary showplace. A large group of men mixed with a few stalwart females crowded at the front door. All appeared eager to get in.

Each side of the door was braced by oversized men of hard disposition. They checked names against clipboard lists before allowing each one inside.

Randall knew he was not on that list. But oddly enough, Jacob Prohaska, someone he did not expect to be there either, strode ahead directly to the largest of the two men and said something close to his ear. The man stood straighter, snapped his fingers to signal his partner to take over for him, and politely escorted Prohaska through the crowd. They disappeared inside.

Now this is interesting...

He waited for several minutes, hovering in the background while the rest filed on in. While he watched, nearly everyone who showed up was admitted, but a few were turned back. A few of them walked away looking embarrassed and angry.

With most of Randall's twenty years on the force spent on the streets, he had learned to read people with a glance, sizing up their propensity for actual violence as opposed to the idle threats. Puff and sound had nothing to do with it; anyone could put on a show. The rest was in the eyes, and Randall was alive today because of the countless times he successfully dodged a flashing razor or grabbed a partially pulled pistol because he saw the action coming in the eyes.

He thought about stopping one of the rejected ones, just to see what he could learn about the event. Maybe use their cumulative anger to get them to spill more than they ordinarily would. It was tempting.

But no. He couldn't have it start going around that some freelancer was outside asking questions of people who were turned away.

So he faded into the background. Though he never smoked at home, experience had taught him a good cigar could take a lot of the sting out of waiting around for something to pay off. It could also give an otherwise suspicious person a convincing reason to hang around any given place.

Half a plan being better than none, he elected to hang around for a few minutes and see what developed. The bouncers were too busy looking dangerous to the people in front of them to be observant of people in the background, so they never took note of his presence.

Luigi Galleani stood in the little blast area below the thick concrete foundation of the San Francisco Mint. The freshly dug circular cavern was carved out beneath the ground slab. With a diameter of eight feet and a height of about six, it was just large enough to allow one man to move around the perimeter of the amazing new bomb it contained. The bomb itself rested on a stack of bricks with the tip of its truncated cone touching the underside of the slab itself.

His only regret was being unable to stay and watch the bomb do its magic when the carefully shaped charge directed the blast straight upward. The liquified aluminum of the inverted cone inside the bomb would shoot upward in a high-pressure blast of molten metal, crumbling the slab and blasting most of the debris upward and away from the tunnel.

With the tunnel itself venting the rest of the blast wave, everyone had to be out of the stable, horses kept at a safe distance. Then, even before the dust settled, the large and steady-tempered beasts would be driven right into the dust cloud and up to the tunnel entrance. Twelve trusted men would clamber into the tunnel and make their way into the Mint, shooting down the surprised and unprepared skeleton crew of guards.

They would have plenty of time to load the wagons one at a time, with the city in chaos and the police and firefighters overwhelmed and ineffective. They would climb aboard in teams of two and pull each wagon away from the tunnel while bringing up the next, keeping up the process until they had all six wagons loaded. Eight thousand pounds per wagon. The terrain between the stable and the docks was fairly even, so any four-horse team of Percherons was capable of pulling the load.

Forty-eight thousand pounds, sixteen ounces to a pound. The projected take would barely dent the holdings in the building but was large enough to panic the countries holding their wealth there. Better yet, it would severely damage the symbolic value of American "protection" in international eyes.

Of course, the money taken from the Mint wasn't enough to let all the conspirators retire stinking rich, as promised. They would be quietly eliminated with a special group toast after the ship was at sea. It might use up half the winnings to buy off the captain and the rest of the crew, but there was enough to do that and leave Luigi Galleani devilishly well set for life.

Politics had grown tiresome. The truth was that the challenge of motivating a population to stand up for themselves had worn thin. The game was always invigorating, but the purpose felt stale. He was torn by doubts and haunted by the question, did the general population even *deserve* to break free of their overlords?

Luigi Galleani would see them all in Hell, if there was such a place. And if there was, his consolation for being there himself would be that he had sent so many on ahead of him.

10

OFFICE OF THE DISTRICT ATTORNEY

* July 19th, 12:30 p.m. *

DISTRICT ATTORNEY CHARLES FICKERT felt as if his blood was about to explode from the top of his head. Betrayal surrounded him like rising tide on a spit of sand, but there was no way to know where the tide was coming from. This despite the so-called protection from the two young men standing before him, Thomas Winkle and Donnie Marsden, his closest advisors. Their principal job was to protect him from such betrayals, but today their performance was a strange study in failure.

They were supposed to be up-and-coming young guys, stallions, part of a fresh generation with bold new ideas, but so far he hadn't found any of their ideas to be especially new or all that bold.

Sure, they were green. Wet behind the nutsack compared to the calloused men he tended to favor. He only made the rare bow to City Council pressure and risked making them his main advisors in order to help him slink past a rough political patch generated by some unknown outside force he could never identify.

And yes, as soon as he took them on, their advice worked like a charm.

The formerly scathing news editorials somehow turned themselves around, and the news editors now bought into his projected image, thanks to the two of them. Clever bastards, both.

But now this. He looked again at the paper pamphlet he had been handed, a sample of many such found along city streets.

We are going to use a little direct action on the 22nd to show that militarism can't be forced on us and our children without a violent protest.

That was it. No other explanation.

"So you're saying we're supposed to take this seriously? This isn't an empty threat? Run-of-the-mill garbage?"

"We take no joy in bringing difficult news, sir. But this is all they put into writing. There is more, but we don't know if it's reliable. It comes through third-party informants."

"I need something a hell of a lot better than this! More evidence. Things I can show a judge and jury. And I tell you, if this was coming from just one of you, I might content myself in the thought that you've likely lost your senses and send you to see an alienist. But then there's this..."

He took a deep breath and picked up a postcard from his desktop. "Yesterday's incoming mail included this lovely card. And some of our business leaders have apparently called here to say they received a copy of the same thing."

He perched pince-nez glasses on the bridge of his nose and began to read: "Our protests have been in vain in regards to this preparedness propaganda, so we are going to use a little direct action on the 22nd, which will echo around the earth and show that Frisco really knows how and that militarism cannot be forced on us and our children without a violent protest. Things are going to happen to show that we will go to any extreme, the same as the controlling class, to preserve what little democracy we still have. Don't take this as a joke, or you will be rudely awakened."

D.A. Fickert turned to the others with an angry sneer. "So a little group of men is going to turn violence upon innocent people in—get this now—the name of democracy. Right? Do you read for pleasure, gentlemen? Because there is this old book written back in 1865, *Alice in Wonderland*. Ever heard of it?"

"Oh. Well, yes, sir," said Marsden. "In childhood, you know. Children's book."

"Children's book, is it? I suggest you get a copy. Because we are 'through the looking glass' here, gentlemen. Anything that isn't broke is running backward. May I point out that your specific purpose in my working life is to prevent this very situation?"

"Sir. We wrote out every scenario we could think of to oppose this thing, but these people are so entrenched at every level... Any resistance you put up will be turned against you."

"Agreed, sir. These people will accuse you of the very things they themselves are doing, in order to confuse public opinion. They can do it, too. They're getting money from somewhere to print their propaganda and send it all over the world."

"Well, then, maybe we should start by finding out where that money comes from. Maybe shut down the supply? Get a team working on that."

Winkle responded, "Sir. Um, no. We went that direction already. The sources are known to be Eastern European, beyond the reach of Western law enforcement. All the printing presses are small operations running in secret."

Fickert glared at both men for a moment, then began pacing the floor and rubbing the back of his neck, lost in thought. "But, but they're godforsaken *anarchists*, for crying out loud! I've heard all their rallying cries about the unfair conditions for the working people, but their stinking solution is *chaos*!"

Marsden held up both hands in surrender. "Of course we agree, sir."

Winkle added, "They want to drive a wedge between business and labor, and between government and the people."

Fickert snorted. "And they do this as if, once they destroy everything, people are gonna simply divide it all up and live like a happy congregation? As if people are going to ignore personal aspiration? Greed and envy will just disappear? Idiots!"

"Goes without saying."

"So why can't you create any alternatives for me?"

"It isn't you, sir."

"No, sir. Not you. It's them."

"I swear you make one more oblique reference because you're scared to speak plain truth to me, I'm gonna send you packing!"

The temperature in the room took a dive. A moment later, the one called Marsden spoke up. "All right, then, here's the hell of it, sir. Every contact we get is a message through some street bum hired by another street bum. They couldn't betray the people behind them if they wanted to. Our contacts tell us if these people, these forces, really, don't get what they want from you, their plan is to proceed anyway. Plus..."

Winkle picked it up without dropping a beat, smooth as a polished dance move. "Plus they claim to know exactly how to blame it on you. They have bank documents proving that some of the funds raised to assure your reelection came from foreign governments hostile to America."

"*What?*" Fickert ground his teeth and began to pant hard. "You get me the name of the two-bit, back-alley bastard who ever spoke those words about me and I'll remove his balls! That is the first I heard about such a thing!"

"We had him arrested, of course. The same day he showed the papers."

"Good. Where is he now?"

"He was accidentally released and took his papers with him."

"... Released. By our own jail staff?"

"Well. Accidentally, though."

"We searched for him later. He left town."

"Sir, the point is you can't...ah, we can't prove what you did or didn't know; proving a negative is just impossible. So whatever the truth, you will be made to appear guilty. The real threat they're making is directed at your political and professional future."

"God almighty. Who the hell is behind this?"

"We would respond with a publicity campaign, of course, sue everyone involved, file charges where possible. The problem with all that is only nuanced thinkers will understand. So public opinion will move on, the way it always does."

"While the smear remains on you."

When Fickert spoke, his voice was tight and strained. "I spent all these years watching every move I made, gentlemen, so my reputation would allow me to ascend to an office like this one. Can you give me alternatives, or at least *speculations* on how to avoid cooperating?"

"None this time, sir," Marsden replied.

Winkle nodded in agreement. "Not this one time."

"What makes it 'this one time,' though? Who's to say they won't be back again and again?"

"Well, sir, in the long view, we'll make sure City Hall cozies up to the California papers. You can go easy on civic regulation of construction, stay blind to their crime reporters when it comes to how often they break the law. But that's in the long term. For now, we have to accept that anyone can become the next target and find themselves cast in some evil light. The opposition will do it simply by lying and then swearing to it."

"All right, I get it. The papers get to say who the credible sources are."

"Yes, sir, but more importantly," Marsden added, "they become the sources themselves."

Fickert chuckled, but the sound carried no humor. "We're not talking about the Opinion pages, are we?"

"No, sir. This organization is already known to be doing this in other major cities. With such great influence over the daily news, they will step up their writing about you and your administration, and everything they write will be slanted against you. Everything."

"It doesn't have to make sense, sir. It only has to sound good to people who look for scandalous stories with simple plot lines. People who already want to believe what those stories say."

D.A. Fickert condensed it. "So for me, the message is there's no alternative to cooperation. To going along with the plan. They could destroy us all and leave us in prison somewhere."

Marsden brought the message home. "This is what we know at this moment. In three days, there is going to be a major event during the Preparedness Day Parade. The note's not a prank."

"Mm. And what sort of major event?"

"We don't know. But your office is to make a series of arrests immediately in the wake of it. Names have been supplied."

"Uh-huh," Fickert softly responded. "Does it matter if they're guilty?"

"No."

"Ah. Well, then."

"Please, sir. The men to be arrested are named Thomas Mooney and Warren Billings. Arrest a few others if you like, and use them to fog the field, but get these two. Here are sketches. I'm told the likenesses are accurate."

"Hold on. I know those faces. These two are a couple of troublemakers for organized labor. Radical union, anti-business. Petty criminals. We arrest 'em once a month for getting 'over-enthused.'"

"So. Good riddance, then, sir. Yes?" asked Marsden.

"Oh, and, ah…," added Winkle, "this office is to continually update the newspapers on your progress of the case. The papers will see to it a jury is impaneled who will give us a guilty verdict." He clapped his hands. "That's it."

"It's true," agreed Marsden. "That's all there is to it. Not such a hard way to go, is it?"

"Not such a hard way…?" echoed Fickert, looking as if his lunch could reappear on his shoes. He stared down at the street, out toward the ocean. His mind left the building and cruised the wavetops with the gulls. Another long pause filled the room. Enough time for pictures to form in one's mind, thoughts to flow, attitudes to change.

All this was beyond his control, beyond the grasp of any district attorney. The essence of his authority presumed a command structure of loyal professionals, ideally a group of people committed to the good of all concerned. Instead, he stood on a shaky platform and didn't even know who the enemy was.

They evidently reached into places high enough to make things happen in government and business that ought not happen at all, and to keep justice from appearing when they did. Now these people, this group, whoever they were, had entered his city like a pack of wolves surrounding a tent.

Fickert took a deep breath. When wolves close in on you, even in pitch darkness, there's no need to see them to know they are there. The sound of their breathing alone will freeze your blood. You already know what they can do to you.

Fickert was confident he had never made an enemy who could have any sane reason to hold such hostility toward him. This had to be coming from a large group. It took a lot of people and money: bribing or outright buying the main news sources; infiltrating government; threatening duly elected representatives.

How could such things even be possible? His eyes never left the outdoor vista while his mind raced. Sheer instinct told him everything he needed to know. Until he had proof that this plot was a toothless trick of some kind, he had to give in and step back.

Time to dance the girl's part. The best fighters know when they're over-whelmed. Fools deny it and fight to their death, but great fighters take the minimum beating necessary, then return later for vengeance.

Clearly, there's nothing left to do here but go limp and take that beating. Once it's over, rise and work your way back on top of things. Then when the chance comes, attack your adversary without warning. Strike back as hard as you can.

Plus a bit more.

No other way to keep your dignity in this world.

He slowly turned from the window and back toward the others.

11

HOME OF GALLEANI'S HOST, COUNCILMAN CINQUEVALLI

* July 19th, 10:30 p.m. *

LUIGI GALLEANI STOOD IN HIS GUEST ROOM while his mouth went dry with shock. His copy of *Electrical Experimenter* magazine was missing. The periodical held the design schematics for his new portable radio transmitter and ought to have been lying open as he left it. He stood alone and struggled to grasp the situation.

Had he moved it? No.

Was he sure? Yes.

Could it be an accident? Removed by some third party? Of course not. Here as a respected guest in the home of one of the city's elite? *Il Signore* Galleani was the world traveler who kept them titillated with stories of social injustice and the brave warriors who set off bombs to wake people up. When he told his tales, men sat up straighter, listening. Women tended to keep one hand touching the décolleté while their breathing grew shallow.

Thus no. No maid, no butler would dare move his belongings, large or small. All they needed to know was the obvious fact that it was the private property of their respected visitor, Luigi Galleani. *Either you respect private property or you do not.*

Yet someone clearly did not, eh? The empty little space mocked him, tormenting him with nothingness.

He had deliberately left the magazine open to the article with the designs for miniature portable radio transmitters, and why not? He was a proud owner. These devices were sure to become the standard in future missions.

Of course nothing was without complications. His Chicago contacts were willing to reimburse the cost of the rest of the radios for the approaching mission, but they had questions.

They were skeptical of the claim that his compact radio set could actually be powered by six batteries of four and a half volts apiece well enough to send a suitably strong signal. And as a major question, did the receiving units have to have their own source of power, or would the crystals really activate on the energy of the broadcast itself? No batteries for the receivers? It had sounded to the Chicago men as if Galleani were asking them to rely on prestidigitations. Crystals, the stuff of magic wands.

He had answered all their concerns by wire, of course. And once they arrived for their visual confirmation, a quick demonstration of the radio's abilities would make believers of them, no matter how tough and cynical those hog butchers fancied themselves. He would also verify the power of the transmitter unit, including the ability of the receivers to function without *any* source of power. Nothing at all! Few people in the world had one of these devices, and almost nobody knew about them. Galleani was a pioneer in all things.

Then it struck him—the missing magazine. It had to be related to his big meeting the following day, when he was to give his demonstration to the three Chicago reps.

So it was sabotage, then? Possibly. It would hardly be the first time. Challenges to his authority were a familiar part of life. The smart thing to do would be to postpone meeting with the Chicago men and get to the bottom of this theft. Snuff out whatever little flame this happened to be and then get on with the larger work. This was no time to attract attention from any of the authorities who weren't already in the fold.

But if Galleani played his dice right, the Chicago men sponsoring him had the power to send a single telegram back to their home base. From there, a quiet signal would be passed to a building in the nation's capital where Galleani's anarchist sympathizers were already working undercover in Congressional offices, involving themselves with allocations in charity work.

And with that connection established and approved, money would begin to flow from US taxpayers, routed past the intended charitable causes and straight into the coffers of the Galleanists. The anarchist movement would become a powerful national force unbeknownst to anyone outside a very small circle of friends. All under the eyes of the American government.

That was ample funding to spawn a thousand more bomb projects just like the one coming in San Francisco. Bigger. Coordinated. Radio controlled. Even as he directed them from the safety of a faraway mansion.

And yet he stood gawking at the vacant space atop his reading pile where the magazine and its schematic drawing ought to be. *Right there*, damn it, atop the well-dusted floorboards.

The burn of frustration rose in his throat. In the best case, he should do nothing else until he found out how this happened and what he had to do about it. Safety was the wise course. But in truth, that avenue was closed to him. The Chicago men would be here tomorrow. There was no other course of action, no way to excuse himself out of this. His fingernails dug into his fists.

Was he being watched, just then? Was someone outside? In his position, the prospect of being secretly surveilled was deadly. *It slits your throat with uncertainty.*

His wounds were further inflamed by having to quell his need to hunt down the perpetrator and throttle the bastard into a condition of clarity about stealing from him. That had to wait while the mission proceeded.

Not the Parade mission, either. The real mission. His mission.

He would see to the funding of future anarchists while he retreated to an island somewhere, a place where there was no government problem because the only government was him.

And so the men tasked with draping the hundred-foot antenna wire from the top of the Clock Tower Building would have to complete the job without his oversight while he stayed inside and tried to work out who might have invaded his room in such a way.

The terrible aspect of this was the unknown identity of his opponent. These political situations. He felt a passing moment of gratitude that there was no God. Such misfortune hurled by a deity would make this ongoing run of disappointments all too personal. He didn't need the extra pressure. As of that moment, it was daunting enough to find whoever dared to penetrate his private room and remove his important periodicals. Taunting him. As if to say, "*I can get to you any time!*"

His chest jerked upward in a hard sigh. He couldn't avoid grinding his teeth in frustration. After a moment, he lowered his head like a horse turning into a storm. Resolved, then, he would force himself to forge onward no matter what this thing turned out to mean, and he would do it under outrageous time pressure, just as he had done in the past.

The demands on him would ease, once he succeeded. Then he could savor the results and, before buying his private island with the incalculable wealth his mission would provide to him, he would hunt down the arrogant pig who did this disrespectful thing to him. This troubling thing. A strike too deliberate to ignore. Strangely precise, deliberately provocative. There was a mind here, and it had issued a declaration of war.

But who, then? Who indeed. Something told him his potential for success resided in the answer.

Randall hurried out to pick up his own copy of *Electrical Experimenter* magazine soon after Vignette brought home the magazine from Galleani's guest room. He was eager to see a clean version, and Galleani had scribbled all over his.

Taking action was better than hanging around wondering if she would be bringing the authorities down on them with that "moving things around" thing of hers. Not that he would keep her from doing it even if he could. Her results were generally solid, and he knew his own ghosts too well to judge hers.

But the magazine! He was elated to have been led to it. Published only a month earlier, its design for a portable radio laid bare the workings of a piece of leading-edge equipment for a reading audience who was just beginning to have an idea what radio waves could do.

And then there was the note to Galleani from someone called "Hemo." Bombs. Fires. He fought the sense of frustration. What were he and Vignette supposed to do against a plot of that size?

So if Galleani already knew the magazine was missing, would he stop to consider that his radio communications might now be overheard? Would he abandon the use of his radio? Or would he dismiss the theft as the act of a petty thief? Either way, Randall found himself feeling glad the old revolutionary had put this new dimension into play. It could work both ways.

The speed of a private courier had been replaced by the speed of light.

It was as if the distant future had already arrived.

12

DOCKSIDE UNION OFFICE

* July 20th, 12:30 a.m.*

THE DOCKWORKERS' TINY UNION OFFICE sat at the entrance to Pier 2 on the Embarcadero, across from the post office. Randall knew from years of night patrols that the office was kept open day and night to address work injuries. He banged on the door as hard as he would for a police raid, and within seconds, a harried-looking young man in a rumpled suit opened up. He looked angry enough to throw a punch.

"Hey! It's the middle of the night!"

"I knew you were open."

"No reason to beat on the door. Who the hell are you?"

Randall just looked into his eyes and spoke in a flat voice. "My name is Randall Blackburn. Recently retired from the SFPD."

The man's eyes shot open. "Blackburn. Yeah, I know that name. I know all about you. People still talk about the time you cut off that rapist's balls!" The union man laughed at the thought.

"That was never proven."

"Ha!" The union man gave him an oversized wink. "No arguments from me!" A sudden question seemed to trouble him. "Uh, you looking for something special down here? I mean, at this hour?"

"No, I'm not looking for anything. I'm here to leave a message. I need you to help me spread it."

"Me? Sure! I mean, Randall Blackburn! Hell yes! But you know we're just a field office here, right? The only reason we're open is in case one of the guys is injured. My job is to make sure he gets the right care. The owners would just roll the injured guy into the Bay and hire somebody else if they could."

"Tonight you've got a far more important job." He pushed past the man and stepped inside, then pulled the door closed behind them. "So I told you *my* name..."

"Randall Blackburn! Yes, sir!"

"I meant, what's yours?"

"Oh! Ha! Of course! Silver! Joseph Silver! Call me Joe! Used to be Silverstein, but my father shortened it. He was nervous about being known as a Jew. I don't think shortening the name helped with that, though. Me, I wear a Star of David around my neck all the time. See?"

"Joe. Joe, look at me. Stop talking for a minute, will you?"

"Ha! My fault, that one! Only time I get visitors here is when the ol' fecal matter flops onto the spinning blades. Sorry. What were you saying?"

"Joe, how many dockworkers are on the night shift down here?"

"That's easy. An even hundred, until daylight. Then we double up."

"Let me see the duty roster."

"Ah, well, Detective, I am not permitted—"

"Joseph Silver, I want to make it clear that you are the most important man on the Embarcadero tonight. You recall the Great Fires after the earthquake ten years ago?"

"Like I could forget?"

"You are going to help me stop another out-of-control fire in this city. There are known firebugs working down here, and I need to have a chat with them."

Silver regarded him with a blank face for a moment while the wheels turned, then he quietly stepped to his desk, picked up a large canvas folder, and handed it to Randall. "Firebugs. Yeah. As it happens, that's something we struggle with in our attempts to strengthen the union down here. We want all our workers to get a fair chance, but the firebugs and the guys who drink on the job, they keep giving the bosses an excuse to hold us down."

"You know who the firebugs are, Joseph?"

"Everyone knows, Detective. We support our brother workers, but we also know a few of those same men will set fire to the place if we turn our backs. It's a disease or something."

Randall ran his finger down the list of names, then reached up and pulled a pencil from behind Silver's ear and checked off one name after another until he had ten of them. "Go put out word on the docks for these men to report to this office. Say it's urgent."

"Might take half an hour or so."

When Randall gave no indication of changing his mind, Silver shrugged and said, "Have a seat. I'll get them here fast as I can. As my rabbi says, this ought to be interesting as hell."

It took closer to an hour for all ten men to show up, but they each appeared as summoned. From the looks on their faces, Randall thought Silver must have suggested there might be something in the offing, like a raise or a promotion.

Oh, well. He was about to serve up a steaming pile of disappointment. The last of the ten walked in, and Randall checked off his name. Then he called out all ten names and asked each man to raise his hand for it. Most of the men made no reaction to seeing him, but he recognized three of them from separate arson arrests he had made over the years. Those men were far more grim and apprehensive than the others.

"I will not keep you in suspense. Here's the news. This is a great day for you today. A day of salvation, a day of grace, a day for you to dodge consequences you may well deserve but will not receive."

"See?" called out one of the men who had no idea who Randall Blackburn was. "It's a promotion! I told you!"

The other men who also had no idea who Randall Blackburn was grinned in appreciation of their union brother's audacity. Nobody liked being summoned off the job, but so far this wasn't looking too bad.

Randall smiled a smile three times larger than appropriate. "It *is*, my friend! A promotion for you, from being a neutered corpse floating in the

Bay to a new life as an honest man with a good job who gets to go home alive. I ask you, is that a great promotion or not?

"Oops. Forgive my manners. I failed to introduce myself." He put a playful singsong tone in his voice. "Except I think a few of you know me..." He allowed the phony smile to melt off his face and dropped the playful tone. "But in case the others got the idea I'm with the union, let's clear that up. Mr. Silver here is your man, he doesn't have any part in what I'm about to tell you, and none of it is directed at him.

"But as three of you already know, my name is Detective Randall Blackburn. I was with the SFPD until last year, and now I'm a private dick. I don't remember my late mother, but my father told me she said I was a bad kid."

He began to slowly step from one man to the next while he spoke, deliberately invading their space and glaring into their eyes. He spoke softly, forcing them to listen.

"I know you all heard the story I'm gonna tell you here, because I walked this beat for years and I know this place trades on gossip like a ladies' sewing circle. So here it is.

"For a good long while, nobody could stop the rapes going on down here. Especially the attacks on prostitutes. It got to where it was some kind of sport for every foul excuse for a man in the region to come down here and do anything he wanted to the first female he came across. I know you remember. It's only been four years. You remember."

"Like we could forget? You kidnapped that man, Detective! And cut off his balls!"

"Never proven."

"Word is he was still alive when you castrated him."

"You should hear what the ladies' sewing circle says. Now..." He dropped the soft tone and bellowed at the top of his voice, "*Listen* to this! I know what you are. Not just you three. Every one of you!"

The impact set them all back on their feet. Randall didn't need to see a mirror to know they were staring at his Crazy Face. He dropped his right hand onto the butt of his 1846 Walker Colt revolver and lowered his voice to a near whisper.

"Some of you have been hired to do a job. Already been paid, likely. That's good. If so, you can keep the money. But that's only if you walk away, right now. I mean walk away from everything you have been asked to do and walk away from the people doing the asking."

"Mister, I haven't had anybody ask me—"

"Stop!" Randall stepped to the man doing the protesting and got close enough to bite off his nose. He continued in a whisper, but his voice shook with fury.

"I don't know which of you got the job, and maybe there are others who also got the job but aren't here tonight. Doesn't matter. They're going to get this message, and you are going to give it to them.

"I am not bound by the law anymore. And if you don't back down from the parade day job, I will find you. You know my reputation, and I am *promising* you I will find you, no matter where you go. So keep that in mind, and I'll tell you what I did to that rapist. No more rumors; you might as well hear it from me.

"I brought him to Lazy Ana Bone's place and gave him the opportunity to lie on the ground and apologize to his victims there, between screams. Bless their hearts, they've never spoken a word of that, have they? Prostitutes with more discretion than any of you.

"Then when we were finished there, two of the larger ladies helped me stuff him in a trunk and get it onto the seat of my car. Back then I was driving this Model T, and it was a tight fit. Had to leave the women at the house and drive him down here myself. Just down the road there, in that turn-off.

"Dark that night, lots of fog. Dragged the trunk to the edge of the dock, nobody around, guy bound hand and foot. So I took out his gag and thought maybe I'd give this guy a chance to talk his way back to life.

"But first, I told him since he's such a dedicated rapist who goes after his crimes like a glutton goes for food, I want him to answer the question of how long he's been doing this. I let him know this is his one-and-only chance to walk away from this in a single piece. To start off, I ask him how long he's been living in my town.

"He says he's been here since before the Great Earthquake and Fires. I ask him if he was going after females back then. He starts crying and says it's a curse. He tells me the other monks were praying for him to be cured of the need.

"I say, *Monks?* He tells me yes, he tried to cure himself by becoming a monk and living at St. Adrian's Home for Delinquents and Orphans. He pronounced the name of the place like he thought working at an orphanage proved he was worthwhile. I tell you, looking back on that moment now, I think he honestly believed he was speaking some sort of magical spell that would dissolve his problems. *Abracadabra, I was a monk in an orphanage. Poof!*

"So, yes, the rumors are correct in so far as he was alive when I castrated him. Messy job. He was still alive when I tipped the trunk over and let him drop into the Bay, too. Any of you Catholic? Who's the patron saint of fish food?"

The men's expressions made it clear nobody felt like trying to answer that one.

Blackburn continued. "You boys feel like you need to burn things to make life worthwhile? Go light a bonfire on the beach. Do any more than that, and I am here to give you my solemn word: you will be the topic of dockside gossip for many years to come."

He took another pause and looked each man in the eyes. "Remember, he was still alive."

One of the men jumped to his feet, pointing straight at Randall. "He's crazy! This man's out of his mind!"

"*Yes!*" bellowed Randall. "Plus keep in mind, this isn't your fight. It's just a paid freelance job for you. So keep the money and walk away. It's nothing to die over."

Everyone noticed his hand resting on the handle of his revolver, but the thing that captured their attention was his voice. It was the command voice he had used in countless situations where he was outnumbered and could have easily been overwhelmed if not for the intimidation factor he projected.

"Due process is for cops and the courts. I don't always have that kind of time. So know this, gentlemen, if there is one flame, one spark coming from any of you on parade day, then *I will find you*. And that's all the due process you get."

He opened the door and walked out without bothering to close it.

13

BLACKBURN & NIGHTINGALES –
PRIVATE INVESTIGATION

* July 20th, 3:00 a.m. *

IT ALWAYS STARTED WHEN SHE WAS deeply asleep. A faint warning cramp in her lower legs, barely strong enough to wake her. This time it hung there for a few moments, offering a preamble of things to come. At first she was too sleepy to heed. But then steel talons of pain dug into her muscles with cramps so fierce it felt as if they could snap her bones.

She had been five years old, maybe almost six, when she was introduced to sex by force. And while the experience terrorized her and left her in shock, those weren't the real attacks. Not the way she saw it. The real attacks came later.

It was only once her body began to show some capacity to endure the physical assaults that they struck with the real attacks. Plucked from her bunk, blanket over her head, hauled away and into a place of chilled air and the smell of motor fuel.

And still that part wasn't the true nightmare yet. The one that would ride around inside of her skull for many years to come. It was only the prelude.

Because inside the sudden torment of the old recurring nightmare and her spasming muscles, Vignette's memory tried to scream in pain but could not. She tried to relax her body out from under the cramping, but her smaller muscle systems were now seizing up along with the legs. There was no bargaining to be done with her past.

Inside the nightmare, her cramping muscles are restrained by force, and her arms and legs held down by strong hands. More than one attacker. She can barely breathe, sneaking in air through a tiny slice of airway between the edge of her nose and the enormous hand clamped over her lower face. Another hand covers her eyes.

They are on a hard bed, maybe a mattress on the floor, the hands holding her ankles in place have forced them apart. Then one of them is on her and then he trespasses inside of her because there is nobody there to stop him. He enters her in a manner certain to be painful, and so it is.

On this night, with those days mercifully behind her, the nightmare began to release her and evolve into other imagery, replacing the memory of terror with the memory of the chaos following the Great Earthquake and Fires. Back to the night she took advantage of the chaos of the earthquake and fled St. Adrian's forever, dropping the false name of Mary Kathleen and taking a name of her own choosing.

Fleeing the place saved her body, and changing her name saved her sense of herself. So did lying about finding a piece of paper in the now-burned offices at St. Adrian's, a document supposedly proving her to be Shane's younger sister. So did lying to Shane about it and then to Randall. So did the last ten years of living the lie under the protection of the only two males in the world she had ever been able to trust. She loved them both so much it hurt her heart to think of it.

Down to one, now.

14

BALLOON-FOR-HIRE, TELEGRAPH HILL
1,500 FEET OVER SAN FRANCISCO

* Sunrise, July 20th *

MARIO BUDA AND LUIGI GALLEANI had perfect protection from unwanted ears, but Buda was doing everything he could to avoid panic. He couldn't recall the specific word for the fear of heights, but he had that fear in spades. Their eight-passenger balloon car, the "Family Fun Basket," was otherwise empty while they hovered fifteen hundred feet above Telegraph Hill. The balloon had no trouble holding them aloft. Both men had noticed its powerful lift while the safety line played out on the rising portion of the journey, and they hit the end of the tether with a stiff jolt. Now the balloon hung in place at the end of the safety line as if waiting for its cue to either break for the open sky or fall into the ocean.

Buda had tried objecting to getting aboard, but the balloon ride operator quickly assured both men he had safely sent entire families up in the "Family Fun Basket." Many times. So many times. No problems at all. Children. Babies, even.

And then they were up there, in this completely unnatural place where only birds were meant to go. The experience of flight stimulated vastly different reactions from the two men. Galleani was elated, babbling with excitement over this unique experience, but Buda's survival instinct screamed at him and panic loomed.

He felt shamed by his inability to control his fears in front of the powerful man who summoned him to that place. He had only showed up at the top of Telegraph Hill in response to Galleani's note, delivered by some damned messenger. What were you supposed to do when a note got handed to you at your hotel room door by a personal messenger? How many people ever experienced that? He knew it was how all the swells communicated back and forth. But not guys like him. Anytime a swell needed to communicate with Mario Buda, it would be in a dark room somewhere. And nothing would be written down.

Therefore Buda saw the delivery of the note for what it was: not exactly an invitation, more of a command. He was all too aware of the deep debt he owed to Signore Galleani for loaning him the digging crew. The wording of the summons didn't sound regal, but the sender was a man many people called the brightest light in the realm of anarchists and the leading vessel of their global plan to save humanity from government and install worldwide Utopia. That was royal enough.

His reasoning was sound, he reminded himself, because whatever the point of this meeting happened to be, why, when a note was presented like this—the way one society gentleman corresponded with another—what else could it be besides a herald of something good?

Plenty of things, responded his inner cynic. Nevertheless, this call was from Luigi Galleani, one of a short list of people who could instantly get the bomb maker's attention.

The moment he arrived at the prescribed meeting spot, his concerns went to full alert. Telegraph Hill was an open hilltop exposed to the shoreline winds. Why this place?

He was additionally concerned over the presence of a small amusement ride operation set up nearby. Camped out, obviously. Right there in the proposed meeting place. Hot-air balloon rides, of all things. These people were trespassing, of course, unlicensed, no doubt, capable of popping up in any location where it might go unnoticed long enough to milk the locals for their pocket change. This one even had brightly colored banners boasting:

Hydrogen Balloon Ride - Giant Passenger Basket - Seating Eight (8) Adult People! 1,500 ft. Line! Diesel-Powered Winch!

Mario Buda glanced out over the Bay, where a small coal-fired fishing boat was barely visible through the morning fog. Its smokestack trailed a lazy black tornado while the vessel headed toward Alcatraz Island. The little vessel might be ferrying more prisoners, some supplies, or maybe the executioner himself. Buda could not repress a little shiver at the image of the Grim Reaper riding the ferry over to Alcatraz. It felt like a dark omen. Buda hated water too deep to stand in. In his world, you rode on boats and ships only because you had to. A good day on the water was the day you stepped back ashore.

A meeting place like this one made no sense to him, with that carnival ride set up and running. Wasn't the spot supposed to be selected for its privacy? He feared the amusement attraction would cause two men to stand out who didn't have family or friends with them.

Then Galleani came driving up in a car he must have borrowed some-where. He leaped out, all smiles, pointing at the balloon ride and shouting, "*Paisano!* The balloon! You must come with me!"

It turned out Galleani didn't care who might see them. The men who were operating the ride were Galleanists. Buda began to ask what happened if random people showed up for the ride, but Galleani scoffed.

"What? No! You don't understand; American pride is all wrapped up in being able to do what you want. So there are two friends who want to see the sights at sunrise." He threw his arms open wide and beamed. "So what? Eh?"

Buda attempted to protest and even planted his feet for one failing instant. Galleani managed to force him without using actual force, and Buda found himself inside the basket trying to control his breathing.

He could not make himself look while the balloon was released and the winch began to pay out line. The basket rose with alarming speed.

Now, *fifteen hundred feet over the earth*, their balloon kept gravity from killing them while the restraining line kept the balloon from riding the seaward air currents to an eventual water landing and death by drowning. Buda had to clench his lower muscles to keep from blowing a load of personal humiliation into the occasion.

He mentally pulled his bomb maker hat down low while his strained nerves held him in check. He remained marginally in control of his innards while he pretended to attend this little moment of lecture by *Il Signore* Galleani, who waxed on about politics and boring details of international banking tricks that were of no concern to a man of action like the Bomb Maker Nonpareil.

But before long his attention was captured by the sight of San Francisco's Embarcadero district shimmering below them. Far below them. Through the swirls of morning fog, questions yawned up at him and grabbed him by the face. Their power put him in touch with his mortality so fast it gave him vertigo.

Is it crazy to hate being up here like this? Is it wrong? Who is this celebrity anarchist, "The Great Luigi Galleani," anyway? Is he worth dying for, right now, by falling out of the sky?

Buda couldn't help but think of all the great work ahead of him that would go undone if that flimsy bag of hydrogen gas above them went bad for any reason. Lightning strikes? Had he read somewhere that lightning strikes were more prevalent near the ocean shore? Saltwater or something?

"You don't look like you're listening."

"What? No. I'm listening."

"Ha! I think you are not! But cheer up! The owner is a Galleani *good friend*. He says we're safe in this balloon." He laughed. "And you can bet your last dollar nobody will listen in on us up here!"

Buda strained to avoid looking out the basket windows anymore. He cleared his dry throat with effort. "So then, Signore Galleani, here we are, as you requested. Whatever is so secret, please just say it, if you don't mind. Please. I want to get back down as soon as we can."

"Relax, Mario! Now is not a time to hurry. It is time for you to get the full story."

"Full story..." Buda responded. A vague feeling of suspicion tickled his nostrils like a feather.

"Oh yes! The Preparedness Day Parade. I have men ready to put your bombs in place along the parade route, but a few of our helpers have gotten nervous. I need another man who is absolutely committed to perform the most important job of all of them."

He leaned close to Buda, although no one else was there. "That man is you."

"I see," lied Buda.

"Not yet you don't."

"My apologies, you are right. I do not."

"Ha! An honest man! Give me a thousand of you and I would take over this sorry excuse for a nation and kill everybody connected to the government. All of them!"

He gave his face a moment to lose the grin and reflect sober thought, then got down to business. "Mario, it's time for street action from you. I have something I cannot entrust to anyone else. Only you, Mario. Only you."

Buda stiffened. He was the Bomb Maker Nonpareil, but street action? His short body and slight build were not those of a rebel soldier. "Thank you," he lied again. "But may I ask, what makes you trust me so much?"

"Your reputation."

"Because I build bombs that work?"

"No. I mean your future reputation. I know you want to sustain it. You want to keep your credibility with all our brothers and sisters around the world. With people who will hire you. What's that thing you like to say? You'd 'rather die than fail'?"

"Right," Buda acknowledged with a smile and a nod, now wishing the remark had never occurred to him. He had felt so clever the first time he said it. "But what are you specifically—"

Galleani broke in. "You will meet with the other men on the day after tomorrow at the Embarcadero at one p.m., half an hour before the parade begins. There will be a sausage stand set up next to the Clock Tower."

"Sausage stand?"

"Yes. Nobody will notice a bunch of men congregated around such a place at lunch hour."

"Mm."

"The bombs have been hidden down at Pier 19 since you delivered them to me. On parade day, you will take them to the Embarcadero and distribute your creations to the men, who will each put one in place."

"Yes, but where will they put them? The location has a great deal to do with the effects of the blast, Signore."

"Location choices are my concern alone, my friend. None of the men will know until they take possession of their device."

"How can that work?"

Galleani emitted a proud smile. "I have placed your creations in larger suitcases, which hold radio receivers. Once the folding antenna is extended, they will act as remote detonators."

"Why? I supplied you with timers."

"Unnecessary. There will be a thirty-meter antenna wire hanging from the tower, which is long enough to guarantee the signal hits every part of the city."

"You want me to deliver one of the bombs...with no timer on it?"

"Timers! Mother of God! It's more important than that, Mario. You will be the one to take the portable radio to the Clock Tower, connect it to the antenna wire, and set off the grand detonation. No timers, Mario. No need."

"Signore Galleani! I am only a—"

"I must oversee the entire mission. There will be too many obligations to guarantee I can be at the Clock Tower and do it myself, as much as I would love the honor. It needs to be timed precisely for the start of the parade. Each carrier will be given their target location when they pick up their suitcases. I have written those addresses inside them. The men will take your bombs to those places, extend the antenna, and leave."

He focused on Buda as if he could see the future in his eyes. It was his most effective facial expression for manipulating others, and it seldom failed.

"For you, as my most trusted one," he continued, "I will see to it the others know it is the Bomb Maker Nonpareil who will detonate the weapons they deliver. You see, don't you, Mario? They will want to live up to your reputation! And so they will not lose courage. They will stay on the mission and deliver their devices."

"What's the point of the secrecy among us about our locations?"

"Simply that if anyone gets caught, there is no way he can tell the authorities where the other bombs will go. They'll have no time to stop them from going off."

Buda spoke carefully. "All right, Signore, this time I really do see what you mean. And I am grateful for the opportunity. But did we really have to come up here for you to tell me this?"

"No. We came up here so you understand why I have to depend completely upon you. There's far more riding on this than you know."

"We're already going to bomb hundreds of civilians. What more could be riding on it?"

"Far more, Mario. The people driving this and sending our funds from Chicago don't come from there themselves. They just route things through that city so nobody outside their system could ever check their bank accounts and get close to a straight answer."

"But they're fellow anarchists. Correct?"

Galleani gave him the indulgent smile usually visited upon sadly ignorant children. "Welcome to your first day of school, Mario. Now please listen. Anarchy is a means to an end. A means to an end, Mario. Surely you realize that."

Silence. Mario did not move. Neither did Galleani.

The shriek of a seagull erupted close by. The call continued and grew nearer, with the bird passing only feet from their basket before diving down and away, pulling its birdcall down with it in volume and pitch.

Galleani smiled. "Lovely demonstration of the Doppler effect, don't you think?"

Mario was momentarily speechless. He had no idea what Galleani was talking about and absolutely no interest. His heartbeat spiked. Did he hear Galleani right when he said anarchy was only a means to an end? To hear this from the great Luigi Galleani was unreal to him.

"Means to an end..."

"Mario!" Galleani shouted. "The Germans have an old saying. It's a good one. '*We are too soon old and too late smart.*' We're both too old not to see that although chaos can destroy a corrupt system, chaos can't *build* anything. Something has to come *after* the chaos. That's why we need this war."

"What?" Buda gulped. He was gobsmacked. His brain was nearly bleeding over this. It didn't matter that Galleani was so far superior to him in the international movement; he fought the desire to grab the great man and shake sense into him. "*Need* this war? We're trying to stop the damned thing, Signore!"

"Of course we are trying to stop it!" Galleani cried out with genuine glee. "And we will fail to stop it, my friend! What we succeed in doing is to push the conflict into pure chaos. The result is the same for us. Are you listening to me, my young friend? Either you control power or it controls you."

"Signore Galleani, my entire life has been a call to revolution! But this…"

"Yes! Yes! Yes!" shouted his host. "And then when the revolution is over, someone has to chop the wood and carry the water, do you understand?"

"Chop wood?"

"The functions of society, Mario! They have to continue in some fashion or other, yes?"

"Maybe they would be better if people just, you know, worked things out as they came along and didn't use all these government systems. Isn't that what you want? No governments?"

"Damn it, Mario, we are not children! Somebody has to run things because far too many people *are* children."

"I don't know what that means, sir. I am not a philosopher."

"Then just listen. The bankers who fund us have decided America needs to get into this war. People in Washington, DC, are looking for a way to get into the war, itching for a way to get in because they represent the industries that will fire up to feed the war machine. And we're going to provide that for them. That's what our mission will help them do."

"I beg your pardon, Signore Galleani, but I can't believe what I'm hearing, here. I built those bombs to help convince America to stay out of Europe's war. But you mention *helping* bankers? The people who created this misery?"

"Mario, the Rothschild family in Britain is funneling money to the British military."

"What does that have to do with—"

"And the French side of the Rothschild family is funneling money to the French military."

"Both of them?"

"Yes. And the German Rothschilds are funneling money to the German military."

"One family?"

"Branched out through marriage. One big happy. And the American Rothschild family is funneling money to all of them, making sure they all have enough to fight their war."

"We now work for *banks*?" He sat without moving for a few moments, then slowly shook his head. "My ears cannot believe this, Signore. Not from you."

"We do not work for 'banks,' we are working with the Rothschild international system of banks. It's the difference between working for a farmer or working for a king."

"Sir, Signore, who can believe the US government will ever allow any bank to hold so much power over it?"

"They already did. Rather, it was already done to them."

"The Americans let this happen? I have heard nothing—"

"Not the Americans, Mario. They are irrelevant. This was done while they slept. The Rothschilds hired an attorney named Samuel Untermyer right after President Wilson's inauguration. He delivered the message that Wilson was being blackmailed by a former fellow teacher he had an affair with years ago. Heh. Married lady, yes? Now Untermyer, Esquire, reported it as his sad duty to demand, on her behalf, the sum of forty thousand dollars from Wilson. Or else she would remember him in public. And keep on remembering him.

"Woodrow Wilson has a humble background. Untermyer knew he didn't have the money. What Untermyer did was, he told the new president he would pay off the woman for him, but of course with a condition: Wilson had to promise Untermyer that when the next seat on the US Supreme Court became available, he would have the power to select the nominee. Last month, Mario, on June first, Louis Brandeis was seated on the Supreme Court."

"Recommended by Untermyer?"

"Oh yes."

Buda exhaled hard. "Now that you mention it, I recall reading about that in the newspaper. Small item. Inside pages."

"Justice Brandeis has sent a secret delegation to Britain promising to deliver the United States into this war. Do you think he wants to be proven wrong?"

"Of course not."

"And yet, no Justice on the Supreme Court can guarantee such a thing, correct?"

"I suppose not."

"Of course not. It takes vast amounts of money and political power to guarantee such a thing. It takes the ability to affect manufacturing, banking, governmental decrees, and a good portion of the national news media."

Buda couldn't believe his ears. "You are going to tell me these Rothschilds, they have all that under control too?"

"They also control all three of Europe's major news agencies, as of today. Plus over the last few years, they have placed retainers in major editorial positions at twenty-five of the most influential newspapers in the United States. So far."

Buda struggled for breath. "Signore Galleani, I...I think this point of view may be extreme. Anything that leads us closer to dealing with banks is simply—"

"You may recall, until recently, the American people wanted nothing to do with the war." Galleani's eyes narrowed. "'Isolationism' was the word of the day."

"Right. Then came all those stories about German atrocities on captured soldiers and civilian families."

"People changed their minds."

"Yes."

"How did they learn about it?"

Another gull went dropping past them toward the water, shrieking in fading tones. "...Oh."

"All those stories. Were they true? Untrue? Exaggerated? Oh, well. Whoever controls the news reporting controls the minds of the People. And now the American public is so full of rage at Germany they are practically spoiling to go to war. The Federal Reserve is eager to approve financing behind the scenes because it's a Rothschild-controlled entity. And here's the genius behind all this: the Rothschild banking system and their proxy, JP

Morgan Bank, will make vast fortunes no matter who wins. Ha! Either way!"

"Signore Galleani, I am a simple man. You want a fine pair of shoes, I make them for you. You want fine explosions to occur, I make them for you too. But you play with fire if you get close to such wealth! It's an entire class of people. They hold us in contempt, you know."

"Yes. The whole point, Mario. It's much more than mere wealth; it's genuine political power. The kind of power that brings down nations and creates new ones."

"Bringing down America, then."

Galleani gave a triumphant smile. "*Voila!* Now you see. Bringing down America along with much of what we now call Europe."

"How did you know about this?"

"Who am I, Mario?"

"All...all right. A new plan, then?"

"The same plan. Bombs on the parade route. It's just that the man who made them will also be the one to detonate them." Galleani stared and waited for him to get it.

"Yes, yes, and I thank you, but my question is this: By helping the banks and by accepting their money, we get the result we need?"

"Exactly, comrade. One step back, then three steps forward."

Buda broke into a cold sweat. He was right about being a simple man, but nobody ever said he was stupid. How was this madness about working for a bank *not* blasphemy?

"And you believe, Signore Galleani, you actually believe these *bankers*?" He bit off the last word like the head of a snake.

"Of course not. They're bankers. But tell me, Mario, what do you consider the most powerful human emotion? The prime motivator of human actions?"

"As I say, I am no philosopher, Signore."

"Guess."

"Um...well, would you mean the loyalty between people with a common cause?"

Galleani exploded into such sudden laughter, a glob of mucus flew from his mouth and hit Buda in the left eye. Buda wiped at his eye and gritted his teeth while Galleani continued to laugh for several long moments. At last he caught his breath.

"Greed, Mario! Greed is the only fully reliable human characteristic. Loyalty is a passing joke. Love sours, anger dissipates, envy grows bored with itself. But greed, Mario. Anyone's greed. Everyone's greed. The greed of our supporters. I would trust the predictability of their greed with my life, Mario. And so should you."

Galleani studied Buda's face for a second, taking in the younger man's state of shock. He laughed again, as delighted as a big kid who just wised up a little kid to the fact there was no Santa Claus.

Buda's cold sweat began to make him shiver. It had nothing to do with the balloon's altitude. His mind reeled so wildly he was close to passing out. He grasped the honor of being taken into the leader's confidence and performing the first radio-controlled multiple detonation, but for this? *This?*

"Signore, please. Why would we want to support that?"

"Perfect question! Answer: we don't. Are you listening to me? We don't! We want the *chaos* it will cause!"

He leaned toward Buda and whispered, for no other reason but dramatic effect, "Inside that chaos, true opportunity awaits for all who play their part. You should heed that, Mario. Endless challenges for the Bomb Maker Nonpareil."

Two more screaming gulls went diving by, repeating the same squawks and dropping down the tonal scale. The sound somehow reached into his skull and seemed to pull the blanket of ignorance from Mario Buda's eyes. And then he saw.

Ah-ha! How badly he had misunderstood! Galleani was no traitor to the cause! He wasn't trying to recruit him to be a turncoat and work for the banks. No, it was deeper than that. The product of a mind much smarter than his own.

He was being advised to use any means necessary to achieve their ends. Working with the interest of banks was merely a temporary ruse! A sensation of illumination overwhelmed him. He felt himself glowing, radiating delight. He and Galleani's men were only *appearing* to cooperate, while in fact they would be using the lifeblood of their enemies against them.

This, he realized, changed everything. Here was a stunning example of what made Luigi Galleani the important thinker that he was. An invaluable ally to the anarchist cause. A rush of humiliation chilled him when he realized his error.

"I see, Signore," he replied, his voice cracking with emotion. "Forgive me for being slow to grasp your vision. And I will make sure the bombs are detonated, no matter where you need to be at that precise moment."

"The men will meet you under the Clock Tower at one p.m. The parade starts at one thirty, so you'll have time to carry the transmitter up into the tower and over to the antenna wire, attach it, and send the signal at the stroke of one thirty. Just as the parade starts."

Buda took a deep breath and steadied himself. Between his acrophobic reaction to the balloon's height and the intimidation factor of sitting alone with Luigi Galleani, he was having a hard time following the conversation. "Yes. Of course, Signore! My apologies. It's the, ah, height up here, I think. Making me so nervous."

"Curtail your nerves. There's no room for mistakes. This is the key to the sausage stand's lock. Take it. You will be inside the stand when the men show up. If any real customers appear, tell them you are still cleaning out the rat's nest you discovered inside. That will get rid of them. The others you'll simply greet so they know it's you. They will say your name, you will give each one a suitcase. With that done, proceed over to the Clock Tower and climb to the second floor. You can reach right out and snare the hanging wire. Attach the transmitter, turn it on, and press the red button."

"What if I am seen?"

"Doing what? The explosions will be far away from you. What you have there is equipment for measuring weather. Understand?"

"Yes, sir. Yes, I will, then. I'll get down there early."

Galleani placed his hand on Buda's shoulder like a father who would, for the cause, gently slit his throat. "We will be in the wind before the police know who we are. And *you* will be the one whose brothers and sisters sing your praises, Mario. *You* will be the one they call upon to repeat this bold act in every city on this continent while the war rampages over Europe, until all these corrupt Americans cry out for safety and protection of anyone who can return them to their quiet lives. Now you see it, Mario. Now you know."

Buda's sense of himself took such a growth spurt behind Galleani's flattery that he now forgot his nausea and fear of heights. The backrooms of his mind swung open. Energy flooded into him as if hydrogen filled his skull, lifting him far above his countless concerns.

What were the nagging fears of acrophobia next to an imagination tumbling with visions? New cities, new countries, perhaps places without governments at all. Utopias galore, just waiting to be opened. Best of all, his own bomb-making skills would help level the foundations for every new castle.

And Mario Buda's brain lit up most brightly while he grasped the potential of radio for the transmission of trigger signals. Thanks to Signore Galleani, he saw the countless uses for remotely detonated bombs. He felt like a caveman who had just seen fire made for the first time.

All of it was brilliant to the core.

His entire universe transformed itself. Now the world was rife with scenarios for the Bomb Maker Nonpareil, more than enough for him to permanently kiss the cobbler's life goodbye and embrace a lasting state of nobility.

He barely noticed when the powerful winch began to reel the balloon back down to the ground. His once-in-a-lifetime view of the Embarcadero shoreline displayed itself unattended while visions of the future covered his eyes like stained glass.

Enchantment prevented him from taking in the look of satisfaction on the face of his host, or noticing the accompanying whiff of contempt.

15

GALLEANI'S BORROWED CAR

GALLEANI GENEROUSLY OFFERED BUDA a lift to his hotel in the borrowed automobile, though he made Buda crank the engine. The ride to the cheap Tenderloin district taxed Galleani's patience with Buda's company, but the older man made it a point to slather on a few more compliments about the importance of Buda's work.

Despite his revulsion over politicians, his success as a public speaker was based upon the power of attentiveness and the ability to listen with the appearance of giving serious weight to whatever was being told to him. His skill prompted him to do just that while also taking note of the obvious pride on Buda's face over being called for this solo audience.

Almost worshipful. Right at the level Galleani liked it to be. He savored the satisfaction of successfully enlisting another suicide drone. The sensation melded with equal contempt for the enlistee, a common man with talents no greater than any trained army sapper. An expendable lickspittle gulled by flattery.

Upon first meeting with Buda some months ago, the younger man referred to himself as "Bomb Maker Nonpareil." Galleani had no idea whether such a claim would prove out, if tested. To him the meaningful information was the simple fact that this Mario Buda fellow was desperate for self-respect and dreamed he could gain it from Galleani and his movement. So be it, then. Naturally the man was a lunatic, but his lunacy was the broken window that allowed Galleani to penetrate his skull and take ownership of his soul. He considered the irony of owning Buda's soul while also not believing he had one, and it caused a smile to spread across his face.

"What's so funny?" Buda asked.

"My wife," Galleani lied with ease.

"Wife? I didn't know you were married."

"I'm not. Why do you think I'm smiling?"

The two men laughed like the conspirators they were and even the friends they were not. Galleani pulled to the curb at Buda's hotel and parked between two hansom cabs. Both of the big draft horses eyed the machine with suspicion but lost interest when an ordinary human stepped out. The beasts turned away while Buda bent down to the driver's eye level and called his thanks back into the vehicle.

Galleani waved in reply, smiling once again, this time at the pleasure of knowing this dangerous *idiot savant* or whatever he was would soon be blowing up along with his last creation.

Because Mario Buda knew bombs, not electronics. Galleani's transmitter would send out its signal at his command, but that same command would also set off a three-second mechanical timer and then ignite the small piece of Buda's own dynamite hidden inside the radio casing. At least Galleani's experience in building the radio was paying off, even if in unexpected ways, such as taking apart the transmitter, then placing the little surprise and sealing the device back up so it looked right. There was no need for a large blast radius. This one would only be lethal within a few yards. Plenty. The man knew too much to risk capture and interrogation.

Besides, he would fit the profile of the parade bomber and take blame for the whole event so much better if he was dead when they found him. Or when they found what bits might be left of him. And if Mario Buda truly believed in the cause, he wouldn't mind dying that way, would he? Going out a martyr and all. One harsh kiss from Death, the immediate embrace of oblivion, the loss of all cares, and an enduring legacy celebrated by those he admired most.

Why, if Buda knew in advance (which he would not), the man would owe Galleani a bottle of port and a box of cigars. That one made Galleani smile, and this time the smile was real enough.

He guided the auto out into the traffic flow, motoring carefully around the slow horse wagons. It was vital to stay away from the police and avoid all contact with other vehicles or pedestrians. There could be not so much as a scratch on his front bumper. His wealthy host's generosity would likely dry up if he failed to return the car in pristine condition.

He knew his value as a dinner guest and a party oddity had a short life-span. There was a cycle to it, one he had repeated other times in other places. At first, a wealthy person or persons befriended him with their sincere desire to understand the political power of being a "subversive," as he called himself and his *Subversive Chronicle*.

He endured their company as a guest because constant contact provided endless opportunity to teach the gospel of Galleani. He succeeded in beguiling by never really answering any of their difficult questions but instead ranting on popular social positions. His viewpoint was respectable enough, and any boundaries he pushed were always done for "the benefit of humanity."

It was in the pushing of boundaries where the art of it lay. *A little bit titillates, but too much offends.* The truth of that was so much a part of him it could have been tattooed on his face. He knew any person who was unusually interested in subversion was also a malcontent of some kind or other, and it mattered not if that person happened to be wealthy or to hold worldly power. It was the *feeling* of discontent that brought them to Galleani, and he was bright enough to address their wounds by giving them the salve of impropriety and an important implied message: *Don't worry, you are special among your peers. You see deeper into things. You are more aware of the world than they are.*

A smidgen or two of the old cow flop, not too much, just enough to provide them with that addictive feeling of being dangerous animals for a few hours, in Galleani's company. Leaving them a bit guilty the next morning. Just enough to provide them the sensation of being on the forward edge.

Heady stuff, revolution, for those with warm homes and a full belly. Better than a night at the theater.

Some of them were so hungry for that sensation, it was as if he offered opium to dope fiends. For a few evenings of dinner conversation, perhaps a couple of weeks of hovering, the wealth-insulated popinjays basked in the naughty perception of themselves as smart folks riding on the leading edge of social thinking.

After a second week or so, when some began to tire of his slogans and a few began to form a detailed picture of where he might be going with all this, they tended to get nervous about having him around. They were not his core supporters and never would be.

No, it was the true desperados—culled from smart young men and women who were bright enough to be upset over the condition of the world but baffled as to what to do about it—those were the ones he converted to his cause, hijacking their hunger to hear a Voice that could sum it all up for them.

And tell them what to do.

That one made him smile, too. He was smiling a lot more these days, and it felt good. *Why not? You could get an attack of something, being angry all the time.*

The unfamiliar sensation of joy graced him; it was impossible to avoid noticing that he was about to become the first fighter in history to cause a simultaneous detonation of a series of bombs, on command, against a civilian population. So Buda would pull the trigger, so what? He was a Galleani puppet, the most essential puppet of them all. The entire parade attack could only function as a diversion for the real act if it was a Grand Display that would compel civic attention for hours. The plan needed law enforcement overwhelmed, all day.

Hundreds killed or wounded would place his true objective within reach. His sappers had finished the blast-tunneling on the real project during this year's Independence Day celebration. They were not only skilled workers; each one carried outstanding criminal charges that made it highly unwise to work on the open market under their real names.

Galleani also paid them to stay around long enough to guarantee the workplace for Buda and then to disappear. It was worth it to capture Buda's loyalty. Galleani was fat with European donor cash, and while he needed little for himself, he spent lavishly on the subjects of his briberies. It was his experience that most people loved nothing more than being handed a wad of cash and told all they had to do to earn it was to just go away. Just dissolve away. If the wad was fat enough, they always did.

And now the parade detonations would all be triggered from the Clock Tower, and at the same moment he would use his own detonator switch to send a wired signal down the long copper line extended along the two-hundred-foot tunnel running from the stables all the way to the Very Special Bomb underneath the San Francisco Mint.

He reached the home of his host and drove backward into the garage, returning the car unspoiled after filling the tank with gasoline from the new petroleum store on Grant Avenue. He hated the places. They ruined the look of every neighborhood they were built in. Ugly reminders of the ugly things coming out of the engines they fueled.

He stepped out, closed the door with a snappy flip of his hand, and polished the edge of the window with his sleeve. *Done here.* He was now through with the attention-sucking beast, and he had kept mishap at bay. Someone else could take care of it after this.

It felt good to shrug it off and walk away while he dared to dream out his vision. His steps felt light. Usually his old injuries tended to ache in the San Francisco chill and make walking painful, but today they felt just fine. He strode like a younger man.

How many years in a cold cell would the Americans give him, just for what he had accomplished in this city so far? Even though all of it was merely the starting ramp of the race.

On parade day, with the teams harnessed to the wagons and lined up in Mint Alley, with the men standing by to run the underground carts and load the wagons, the only statement that mattered would be made, and it would come from him.

He stepped inside the city commissioner's home and greeted the missus in passing while he made his way upstairs to privacy. His thought train was too good to interrupt with mindless balderdash.

The detonation area beneath the mint was reinforced with double layers of railroad ties to make certain the tunnel stood up to the overpressure of the blast. The Very Special Bomb guaranteed the floor of the Mint would give way to the explosion, blasting upward like a volcano. And the fact that his puppet would be detonating the parade bombs, screaming at the sleeping Americans on his behalf and then terminating himself in a blast cloud? Sublime.

What a time to be alive!

16

MINT ALLEY

IN THE PITCH-BLACK ALLEY behind the San Francisco Mint, far from the weak amber streetlamps running along Mission Street, the commercial stables of the Yerba Buena Hauling Company stood silent in pre-dawn darkness. The wooden building stabled twelve massive draft horses and six double-team hauling wagons. Four horses currently lay asleep on piles of straw, while the other eight employed their ability to lock their knees, relax their muscles, and doze upright in their stalls.

These massive beasts were the thick-necked Percheron breed specially imported from France: powerful, docile, able to pull heavy wagonloads all day. They blended in with city traffic well enough. Any local resident who happened to see one at work on the streets might feel a moment of envy for an owner who could afford such a magnificent beast of burden, but there would be no questions asked. Horse-drawn work wagons were still so much a part of daily life, they were practically invisible to the population.

Plenty of working men, hard men, were seen coming and going from the Yerba Buena Hauling Company, but this was expected at a commercial hauling operation. If anyone was troubled by something they saw, nobody spoke up about it. Even if they did, apparently nobody listened.

And if someone had in fact listened, for reasons unknown they failed to respond.

During the two months since the horses were brought in, they had so far hauled only loads of dirt, the sort of work any heavy horse might do. The true action of the place was concealed by the clever use of timing in their departures and returns, along with the false bottoms in the big wagons. These effectively concealed the fact that there was no commercial hauling being done from there and that the receipts for fake work orders were cleverly forged.

All the dirt was coming from the stables itself and moving to a landfill on the South Bay. It was generated by the excavation of a tunnel dropping twelve feet under the stables and then roughly two hundred feet east, to the inner garden of the San Francisco Mint.

Vignette's nightmare left her with an emotional hangover that refused to go away. Even awake the next morning, she felt it hovering in her awareness.

For once, her waking mind was able to access the full library of her unconscious, as if some part of her dream mechanism were still active in her waking state. Flashes of the fierce demon, the one she first met at St. Adrian's. Flashes playing across the faces of regular folks, people who otherwise seemed decent and who probably thought of themselves that way.

Always the demon face. So many different people flashing that same expression. Just an instant, a second or two out on the street, in a market, a church. Anyplace at all. The demon face was there, and then it was gone.

But oh, what things the one playing host to that demonic urge would do to you, in that moment, if only they could. She supposed a mix of civilization and personal guilt held most of them in check.

Held her in check also, after all. Partially in check.

Because even as grateful as she was, and loving Randall Blackburn as she did for taking her in as his own, whenever she was out in public, the glimpses of the demon face still appeared too often. Those damned faces had kept her distant from other people for the last ten years.

It was why she knew her future in the world was dodgy at best, especially regarding employment, until Randall gave her a real chance at life with this detective agency. She was determined to keep those demons under control and do it as an act of gratitude for Randall. It made no difference whether he ever knew about her demons or not. She was going to get it right, from her soul to his.

Still within the hangover of her old nightmare, the demon face came to her. *You think you see me too much, but you missed me. I was right there before you, and you missed me!*

A splinter of evil knowledge pierced her brain and lodged there with a single image: Prohaska, the US Customs officer. Not that she actually missed him, more like she didn't follow up on her instincts.

Prohaska had struck her as a driven man, strangely intense for one who supposedly spent his working life tracking tax receipts from new arrivals. She did not believe the man was acting on his own by enlisting their aid. Something compelled him to do it. On that first day in his office, whenever he looked out the window and seemed to relax his guard, the demon face flashed.

Why hadn't she realized what she was seeing right then? Maybe Randall was right when he told her she needed to get out more, to develop her observational skills.

Because she saw it now. Something dark had connected to Jacob Prohaska, vibrating in unison with his own dark side. Just because Prohaska enlisted their agency's help didn't mean he wanted them to succeed. Maybe the opposite, in fact. His actions might have been intended to serve as cover later on.

Leaving the question: Cover for what?

Fifteen minutes later, she and Randall sat bleary-eyed at the kitchen table while she explained her dream and the insight it provided about this Jacob Prohaska. Randall listened carefully. He knew Vignette's gifts well enough to show respect on the rare occasions when she called upon them.

"All right," he replied, rubbing his eyes. "Let's see. Prohaska's originally from Chicago, isn't he?"

"He mentioned that. What's it mean?"

"Can't say. Maybe nothing. But I still have a contact in the Chicago PD. We worked together here in town for years. I can call him at his office."

Vignette grinned at that. "Hey, for the first time, I don't regret having a telephone in the house."

At the stable in Mint Alley, the true purpose for the powerful Percheron draft horses would soon require their fabled strength. They would be making a single trip from the Mint Alley stables over to the Embarcadero, Pier 19.

Such a small distance. But the wagonloads were going to be far heavier than the usual dirt piles and garbage stacks. And once they reached Pier 19, while every emergency vehicle, fire engine, or police car in the city flooded the parade route to deal with the bombs and the bodies, the cargo would be driven out onto the deserted dock and loaded onto an ocean-going vessel purchased for this single journey. The drivers of the wagons were the ship's crew, and each one knew if he did his job right, he would never have to work again.

The empty wagons were to be abandoned there and no doubt quickly stolen by hustlers from the Tenderloin district. Nature regenerating itself.

During the six months of new tenant occupation at the stables, neighborhood people saw the heavy work wagons roll in and out all day. Nobody would ever know anything beyond the rumor that the property was being leased by a mysterious charitable organization paying *ten times* what the owner could earn there in a year. Suckers from the East Coast.

A year was the shortest span of time Galleani's men could believably engage to rent the stables. They had calculated the soft-core tunnel work would only require half that, but this left a comfortable margin.

With payment in advance, no questions were asked. The owner was delighted that the new tenants also planned to maintain a commercial stable. He saw no reason to do anything other than sign off on the proposal, run home to kiss the wife and kids, then treat the family to an extended holiday. All courtesy of the idiots who overpaid him.

Naturally everyone wanted to know how the owner did it. But they didn't move quickly enough. By the time anyone came sniffing around for a clue, he and the family were long gone.

Now at this darkened hour inside the stables, silence was perturbed by the metallic rattle of a key tumbling a lock. Pitch black lifted by the merest degree when faint starlight defined a rectangle at the front door. The silhouette of a solitary man stepped into the frame. He turned this way and that in the cautious manner of a prowler, even though he had just opened the front door with a key. He carried no lantern.

He swung the door shut and paused for a moment in the gloom. The standing horses could see better in the darkness than humans could, but they made no skittish movements in reaction to his presence. Not even when he struck a wooden match on the sole of his boot.

Luigi Galleani was a familiar figure to them.

He glanced around and decided everything appeared as it should, then padded over to the large trolley door hanging at the front of the tack room and used a second key to remove the thick lock on that door. He puffed out the dying match, struck another, then stepped through the door and slid it closed behind him.

He extinguished the second match and picked up an electric torch, one of several on the wall. When he pressed the switch, a pale yellow circle appeared on the floor, as wide as he was tall. He cast the light around. The room was empty, save the black square on the floor over in the corner with four feet of wooden ladder protruding from the edge. Once he stepped closer, the shaft revealed itself when the torch flashed glimpses of the reinforced sides leading downward.

His men really did do an admirable job of cleaning up after themselves. No loose soil visible anywhere on the floor, all signs of digging gone but for the shaft itself. His carefully selected workers were loyal Galleanists, young single men well rewarded. They currently lolled in prepaid hotel rooms around the country, resting up on large expense accounts after their weeks of heavy back work.

Galleani allowed his light to play around the stable, confident he remained hidden from outside because the tack room was built without air vents atop the walls. Galleani loved the affirmations from lucky little breaks like that. The owner had been too cheap to extend the overhead vents into the tack room. There was nowhere for traces of light to escape. Out in the rest of the stable, the louvered ceiling vents that kept the air breathable could also emit traces of light, the definition of a dead giveaway.

He lit another electric torch that hung from the top of the ladder, leaving it on as a sort of beacon. It was safe to go down and do another check. He reached the bottom of the ladder and turned to face into the tunnel itself. Strong wooden braces held it together. The earth there was a combination of ancient deconstructed sandstone and man-made land added to the existing shoreline. This resulted in ground that was quick and easy to tunnel through. But the stand time for the structure was short. And while the bracing system would support the roof, it was most fortunate that the dry season was upon the land. Water could weaken the entire thing and cause a massive collapse, braced roof or not.

It gave him a claustrophobic sensation, almost as if he were choking, but he forced himself to walk the entire two hundred-plus feet of it. He walked between the simple wooden track boards that had been put in place so very heavy loads could be pulled on the wheeled carts currently stored inside the stables, waiting to be loaded with bricks of gold.

By the light of his torch, it all looked plenty solid enough to stand throughout the mission. His sappers were the best. The tunnel would endure the explosion when the blast vented itself, and it was strong enough to tolerate the vibrating passage of so many carts in a short period of time.

This place had that sort of strength. It made him proud. Look at the way the joints were cut to fit. Look at the extra-thick walls, sturdy beams, hard-grained timber. This was all he needed, plus a mere three hours of work time after the blast. Extract enough bullion to maximize the draft animals' capacity. Once they were gone, nothing mattered.

He finally reached the tunnel's end, squarely beneath the Mint's foundation. He knew the location topside would be the middle of the Mint's center garden, the part of the building least able to resist an underground explosion.

He came to the Very Special Bomb sitting where he himself had dragged it earlier. No one else could be trusted to handle it. Buda was out of the question, since he knew nothing of the stable or the tunnel itself.

Galleani had sent the bomb maker off on a harmless chore to get rid of him while he finished setting the stage.

This bomb was beautiful to look at, even though Galleani had only a passing knowledge of explosives. Its beauty came not from the strange appearance but from the results it promised to create. He knew the concrete pad directly over his head was five feet thick. Back when the Mint was opened in 1874, that was plenty thick to thwart any invasion from below.

But in the years since then, scientists had discovered certain strange and powerful effects in explosive chemistry. This was knowledge the Mint's architects could hardly have possessed. Certain mining engineers of the time had mastered a new discovery called the Munroe effect, but it was not yet widely understood.

The fundamental truth of it, however, was simple.

With this discovery, an explosive blast no longer needed to render chaos in all directions unless that was the desired effect. In situations where such a blast would be undesirable, such as a soft-earth tunnel, the blast wave itself could be shaped to send its greatest force in a single heading. The Munroe effect therefore created an invisible cannon barrel to guide the explosion in the desired direction.

The bomb was made of sticks of dynamite fastened to a wooden core that held them in a cone position. The inverted downward-facing cone was made of shorter dynamite sticks and lined with an aluminum cone that would liquify upon detonation and form a white-hot jet of molten metal to shoot upward and through the concrete pad. Five feet of concrete would come down in small pieces, and the hole would be plenty large enough for his men to surge through, then overcome the skeleton crew at the Mint (closed for the holiday parade). Their orders were stark: tie up the workers if they cooperate, kill them if they fight.

Then they could finally begin loading gold bricks onto the Mint's push carts, hauling them to the hole, loading their contents into the tunnel carts. Pull the carts through the tunnel to the shaft. There, pass them hand over hand up the ladder and load them onto the waiting wagons.

If some hero in the Mint tries to find a telephone and call the police? Well, the transmission lines will be overwhelmed. If they get through, the police sergeant will be overwhelmed. If they get the attention of the sergeant, his police forces will be overwhelmed. And even if he can somehow muster police forces, the streets between here and the police station will be overwhelmed by the results of the bombs, the fires, and public panic. Beautiful.

And his plan only needed three hours of working time. Three hours of the city's victims screaming on the ground and bleeding to death by the hundreds, clogging up streets and sidewalks all over town while gold bars fled the Mint.

How much gold? Enough to be worth many millions of American dollars. His contacts in Germany at the Rothschilds' Deutsche Bank had tipped him to the astounding news that the major governments of Europe had moved their gold supplies to the San Francisco Mint for safe storage while the war rolled over their land. The governments reasoned that if one or more of them were defeated, they would still be able to rebuild and govern in absentia—so long as they retained substantial treasuries.

He didn't need to take it all. He only needed to dramatically deplete the stash. And if the chaos in the city was deep enough, he could always send the wagons back for another load...

As soon as word of the Mint robbery got out, nobody would believe anything about how much gold was actually taken. Name the amount! The more the authorities tried to play it down, the higher the figures of speculation would go. Rumor would become the same thing as reality, capable of rendering damage just as great because so many people loved to be outraged about things and thus feel assured of their own worth.

As for this bogus war in Europe? Armies couldn't fight for governments who couldn't buy ammunition, weapons, or even food for the men.

Preparedness Day Parade. The name alone was offensive to him. But as a bonus, the explosions would also mock the name of the event, since "Preparedness" was exactly what San Francisco lacked. This in spite of the solid lesson in the hazards of being caught unprepared when the Great Earthquake and Fires struck only ten years earlier. Ten years! What did they learn? What were they "prepared" for?

Nothing. His true mission would make that plain.

17

THE RUSSIAN HILL HOME OF THE LATE HAROLD SAUNDERS

* July 21st, 8:00 a.m. *

VIGNETTE STOOD IN THE RARE GLARE of direct morning sunlight with her nose inches from the front door of the Saunders home. Usually, her great preference was to sneak into anyplace she needed to be and then let things roll out however they would. She had already done that much here. She had always been able to jump at the last moment when things turned lousy, anyway.

She had never killed anyone, and so far she caused only minor injuries to a handful of penises with bodies attached to them. The injury list also included a few gormless females who should have known better, but as far as Vignette was concerned, the moral scoreboard looked good for her. What she was about to do made perfect sense.

Because good people existed in theory, but she knew demons moved invisibly among them, dangerous beyond description. Some even had the nerve to call themselves monks, like the ones over at St. Adrian's Home for Delinquents and Orphans. From the age of four or five until she fled at age ten, there was no one to stop it. Just a few other terrified kids who didn't want to talk about what was done to them in the darkness, either. In the alone time.

She never spoke of it. Not to anyone. And anyplace else but alone with God, she never would.

Vignette knew she was crazy by the world's standards. The knowledge helped her feel better about herself when she looked around at the world.

What the hell, she thought, and rang the bell. She mentally slipped the old mask of benign affability in place, the way Shane had taught her to do, reminding herself to keep it on.

After she rang the bell, it took a minute for the door to open...then with two clicks and a swish, the door swung back and there was the face of Mrs. Felicity Saunders herself, already talking. "Well, you're the last one! I was waiting..." She stopped, staring at Vignette, clearly expecting someone else.

Vignette was equally surprised to see the woman of the house answering her own door. Apparently not even a butler or maid was on duty here.

"Hello again, Mrs. Saunders," she began in her best imitation of a disarming smile. "Vignette Nightingale. We're acquainted through your women's suffrage group."

Saunders's face remained impassive. "The bicyclist."

"Well, no, it's a...anyway, I know I left things in an awkward way at the last meeting, and I felt compelled to personally extend my deepest condolences over your loss."

"Miss Nightingale or Mrs. Nightingale?"

"Miss."

"Still single. Good for you."

"Indeed." Vignette handed her the agency's business card and adopted a secretive tone. "I would never intrude on you at such a time, except we've been left no choice. One tragedy does not prevent a second."

She dropped to a whisper to prevent anyone inside from hearing. "Our agency has reason to believe your husband's reputation may be badly smeared in the wake of his passing." She leaned in closer. "And I mean smeared with charges so terrible the memory of them will outlive both of us. Not his fault, of course," she lied. "Not at all. Your husband had no idea how dark the forces around him would turn out to be. I mean, simple theft is nothing at all like…"

The Widow Saunders's eyes grew wide with concern. Vignette said nothing to console her. If Mrs. Saunders felt fear, it would be harder for her to lie well.

Felicity Saunders's heartbeat surged, but old habits drew a waxy calm across her. At the well-formed age of forty, she still had no doubt that she could give an effective performance. She was just so tired. Sudden widowhood was a staggering burden. Years of disgust under Harry's nose should have ended with a sense of freedom and release. But now, so close to the big event, it felt as if he had not merely struck out at her with his suicide, if that's what it was, but with the timing of it. Once the big event was pulled off and she disappeared from San Francisco, he could have killed himself a dozen times for all she cared.

Moreover, a couple of important friends had failed her, and these were women she ought to have been able to trust. Instead they took their cue from the shame of Harry's suicide and disappeared on her. Left her to suffer through an avalanche of last-minute arrangements without them. She looked this unexpected new visitor up and down. Whatever the young Nightingale woman had in mind, she never brought anything but personal resistance and an argumentative nature. She needed to be dismissed so Saunders could get back to her preparations.

"Miss Nightingale, this house is in mourning."

"Yes, ma'am," the impertinent visitor hurried on, "and I repeat, I would never presume to bring this to you, but the people who want to destroy your late husband's reputation have no respect for social conventions."

"Mm. And may I inquire what this has to do with you?"

Vignette checked herself. She knew her Achilles' heel was an inability to suffer fools. With a calming breath, she cranked her smile back up into position like she was starting a Model T and replied, "Of course. As soon as I got the news about Mr. Saunders, I realized there might be an opportunity to offer our assistance at the Blackburn & Nightingales detective agency. Gratis, naturally."

Saunders could almost feel the gears turning in her skull. *Watch out for her! Who approaches this way?*

"Miss Nightingale, I've heard nothing of such things regarding my late husband and can't imagine requiring a detective agency to defend his name after what he did to it with his thievery."

She paused and studied Vignette for a moment. "However, I wonder if you have a desire to be of great service on a private level? Simply one woman to another?" Saunders held her breath without letting it show.

"Oh. Well, then," said Miss Nightingale with a smile that looked relieved somehow. "I'll do my best to be of assistance."

Saunders looked hard at Miss Nightingale, who may or may not have been telling the truth. The young woman's smile was tentative but not shifty, more like a shy young person unused to social interaction, unschooled in how to address those of a higher class. Saunders decided to proceed. "If you are at all sincere in your desire to be a sister in this hour, please return at nine o'clock this evening. I'll be free by then. Let's talk. Explore the best ways to gain more freedom for women."

"I can't speak to that with any knowledge."

"Nonsense! You are a female detective, and a young one at that. I'm certain you have many personal experiences of things which are of great concern to me and many others. Things you may not realize. As you rather rudely said, look at how behind we are in this society. I realize Norway approved women's suffrage three months ago. Now is not the time to take a furlough."

Felicity Saunders knew this was the test; if Miss Nightingale was put off by the thought of conversation deeper than sympathy chitchat, she would create an excuse to refuse and thereby reveal herself as a social climber who had just made a clumsy blunder. A troublemaker.

Instead, the young woman looked pleasantly surprised. "In that case, of course, Mrs. Saunders. I'll be happy to return this evening."

"Good, then. The best antidote for despair is an idea we hold with passion. Let's turn our attentions to such things."

"Happily. To, ah, help a sister keep grief at bay."

"No need for melodrama, my dear. I rarely saw the man, and I'm quite sure he has prostitutes who are more bereaved than I am. Everything about him was a pose." She allowed herself a sneer. *Why not? It won't give away anything.* "Including his role as an astute collector who acquired fine things at bargain rates. I am only fortunate the prosecutor realized I had no part in the crimes."

"I assure you, Mrs. Saunders, I know how terrible it is to be betrayed by those closest to you."

"Mm. And so often the problem is men. Isn't it?"

"Ha-ha. Well, yes."

"He surprised me with a gift now and then and made it seem romantic. I now know, along with the rest of the world, that such things were only a few baubles out of a king's ransom in stolen booty. I don't know how he kept the source of it all from me."

"I'm so sorry. And I can't understand it either."

"Yes, deception. It's what men do if you give them the chance." She forced a quick dismissing-the-help smile. *I've pretended we're sisters. Now go home.*

Miss Nightingale caught the hint. "Well, then. Until this evening?"

"In the meantime, please give thought to all the ways society forces us to submit to men. Without logical cause. Mere tradition."

"Tradition. All right."

"Ask yourself what things would be like if it all was different."

"Different in what way?"

"Imagine a situation where things change so much that we redefine the notion of what it means to be a woman." She offered Vignette a confidential smile. Ersatz equals.

"I see. Well, then, I look forward to it. Good day."

This time the young Nightingale woman turned and walked away. Saunders stepped back inside, closed the door, and left it unlocked. Although personal safety was a bit of a concern, with the help dismissed following the seizure of Harry's bank account, it felt good to enforce her laziness on the house. The idiot had unwittingly provided her with the perfect excuse of appearing too broke to maintain a staff while she was actually preparing for her own departure.

The silent house surrounded her. She savored the peace for a moment. It would not last and was all the more valuable because of that. She stepped into the front sitting room and came to light on one of the matching Queen Anne chairs, took several deep breaths, and allowed her mind to drift.

Everything was different now. All plans shifted. Until she was abruptly widowed, the idea was to remain in the city for another year or so until everything had all cooled down, then take her share of the payment, leave Harry, and disappear, never to return.

How glorious it would be if everything had turned out the way it was supposed to. After all, sometimes things did, didn't they? God, Fate, even Random Rotten Luck—they didn't always ruin everything for you. Not every time. Sometimes they allowed things to work out the right way.

And this time, if they did—if they only did in spite of Idiot Harry—life could finally become good for Felicity Saunders. He nearly took her down with his carelessness and greed, but she effectively maintained her innocence and stood smiling while the detectives collected the rest of his booty.

She took shelter in her status as "an innocent woman deceived," knowing how the public gobbled up such images, and Saunders was happy to provide them. The promise of the big payoff and all the freedom it represented had pulled her in, years before, and she had invested far too much time to miss the payoff.

Otherwise she never would have been seduced into giving up her career as an actress, stalled though it was, to be paired up with Harry and to spend years playing out the role of his wife. Hiding in plain sight until The Day came.

Her part in it was mostly over now. Nothing left to do but finalize the escape.

It was all so pleasant to consider, this newly re-envisioned future, here at long last. Of course she had no intention of keeping her appointment with the young detective, interesting as she was. The time to indulge in mentoring impressionable young minds was over. The offer itself was little more than a means to remove the young woman from the front porch. In Felicity's New Life, she planned to get as far away from politics as possible.

Despite the uncomfortable Queen Ann chair, she felt herself drifting off to sleep...but jerked her head upright with a startled snort. *No. No sleep. Back to it.*

Saunders had no reason to go downstairs to the basement before climbing the stairs to the top-floor bedroom, and so she failed to see the same outfit Miss Nightingale had been wearing at the main entrance a few minutes earlier now lying folded at the bottom of the basement steps. She would have had to go all the way down to the basement level to spot the unlocked door handle and be reminded of her late husband's paranoid insistence on keeping those doors locked, always locked, no matter what. It felt so good to no longer follow his annoying habits, and so she did not go down to check.

Instead, her next task was upstairs, to stow the extra steamer trunks back in the attic after packing one of the others for her escape. She had brought them all out before she knew how much room was needed. After she surprised herself by fitting everything inside a single trunk, she placed it at the base of her bed like a piece of furniture.

That meant all the empty trunks had to go back to the attic. Saunders was as strong as most men, but it was still a daunting task, necessary since the house had to look normal in case any more investigators came her way before she made it out of there. Everything about the interior of the home had to reflect the daily existence of a recent widow, a longtime member of the community.

She had been stuck in town because of the idiot, but now she was free of him and free to go. And in this new life, she would never need to hear herself addressed by the ridiculous code name of "Rogue."

Felicity Saunders was lost in thought while she made her way to the top floor and so failed to notice the young woman attired in dark long johns perfect for sneak work, skillfully blended into the shadow of Harry's ancient grandfather clock. She slipped back into the basement without a sound.

18

BLACKBURN & NIGHTINGALES –
PRIVATE INVESTIGATION

* July 21st, 9:00 a.m. *

RANDALL OPENED HIS FRONT DOOR wearing a thick house-robe and holding a cup of coffee. He immediately looked confused. "Have to admit I wasn't expecting to see you."

Jacob Prohaska was still in the same clothing he wore earlier. He appeared long overdue for sleep and was now two or three shades dingier in all respects.

"I came here planning to wait for your return, but here you..." He stopped and exhaled in frustration. "Mr. Blackburn, why are you home now? I mean to say, why aren't you out...you know...investigating?"

Randall gave up a tired smile but didn't move to invite him in. "Mr. Prohaska, I'm stuck here waiting for a long-distance phone call from Chicago. And out of courtesy to you, I will tell you that the call will be very much a part of the investigation."

"Chicago? You've heard, then? The trouble's coming from there? Points east. Maybe the whole country?"

"I haven't heard anything, yet, except that my associate in that town responded to my phone call by telling me he could get information about some of the people from there who are recent visitors to San Francisco." He looked straight at Prohaska. "A fella by the name of Luigi Galleani, for example. Been making a lot of noise."

Prohaska's face immediately went beet red. Randall figured poker was not this man's game. He decided to push him a little and see what else his face revealed.

"They're putting together a report on him for me. But maybe you can fill me in. You know. Before they call."

Prohaska blanched. "Me? Why would I—"

Randall held up his hand like a traffic cop. "On second thought, don't bother. We'll make it short. I saw you yesterday. Yep. Right there at Luigi Galleani's exclusive little rally. In the warehouse over on Mission Street."

Prohaska took a deep breath, taking just enough time for the universal *oh-shit* to strike. It smacked him hard. "I...I only went to see what he, he... For crying out loud, Mr. Blackburn! He is one of the worst examples of, of, of the very sort of thing I told you about! He comes here, but he hates us! I wanted to know why."

"Mm. Except the event was invitation only. The door guards had checklists. And they not only let you in, they stopped what they were doing and escorted you inside."

"You saw...?"

"I just said I followed you."

Prohaska winced. "All right, then. I'll tell you, if you're so keen to know. Galleani sent me a written invitation. Never seen such nerve in one person. I couldn't believe it. But it seemed like a perfect time to find out what he's doing here."

"And did you?"

The question seemed to give Prohaska back some of his nerve. He lifted his chin. "I did. And I came out knowing much more than when I went in. But I tell you, it's not nearly enough. Mr. Blackburn, he's definitely got some kind of nasty plan for the Preparedness Day Parade. Tomorrow. It's not a rumor."

"Oh, he told you that?"

"Of course not. He taunted me for the amusement of his companions. I swear, the man called me to meet him just so he could gloat about how easy our government makes his job."

"What job is that?"

"He didn't say. He just turned away from me and began talking to some other men, as if I had disappeared. The thing is, I overheard snatches of conversation from the other men who were waiting around. Enough to know something is on for the parade. Something bad."

"I'm sure we can trust that it's not anything good. So you're telling me your suspicions sent you there?"

"Yes! To check on things! To see what progress has been made! For God's sake, you need to get out there and search the parade route and interview people!"

"Search the parade route. Is that how it's done?"

"There's no need for sarcasm, Mr. Blackburn. Something terrible is being planned for tomorrow, and with a man like Luigi Galleani, it's almost certainly going to be deadly!"

"Go home, Mr. Prohaska."

"I beg your pardon?"

"Go home, or go back to the office if you like. Go somewhere and check your own sources and see what you can learn."

"Now listen, I have no such investigative experience!"

"Then you listen to *me* for a moment. Surely, out of all the people you know, all the people you've been meeting in your line of work down through the years, surely one or two stood out as people you can trust. Yes? You know, people who will talk to you and be truthful about it. Amazing how much important stuff people know without realizing it."

He leaned in close and dropped the pretense of a smile. "Go now. Find somebody who knows something. They have to be out there. I need the information I'm expecting in that phone call, and until then, I can't leave here."

Prohaska exhaled hard. "Will you at least check with your Chicago contact to see if they heard anything about the parade?"

"Yes. I'll do that. Now go home, go to work, go someplace else." He reached over to a small table by the door and picked up one of his business cards, handing it over. "My telephone exchange number is on that card. If you get any more information, try calling me from your office phone. Save yourself a trip. One of us is usually around. Now go get 'em."

Prohaska thanked him and turned to go, but his posture was devoid of confidence.

Randall couldn't help himself. "Tally-ho!"

Prohaska doffed his hat without looking back.

Inside the house, Randall walked back to the kitchen carrying his coffee cup and rinsed it in the sink, asking himself why he didn't believe anything Prohaska told him. The man was too intense, pleading his cause too hard.

Blackburn was still there when the phone rang from its trusty location bolted to the wall. He hustled over to pick up the earpiece and put his mouth extra close to the telephone's microphone apparatus because the call he expected was coming from so far away. He raised his voice to make himself as clear as possible.

"Ahoy-hoy!"

A woman's voice came over the line. "This is the long-distance operator. You have a collect call from Chicago, Illinois. Will you accept the charge?"

"I guess I have to. Go ahead."

A man's voice was now heard. "That you, Spike?"

"John Maxwell! Good to hear you again! Is this line coming in clear?"

"Good enough for the likes of us. You sound like you're standing right next to me and we're both in a tin can!"

Maxwell had trained under Randall as a rookie officer, down in the brawling Tenderloin district, back before he got tired of taking punches from drunken whores and their knife-wielding pimps. He married and moved to a soft desk job in Illinois. Blackburn regretted that then. He was glad for it now.

"All right, so what can you tell me?"

Now Maxwell's voice came over the line in soft tones while he lowered his voice to a near whisper, just loud enough for Randall to make out, which seemed very odd. It sounded as if his old friend feared someone else could be listening.

Or perhaps Maxwell's caution was merely because of the white-hot information he was about to deliver. "All right, Randall. You've heard of the Rothschild banking family, haven't you?"

"Sure. Rich people. Extreme wealth."

"Yeah. Well, you should say that a few more times. But your troubles there in Frisco aren't really about money."

"Aw, don't say 'Frisco.' You lived here; have some respect. And in my experience, crime is almost always about money."

"Sure, but what's money good for? I mean real money, get me? Mountains of gold!"

"Well, you can't eat it or screw it, so that leaves power."

"Power! Yes. Let's talk about power. This family's got branches in France and England supporting the armies of both nations with cash loans. Basically financing their combat efforts."

"Figures. They're bankers."

"Yes, but...they also have family branches in Germany and Austro-Hungary, supporting *their* armies. Against the English and the French."

"What, both sides?"

"They win no matter how the war goes."

"I am outraged and will write somebody a very angry letter. But what's that got to do with us over here?"

"Oh, not much. Just that the Rothschilds already have control here in the States, too. They get it through that new Federal Reserve Bank thing, which they created three years ago and which *they* forced into place! The American people didn't ask for it, didn't support it, and hey, you can ask around if you don't believe me—most people have no idea what the Federal Reserve even does. But the Rothschild banks control the board, meaning they control the entire Federal Reserve itself. They have all this even though the American voters never agreed to it, and isn't a 'reserve' because it's got no money. It just has the authority to mess with the money everybody else in America has, for a hefty fee. Get it now? Is the fog lifting?"

"Damn it, John. How can you know all this?"

"Because up here in Chicago, we're in factory 'n' farm country, Randall! For us, the hot button is Labor with a capital *L*! You can feel the heat. There's some powerful employers up here, and they's got tens of thousands of able-bodied young men on payroll. If the banks want war, those same able-bodied fellas are gonna get sucked right out of our factories and off of our farms and shipped off to Europe! We're into this one face first.

"Now, I've got enough juice in town to see that the powers-that-be are rigging the warships, but I don't have enough to stop it. Neither do you. Neither does anybody you know."

"Look, John, but why not just go to the newspapers with this? I'm sure the population has no idea."

"Great idea—except they already thought of it. They purchased twenty-five American newspapers through their holding companies."

"When?"

"Just before all the reporting took on a war footing. They had to counteract the population's desire to stay out of war. Get them fighting mad."

"You think they're behind sponsorship of this parade?"

"It didn't create itself. Who benefits most from it? If we follow the flow of power, we can say sure, have a parade. Why not? But after what I'm seeing here, you folks in San Francisco need to ask yourselves, if a big parade can help convince pacifists to accept a coming war, how much better if something terrible happened during that parade!"

"Bombs? We've spotted that fellow Mario Buda here a couple of times lately."

"To the point, then. He also appears here in Chicago a lot. Nothing good ever happens with him around."

"Bombs on the parade route, then. Not just rumors."

"You have to consider it."

"Ah, hell." He vigorously rubbed his face with his hand. "All right, John, thank you for this. Can I ask one more thing?"

"Sure." He sort of chuckled and added, "But after that I have to charge you."

"Fair enough. For now, please give a phone call or send a wire to anybody who's got anything to do with law enforcement in New York City. Ask them, are they seeing any of this?"

"I can do that. Might take a day or so."

"Needs to be less. Please."

"I understand. So when are you coming out to visit the Midwest? Bring your, ah..."

"Vignette."

"Yeah, bring her. We can catch a baseball game over at the new Weeghman Park. Right over by the lake."

"That place open for business already?"

"Two years ago! The whole Federal League just went bust, and there's talk of maybe moving the Cubs over there."

"Well, if you help us out with this, we'll visit, and the tickets and beer are on me."

Maxwell laughed out loud. "And lunch!"

"All right."

"Ha! Dinner, too!"

"All *right*."

Maxwell disconnected the call still chuckling. Blackburn replaced the tube-shaped earpiece on the nickel-plated holding fork extending from the side of the telephone's wooden body, then stared into space and thought about what he'd just heard.

19

RUSSIAN HILL

* July 21st, 9:15 a.m. *

RANDALL DROVE THE WAVERLEY OVER the rough streets toward Russian Hill on his way to have a little chat with the City Council member hosting Luigi Galleani. Councilman Vincent Cinquevalli was an affluent son of European show business royalty, the great juggler Paul Cinquevalli. Which prompted Randall Blackburn to have questions about how a local elected official arrived at the point of harboring a man who was openly willing to commit evil against the people who elected that official in the first place.

The Waverley was so quiet, its presence was announced on dark or dimly lit streets by nothing more than the faint noises of rolling rubber tires and the car's squeaky springs. Once he reached the Russian Hill area, he looked for a place to park away from all the accumulated horse flop that city workers had swept to the side of the road. He found the spot and parked, then set out on foot.

He cracked his knuckles and rolled his shoulders while he walked, loosening up for action in case he was met with violence. Randall's twenty years of hand combat with people of every form and persuasion had convinced him of the existence of the darkest side of human behavior. The only thing different about the Tenderloin district was the thinness of the veneer of civilization.

———————

Felicity Saunders stood before a full-length mirror with one foot in front of the other, twisting her body this way and that. She spoke out loud to herself, which was all right since the house was empty, what with hubby dead and all of the staff released to the wind.

Her present circumstances, which some might call a widow's isolation, felt to her like taking in a huge breath out on the back porch on a beautiful spring day. It was nothing she needed to be cured of. But beyond the isolation and the respite it offered, on some level she also understood herself to be coming apart, way down deep. The feeling accounted for her solitary status more than anything else.

It was the pressure regarding the upcoming attacks, of course. Doubts had come to rest upon her shoulders like invisible boulders. They combined with the weight of the obligations she had already taken on and formed a crushing burden.

This rehearsal before the mirror was necessary because if she wanted to position her escape in the proper light to Hemo, she needed to make sure her verbal powers never failed her during this brief meeting. She needed all her rusty old acting skills. She knew the way Hemo was; her fate would be decided in two or three minutes. Maybe less. The rest was decoration.

Tonight's meeting was scheduled for the same fancy hotel room as last time. And she planned to attend the meeting as if everything was hunky-dory. Her secretly packed carriage would wait outside while she went in and explained her change in plans to Hemo and the others. She was all too aware that the people he worked for had the power to track her movements. Have her reputation ruined, have her killed. Thus her reason for leaving town had to satisfy Hemo along with the others before she could safely flee.

"You should keep in mind," she announced to the mirror with sudden inspiration, "that I served alongside that fool for six years. I kept up the illusion of marriage, and he kept up the reality of the infiltration at City Hall." She nearly spat the next words, "But my marriage was to a gaudy moron who brought himself down because of a fetish for shiny objects."

She allowed acid to drip from her tongue to add, "Like a crow."

With that, she spun around and put on a different voice, serious, composed, trying out a new tactic for her imaginary audience. "I endured the sacrifice for one reason only: to smash the status quo and get women the vote. The fact that women are still not permitted in voting booths is criminal. I understand that political statements have to be made, but please tell the committee to make them without me from now on, that's all."

Now she mentally turned to the others on the committee or the group or the gang or whatever it was she and Hemo's crew had allowed themselves to become. "Of course I will never speak to anyone about you, because I still believe in what you are doing. So you see? I remain a friend. A silent friend."

She studied the trim lines of her reflection again, repeating "silent friend" in a little whisper while she looked over her shoulder at her reflection. Even in the midst of this attempt to flee her dreadful situation, she felt consoled by the sumptuous feel of the extravagantly expensive jacket-and-skirt combination.

How could she not? Anyone with skin could feel the difference between these fabrics and everything else they owned. The entire outfit was from a new fashion house located on France's Basque Coast. The store and the design were that of a beautiful young designer named Gabriella Chanel. The lines were cleaner than Victorian style, and the fabric was so soft, it caressed the skin instead of punishing you.

True, the outfit had been a gift from her late husband. It was far too big at first and had to be taken in to give her its current tasteful fit. She refused to consider how he obtained it.

Simply put, the sense of style and personal confidence it rendered was so finely wrought, the impact of its obviously high price was so impressive, there was no way on this green outhouse of a planet that she could allow the idiots at City Hall to stuff the garment back into a box in their stinking evidence locker.

Her taste was ahead of conventional fashion, but it was hardly unique. Since the Chanel store on the Basque Coast was just north of the Spanish border, it had already become a major attraction for wealthy Spanish women, and wealthy American women had noticed. They embraced the entire Chanel line with the same enthusiasm as Saunders and her social set. In Europe, these upper-class women loved the way the Chanel extravagance helped them forget the nastiness of the war and the tragedies of those poor working folks dying in it: soldiers, innocent families, farm animals, whatnot.

She did a few more half-turns for the mirror while she whispered to herself. "A silent friend. A silent friend."

The sound of her doorbell startled her even though its warm tones were like church bells. She turned from the mirror toward the downstairs front door and felt a rush of foreboding. If that Nightingale woman had returned so soon, then something was almost certainly wrong. Her mere presence once again today would indicate that some deeper form of suspicion had fallen onto the Widow Saunders.

If the detective's true interest in Saunders had to do with the Preparedness Day Parade, it would be a terrible sign. Even if the interest was only from a private detective agency, it could have only one meaning: *Somebody knows.*

It would also point to far deeper problems for Hemo's faceless anarchist masters, an organization of people who hate organizations. These were not people to accept defeat. No matter what part of the knowledge was revealed, far deeper darkness would have to follow in retaliation.

20

HOME OF THE WIDOW SAUNDERS

* Immediately Following *

FELICITY SAUNDERS RECOILED WHEN SHE opened her door and saw this was not a repeat visit from that young private eye. Unbelievably, Hemo was there. *But no.* Not only had Hemo never been to her home before, he had always emphasized that there was never to be any visiting between team members.

After so many warnings, why would Hemo appear at her door? His face formed a smile so intense it made her wince.

"Well, hey," he called out. "Good morning there! Surprised to see me?" He leaned forward and added in a melodramatic whisper, "*Rogue*?"

Her startled reaction made him grin. "Relax!" he said with a chuckle. "No one can hear me. Relax and rejoice, comrade. Surely your nosy neighbors won't have any suspicion over a bereaved woman such as yourself receiving a visitor at this hour?"

"Oh, for God's sake! Get inside." She pulled the door open wide and stepped back.

Hemo let out a little laugh and swept himself into the house like a landlord come to claim back rent from a tenant he didn't like. His ease of movement belied his powerful build and added to the sense of exuded menace.

She kept up a stately front to conceal her dread but couldn't believe the timing. *Is he psychic? Did he have a revelation that I'm about to run? How the hell does he know to come here now?*

"Well!" he cheerily announced. "I'll not keep you in suspense. Of course you're wondering why this violation of the 'no personal visits' policy, true?"

"It's your policy, I suppose you can violate it. But I am wondering what you—"

"I'm here because the hour is upon us and things are crumbling. We are on the eve of tee-off time, as all the decadent golfers say. What is your operational condition?"

"Just as I assured you, all three women came through for us." She had no intention of passing on their doubts.

"Excellent…"

"The escape kits are in my basement at this moment, packed in cloth shoulder bags. Since you stuck me with keeping them, the men can just come around to the back door through the alley and pick them up whenever they need to get them. I'll unlock the door as soon as the parade begins. Just pass the word along."

"I already have."

"You what?"

"They know to come here."

"And to come to the basement door?"

"Maybe."

"How could they know that?"

"They might come to the front door, so what? Just send 'em around back."

"Oh, and now I am supposed to be seen interacting with them? I have told you repeatedly that in this neighborhood, residents will absolutely notice if six strange men come strolling up to the door one after the other."

"Yes, and what you will tell anyone who asks is that they are friends of your late husband, coming to pay respects. The fact is, there may not be any of them showing up here at all. The ones who do may or may not have executed their missions, but they will all be looking for a fast way out of town at our expense, to avoid getting hauled in for questioning. Leave it at that."

She hesitated, breathing a bit too hard, trying to read his face, but it was like trying to look through a wall. "You're telling me we have spent weeks preparing to help your firebugs, but now they may not show up?"

"That private detective, Randall Blackburn. Somehow he got wind of things and sent out a warning at the docks and all through the Tenderloin. Apparently he's got a fierce reputation. A couple of my men have disappeared altogether. Others I've checked with are spooked. We may not get any fire, but we still have the bombs. The bombers won't turn yellow because they can stay invisible and fade back into the city, but a few might want to escape anyway. If they show up here, give 'em the kits first come, first served. They're better off gone."

He turned toward the door as if to go, then turned back, faking an afterthought. "Nice of you to have changed your mind and allow us to keep the bags here..." It was not a compliment.

"Mm." She figured there was no use in having a discussion about the difference between changing your mind and following an order.

Hemo added, "Just remember you are distributing the kits to our brave men for the greater good."

Saunders gave a grim nod. "If any of them show up, they'll get their escape kits, as I planned to tell you this evening. Then my part of the mission will be over."

"Over?" His tone of voice dropped by a couple of notes, "*You're* not having second thoughts, though? What with the shock of Harold's death and all?"

"You can't go into shock from feeling relief."

"Heh. Your manner of grieving is strange."

"It's just that I—" She closed her eyes and exhaled sharply, then opened them and continued. "My husband's death changed everything. Something like that shifts one's concerns."

"No doubt, in a real marriage. But I understand you hated old Saunders."

"Brilliant insight. Any woman would hate having to pose as the wife of a man who held his position by being a violent thug. And when he took his life, for all he knew, I could have been dragged down with him."

"I realize the worst part of your assignment was being stuck in a fake marriage."

"That's right. But now, today, I can look anybody in the movement right in the eyes, because I stuck with it. I can tell them about the contributions I made to the cause. The sacrifices."

"Oh, agreed!" he looked her up and down, then looked away, scanning around the large entry room. "I'd gladly attest to it," he said over his shoulder in a tone that convinced her he would do no such thing.

She realized she had pushed his pride too far, so she took a long step back, softening her voice, "Although I shouldn't speak of sacrifice to a man who intends to die in the field."

He gave her a moment of eye contact, then looked away again. "My end will be glorious. Because no matter how well our fighters make their statements," he leaned close and whispered, "we can't achieve maximum chaos unless the city's mayor dies at the same time."

"The mayor. He's your target? That's why you expect to die?"

"This city's mayor is no figurehead; he's got far too much power. It reaches into every part of city life."

"You mean because he has the power to stabilize things afterward?"

"Yes! We need maximum confusion to continue for as long as possible." He reached into his jacket and pulled out a folded newspaper, worn and dog-eared. "This is the headline page of the *San Francisco Call* from three months ago. See? It says Pancho Villa has been killed! Is it true? No! Villa is alive and well! The story is all garbage."

"What's that got to do with—"

"The people we work for don't report the news, they control it. And three months ago they needed for the public to get past their outrage over Villa's crimes against innocent people. Faking his death got people talking about something else. See? False justice works as well as real justice. And in the aftermath of the parade attacks, the stupid public will want justice so bad they won't care if the justice they get is real or not."

He leaned in so close to her that when he exhaled, she felt the warmth of his breath on her neck. It smelled of halitosis and cloves.

"I keep this headline page with me because this is the kind of so-called reporting that will be done on us. It's what they'll do after we strike. They'll blame whoever they most want to send up the river, or maybe put to the rope. Now, we have half a dozen radio-controlled bombs packed in ordinary suitcases waiting for the bombers over on Pier 19. The whole pier is closed for repairs, so it's a good location. But after the attacks, it's better if we guide the men away from that area and up here instead, where it will still be quiet."

"Isn't the public you'll be bombing made up of the same people you are trusting to form a new and better world after you bring the system down?"

"Of course!" he laughed. "All but the stupid ones, ha-ha!" At that moment his gaze fell upon the last remaining steamer trunk waiting by the banister at the top of the stairs. The only one she hadn't yet dragged back to the attic.

His laugh stopped short.

Felicity Saunders followed his gaze and felt her blood turn to ice.

He made no reaction at all, at first. Then he pushed a weak smile onto his face. When he spoke, his voice was so strained it almost cracked. "Planning a trip, then. Are we?"

Saunders felt her face flush. She knew her damned skin was beet red. Of course he saw this in her demeanor and took note. The old curse of blushing under stress. It was her true weakness, always a dead giveaway at the worst possible moments. It had been that way all of her life, and no amount of practice ever stopped it.

Fear overpowered her while her mind spun. *Idiot! Idiot! What have you done?* The floor fell out from under her. All ability to think up an acceptable answer was gone. She might have offered up a harmless story about using the trunk for storage of "unused marital bedding," effectively using propriety to put a taboo on the topic. But the words to any such tale stalled in her mouth.

This was doubly frustrating because her forte was acting. Pretense, acting on the stage back in her early life, and later acting in the real world. The challenge before her was nothing more than what she had dealt with every day for years.

But stage fright grabbed her hard. Access to charm failed her. The icy weight of dread returned. It quickly began to spread, as if some unconscious part of her knew something bad about the immediate future that the rest of her could not grasp.

The sickly waves of mortal fear delivered no usable information. Panic began to claw at her.

At a loss, she allowed desperation to push her into trying blunt honesty. *Why not?* The seductive power of plain speech was strong in her after being absent for the years of her false marriage. When it came to feeling the need for honesty, she was underwater hungering for air.

Felicity Saunders made a quick decision to come out of hiding and swim to the surface. "All right, then. I'll tell you. It's time for me to go somewhere and make a new life."

Hemo's posture stiffened, but he did not move.

She went on. "Harold's death changed everything for me."

With that, the air in the room soured. Hemo's voice was soft but tight. "It changed nothing."

"Not true. It freed me. He did this. He ruined himself. I had no part in it. I did my job, by God! He ruined himself, and the last honorable thing he could do was shoot himself to keep the investigators away from our mission."

"You think he had the nobility to shoot himself to protect us?"

"What do you mean? Look. At least it worked. As you see, no one is stopping the mission, are they?"

"Rogue, our leaders are—"

"God almighty! Do you refuse to address me by my name inside my own house?" She noticed she was panting already, so she made herself pause for a breath before going on, "By the way...when it comes to names, are you ready to tell me yours? Here on the eve of everything, are you ready to come clean with me?"

"Our leaders are counting on you to continue working here after the attacks. You know this! You are all to stay in place until chaos reigns and the national transformation begins. My work will have already been done! But only then will you have completed yours. Only then!"

He turned away from her, fuming, then added in a near whisper, "I can't risk your betrayal. Shadow tried to betray me. Us. All of us."

"What? What happened?"

"For some reason or other, he found himself overcome with the jitters. I'm aware of the phenomenon. Happens with soldiers when they first experience combat. Training is one thing, but enemy bullets are another. Sometimes their patriotism turns to shit and runs down their legs."

"Yes, but...what are you telling me?"

"He turned into a brainless moron, Rogue."

"Once again, you shall address me in my home as Mrs. Saunders."

"Of course." He gave a cynical bow which managed to mock the process of bowing. "Shadow actually looked me in the face and asked me to go to the police with him and get them to help stop the others. Kept talking about children."

Hemo went on. "He was a miserable little man. A traitor who went back on his word. He was unable to deliver the firebugs he promised, and there's no time to enlist new ones. We will have to rely on the bombs alone."

Saunders had always possessed enough intelligence, poise, and essential backbone to navigate the social minefields of polite society, but none of it gave her any insight into how to deal with this man.

In the space of a split second, she decided all she was feeling at that moment was her own nerves over this great change about to come to her life. *Courage. Back straight, chin up. You are not abandoning him prior to the attacks the way Shadow did. You are not telling him to go to the police...*

She paused in that thought to absently watch a fly crawl along a nearby windowsill. She was still watching that fly when she made the most fateful decision of her life.

No more deception.

And so, quietly, she began: "I mailed a letter to you. It will turn up in a day or two. Explaining everything, why I'm leaving. But since you're here..." She tapered off.

Hemo responded in a whisper. "Yes?"

The gnawing dread was ferocious. It ought to have been enough to stop her right there. It would have, any other time. But some part of her, long since forgotten, had seized control of her emotions. That part needed to believe sunlight could fix this. It hungered for sunlight. After staying silent in the darkness too many times for far too long, it was starved for sunlight now. And so she kept going when she ought to have stopped. The words came out as if she were letting him in on a sweet little secret.

"I hired a private background-checking agency to have you followed. And then to track your origins. To obtain your true identity, Mr. Byron Morrisey. You live in Chicago and you work from there, but you grew up in Washington, DC. You probably picked the name 'Hemo' because you studied ancient languages at Georgetown University."

Byron Morrisey regarded her with a perfectly blank face. His features could have been carved of wax.

When he failed to speak, she continued.

"You supposedly work for the government in the nation's capital, but you're like my former false husband; nobody really knows what you do. It doesn't matter. You made the most radical *anarchist* move you could, getting that job, because you got yourself into a position where the taxpayers pay you to destroy their way of life. Ha-ha."

"Bravo," replied Morrisey in a dull monotone.

"And since you expect chaos on a national level, there must be a series of these missions planned for cities all over the country."

Hemo stood straight and offered up his best sneer, but without realizing it, he placed his hands together and folded them in front of his crotch. "That's going to depend on whether we succeed here or not."

"And then I realized the only thing that can support an organization so complex is big money. Major funding."

"Stunning insight from a woman. A housewife."

"An actress playing a housewife." She missed the opportunity to take note of his tone, his expression. The eyes most of all. And because she missed it, she went on.

"But this is where the horse hit the fence in your grand plan: business and industry won't pay for chaos. Come on! They don't want anarchy. They can't make money from anarchy."

"Only half right on that one, Mrs. Saunders. Small businesses and local industries can't make money from anarchy."

"They can't." She smiled, folded her arms across her chest, and looked him in the eyes.

"However, big industries and businesses can make unlimited amounts from war. Did you think of that?"

A moment of silence passed before she responded. "Exactly who are we working for, here? Who controls us? Who controls you?"

Felicity Saunders had no time to wonder if it was the unnecessary addition of her triumphant smile which added too much weight to the branch she was perched on, or maybe it was just her challenge to the identity of their masters. Either way, it was at that moment when the branch snapped out from under her. And with that, her time for wondering anything at all was gone. The branch fell, and she dropped with it.

Morrisey made his renowned lightning-fast attack. His powerful hands had choked out many unwitting victims before and had lost none of their strength since. The hands and his ability to use them were the primary reason he got himself selected for this mission: a discreet loner who dispatched a human target with the same indifference Saunders would have felt in going after that fly on the windowsill.

Byron "Hemo" Morrisey was in his true element now, doing what he did best, keeping all the structural points of this mission clear of troublemakers. And on the eve of execution, his primary job was to make obstacles disappear.

Which is what he did. Snatch and squeeze.

He even maintained strict personal discipline while the pleasurable sensations of her death struggle wafted through him. Something inside of him had always realized only insane people relished killing. On the other hand, people like himself, destined to get on well in the world, were merely *proficient* at murder; they took no succor from the deed. Like any other essential job skill, they never confused it with a hobby.

Thus by holding her at stiff arm's length, Hemo was able to unleash death upon her at his leisure while she clawed the air in front of his face, striking nothing, growing weaker, quickly weaker. Then came the useless flapping for a moment or two, followed by the draping off of arms to the sides, beautifully impotent. And then silence from which there was no return.

Job well done, then.

Byron Morrisey would never let it be said that Hemo was a necrophile.

No to that, full stop. Murder and morality did not have to be mutually exclusive. And for that reason he left the late Widow Saunders fully clothed, just as she was. Not so much as an unnecessary squeeze.

Instead he lowered her to the floor and began to drag her body toward the basement, holding onto her arms and pulling her down the stairs behind him while he hurried ahead of her bouncing form.

But near the bottom of the steps, he slipped for a moment, and the sliding corpse overtook him, knocking him to his hands and knees on the floor. He rose, brushed some coal dust off of his trousers, then bent back to the job and pulled the body away from the steps, feeling glad there was nobody to see him get run over by a dead woman.

On that lower level, the tiny basement windows allowed no more than a deep twilight, so he struck a pocket match and looked around.

The bags. There they were, all right. Lined up against the wall beside the exterior door. Morrisey counted six cloth carry bags, purportedly stuffed with supplies for each of the escaping arsonists. He blew out the match, then stepped back from her corpse, which would go unseen for hours and perhaps even for days. More than enough time.

He stepped back over to the basement door. A small utility table had a dress folded on top of it, but it didn't seem to mean anything. Nothing else was with it. He dismissed it and leaned over to check each of the bags to get a general idea of their contents. It all seemed to be just as ordered.

After he turned the door's lock back and forth to be certain it would open from outside, he had to strike another match. It threw its circle of dim amber light seven or eight feet, so he gave a final look around at as much of the basement as he could see amid the inky shadows.

Yes indeed. All done here. Time to go.

Out through the basement door, gently closing it behind him, and then he was gone. He made no attempt to sneak away, and cast no furtive glances. Nobody who caught sight of him would see anything suspicious. He sauntered like a guy headed home because he got the day off early.

Nobody rose to a position like his by being stupid. He knew the importance of blending into the crowd, *never act as if you're doing anything wrong, even if you're setting fire to the place.* Therefore, the sprightly tune he whistled while he walked down the street was an effective reassurance to any and all onlookers. *Nothing's wrong here, folks. Look how happy I sound...*

It was a masterful performance while he battled panic. His end of the operation appeared to be crumbling, all through no fault of his own, due to the ineptitude and lack of commitment from a pack of fools. He could not allow it. He had earned the title 'Hemo,' and there would be blood.

Starting with that bastard private detective.

The basement remained soundless for a full minute after Hemo's departure before Vignette slid from the deep shadow concealing her, gasping as if she had held her breath too long. Her muscles contracted in jerky motions while she walked. It was all she could do to keep to her feet. She stepped on out into the room, shaking with spasms of fear while she hurried to the door and snatched up her folded outer garments.

What was the next action to take in the wake of something like this? Memory and imagination had nothing for her.

She heard the crime take place but saw nothing. Her hiding place kept her out of the eyeline. Nevertheless, the big wooden house magnified every sound. She had picked up on every noise made by their struggle, every gasp. There was no way to avoid hearing the full attack, the final sounds of desperation, and then the terrible silence.

The sudden and brutal manner of Saunders's death set off mortal terror in Vignette, rising out of places deeper than anything she recognized in herself. Still, those noises conveyed one emotion even stronger than her fear, and that was her disgust with the man calling himself "Hemo, Greek for blood," who had just proved himself to be more than a killer for a cause. No, he was just as deadly to the people working with him. To anyone.

She glanced around the basement and decided the first order of business was to move the escape kits where the men on the run couldn't find them. She grabbed the whole lot and pulled them over to the large coal pile next to the oversized heating furnace. Within two minutes she had all the bags covered with enough coal to completely conceal them. She muttered under her breath, "Good luck hunting for them, guys."

Then she stepped back over to the body of the recently late Felicity Saunders and was just about to grab the ankles to pull it closer to the door. Just before touching the body, she realized her hands were covered with coal dust and she noticed Hemo had left black handprints on Saunders's clothing. Without hesitating, she pulled off her jacket and used it to cover her hands while she pulled the corpse out of the hiding spot and onto the main floor. There she placed the body in plain sight, having left no marks on the corpse at all while leaving the large handprints left by Hemo plain to see. A picture of the hands that killed her.

Vignette wadded up the jacket with her handprints on it and tucked it under her arm to carry away. If those fleeing arsonists ever actually got as far as this house, they would not only miss out on their escape kits, they would walk into an unmistakable crime scene. *Oops, no comfort for the firebugs if they show up here.*

She wondered if any of them would still come around after being warned off, or if one of them might report the body if they found it? A note? A phone call? Like her, their problem would be that they weren't supposed to be there either.

It seemed most likely that any one of them would open the door, find the body, stand in shock for a few seconds, then glance around the basement for the expected bags of provisions and realize it had all gone wrong. If the guy had any brains at all, he would also notice the dark palm prints embedded in Saunders's sleeves and instinctively avoid any contact with her body. If not, this single-use soldier would prove himself too stupid to live beyond the mission itself by voluntarily walking into the middle of a murder investigation, and to hell with him anyway.

The wiser subjects would forget about the luxury of pre-assembled escape kits, get the Sam Hill out of town, and keep going until they were out of state. Drop out of sight. Live to fight another day and all that.

If they were not wise and instead did something rash that got them caught, well then, the public would likely lynch them before the law got the chance.

21

HOME OF COUNCILMAN CINQUEVALLI

* July 21st, 10:00 a.m. *

VINCENT CINQUEVALLI STOOD FIRM in the doorway of his prestigious home without stepping aside. Randall was fine with not being invited in. He didn't like visitors, either.

The man's appearance was polished, but his voice dripped with boredom and arrogance. "Yes, that's correct. Signore Galleani is residing with us during his stay in San Francisco. I had thought it was going to be something of a secret, given his controversial, ah, reputation." He ran his gaze over Randall. "Seems the word is out."

"Yeah, he hasn't exactly been playing it close to the vest, Mr. Cinq...uh..."

"I'll say it slowly: *Ching-kway-VAH-lee*."

"*Ching-kway-VAH-lee*. Good. Anyway, fact is, I'm here because there is some official interest at City Hall in the death of Harold Saunders."

"Yes. The mayor's man. Would've looked bad for Sunny Jim if ol' Saunders didn't exonerate him, eh? And you're here to see me about it because...?"

"Oh, it's not you. I mean, no. I'm sure you'll be eliminated as a suspect. You know, soon."

"A what?"

"No concern necessary. They have to look at everybody who worked with him. All very standard procedure."

"Standard, except you are a private sleuthhound. Are the police short-staffed?"

"Always. Now, the way Mr. Saunders died—"

"Suicide. We all know."

"Maybe. You must have seen him around City Hall from time to time in the course of doing your business? Yes, no?"

"Detective Blackburn, is there something wrong with hosting Signore Galleani for a few days in my home? Because that's *really* why you're here, is it not?"

"Oh. Oh, *hosting* for a few days? All right now, see that? *This* is why we conduct investigations. I did not realize, you know, how it's only been a few days."

He dropped his voice to the level of a father confessor. "Because I hear he's been around for several weeks already. Here in your home."

There was a nasty pause. Randall briefly considered punching the man in the mouth on a TBNI (The Bastard Needed It), but then the interviewee spoke up. "Technically, yes. I guess. It was only supposed to be a few days. I don't know, what can I tell you? The man is persuasive!" He dropped his voice to match Blackburn's whisper. "It started when I heard him speak at my *alma mater* on the East Coast, and when I learned he wanted to come to California, why…"

Blackburn interrupted in full voice. "I'll cut straight to it, sir. Are you aware of any direct contact between Mr. Galleani and Harold Saunders?"

The city councilman gasped and recoiled like a man sucker-punched in the chest. "Wait a minute, now! I…I…you mean, as if Signore Galleani might be involved in Mr. Saunders's death? As if my household is harboring a criminal?"

"No. I mean are you aware of any direct contact between Signore Galleani and the late Harold Saunders."

"My household does not harbor criminals!" He swallowed hard and took a deep breath. "I am simply interested in the thoughts of anyone as passionate about human rights as he is."

"Hold up. 'Human rights'?"

"Familiar with the term, are you? The poor, the downtrodden, the disadvantaged? Or do you imagine that simply because I am a man of means and success, I have no compassion for my fellow human beings?"

"No, sir, I'm actually here to ask you why you don't feel the same passion for all the innocent people Luigi Galleani is suspected of killing. All the innocent people he wants to kill in the near future. The immediate future, sir. Compassion."

Cinquevalli glared hard at Randall and took a deep breath. "I'll tell you this much, Mr. Unofficial Detective With No Police Authority: I am so glad we have free speech in this country, because there is nothing to prevent me from telling you this: in my household, we consider patriotism a mark of low intellect."

His face took on the expression of a man smelling something nasty. "And even more so, we see this thing you call 'patriotism' as a mark of low character."

"Understood. And as soon as you're better than someone else, you can kill them. Why not? Even if the victims include the poor, the downtrodden, and...who else was it? Oh yes, the disadvantaged."

"You're talking nonsense!"

"How is it nonsense when those are the very people he intends to blow up, sir?"

"Pity your profession doesn't require more education, Detective. Knowledge has a way of stabilizing a person and guiding them away from hysterical fears."

"Well, yeah. I hear only one out of ten people finishes high school in this country. I was one of the lucky ones. My father believed in education because he didn't have any. Funny thing, though, you wouldn't know it to talk to him. I mean, he spoke like an educated man. Read books all the time. Books about anything."

"Next you'll want to tell me about your mother."

Blackburn took it as an invitation to improvise. "Never knew her. Dad would only ever say a demon got ahold of her—his words. Said he caught her about to dump me in a soup pot full of boiling water. She told him I needed to get clean. They took her away somewhere, and she hung herself."

"Good Lord…"

"Yep. Now that we're friends, would you like to tell me why you're harboring Luigi Galleani?"

But without another word, Councilman Vincent Cinquevalli, pronounced *Ching-kway VAH-lee*, stepped back and swung the thick door closed. Randall heard the heavy deadbolt slide into place.

A couple of newsboys hanging on the corner in the Russian Hill district watched while Vignette stepped up to her Harley and climbed aboard. They tossed some banter back and forth, which she couldn't make out, and shared a nasty laugh. Then they went hog wild when she jumped on the kick starter and fired the engine.

She ignored it all. The sound of the engine drowned out their hoots while she rode away.

But a little girl sitting on the curb stared with wide eyes while the young woman in boy-pants charged away on the big, loud bicycle thing. The girl kept her gaze on the rider until the loud machine rounded the corner and disappeared.

Vignette had only traveled another block when the unusual sight of a rare Waverley electric automobile caught her attention. As she brought the Harley to another angle on the car, she recognized Randall sitting at the wheel, left elbow resting on the open window frame. His hand was to his forehead, and he appeared deep in thought. He noticed the unique sound of the Harley as it approached, and he looked up to see Vignette wheeling over to his side of the street and climbing off the bike.

"Hi," she called out with a cheery grin. "Are you finished with all three of them?"

"Yeah, just finished with the one that matters. We'll get more cooperation from a wet sandbag. Learn anything worth knowing from Felicity Saunders?"

"Brother, did I. You should sit down."

"I am sitting down."

"I should sit down, then."

She stepped over to Randall's passenger side, got into the car, closed the door, and took a deep breath. "Who goes first?"

"You wanted both of us to sit for this, so I guess you should go first."

"Okay. Here we go: Felicity Saunders is dead."

"Vignette!"

"Not me! Not me. It was some guy named Morrisey. Byron Morrisey. I heard them talking, but I never saw his face. He had this nickname, 'Hemo,' and he called her 'Rogue.' Definitely something is going on that's a lot bigger than those two people."

"What the hell happ—"

"I was hiding in the basement."

"Why would you—"

"She left the basement door unlocked, and I didn't believe a word she was telling me at the front door, so once she thought I was gone, I snuck back in."

"All right, not really surprised to hear this, but did you consider the danger of getting spotted inside the house? Visitors? Servants?"

"Nah. The place was empty. She wanted it that way, but not because she's in mourning. She hated her husband, and she's glad he's dead. Or she was. This guy Morrisey! He's some sort of bastard, I tell you. But it's all..." Her breath was coming too fast. "I don't know where to start."

"Easy. Tell it the way you heard it."

"Right. This is the gist of it. The mayor's adjutant didn't kill himself because he was busted stealing from the evidence locker."

"Sounds right."

"It is. And it was much worse than theft. We know there's no proof he killed himself at all. Now it appears death was delivered to him, perhaps by his secret employers."

"Secret employers? Ah, hell. I always hate hearing about secret employers. I've never heard of a secret employer getting caught feeding starving kids."

Vignette nodded. "Especially not these pigs. I tell you, whoever, wherever they are, the way this Morrisey fellow described them, they sound ready to kill as many people as they have to, to go after what they want."

Vignette went on to lay out everything she overheard about the conspiracy to bomb the Preparedness Day Parade on the following afternoon. And while six arsonists were taken out of the picture, there were still six bombers supposed to disburse explosives. She told Randall how the man spoke of using similar attacks in cities all over the country, if this attack proved successful.

Randall shook his head. "We can't trust the infiltrated police, so we can't report this to them without letting them in on what we do, step by step. We also can't trust the infiltrated City Hall, because there's no reliable way to warn anyone in that place, from the mayor on down."

"You mean because for all we know, we could be giving them advance warning?"

He nodded. "And we can't trust the infiltrated newspapers because their editors are either paid off or blackmailed into going along with the pro-war drumbeat."

"You think that includes our city papers?"

"Only way to find out is to tell them, then see if they betray us."

"Wonderful. So we can't trust that avenue, either."

"We could do everything we need to if we had more time. We could sort out the good people. I know there are loyal cops you can't buy." He checked his silver pocket watch. "But it's eleven fifteen in the morning and the parade starts tomorrow at one thirty. Just over twenty-six hours."

"Which rather kills any chance of running experiments to see who can be trusted."

"There's one thing: the bombers might get their explosives planted, but unlike the firebugs, they might not even run. They aren't known as bombers; they're ordinary dockworkers. And they have to return to their jobs as if nothing happened."

"That's your silver lining?"

"Nope. The silver lining is that they don't have the luxury of flight. They can't run. The disappearances would indict them. No, they'll hang around, at least some of them. And eventually one will talk."

"Randall, this is all starting to sound, I don't know, how are we supposed to cope with this? Surely we can't run this thing to ground on our own. Hell, not if we had a hundred investigators."

"Nope. Or a thousand. I've never asked you how much you remember about the aftermath of the Great Earthquake and Fires. It's more than half your lifetime ago."

"Well, I know within a few hours of the quakes, there were roving gangs of armed thieves prowling the streets."

"I wouldn't blame you at all if you had put the whole thing out of your mind. People looting dead bodies. Army soldiers had a 'shoot to kill' order against looters. Countless fires started from the broken stoves and ruptured furnaces. And as for the parade, if they set off enough bombs in the right places, especially next to flammable things, you'll still get fire even without the arsonists."

"Randall! That's what they're trying to do, isn't it? Chaos. Like the earthquake ten years ago! Another full civil breakdown!"

"Sure seems that way. They don't want to just make some angry statement. They want to shock the whole city, maybe the country."

"All right now, just between you and me, this feels ridiculous. How can we do anything to stop this? How can anybody stop it?"

"We could stop the attacks before they take place, maybe with a dozen tough sharp-shooter agents and full backup from the police department. Assuming you have officers you can trust."

"It's strange to hear such a negative outlook from you, Randall."

"Right. Sorry. True is true."

"Hearing it out loud makes it feel closer."

He sat staring into space for a few moments, then his jaw flexed with tension and he shook his head. "The parade route runs all through the Embarcadero district and then off into the city. It's been printed in all the local papers. We could probably trust help from the army, and I'd appreciate a couple of platoons from Fort Mason. Put them in designated neighborhoods and go house to house."

"Great idea!"

"Might have been. Problem is, after the Great Earthquake, the army really took heat for providing soldiers to patrol the streets. Now they won't come out for a civil disturbance unless the governor authorizes it. You realize how many flaming hoops we have to jump through to talk to the governor?"

Vignette let out a heavy sigh. "Oh boy. I sure hope you see something here that I can't see. We're stuck."

"Yes. Stuck, within the current requirements…" He waited for her.

Vignette caught the wave and beamed. "So we change them!"

"Which is why I love private work."

"Let me guess: we 'require' less safety for ourselves, and instead we take the chance to bring someone into our confidence?"

Randall smiled and nodded. "After all, the city has this new 'strong mayor' thing they voted in, so maybe it's time to see if we can get him to show some strength."

"The mayor. All right. I thought you were going to say the chief of police, but they're both powerful."

"Except this Morrisey fellow intends to kill the mayor and says he expects to die in the attack. He didn't mention the chief of police. That pretty much proves the mayor isn't one of them."

"And if we protect the mayor, he becomes our friend. Brilliant!"

"Why, thank you. Especially so, since this Morrisey fellow is an otherwise unstoppable attacker who claims he will die in the attempt."

"I tell you, the way he strangled the Widow Saunders… One moment they were arguing about something or other, and the next all I hear are her choking noises. I knew they were her death sounds as soon as they began. You could just tell. Then he dragged her down into the basement where I was hiding. I barely had time to get out of the way."

"You what now?"

"He dragged her like a sack of rocks."

"How did you avoid him?"

"It's so dark down there, he just never saw me. Heavy shadows, even in the daytime."

"So he just passes you right by?"

"Well, he had just strangled a woman to death with his bare hands. It seemed to take up all his attention, plus dragging her body around."

"And he left right after that?"

"Snuck out after leaving her body in front of the door where nobody could miss it. When the firebugs showed up to retrieve their escape kits it would have been too bad for them. No bags, just a fresh body. I must say, each kit had fresh bread included. You could smell it. Nice, fresh-baked smell."

"Leaving the question, what was he going to do with the men who delivered his bombs, if the firebugs came through for him and picked up their kits and disappeared? Only six bags. I think this proves the bombers will go back to work and disappear on the docks. It's only the firebugs who have to run, because they're already known to the cops."

"He never said, either way. But the bombs themselves are stored, right now, in big suitcases down at the Embarcadero. Pier 19. The pier is undergoing repair, so nobody goes there but a few workers. Which is good, because therefore people in the area don't expect it to be completely deserted."

"So if the few legitimate workers at Pier 19 are scared off, or bought off..."

"Or killed off."

"Or killed off, the entire pier becomes a workable staging area for battle. Right under the city's nose, they'll be free from interruption."

"It's pretty clear the guiding attitude here is, 'I don't care if I die fighting you, as long as you die first.'"

"That's it, then. I'm going to see the mayor and hope he's smart enough to know a hard truth when he hears one." He moved closer and said, "You go over to Pier 19."

Then he continued in a tone she would hardly tolerate from any other male. "Damn it, listen to me this time, Vignette: you *observe* and that's all. What you are doing there is looking for anyone who moves on or off the pier. If they go in, see how long they stay. If they come off carrying anything, try to get an idea which way they're headed. But all that, you do from a distance. You hear me?"

"I hear you."

"Whoever we're up against here, they're determined. They're killers. We won't help anybody by getting ourselves planted."

"Meet you back at home, then. Yes? Say when."

He checked his watch again. "One o'clock. Gives us almost two hours."

"We'll have to hope that's enough time to learn something useful and still be able to do anything about it."

Randall reached over and put the car into forward gear, holding it steady with the foot brake. "Two hours, Vignette. You can stay out of trouble and do a simple reconnaissance mission, yes?"

She gave him a smart mock-salute, "Reconnaissance only. Home at one in the p.m. Aye-aye!" She gunned the engine of her Harley and took off toward the Embarcadero.

Randall steered the electric Waverley toward the mayor's office over at City Hall. It wasn't far. The journey was barely long enough to give him time to gather his thoughts.

He had only met forty-six-year-old Mayor James "Sunny Jim" Rolph a few times over the past few years, and he enjoyed a hint of credibility with the old politician as a result of his solid reputation with the SFPD.

Although Rolph had been mayor for over four years, there was no reason for them to have more than a passing acquaintance. Today, with luck, he would trade on his standing as a former police detective just long enough to hold the mayor's attention while he tried to generate the necessary urgency. With luck, the man would realize the wisdom of cooperation and get all of his resources on top of it, leaving Blackburn enough time to join Vignette down at the docks.

With a little luck, he told himself, *the mayor will have somehow been spared the corruption riddling City Hall. It could happen. Even a pig will fly, if you throw it hard enough...*

He parked the Waverley a full car-length back from a worn livery carriage and a crapping horse, then turned off the silent motor, set the brake, and headed into the building.

22

PIER 19 – EMBARCADERO DISTRICT

* July 21st, 11:30 a.m. *

VIGNETTE PARKED HER HARLEY on Filbert Street just past Pioneer Park, leaving only two blocks to the Bay. Her spot was far enough away from the pier to keep her cover, and it felt like good fortune to find a place without buildings or vehicles in the way.

She left the heavy bike in the shade of a wide oak tree whose branches extended well out over the street, then pulled a pair of low-heel leather slippers from her bag and put them on after tucking her boots under the bike. The slippers were designed for indoor wear, but for her they were perfect sneak-shoes. Their light soles protected her feet, while the uppers were of leather sliced so thin it felt like another skin laid over hers. She permitted a quick sigh of relief.

The footwear gave easily with her steps instead of fighting her motions. It was impossible not to smile when it occurred to her, *This is pure luxury for any woman, no matter how much money she has...*

The morning fog was likely to burn off soon. She could already see anything going on outside the pier from right where she was. Observational hypnosis creeped over her and made the entrance to Pier 19 loom in her vision. It beckoned like a warm donut on a chilly morning. It was one long city block to the pier's crumbled entrance.

The aging gateway must have been impressive once, but was one of the places needing major overhaul. The sides and roof of the long pier had been done with the same construction techniques as the covered bridges back on the East Coast: thin wooden walls supporting a roof of planks sealed under tar paper.

From Vignette's tantalizing surveillance point, the plan to store the bombs there for a short time looked perfect. The pier was marked closed for construction, but the public would find no cause for concern if they did see a few workers milling around, guys who looked to be there on the repair job. If the bombs had to be moved, well, everyone expects construction guys to carry things around.

Intuition told her something was going on there worth observing. She walked closer on legs she sort of controlled but not really.

Before she made it halfway to the pier's entrance, she saw two men walking in her direction up the Embarcadero. They each had light hair and were slight of build. They could have been brothers. She melted into a shadow of construction fencing and watched.

The pair strode past the other pier gates until they reached Pier 19, then let themselves in through the padlocked gate and proceeded straight through the entrance. Even from her distance, she could tell they had carried a key with them.

That made them legitimate, did it not? But then they laid the lock aside and left the gate ajar, as if expecting others to follow.

Vignette's adrenaline surged. *Those weren't a couple of dockworkers. Dockworkers don't dress that well. Sure, they could be the owners or something, but they could also be perpetrators operating right out in daylight.*

She started to return to her bike to hightail it back home so Randall could figure out what to do. She only got a few steps before her feet stopped all by themselves and left her standing to replay her thoughts: *Wait for Randall so he could figure out what to do?*

If she wanted this agency to work, she had to do better when things got slick. Right now, assuming she played the ingenue part and put all this on

Randall's shoulders, what would she actually be delivering to him, in terms of information he could take to the authorities? She was asking him to do magic. Was there even any point in reporting this yet?

What could she "report" to any third party? Specifically: (a) some guys milling around a deserted dock; and (b) a few hunches.

She felt a flush of embarrassment at the mere thought of trying to air those ideas in public. She already carried the sense of being a freak in the world, now she could add the image of a buffoon. *I really should get out more*, she thought for no reason.

In spite of anything else, the oncoming locomotive was headed right for them. Nothing in the difficulty of the situation made the challenge any less real. Unless they stopped the attacks, the results would be worse than anything she could let herself imagine.

Of course Randall had been clear. Unequivocal. *Do not go inside.* Observe from a distance.

And yet...the situation here was fluid. It was Randall who taught her all about handling fluid situations when a chase was involved. Especially when the prospect of violence was there. He understood that in an instant, a good order could become irrelevant. A good order could become wrong.

The city was stuck on an unforgiving time clock, with the moment for the starting gun closing in on them all. She told herself Randall would understand, given the facts in front of her, and she remained aware of his instruction to avoid the scene and not contact anyone.

She reminded herself she was not some ungrateful uppity kid. She would punch the face of anybody who suggested she was.

But how could the police and their iceberg bureaucracy get this job done in time if she hung back now after seeing this? If she waited for this to play out because she was female, what would it take to light a fire under them in time to help?

Vignette exhaled in frustration because she already knew the only answer. Even if she could find someone in power who could be trusted, she couldn't go to the authorities and *claim* anything; she had to have something to show. Solid proof and nothing less.

Either you're a detective or you're not. She repeated it under her breath a few times.

She eyed the entrance to Pier 19. A hand-painted sign made of large, sloppy letters on a plywood sheet read: "Closed For Repairs."

Nobody milling around. Nobody visible back inside. Nothing but regular traffic approaching.

Vignette set off across the wide boulevard with her notebook and heavy pencil clutched in her hand, calmly walking toward the entrance as if she had good reason to be there. It would have been great to be able to make herself invisible, but failing that, she would come close to it by becoming something the human eye doesn't see, the human brain doesn't notice. Along with her personal favorite of Moving Things Around, it was a reliable tool among her less-than-legal skills.

She moved with the understated grace of a distance runner, hot-footing across the boulevard and stepping around two piles of horse flop while avoiding a real ankle-turner of a pothole. Seconds later she was on the other side.

The unlocked security gate presented a real puzzle to her, sitting ajar as it was. It was as if somebody inside knew there would be no problem with beat cops sniffing around.

Apparently someone also had no fear of dockside guards; there was no trace of a private patrol. It was as if the entire pier had an unseen "No Trespassing" sign that everybody somehow recognized and obeyed.

But that left the question, what could actually keep unwanted visitors away? Danger of some kind, taking an unspoken form. Danger projected and danger presumed.

Vignette saw it for what it was to the world at large: a fear tool. A bluff.

She also saw it for what it was specifically to her.

A taunt.

23

OFFICE OF MAYOR JAMES "SUNNY JIM" ROLPH

* July 21st, Noon *

THE OFFICE OF JAMES "SUNNY JIM" ROLPH was opulent enough to reflect the newly formed powers of the city's rebuilt government and fancy enough to imply that neither the mayor nor his staff had time to waste on nonsense. Whatever business puny mortals brought before them needed to be damned good.

The intimidation factor in the architecture alone was so intense, it was not a rare sight for workers in the building to see some member of the public come in with a determined stride that soon weakened and slowed while they crossed the big lobby taking in their surroundings. Some stood silent for a moment, then turned to leave without speaking to anybody.

Randall Blackburn showed no sign of intimidation at all, but it was the result of accumulated experience and not physical size. In spite of his six feet and four inches of height and two hundred twenty pounds of what was still mostly muscle, he never raised his voice and made no attempt to intimidate anyone. He just quietly dropped a few names, making sure the right people knew he was in the building. And to the astonishment of the aides who regularly watched visitors being ejected without getting near the top-floor offices at all, the retired detective and active PI got himself ushered directly to the mayor's office.

He had been inside that sanctum only once, years earlier when the mayor was brand new to the office. Randall had obtained additional information on a murderer already awaiting trial, and the evidence he provided turned out to cinch the case for the prosecution. He was summoned to a jubilant City Hall, where he delivered a case synopsis to His Honor the Mayor. Routine departmental praise. Nice, but very cut-and-dried.

He knew today's meeting was going to be nothing like that at all. He stepped into the mayor's new office.

James "Sunny Jim" Rolph was behind his mammoth desk when Randall entered. He slid out from behind it with his trademark wide smile, welcoming him with the demeanor of a happy boy about to receive a birthday present. "So! Detective Blackburn! Man on the beat. Hello, hello!" He grabbed Randall's hand and pumped it like a candidate.

Randall appreciated the greeting but also understood it didn't have much to do with him. Sunny Jim's demeanor was simply the personality trait that had carried him through his career and propelled him into office.

"Great cop," Sunny Jim called to his secretary in the outer office. "Now in private work! Strong! Courageous!" He pointed Randall to a large chair and closed the office door before he stepped back behind his desk to sit.

"Cigar? No? Good man. Wreck your health. Hope you don't mind if I do." He put a match to a cigar tip and took time to properly put the fire to it, took a deep pull, exhaled. "Mm. All right, then. Urgent meeting, you say. Here we are. What can the city of San Francisco do for you?"

Randall paused for a moment, suddenly at a loss for the best way to dump disastrous news onto a man who might not believe a word he said. He took a deep breath and leveled his gaze at the mayor.

"I won't waste your time, Mr. Mayor. So please, excuse me if I'm blunt. This might strike you, in fact will certainly strike you as unbelievable. At first, anyway. It certainly seemed that way to me, until I found out more."

The mayor smiled his famous Sunny Jim smile, all friendliness and concern. "Well, then! Sounds serious. I'm all ears." He leaned forward to indicate full attentiveness, the way he did with interviewers.

"Well, all right, Mr. Mayor. The parade."

"Tomorrow? Yes! Biggest in city history! Yes!"

"Ah, sir, that may well be, but it's actually part of the problem. I mean, the parade may have been selected because of the size of it."

"Mm-hm. Selected for the size."

"We are in an ideal time and place for terrorism, Mayor Rolph."

"Jim! Please!"

"Well, Jim, I mean multiple bombs which can also cause fires, all coordinated to cause maximum chaos, sir."

The mayor just stared at him for a few moments. No movement, no expression, not a sound. Meanwhile the smile melted like ice cream on a hot sidewalk.

"Detective Blackburn...I realize your reputation...I mean, I know when you were on the force, you were one of our brightest assets."

"Not much for flattery, sir."

"Good. Forget the compliment! Multiple bombs and fires? As if we are suddenly living on a war front? Just tell me what would make you say such a thing?"

"I tell you gladly, sir. A few days ago, Jacob Prohaska contacted me with concerns he developed while doing his work for the US Customs office."

"Yes, yes. Rented office downstairs. Nervous fellow. Always skeltering around."

"Mr. Prohaska says things have changed all of a sudden, and there's a flood of people coming into the region who actively want to destroy us, and they are already working on it right here. From within City Hall. Maybe as far as the state capital, I don't know."

Randall noted Sunny Jim's expression remaining pleasant enough, but his eyes were getting glassy. It was plain Randall had about three seconds left before he found himself talking to a wall. He sprinted for the finish line.

"I know it's hard to hear, sir. But Mr. Prohaska was afraid to reveal these things to me in front of his own staff. He was in the same position you have been in, sir, not knowing where trust is to be placed. He says he contacted my agency because he's concerned that he can't make any progress inside the official system."

"Detective, hear me out, now. Have you considered, perhaps, that this grand terror plan isn't really happening? And it may be that your source is wrong?"

"Yes, sir. I hoped for that too. At first. But I'm here to confirm that we have elements in the city who are willing to use mass murder to make a political point. They plan to do exactly that. At the parade. Tomorrow."

"And I'm waiting to hear how you know this."

"A messenger boy was killed trying to deliver Prohaska's warning note to me. The note told about some kind of infiltration going on in this city, supposedly all around the whole country."

"Yes, well, I heard about the boy. One of our street orphans, sad to say. No mother. Father a derelict out on the streets, doing the boy no good. We haven't learned anything about the boy himself, but I surmise he was just trying to survive."

"Sir, the warning note was supposed to be a secret, but somehow these people found out about it. And they had that innocent boy killed."

"The boy who carried Prohaska's warning note to you."

"Well, yes."

"And although they killed him, the note found its way to you anyway?"

"Right to my door. They could have seen to it I never knew about the note at all. Instead I believe they used the boy's body to guarantee I would realize how dangerous they are. If I were frightened enough, maybe I would walk away from all of it."

"And you did not. Good for you, Detective." He took a gilded pen from his desk set and pulled a piece of paper close. "I'm making a note to have your name mentioned when we give out our civic awards tomorrow at the finish line." He smiled the Sunny Jim smile. "A little favorable publicity might send a few juicy cases your way!"

Randall lowered his voice to a level no one outside the office could hear. "Mr. Mayor. Prohaska sent it anonymously. He only came forward after he heard the boy was killed. He said he paid the boy to get it to me instead of using a city messenger because of not knowing who to trust in City Hall."

Mayor Rolph's face paled. He stuffed the cigar between his lips again and put it to a long and slow draw. He stared out the nearest window. "Oh," he murmured. "Who to trust. Yes..."

"He claims your entire city government is riddled with turncoats.

They've either been bribed or blackmailed into going along with some grand scheme to destroy the parade with an act of mass murder. The idea is to use the propaganda value of it to convince Americans to stay out of the war."

"Riddled with turncoats..."

"Not all of them, sir. Some of your people somehow learned of it and refused to play along. They showed personal character in the face of temptations, threats, blackmail."

All of the renowned sunniness left the mayor's face and was replaced by a gray pallor. "You mean...you're saying...that clump of unlucky accidents here, and at the police department? This was...these were the ones who said no? Who simply held onto their sense of honor?"

He paused and stepped to a window to take in a deep breath. After a moment, he let out a sigh so heavy Randall nearly felt the breeze.

"I don't really know this Prohaska fellow, but I can tell you...he's right about the turncoats. I'm seeing indications all over the place that our city government is thoroughly infiltrated."

"Why do you say that?"

"Why do I say that? Let me see: I give orders, they don't get followed. I demand to know why they are not followed, all I get are lies. Of course I have an internal investigation quietly taking place right now, Mr. Blackburn."

Randall noticed that "Detective" was currently dropped from his name.

Sunny Jim spun back around and pointed his cigar at him. "For a long time, I thought we just had ourselves a generation of do-nothings, and so my consistent response was to fire them right and left. But lately the new hires are often no better than the ones they replace. Sometimes worse. Frustrating."

Sunny Jim dropped his voice to a near whisper. "If they really are this organized, then this sure as hell isn't just a few over-ambitious people who want to pull off backroom deals."

"I was hoping Prohaska exaggerated the threat."

"Apparently a hope not to be realized."

"Mr. Mayor, you—"

"Jim."

"Jim. You honestly believe these people, this group or whatever we should call the thing, they possess the gall to do something like this?"

"They have killed my hopes but cleared my vision." He struggled to form another sentence, failed, exhaled hard, and tried again. "There is a cancer in my administration, Mr. Blackburn. I also keep getting indications that it goes far beyond our city."

"There must be people on your staff who aren't a part of this. So why aren't they informing on the others and reporting back to you?"

"Obviously they're cowed into silence. And apparently it's a rational response, since the people we're dealing with killed a delivery boy simply to make a point."

Mayor Rolph looked at him with eyes that bored through him, then he seemed to come to a decision. "All right, then. I'm going to trust you, Detective. Detective Blackburn. Great reputation on you, my friend, I know that. I certainly know that. I have to trust somebody."

He lowered his voice to a whisper and leaned close enough to Randall to nearly touch his shoulder with his forehead. "And I will be damned if you did not just show me you have real courage! To come here and tell me this? Even with no way to know where my own loyalties might lie? You have what I call 'Golden Balls,' my friend! Stand up to anything. Never tarnish, ha-ha! Good."

Randall avoided the temptation to respond and just waited to hear what the mayor was going to say.

Sunny Jim let out a blast of air. When he spoke, it was in a hushed voice. "I know there is a plot against the parade, Detective. We just don't have any relevant details. D.A. Fickert tried to tell me about this, but he's got no more idea what to do about it than I do. We will have patrols all over the parade route, but we can't tell how many officers are compromised. It won't take many to sow chaos."

"Cancel the parade."

"Oh yes. Well. Call off the biggest event in the city's history because of some rumors of threats, eh?"

"We have more than rumors, however."

"Because these last few years, we live in a world where you can't make a political statement of *any* kind without getting a threat from somebody. Between the newspapers on one hand and the unions on the other..."

Randall pushed himself to think of something, of anything to pull the mayor off his rant and get him back on point without showing unacceptable disrespect. "Well, sir, I believe if you—"

"But! If you react to mere rumors of threats and you are wrong, then you display weakness! You see, Detective?"

"I'm listening with full attention, sir."

"Jim. Please. I don't care for the *sir* stuff."

Randall felt himself stare in disbelief for half a second, then he stood up to the occasion. "Of course. Jim. My apologies."

Sunny Jim nodded.

Randall waited for more, got nothing, then continued. "When it comes to motive, here, we can't avoid wondering what the end result of this is supposed to be. Somebody, somewhere, knows the answer to that."

"Can you find them in twenty-four hours?"

Randall mentally sifted the few indicators he had so far, not a single real clue among them yet. He shook his head. "Almost certainly not, sir. Jim. Fact, I hate to say it, but we need something compelling, some solid direction to move in these few hours we have left."

Sunny Jim stared into space, projecting calamity. "What about your street sources?"

"Street sources?"

"Oh, please. We know your work operates on a foundation of street contacts, people living the low life. They bring in tips to trade for a few coins. Keep you wise to the undercurrent of daily life. Business, too, sometimes. I would like for you to patrol your old district and run down everything you can on the story. Take the day."

That stopped Randall cold. *What?! Turn to outdated street contacts who were never all that accurate back in the day, and now somehow gain usable information about a public bomb attack?*

His heartbeat reminded him the clock was ticking. He needed to play along, keeping the mayor on his side. "Well, I will certainly direct all the energies at my agency to your disposal. I should tell you, I seriously doubt that anyone down there has anything we can rely on. Why, the boy's father—"

"An unhappy derelict. The hobo life. Nothing for the boy in a man like that."

"Yes, ah, Jim. And that's the sort of character we tend to get down on the Bowery, when it comes to finding out which way the rats are running."

"Excellent man. Detective Blackburn. Obvious hero. I am grateful for your presence in this thing."

"...I was hoping we could check around closer to your own social circle, sir."

"Politicians and power brokers? Waste of time. How can anyone create esteem in the eyes of the public by blowing up families? Whatever they might gain in horror they would lose in stature."

"Unless they've got no interest in public esteem. Only in public terror. Jim."

The mayor thought a moment, then stood and took a deep breath, suddenly resolute. "Right, then! Let's go see Fickert and get him on board. Pull in Mr. Prohaska, and we will then field a reliable team of four, at least."

"Five," Randall added with a smile, "with Miss Nightingale."

"Five, then. It's a place to start."

"It is. And I've already confirmed that all three City Council members have telephones in their homes, although I have no idea if they're all involved, or just the one I spoke with, so we need to set up phone call interception. Then we can listen in to see if they give away any information."

"Mm. Good idea if we had months instead of hours. Who can we trust to do this? Reliable enough to listen in and report back to us in secret? Can you assign Miss Nightingale to do it?"

"Well, yes. I could. But she has a low tolerance for boredom and would disappear from such duty within hours. Maybe less."

"Why? It seems like a perfect job for a young woman, and an excellent way for her to contribute to the task."

Randall had to laugh. "Oh, she likes to contribute, all right. But sitting around isn't something she does well."

"Who, then?"

"Mr. Mayor, I think we should have the listening device set up here in your office and give you first access. It's a vital function, sir, and we have to have a partner we can trust on the line."

Mayor Jim nodded. "A partner we can trust. Fair enough, I'll stay here, Detective. I don't fancy running around the city trying to play copper and getting recognized by the hoi polloi."

Randall laughed. "You do have that 'Sunny Jim' moniker to live up to."

"Exactly. So! A plan, then. Good-good!" Sunny Jim deployed the famous smile. It had been mostly absent in recent days but now reappeared.

He stepped to his office door, opened it, and called out to his secretary, "Get a telephone engineer up here right away, will you, please? Oh, and call the head of the local telephone exchange. Tell whoever it is that I need a special favor and we have to get it done right away. This afternoon! Now!"

Randall heard the secretary ask a question, but he couldn't make out the words. The mayor's response was succinct.

"No, I said *now!*"

24

PIER 19 – EMBARCADERO DISTRICT

* July 21st, 1:00 p.m.—The Day Before the Attack *

IN THE DARKNESS UNDER THE ROOF and between the walls of the covered pier, there was too little ambient light to determine if the place was fully rigged for gaslights. If so, maybe they worked, maybe not. Maybe nobody had turned them on.

The darkness was a good thing for Vignette and the only reason she had avoided capture so far. She took a quick step backward and pasted herself into a shadow so black it swallowed her whole. From that spot she could see, she could hear, and yet remain invisible to the two large men who were arguing in whispers over her disappearance. They stood only a few feet away.

"I tell ya, I saw somebody back in here. Skinny kid, maybe even a girl. Not dressed like a girl, but..."

"What, guy was by himself?"

"Him, her, I'm telling you!"

"What girl is going to come sniffing around by herself on an empty pier?"

"All right, it could have been a skinny guy. Okay? Skinny girl, what's the difference?"

"The difference is a skinny guy is maybe a solo cop looking to start trouble. A skinny girl is maybe your imagination."

"You think we should get rid of the items?"

"People are coming to move them at daybreak. There's no way to get the word out in time."

"Then just help me look around the place. I'm starting with the pallet stacks at the other end, over there on the right side. You take the left side, will you?"

"Right. Here's the ticket, though; if anybody's found us, then it's down to you and me, and we got to get everything out of here. You know that, right?"

"What I know is if anybody's found us, we have to get rid of *them*. The items stay right here."

The other guy laughed at that and responded in an admiring tone, "You are a madman. Howling under the moon." They both laughed at that.

The pair stomped on down to the stacks of wooden pallets and began swinging their lanterns back and forth to light up the dark corners, leaving Vignette alone with the "items," a line of six large suitcases sitting flat on the floor with their tops open. She had already heard the men mention that each bomb only needed to have its final detonation wire connected, and with that, they would all be ready on command.

Raising the question, whose command?

Vignette bent to the line of suitcase bombs and wondered how many hundreds of deaths they represented. Six bombs delivered by half a dozen operators. Maybe more. For all she knew, this was to be done in teams.

She got the impression there might be a few seconds to play with before the men finished their search, and her heart rate was still at a good level: easy for calmness but wide awake if sudden explosion was needed. Rapid acceleration with plenty of juice for a hot sprint.

The most stimulating sensation in her life was that of running at top speed from someone who dearly wanted to kill her. With these men, she felt certain the only weapons they had were their beefy hands, so without challenging herself as to why she believed that, she decided to stay in place just a bit longer.

She felt her way with careful fingertips through the exposed wiring of one of the bombs, locating several wire connections. She randomly selected two of them and pulled them out, tucking the ends back so they appeared solid. All the while she kept an eye out for the men who, at that moment, were actively searching for her.

She only had enough time to rig that one bomb before the searchers moved back in her direction. The level of risk shot her pulse so high she had to take several deep breaths to avoid passing out. She loved it.

It was only once she finished and was on her way out, light-footing it back through the entrance, when she realized she had once again allowed her love of the energy geyser to carry her away.

A flush of self-consciousness flooded her. *What's the matter with you?*

Randall had warned her that certain bombs were built to explode if anyone tried to disconnect them, but she still had no idea what such a bomb would look like. She could have had one in her hands and it never occurred to her.

It hit her with a gut punch. It was reckless in the extreme for her to pull those wires. She had gambled with her life and gotten lucky. With that, the self-judgment hit her hard.

"It wasn't lucky; it was stupid lucky," she muttered under her breath. Stupid luck was luck you didn't earn. You could never be sure if it would show up for you or not, like the worst fiancé anyone could ever have: there for you in some spectacular way, and in the next moment leaving you to fall to your death.

No more stupid lucky. You got stupid lucky when Randall took you and Shane in, full stop. He's the only man besides Shane you've ever known who can be trusted to be good and kind.

For those first years, she waited every day in the back of her mind for a monster to appear in Randall. He simply never did, that's all. Instead this man, Randall Blackburn, gave her the steady love of an actual father, unlike the drunken animals who savaged her youth. He forgave her the scars from the hellhole and mostly overlooked their effects on her behavior. He loved her anyway.

And so as far as Vignette was concerned, that was *more* than enough stupid luck for one lifetime. She exited the Pier 19 gate and hurried across the Embarcadero, heading back to her waiting Harley. But while she moved, the realization of the risk she took began to weigh so heavily her muscles started cramping and her gait became unsteady. Of course she should never have been so bold around so many desperate men. Her disappointment in herself came through in the form of nausea. It nearly cramped her to a standstill.

She reached the bike on unsteady feet and leaned on the handlebars like someone using a cane. Her hands shook while she pulled the key from her pocket, stuck it in the magneto box, and turned it to the "on" position.

She raised her torso upward using the handlebars, stiffened her ankle muscles, and dropped her body weight onto the kick starter, firing the Harley's power plant to life. The drop starter was a new feature for the Harley "F" model, along with its electrical headlight system. It made for much smoother start-ups than the old pedal system.

On the first turnover, the iron and steel of the power plant reliably took to rumbling between her legs. The transfer of energy helped drive the sense of sickness from her. She loved the sensations of sitting astride a mechanical creation while it was all but begging her to hit the gas.

Shane had taught her well, even recommended the "F" series kick starter. She knew the basics of the engine. At a moment like this, she fully appreciated the fact that this new model blasted the air/fuel mixture into the V-twin pistons with such great efficiency that the beast could respond with a primal growl heard for half a mile on open ground.

And now the beast was wide-awake. Calling out to her, *Twist the throttle! Twist the throttle!*

With the transmission in neutral, she did exactly that and twisted the throttle as hard as any engine's voice could want. Once, twice, three times the beast screamed like a caged beast, startling nearby horses, angering pedestrians, announcing itself to the world at large. Again she felt the Harley's power pass from the engine and into her, through her thighs and her crotch, then up into her hands through the handlebar grips.

She hit the gas a fourth time, then she tapped up first gear. The factory-gray Harley-Davidson peeled out and darted away, weaving through traffic and heading in the general direction of Golden Gate Park.

Now the machine passed the spirit of the warrior into her. All her unsteadiness vanished. In its place she felt a state of clarity and focus. In such a state of concentration she could ride like the Headless Horseman, fearing no ground, no matter how dark or rough. She rode as Shane taught her to ride. This was her flying machine. It was not a mode of transportation, it was a solid object testifying to her hard-won condition of personal freedom. She had caught the bug from Shane and allowed it to possess her.

The urgent problem at hand was to think of a way to present this information to Randall without sending him up the chimney over it. She'd definitely gone too far again, no way around it. She was going to hear about it from a man she hated to disappoint.

Regardless of his potential anger, it was urgent to meet him right away and hit him with her discovery on the pier. Plus the untidy fact that there was no way to tell if she actually disabled that one bomb. Or even whether her attempt to hide the detached wires would fool anybody.

He had to know about them so they could figure out what to do together. Not so he could tell her what to do, but so she could think it through with him and come up with a plan together.

She took a tight turn on the bike and found herself passing the home of one of the many males who couldn't seem to stand the sight of her on a large motorbike. In the past, this one had merely catcalled her when she passed. She always perceived his intentions, but her speed always kept her from hearing most of it.

This time, however, he was just backing a small truck out of his driveway and into the street when he looked to his right and saw her approaching. He grinned and deliberately pulled the truck into her path.

A less competent rider would have collided. Instead she swerved hard to the left, taking much of the weight of the bike on her left leg by pressing her left boot hard to the road, topped by a final thrust with her left thigh muscle to pitch the bike upright again. She immediately dropped the bike's weight to the right this time, to correct for the bike's direction of travel, until with a final kick she went upright and rumbled away down the road. The truck honked in outrage, and that made her laugh. Little victories. The stuff of life.

Her amusement dissipated when she realized Shane had been killed by just such a maneuver, and he was a far more experienced rider. How could he have made such a mistake? Why couldn't he self-correct out of it? She blinked hard to flick the thoughts away and force herself back to the matter at hand.

Maybe, she told herself, *we'll catch a break with those bombs. Maybe the bomb carriers will be so focused on the job that they'll trust the equipment without giving it a thorough check. Remarkably foolish on their part, but what if they've got no expertise? Delivery boys with no need to know anything?*

Could be. The men scheduled to pick up those bombs and deliver them God-knows-where might have been lied to and told their purpose was something relatively harmless, something they could stomach. Like maybe the bombs were more or less fireworks that would merely detonate with great noise and light, scaring people but not killing them. The bomb carriers might be relatively innocent, simply pawns caught up in something far above their understanding.

For now, with no way to know the truth of it, there was nothing else for her to do but assume her little trick failed and all the bombs were still functional; either she had not disabled the bomb or the broken connections would be discovered and repaired. Either way, she would have done nothing to make the public safer.

But as to the power of those bombs, there was no need of an education in such things. Each one was a deadly device. What purpose was served in devising camouflaged portable bombs that went off like a summertime picnic display?

She recalled the detached superiority in Luigi Galleani's eyes. The memory prevented her from believing he held any interest in a symbolic gesture, a fireworks display.

No. If he was involved in this Preparedness Day Parade and explosives were being used, then the story on this was going to be one of the mass slaughter of innocent people. The purpose claimed for it would make no difference at all to the victims.

25

BLACKBURN & NIGHTINGALES – PRIVATE INVESTIGATION

* July 21st, Approximately 24 Hours Before the Attack *

"I FOUND THE BOMBS," Vignette announced while she pulled off her boots at the front door. "Six of them, anyway. There could be more, I guess. But these are definitely hidden down at Pier 19."

"What do you mean you 'found' the bombs?"

"Six, Randall! Packed in suitcases! Basically invisible. You could take them anywhere and not be noticed! I pulled a couple of wires on one, but there wasn't any more time. Two of the guys were searching for me, so I had to take off and beat it back here."

"Oh, two of them were after you. Thus two living examples of why I asked you to observe from across the Embarcadero, *not* from inside."

"Well, I mean...from the front it's just a closed pier, you know?"

"Outstanding. You risked walking into a gang of armed criminals alone. You somehow divined what was inside the covered pier, but in spite of knowing you were looking at suitcase bombs, you made physical contact with one of the devices. You pulled two wires, when you know bombs can be rigged to go off if you try to disarm them."

"Trust me, I thought of that."

"You thought of that but you did it anyway."

"No! *Damn* it! I mean to say...I mean..." She took a small breath and sheepishly added, "I thought of it while I was running out."

"Running out from what was supposed to be a simple surveillance position where nobody would be able to do you harm or even know of your presence."

"Please, Randall. Stop for a moment. We're running out of time, and I wasn't doing any good standing around out there. I'm not hurt, and no harm was done."

"Or should we say *yet*?" He blew a hard sigh and took up his old habit of pacing while he considered his words. "Vignette, if I can't trust you to follow directions, I don't see how this can work for us. Of course I want this agency for myself, but I want it for you, too."

"Randall. Listen. I mean...I realize that. I do. I do. But this thing, it's turning out to be more serious than we thought, and at that moment, you know, in that opportunity, I just had to freelance."

He regarded her in silence, then exhaled and shook his head. "I want you to succeed at this work, Vignette. I know you can. But please, have a little compassion for me, okay? Ask yourself what happens to me if you go off 'freelancing' and get killed?"

He looked into her eyes. "Because after losing Shane, I would not know how to carry that load, Vignette. Neither of us wants to lose the other." He touched her cheek with his fingertips. "If you won't use caution for yourself, please, at least do it for me."

That did it. Her hard shell split down the middle and the emotions burst out. She began to cry like a child and threw her arms around his neck. Her grief over losing her brother blended with her own regret, and she held onto him with all the strength in her arms, as if willing her muscles to say what she could not.

She knew he was right. She felt the truth of it. This time she crossed the line by ignoring the respect she owed to him, whether or not she could believe she owed respect to herself.

Randall had never seen an expression of emotion so strong in her. He felt his lack of expertise as a father. At least he knew enough to go easy with her, and he stood still while he held her, gently patting her shoulders and giving her time. He thought of it like emptying poisoned water from a bucket. Maybe they would both travel lighter for it.

Vignette stood that way with Randall for several seconds, much longer than she had ever allowed a hug to last. She felt baffled by the warmth of the moment. Here she had arrived ready to tell him her story, braced for his outrage and a punitive response. She deserved it. She knew how it all looked.

And then the tricky bastard went and reminded her of his love for her. Vignette could stand firm under the worst verbal humiliations. She could stifle panic and remain rational amid sudden physical assaults. She had proved both many times in her former life. But here Randall Blackburn simply asked her to picture him alone without her, if she threw her life away, and it broke her heart wide open.

Finally Randall whispered in her ear, "I have more to tell you. Why don't I make us some tea? There's something you should read."

Minutes later they sipped hot tea at the kitchen table while Randall explained the new uneasy alliance with the mayor and the district attorney. He was not particularly happy to have to report that Mayor Rolph insisted that the Customs man Jacob Prohaska must be included.

Vignette shook her head. "I have to tell you, Randall, nothing I've witnessed in Prohaska's behavior makes me inclined to trust him."

"Agreed. I believe this is one of those times where it makes sense to keep him close whether he's trustworthy or not. For example, I don't think we should tell him about this." He tossed a small envelope onto the table, already opened, and pointed to it. "Have a look."

The note was scrawled on a greasy piece of old newsprint, with ill-shaped letters that were hardly unusual in a land where few people completed their education before going to work. Still, the few lines it contained were enough to widen her eyes.

The words, as best she could make them out, read:

Yoo peepul shud take a look at a man named Jacob Prohaska. J-a-c-o-b P-r-o-h-a-s-k-a. Guvmint man. My boy heared him say a lot of oter things to sombody on the telyfone line when he dint know my boy was there. Other man is Byron Morrisey. B-y-r-o-n M-o-r-r-i-s-e-y. Call hisself HEMO. My boy told me that night. Came home scared about going back. Sed he coodint tell me what he heard. Next day them two kilt my boy. I told the cops right off but they done nothing.

Randall broke the silence. "Hardly leaves room to doubt, this confirms the Hemo fella is Byron Morrisey."

"Yeah. The man I heard but did not actually see killing Felicity Saunders."

"Meaning he's still presumed innocent."

"Except he killed her, all right. Cold."

"Then here's what we have to do. We can't wait for her body to be discovered at some point after the attacks. As dangerous as it is to attract any attention from the authorities right now, we have to report her murder."

"What the *hell?* Randall?"

"Anonymously! Anonymously. We don't report it in person, and we don't send a note."

"Leaving what option?"

"A telephone call to police headquarters. The police operator won't recognize my voice."

"What if they can tell the call is from here? From you?"

"That takes special preparation. They won't have it in place. I'll just give them the facts and hang up."

"Oh. I guess that's good. I suppose if you don't make the call, she's not likely to be discovered until somebody shows up to reclaim the house."

"By then, one or two steps past the doorway would be all it takes to get the ball rolling."

"I should have stolen those escape kits. We sure don't want them back in the hands of the perpetrators, and there's no way to guarantee where they end up once they go into the evidence locker."

"Right. Of course, the risky part is that if word gets back to whoever's behind this, it might just make them more desperate."

"If only there were some good cops to report all this to."

"There are plenty of them. We just don't know which ones they are, and we can't hunt them down in a day's time. This infiltration, if that's what it is, it has to have been going on for a long time. Years."

Vignette paled at the thought. "The end result being we can't afford to trust any of them."

Randall nodded. "All right, there shouldn't be any real danger in that house for the time being, so you run back and take the escape kits. I'll wait a few minutes before I make the call to the police. They can't assemble a team and get over there in less than an hour, so you'll be long gone before they get there. Just bring the kits back here. That will at least take them out of the picture."

"I'll leave right now."

"Take the Waverley. There might be too much to carry on your motorcycle."

"Nope, thanks."

"Nope, thanks?"

"Prefer the bike."

He grinned. "Holding the bags in your arms and steering with no hands?"

Vignette laughed at that. "Nah. I've got a plan. Won't take long at all." She stepped to the front door and opened it.

Randall called after her. "You taking the motorbike because you're still not tired of getting bugs in your teeth?"

"You develop a taste for them."

"Just come straight back here, because—"

"I understand," Vignette anticipated. "We're running out of time."

26

THE BLACKBURN-NIGHTINGALE & SAUNDERS HOMES

* July 21st, 2:00 p.m.—24 Hours and 6 Minutes Left *

RANDALL WAITED FOR AN EXTRA amount of time—for nearly half an hour—after he watched Vignette peel away from the front of their home. Then he stepped over to the wall-mounted telephone, picked up the receiver, whirled the hand crank to alert the operator, and asked her to connect him with the San Francisco Police Department. A moment later he had the desk sergeant on the line.

"Police. City Hall division."

"I want to report a dead body. Female in her forties. You'll find her in the basement of her home."

"Who is this?"

"Her name is Felicity Saunders. She was the widow of the mayor's adjutant."

"Wait a minute. You mean the Widow Saunders?"

"One and the same."

"And who are you again?"

"I'm the person calling to tell you someone she trusted betrayed her and strangled her."

"You?"

"No. I had nothing to do with it. Just go to the Saunders home. You guys know where it is."

He hung up at that point and found himself breathing hard, as if by physical exertion. He was surprised that his act as an "anonymous informer" hit him so hard. Anonymity had never been part of his skill set.

In an ironic twist, the same scrupulous honesty that once made him widely admired by any fellow officer who wasn't in on the take now came back to haunt him with a sick feeling. He stared out the window and spoke to the killers under his breath. "Who *are* you?"

Today, the old attitudes he had about the city no longer worked. The simple reason being that the same authority structure he risked his life to protect countless times over twenty years now appeared to be turning on its own people.

This line of PI work was never supposed to put Vignette in serious levels of danger, but whoever expected any of this? Their puny team was already far too small for the task before them. So beyond the desperate hope that the rumors were wrong or that the plot would somehow fall apart, he was left with the question, how was he supposed to unravel this thing when the mayor himself couldn't trust his own police force?

The Waverley was still parked out front, so Randall went back outside and climbed in. He drove it down to the electric stable and hooked up the charging cables. There was no need to stand around once it was connected, so he always left the charger in place and walked back. This time he decided to stick around and switch out the hard top for the open-sided soft top. Twenty minutes was all it would take him. He could be home in less than half an hour.

The unlocked basement door of the Saunders home opened for Vignette without resistance. The first sight to greet her in the shaft of light across the floor was the body of Felicity Saunders. Vignette was no stranger to the chemical process of a moldering corpse; whatever she lacked in the language of the white coats she knew from the signs of nature. The cool basement had spared the corpse from visible decomposition beyond its gray-blue pallor, and yet already the withering remains of Felicity Saunders spoke of nothing but deadness. The once-shapely corpse of Felicity Saunders was slowly deflating to gravity.

She had no doubt that by the time the firebugs showed up expecting to find their escape kits, they would be greeted by the smell of death from a murder victim who would be stiff as a board if her rigor mortis had not yet faded. But clearly, no one else had been there since Vignette left.

She skirted her way around the remains and slipped back to the coal pile to retrieve the hidden bags. After dirtying her hands in pulling away the coal lumps, she collected one bag in each hand and one under each arm. She left the other two behind for the moment.

Outside, she made her way to the Harley with the four bags and set them next to it. She had brought a short piece of thin rope along and now used it to bind up all four bag handles. She hustled back to the basement and retrieved the last two bags, returning to tie all the handles together so their combined mass was stable enough to fit on her passenger seat, then tied the whole bundle around her waist to keep the bags on board while they bounced over the bricks to get home. It was a good plan, as far as improvised actions go. Practical. Simply executed.

Her plan worked well enough but never allowed for the possibility that someone might follow, or for the need to watch out for tails. She never saw the two men sitting in a stolen milk truck just down the street, surveilling the Saunders house.

Both men looked as if they were fighting off falling asleep. And then they were wide-awake the instant she passed them. They started up the truck and pulled out into traffic, tailing her at a distance all the way back home.

The truck continued on past when she pulled up and parked in front of her house, but it turned at the next corner. Once out of sight of the house, it pulled to the curb. The driver set the parking brake and killed the engine without the neighbors taking particular notice of the arrival. Both men got out at the same time. Vignette would have recognized each if she had seen them.

One carried a large suitcase.

Vignette left the Harley leaning at the curb and toted the bags up the front steps, opened the main door, and dragged it all inside the house. She kicked the door closed with one foot, then knelt to separate out the bags, opening each one to sort through the contents.

The sight of someone else's careful labor won Vignette's respect. The women who assembled these bags had made a fine job of it. Each one contained the kind of dried food that could travel well: prepared meats, cheeses, crackers, along with two canteens of water. Each bag had a full loaf of bread. There were also blankets, can openers, hunting knives, and maybe best of all, thick hats and sweaters for the deep-chilled Northern California nights. The purpose of the hunting knives was unclear to her, but each was made by a fine hand and sharpened to the point of severing skin by touching it.

She was still on all fours among the escape items when the front door of their home was bashed open by a terrible blow, loud as gunfire. Vignette caught an approaching shape in her peripheral vision and leaped like a mongoose evading a cobra, but despite her speed and agility, the move required her to push herself straight upward from a standstill, reacting in surprise, while her attacker charged her with a full load of attack energy.

In less than a second she was struck from the side, taking a thunderous blow to her rib cage. The force of it knocked the wind out of her and left her lying trapped beneath her assailant, choking. Randall had taught her well that weaker victims were known to die of heart attacks at about this point in an assault. But they tended not to be twenty-year-olds in good health who hated being victimized more than they loved being alive. Her heart went into overdrive and powered up her body. As harsh as the attack was, the level of violence was too familiar to cause her to panic.

There was no denying the difference in size and muscle between her and the attacker. She found herself overcome and physically helpless. A crushing force was closing off her air supply, dragging her away from consciousness. She had an instant or two to find some way out from under this man or she would perish on that floor. Because of her particular history, she knew if she failed to take effective action, the best she could hope for was to be unconscious or dead when degradations were visited upon her.

Oddly enough, with that realization, a cold rush of glee shot through her. She recognized it in her bones and her blood, and the glee came from her certain knowledge of the strength and power to be had in sheer rage. An invisible geyser of energy blasted upward from her toes and out the top of her head, real as lava itself and just as hot.

Experience had taught her well. She knew there was a way to explode and focus the blast of energy in any desired direction. She knew what it was, could picture it in her mind, had the skills in her muscle memory.

Oh, how she loved to fight them. Anytime, anywhere. So all right, then. She had one of them on her back at that very moment.

She also had one of those finely crafted hunting knives in her left hand.

Vignette was ambidextrous.

27

BLACKBURN & NIGHTINGALES –
PRIVATE INVESTIGATION

* July 21st, 2:06 p.m.—24 Hours Before the Attack *

BLACKBURN HAD NEARLY WALKED the distance from the electric garage back to his house when he looked ahead and saw Vignette's motorcycle parked out front, leaning on the kickstand. He was glad for her rare punctuality, because he was still unsure how committed she was to the whole idea of their detective agency. The problem was not that she wanted to do anything else, but in how she chafed under instructions and orders. He had watched her spend so much time inside her own mind over the years, and even more so since Shane's passing. When he told her she should get out more, she jeered at him and replied he should do the same.

They were both right. He never forgot that this injured young female was not his daughter by birth. He simply decided as a matter of his own lifetime policy that it didn't matter and never would. She was his daughter by declaration. He had watched her, beginning as a ten-year-old runaway orphan with moxie and too much adult knowledge, joining Shane in taking his last name and embracing membership in their little family.

A family. As if he was anything but a joke in that regard. But back then, as a thirty-five-year-old bachelor who dealt with the ugly side of human nature every day, he had known something of the horrors Shane and Vignette had each endured.

Which explained his life's work to see to it that this phase was gone, never to return. Ditto why he kept at it in the years since. It didn't matter that he had no idea what he was doing. He figured, then and now, if you strive to do the decent thing, you will not mess things up too badly. The rest was called a life.

A light sea breeze wafted through the air, stirring the trees in the park across the street. July was a beautiful month to be in San Francisco.

But in the next instant he also saw a large man appear from somewhere in back of their house and run across the front yard and up the steps, all the way to the front door. The man ran with determination and without slowing. Randall gasped as the man shoulder-blasted his way through the front door of their home and barely slowed in crashing through the door, taking the door off the hinges as he went. He disappeared inside.

Quick thoughts flashed. Randall knew Vignette was the only one inside, but his gut told him with cold certainty the attack was really intended for him.

He powered his legs through an explosive takeoff, but his joints felt like they were lined with gravel. While his strength was at high levels, his knees felt the effects of years of night shift patrols and countless fights with drunken opponents. His legs nearly buckled, and only a mix of panic and willpower carried him to a full sprint.

He was still fast enough to reach the house in just a few moments, but urgency stretched his sense of time into slow motion. Worst of all for the searing anxiety in his chest, there could be no doubt that the intruder was attacking Vignette at that instant.

Randall flew up the front steps three at a time. By now enough adrenalin radiated through him that his knees felt no strain at all. He kept going and almost cleared the unhinged door, but his trailing toe caught the edge and forward momentum sent him to the floor inside.

His muscular frame protected his bones, and he managed an impromptu somersault to distribute the force of the fall. He had already spotted Vignette and the invader. He snapped to his feet ready to dive in.

But no. No diving…

The man lay on the floor, turned onto his right side, with Vignette holding him down from behind. She had one arm around his neck and one leg around his lower legs while her other leg was bent at the knee and jammed into the small of his back. His face was a mask of terror and pain.

This was odd because he was easily large enough to throw Vignette across the room, but for some reason he made no move to escape her. Blackburn took two quick steps toward them, and the small change of angle revealed the reason.

Vignette had a long-bladed hunting knife buried in the center of her attacker's crotch. It was sunk in about a fourth of the way down the eight-inch blade. Blackburn's adrenaline level still held him in slow time. His mind was observing and calculating faster than he could move.

A blade! Talk about handy. Perfect to have in hand for repelling a street criminal inside one's home.

He had no doubt she could explain it all in a way that would satisfy a grand jury and still manage to be funny, but he had never known her to hang around the house with a knife in her hand. Nevertheless, the giant thug who so rudely infested their place seconds earlier was now a butterfly on a pin. His pathetic cries were caused by Vignette's rhythmic twisting of the blade. Just a tiny nudge back and forth in each direction.

Two seconds had passed since he rolled through the door.

Blackburn hadn't said a word yet, still on slow time. And while it was too soon to laugh out loud, he had already seen enough to hope the moment was coming in a hurry.

The rage on her face was more intense than the agony radiated by her well-skewered attacker. It was an expression he recognized on her, though he was thankful to have rarely seen it. Some very dark reservoir of feeling festered in her, and in moments like these, it came out in full force.

His vision was honed by twenty years of surviving on Bowery patrol. It prioritized the scene for him.

<u>Situation</u>: *Home invader subdued, unable to resume attack; resident apparently unhurt. Perpetrator suffering inconvenience.*

<u>Immediate Priority</u>: *Vignette.*

<u>Secondary Priority</u>: *Information from the perpetrator.*

Following Priorities: Medical help for the injured perpetrator. Well, sure, but the suffering was taking place solely because the maniac crashed into their home and went after Blackburn's daughter, yes, damn it all, his daughter. So there was that.

Actions to be taken:

(a) Check Vignette for physical injury and see about talking her back down to earth;

(b) Question intruder; and

(c) Allow injured intruder a few moments on his own before calling for help, longer perhaps. Assure him the opportunity to bask in the glory of crime.

Four seconds had now passed. He spoke in deliberately soft tones. "Vignette. Vignette, look at me. Can you look at me?"

She spoke in a strained voice, and he wasn't surprised hearing it clenched up tight, the after-effect of a sudden death fight that explodes without warning. It commonly showed up in people exposed to such things.

"Randall! I was just working here! Just...just...just! This piece of..." She began gasping. "This rotting piece of—"

"Okay, listen! Are you hurt? Did he injure you?"

"Hot damn, I don't even know!" She put her mouth at the man's ear. "I've got an earful for you, crackpot! I'm going to let go and give you the chance that maybe you live through this. If you decide to play strong man, all that's going to happen is I push it in and twist it like a corkscrew!"

His cries paused. He gave her a frantic nod of his head.

"All right, then. Don't you dare disappoint me. I'm not the police. I don't have to care what happens to you."

With that, she gradually released her grip on the knife handle, extended her fingers outward, moved her arm away from his crotch while also releasing the grip of her arm around his neck. She rolled sideways to gain some distance, then pulled into a crunch and jumped to her feet. "He tried to put his arm around my neck, Randall."

"Your neck..."

"From behind."

There was a moment of silence while Randall let it sink in. He knew enough to understand there was special meaning for her in being handled that way, rising from deep in her past. "I see. All right, then."

He cleared his throat, glanced around the room in a quick moment of helplessness, then put his hands on her shoulders and looked her deep in the eyes. "Well done, here."

She beamed under his brief words. Not with an open smile, but he knew her well enough to catch it in her eyes. Despite his avowed ignorance of how to be a step-in father, first as father to a girl and later to an emerging young woman, Randall had managed to learn a few things in that regard. Every tip he could soak up was vital in dealing with a young woman who wouldn't last a month on her own in the world.

His love and empathy for her combined with those few little bits of wisdom, those sparse tools were all he had for dealing with something in Vignette which was, as her final schoolteacher assured him, *a disturbing range of potential responses to any given moment.*

"So are we running to find a doctor for you or not?" He looked her up and down.

She felt herself all over, stepping back and forth on the balls of her feet to test her movement, then stopped and grinned at him. "Apparently all is well here. Spare the ambulance and send the doctor home. You?"

"Knees hurting again."

"Oh, sorry. You know the salt baths help, though."

"Thank you. Regarding the criminal element on our floor, he is a stranger to me. What about you?"

"He told me who he is. He's the one who killed Saunders! Felicity Saunders!"

Randall bent to look closer at the man's face. "Oh, that one, eh? From the Saunders house? Well, well. And now he's here in ours. I guess this proves that somehow or other, he found out you were there that day. Somehow."

"How in the world..."

"Doesn't matter. However he found out, someone knew. All we know for sure is the information did not come from us. So there's you, and there's me, and that's about as far as the circle of trust goes on this one."

Vignette glared down at the man as if she wanted to spit. "First words this fool spoke to me today, first ones, mind you, were: 'I am *Hemo*! I am *blood*!' Like I was supposed to scream and cry or something. I just thought, oh, thanks for confirming who I'm dealing with."

"Vignette, this man is twice your size."

"I know. Anyway, along with how he was looking at me, the words were just some sort of ritual words. He was more like a guy going through his prayers or something. Not like he was talking to me. But all it did was stamp him for delivery. Because lo and behold, what was it I was doing when Mr. Blood here so rudely entered our home?"

Vignette leaned forward at the waist and spoke directly into the perpetrator's line of vision. "Why, I just happened to be busily sorting out this impressive display of hiking goods. And hunting knives."

She stood up straight again and looked at Randall, holding up a second knife and stifling a smile. "Six of them altogether. Five now, since one is in use at the moment, wouldn't you say, Mr. Blood?"

"We might need to see to his condition, Vignette."

"Yes! Let's get that blade out of him. Oh, Mr. Blood, tell me, do you have a desire to remove that knife yourself?"

What was left of Byron Morrisey managed a couple of squeaks that may or may not have been signs of agreement.

"Fine. Neither do I." She turned to Randall. "It appears you're going to have to pull it out, then."

Randall regarded the big man who targeted her. "Not in my job description."

He stared down at a man currently in need of medical intervention and pain relief and would have felt far more humanity for an injured dog. He caught the man's eyes and met his gaze.

"Sir, I have to report that people are saying some terrible things about you." He turned to Vignette. "Maybe we leave the blade in place, just in case major bloodlines should be cut in pulling it out?"

She nodded and said to Morrisey, "If we leave the knife, it might keep the bleeding from getting worse. Might slow blood loss, mister! Hear that? I like the sound of it because it also means you might bleed out like a stuck pig anyway! And that only bothers me because this is our floor!"

She turned to Randall. "I believe we have to report this, or we get into some sort of trouble ourselves, right?"

Randall nodded, then gently took the second knife from her hand and dropped it into his coat pocket. "Yeah. No choice. We could never deny we had the chance to report it." He glanced at the wall-mounted telephone.

"Oops. City Hall knows we have a telephone."

"Any crime that occurs here, we have to call it in."

"That telephone, I tell you, it's convenient sometimes. But this phenomenon of constantly exchanging 'Hallo' back and forth to a box seems sort of silly."

"So are you using 'Hallo' now?"

She snorted out an unexpected laugh. "Well, yes, I don't hear 'Ahoy-hoy!' anyplace else but here, Randall. You're showing your age."

"If I were showing my age, I'd use Morse code."

Morrisey interrupted with several pained grunts that communicated little more than a general cry for relief. Vignette just looked away and shook her head.

Randall turned his back on the dying man and sank into himself for a moment, then stood straight again and looked into Vignette's eyes. "First of all, I am very thankful you made it here, however it happened. Second of all, I am thankful for this, ah, I don't know, ability you possess. To get yourself out of tight spots."

"Lucky for both of us, then."

"You're not going to be the death of me, are you?"

"Absolutely not, Randall. I'm sorry for even making you worry like that."

He stared at her without moving. They held each other's gaze without a quiver in their facial muscles. He had been doing this many, many, many years longer than she had. She broke it by snorting and rolling her eyes.

"I mean I will do my best. These things are unpredictable. Unforeseen circumstances can completely alter the landscape of a prior understanding. I'm sure you know that."

Her words appeared to hit Randall much harder than she predicted. He took a sharp breath and spun around, eyes wide. A smile of revelation filled his face. He pointed straight at her.

"Ha! *Attorney*!" He paced away several steps and whirled back around to her, beaming with inspiration.

"What?"

"Attorrrneeey!"

"What are you saying?"

"They don't all have to be men! Not anymore! And a lot of the talent pool is going to be swept into military service!"

"I still don't—"

"We have to get you into law school!"

"...What?"

"And if an attorney has her own shop, she can be—I mean, as long as she gets results in the court system, she can be anyone at all. I'm pretty sure those guys get left alone, as long as they win cases. Have you seen the hairstyles on some of them? You should. It's worth a little courtroom time just to observe."

A loud squeal of protest came from the floor. Morrisey remained in position on his side with his hands gripping the knife to stabilize the blade.

They ignored him. Randall asked her, "Any neighbors sniffing around?"

Vignette stepped over to the door and looked around. "Nothing. It's a great neighborhood." She put her fists to her hips. "But there's also an unlimited number of random people out there in the trees. People who could have seen this man crash in here. So we have to phone this in."

"But the question becomes is it smart to bring uniforms into our house with a dead body? We could accomplish nothing more than get ourselves stuck in a holding cell while this gets sorted out."

"So we can't trust anyone without proof that they're clean of this thing?"

"Yes. And I don't know how to make that distinction." He looked down at the cringing Morrisey and said, "Time to speed things into action!"

Morrisey growled something that sounded like a primal whelp of gratitude from an animal who saw possible escape approaching. He tried to speak, but his teeth were clenched tight enough to bite through nails. All that came out were desperate sounds.

Randall got straight to the task of putting this emerging communication instrument to work at preventing a crime. He removed a reading monocle from inside his coat, tucked it into his right eye socket, and pulled a bit of paper from an inner pocket. He lifted the telephone's listening device from the nickel-plated hook and whirled the hand crank.

Keeping careful watch on a sequence of numbers jotted on the paper, he recited them to the telephone exchange operator, one by one. Down on the floor, the would-be killer shuddered in pain, willing help to come, willing relief from agony. *Hurry! Hurry!* His unspoken pleas filled the room.

Randall directed a quick nod of acknowledgment to the suffering man with the blade in his balls. He held up the listening device to show him and pointed at it, as if that explained any questions the man might have.

He imagined telephone signals flashing down the line to be processed by other devices kept hidden by robed wizards deep within firelit lairs guarded by hissing serpents. All in service to the brand-new Telephone Exchange System. A new era of safety and convenience was upon them.

He could hear the ringing on the other end of the line. Then came the faraway sound of a man trapped in a well.

"City Haw Bahbeh."

"... What?"

"Bahbehshop. Haircuts! You cawled. Need a shave?"

"My name is Randall Blackburn. I am a private detective on the trail of an emergency for the people of this city. This call is for the mayor!"

"Mayor? Call back when you wanna haircut! Or else be a clever devil and just come in and get one! Deadbeat!"

The connection broke off. Randall shook his head. "People seem ruder on the telephone than in real life." He looked down at Morrisey with an apologetic smile and pointed at the telephone, as if that explained everything. "The things can be unreliable."

Morrisey finally got out actual words this time. "You call the police, damn you!" came the weak voice from the floor. "Get 'em to send an ambulance! Call 'em *right now*!"

"Well, he was more clear that time," Vignette observed.

"Maybe he's getting better. He might recover on his own."

"In that case, do we still have to call it in?"

The howl of protest from Morrisey was a mix of whining and screaming. It trailed off into a moan.

"He is a fellow human being, though."

"Yes. Yes, he is."

"Every human being deserves a chance at life."

"They certainly do. But if he lives, the rest of the human beings in town aren't looking so good for a chance at *their* lives, are they?"

"There is that."

Randall held up the slip of paper with the mayor's telephone exchange number written on it. He leaned down and spoke in a loud tone to Morrisey. "One more try. See, the thing is, we can't call the regular police. We don't know how many of you guys are on the force now. This is the phone number for the city mayor."

He got the operator on the line and repeated the number a second time, carefully referring to the paper with each numeral. He spoke to the man on the floor while he waited. "Ever met the mayor? 'Sunny Jim'? Oh, you'd like him. Why wouldn't you? The man smiles a lot."

This time, he heard the phone on the other end of the connection ring two times, and then the familiar voice of Mayor Rolph was there. "Yes-yes? This is Mayor Rolph. Who's there?"

"This is Randall Blackburn, Mr. Mayor! We have a situation here that—"

"What have you learned from your street contacts?"

"I'm calling from my home telephone, sir. There's been no time to—"

"Blackburn! You listen to me! There's *no* greater priority than that! I don't care what it may be! Get down to the Tenderloin and beat the streets! Somebody down there knows how this is going to be done. We have to find them, that's all there is to it!"

"Yes, sir."

"Tell me you are on your way, Mr. Blackburn. Let me hear you say it."

So we're back to Mr. Blackburn. "I'm on my way, sir. But I called because we have a man here in our home who is one of the attackers. He tried to kill Vignette, but she got the drop on him, and, ah, he's injured pretty bad, sir. I think he'll most likely bleed out in a few minutes."

He quickly covered the mouthpiece and looked down at Morrisey to mouth the word, "*Sorry...*"

"Son of a bitch, Blackburn, that man will know something! We have to interrogate him!"

"Now see, that's what I was thinking. And we could postpone the street interviews until we see what this one tells us."

"You could have told me all this at the start."

"Yes, sir. It was a lot of information to—"

"Get him to talk! Now! Drop everything else! And call me right back when you learn anything! Anything at all, Detective Blackburn."

Oh good, back to Detective Blackburn. "I'll do that, Mr. Mayor. I'll call you right back."

"I need to hear from you in a matter of minutes. You understand? If we don't get a grip on this thing, there aren't enough of us to stop it. You realize that, don't you?"

"Clearly, sir. Let's just hope luck is on our side."

"We'd better hope Providence is on our side. I don't think luck will do the job."

Randall nodded and replaced the earpiece on its nickel-plated hook, then realized the mayor could not have seen him when he nodded to signal goodbye. Randall had therefore ended the call without saying anything. This would be an abrupt gesture if he were there in person. Was it rude in real life but permissible in telephone life? What should he do now? He picked up the listening device and held it to his ear, but the call was gone.

There was nothing to hear. It was like holding a rock to his head. A new thing called a dial tone had been invented in Germany eight years before, but the technology had yet to reach the city of San Francisco.

"What's up?" asked Vignette.

"Not sure. Sort of an accident, I just ended the call without saying anything to the mayor. Like 'goodbye' or something. You sure wouldn't walk out of his office without comment, right?"

"Not unless you're angry and trying to make a point."

"Should I call him back?"

"If you do, he's going to think you have information, and you have to ask yourself if a nicer goodbye will make him feel better when you tell him you haven't started on the guy yet."

He met her eyes and nodded. "All right, that sounded like the truth." He took a deep breath and squatted down next to Morrisey. "Hey! You sleeping now? Time to talk!"

Randall and Vignette realized it at the same instant. Their eyes met. They exhaled at the same time.

"Uh-oh," said Vignette. To which Randall could only add, "Ah, shit."

"Any chance he's just out cold?"

But the pool of blood around Morrisey was a bigger loss than anyone could survive. Randall glanced down at the knife, still partially buried in the attacker's groin. He thought for a brief moment, then turned to her and softly asked, "Would you mind checking the front porch and the street for me? Let's make sure we don't see any of his friends lurking around."

Vignette cooperated without a word, stepping over to the door and facing outside to have a look. Randall smoothly reached down to the handle of the knife currently occupying space inside the would-be killer. He gave it a little twist. Nothing. Another twist, a big one. No reaction.

He stood up, wiping his hands on a pocket kerchief. "Nothing more from him, then."

"Information lost. At least we're no worse off than before he showed up."

"Except for the mayor's reaction," Randall replied with a grim set to his mouth. "But I'd say he brought lots of information. He confirmed himself as Mrs. Saunders's murderer, also as part of this plot, whatever it turns out to be. And then he demonstrated again that whoever he works for will kill anyone at all to do what they have in mind. If the delivery boy wasn't a good enough warning, here's another one for us."

He took her by the shoulders. "I'm going to get the Waverley and drive over to the Tenderloin, start pumping the streets. You have to get to the mayor's office and get him to use any officer he can trust and get down to Pier 19. We can't leave those bombs in place."

"A police officer? Randall, we didn't report them because we can't trust the police."

The twin bells on the telephone device began jangling. The sound was loud and caused both of them to jump.

"Damn thing."

"That could be the mayor calling, though." Vignette moved toward the phone but did not pick it up. "Maybe he found out something!"

Randall lifted the earpiece from the receiving hook and put it to his ear.

"Ahoy-hoy, ah, hallo?" Vignette smiled and spread her hands as if to say, *Wasn't that easy?*

"I have a long-distance call from Chicago. Will you accept the—"

"Yes! Yes! Go ahead!"

The caller's voice came over the line, shouting to be heard across the distance and through the hissing static. "Blackburn! Are you receiving me?"

"Maxwell?"

"Yes! Yes!" Maxwell shouted. "Thank God you're there! Listen to me! You have to get out of your house. Now. Right now!"

Blackburn squinted his eyes and concentrated on hearing everything he could. He pressed the listening device into his ear until the pressure became painful. "Talk to me, John! Where are you?"

"At home! I've got one of these things, too! You get out right now and then call me from someplace else! Take your daught—" A wave of static overwhelmed the line for a few seconds, then, "Because they put some kind of listening device on my phone..." There was more static for a few seconds, then: "You shut up and run! Now, Blackburn! *Now*!"

On the Chicago end of that connection, a gunshot rang out in the background. Blackburn had never heard a gun fired over the telephone before. The sound was thin, weak as the snapping of a pencil.

"John! What happened?" he shouted, trying to force his voice along hundreds of miles of wire. "Can you still hear me?"

A moment later, somebody replaced the listening device on John Maxwell's phone back on its receiver. The connection went dead.

Randall and Vignette stood staring in disbelief for half a second before he launched himself at her with more force than Hemo employed to break through the front door. The force of it drove both of them onto the porch.

Vignette had overheard enough of the call to cooperate with the concept, and together they ran down the steep front steps and out across the sloping grass lawn, stretching their legs for distance. Just as they reached the front sidewalk, the ground floor of the house exploded.

With the house perched on a rise up and over the sidewalk level, most of the shock wave went into the air over their heads. They only remained on their feet because they had gained enough distance from the blast center.

And with that passing instant, their home of the last ten years disappeared. Not just the stuff of their personal lives, but every record necessary to run their agency. The blast dropped most of the second floor into the first, mixing with the ground-floor wreckage and leaving a dense pile where the inside of the home used to be. The roof remained in place because the blast appeared to have vented through the windows on both floors, which had all shattered and blown out.

"What? What? Randall?"

"Is your bike okay?"

"Randall! Our house just—"

"Start it up. Make sure it runs."

She stared in disbelief for a moment, then realized that no, he was not fooling, and yes, she needed to comply. She rushed to the curb, hopped aboard, and kicked the starter. The engine fired right up, still warm from the day's riding.

Shocked neighbors began to filter outdoors, wide-eyed. "Mr. Blackburn," one of them shouted after him. "Your house!"

Randall waved his arm in the air, shouted, "Yes! The house! Stay away!" He turned to Vignette. "The blast must have snuffed itself out, so at least we don't have to deal with a gas fire."

"Son of a bitch, Randall!" exclaimed Vignette, releasing a blast of pent-up air. "All we need today is an earthquake."

The neighbor's voice was loud enough to reach them. "Did you see that man who ran away?"

"No, what did he look like?"

"Well. Just...you know. A running man. He was moving very fast." The neighbor pointed up the street. "That direction."

Randall sighed. "Okay. Thank you. Please stay away from the house."

"Mr. Blackburn, what are you going to do?"

"Well, *you'll be one of the first to know*, won't you?"

"There is no need to be—"

"Thank you, then! Stay away from the house! Help the whole neighborhood to keep scavengers away! Put up a 'No Trespassing' sign!"

He turned back to Vignette. "Get to the mayor. Get him alone. Tell him about the bombs, and do *not* let him make you go with the retrieval squad, not to show them the way or to do any such thing. You can describe it just fine."

"What are they supposed to do with the bombs?"

"Well, since they're down on Pier 19 already, I say why not row 'em out into the Bay and put them over the side? It has to be safer to tow them over the water than to bounce them over the streets. If the mayor doesn't like that idea, just tell him to take them someplace where they can't cause any real damage if they blow. He's got to know a secure place. Bastard has to be good for something. Don't tell him that. As soon as I'm done with these interviews, I'll get back to his office, and we'll meet there."

"I could go with you."

"Forget it. There's no time to gain their trust. I have to solo this one."

"Our house…"

"Stay away. These are murderers. We don't know what else they might have planned for us. Hell. We can't go back there at all until this is all over."

"Not even to get our—"

"Nothing. We get nothing. You have your wallet, yes?"

"On the bike. Locked in the tote."

"And mine's in my pocket. We can live without the rest of it until we figure out what to do."

"Holy Mother of—"

"There's no way to know what else is planned here. We don't go near the house until the parade is done."

Vignette slumped over the handlebars and shook her head. "This thing is so much bigger. So much bigger…I mean, I was getting good at following married men who have second families. I'm qualified for about that much."

"All right. For this case, just pretend there are an endless supply of married men with second families, and they're willing to kill to protect their secrets. You'll be aiming in the right direction." He stepped close to her and did the almost-hug by leaning into the space close around her and speaking in a voice no one else would have heard, even if anyone was there.

"Vignette, I never wanted you to have to take on something like this without gathering a lot of experience first. Years of experience. Now that's a luxury we don't have. I need you to stand tall and deliver this thing. I hate that we're in this position, but here we are anyway."

She took a deep breath. "Take it easy. I told you before, it's all jake. Truth is, I'm glad for the chance to fight people like these."

"You don't know who they are."

"Doesn't matter. I know *what* they are."

"That worries me, too. We have to promise each other not to die behind this. You've seen what we're dealing with here. We're private detectives, not combat soldiers."

The almost-hug didn't appear to be sealing the deal for him, so he pulled her close to him for a rare embrace while he kept his voice gentle and calm. "What we will do is finish this, whatever it turns out to be. And once it's over, we'll come back here and see if anything is left at all, and then we will get ourselves a new place to live."

She gave him an even more rare return on his hug, speaking in a voice that probably sounded like the little girl who took off from St. Adrian's Home for Delinquents and Orphans on the heels of the Great Earthquake and Fires.

"Because we made this our home for ten years and nobody gets to chase us out. Right?"

He nodded. "Yes and yes. For now, you get to City Hall. I'll meet you there as soon as I can."

She grinned and gunned the engine in response.

"Damn it, Vignette, let the cops do the bomb retrieval and stay with the mayor! Wait for me before you take off somewhere!"

She waved agreement, gunned the engine twice more, and sped off. Blackburn turned and ran toward the electric stable while another helpful neighbor called out, "Mr. Blackburn! Your house! What are you going to do?"

This time he just kept on going.

28

LAZY ANA BONE'S PLACE – TENDERLOIN DISTRICT

* July 21st, 2:30 p.m.—23 Hours and 6 Minutes to Go *

IT TOOK A FEW MINUTES after the house exploded for Randall's hands to begin shaking. The tremors kept up throughout the drive to his destination. He told himself it wasn't too bad, but now as he stood alone at the doorway to Lazy Ana's place, he also noticed a faint smell of smoke rising from his coat. A remnant of the bomb blast. For a moment he hoped other people wouldn't smell it, then realized that he didn't care if they did. How are you supposed to smell after your house blows up?

There was nothing to be done about it while he waited at the door of the respectable-looking house where he had once obtained a lot of his workable street information. After knocking in the old code: tap...tap...tap-tap-tap...he followed it with the required soft kick to the brass plate at the bottom of the door.

He hadn't visited in years, since the last time he was there as a city detective. Back then, he was a large part of the reason the men who thought this neighborhood was a place to anonymously do evil to women often ended up learning a harsh lesson: if they tried, they were taking a chance with their own lives.

Years ago, before he softened, Randall Blackburn had sometimes found horrible ways to punish men who abused the Tenderloin prostitutes. The cowardice of those men was betrayed by the drop in assaults to the women who lived and worked there. His reputation had hovered over the district: *The man doesn't care. He's an outsized brawler.*

Today, there was no telling if that reputation still worked. Although his larger-than-usual size had not changed, he wondered if there was anyone left inside this establishment who still knew him at all. Life expectancy was terrible in the Tenderloin.

He tried again with the knocking code: tap...tap...tap-tap-tap...not forgetting to lightly kick the brass plate at the end. This time he heard a hearty woman's laugh bark from behind the door.

"Mah-hahhh! So it *is* you!! I see you coming down the street and I think to myself, there's a face gone from this lifetime! Can't be him! But then you step up to my door and use a code I ain't heard in years!"

The woman threw back the door and laughed again. "We're closed, but I guess I'll make an exception here."

He recognized her face across the years. She was aging well, this doyenne of the sex trade and all things illicit. She bellowed another laugh, then added, "And I mean I ain't heard that knock code from *nobody*, Detective Blackburn. You still Detective Blackburn, are you?"

He gave her a warm smile and added, "I am, but I carry a private badge now."

"Private detective! Good for you! I'm bettin' you like private work better, eh?"

"No comparison."

"I'd figger as much. Us folks who's self-employed know the real score on things."

"Right you are, Miz Bone."

"Miz Bone? *Miz Bone?* That name just come outta your mouth? You ain't a copper no more, why are you so formal on me? You can just be callin' me Lazy Ana like everybody else!"

"Um, right. I'm sorry." He grinned, unsure why. "Lazy Ana it is, then."

"Ha!" She opened the door and stood back for him. "So come on in."

He removed his hat and stepped inside while she closed the door behind him. The transformation was immediate; the perfumed air, velvet-lined walls, and mirrored ceilings of Lazy Ana's House of Ill Repute, which it might have been named if signage were allowed, announced without a word that this place was unlike any other, even among cathouses. The building's exterior reflected ordinary propriety, while inside, available services were advertised in silence by the decor: *For the right price, we do almost anything for almost anyone who pays. Working gentlemen will please keep their boots on.*

The message radiated itself like the spread of perfume, powered by an explosive mix of lust and an open secret. There was never a dearth of high-paying customers at Lazy Ana's place, male or female. Even respected businessmen were seen coming and going through the active front door. The more fearful of them came around to the back alley and in through the service entrance.

Blackburn knew Lazy Ana Bone's real name was Louisiana Bone, but the sort of folks who love to make whores feel bad had done it to her so often—switching "Lazy Ana" for Louisiana—she eventually tired of correcting them and instead adopted it for herself.

Lazy Ana Bone, then. Progeny of a father with an unfortunate surname and a mother who shot for the moon by giving her baby the lofty title of the state where she was conceived. She ended up with a name that actually earned money for her. Who ever knew it was such good business to have a catchy moniker?

Lazy Ana's place flourished without commercial advertising of any kind while the warm waters of permissiveness gave tacit approval to drunks asleep in their own puddles beneath the docks as well as cathouse customers from every walk of life: *Come in search of a few moments of release from the constrictions of your lives. Or stay for hours. Stay for days if you can pay...*

The district's constant flow of pass-through visitors was described by people with manners as, "hearing the call of the wild." And so long as the proper bribes were paid to the right people, it all took place in a whirlwind of personal sins with nary a police uniform to be seen.

However, today, ten minutes into the conversation with Lazy Ana, Randall had the uneasy feeling that the regulars at this establishment hadn't done any talking to the madam. So he asked her to bring down all the working girls to meet him, just in case they caught something she missed. She did, but they had no appreciation for having their off-hours interrupted. He put each one through a line of questions about the upcoming parade. Had anyone spoken about it? Any mention of violence? Any mention of a big "surprise" coming to the city?

Over the years he had learned these women heard about most everything going on in the city. They got information because when lips were loosened by alcohol and overconfidence, something usually leaked out.

This time he got back nothing. It seemed impossible, but not one of the women could recall anything being said about the parade. Nothing at all. The silence of it painted a dark picture for Blackburn. Everyone involved in this plot, whatever it turned out to be, felt motivated to maintain silence even in the company of anonymous prostitutes.

Randall knew human nature too well to believe a group of any substantial size could keep a disciplined silence unless they were afraid to disobey. They had to be certain of retribution.

Lazy Ana thanked the grumbling ladies and sent them back upstairs, then turned to Randall. "Still early, but maybe you need a drink?"

He exhaled hard in frustration. "Tempting, but no, thank you."

"Sure you don't want to tell me what it is you're trying to find out?"

"For now, just say I'm looking for anything on the parade. Anything at all."

"Mm. We can usually deliver on the gossip front. People come here and confess things you would not believe. Maybe it's the red velvet wallpaper. They somehow get the idea that nothing they say matters here, just 'cause they can pay a fee and pick a girl."

"I was sure hoping somebody bragged about it."

"In that case, I apologize, Detective. You was always straight with me, so I don't mind helping you. Wish we could have."

"Oh, you still did, Lazy Ana."

"How's that, then?"

"Your ladies taught me the people I'm looking for have a highly sophisticated operation, probably using out-of-town criminals, who have shown organization and discipline by keeping quiet and staying out of bars and, uh..."

"Cathouses?"

"Thank you."

"Around here we call things by the right name."

"Good. Yes. Anyway, our visit today told me I'd be wasting my time to run down the Embarcadero and stop local people for questioning. Nope, your ladies have simplified my job today, even if they can't point me toward the perpetrators."

He slapped the table for emphasis. "I'm glad you were here this afternoon. This helps."

Lazy Ana gave him an appreciative up and down. "Well, if you have some extra time, perhaps we can—"

"Miss Bone. So far we know they have stockpiled bombs as well as escape kits for getting out of town afterward. We got some of their bombs and escape kits, but there's no way to know if there's any more of them. There's also been talk of arson attacks. I've tried to snuff those, but we'll have to see if it worked."

"Well, son of a bitch. It always comes from somewhere, don't it?" She pinched the bridge of her nose between her fingertips for a moment before she went on. "Now you got me scared, Detective. I was gonna give my ladies the afternoon off for the parade."

"Personally, I never understood the appeal of a parade. Hate standing around."

"I like to go. I mean, I always did. Happy people."

"Lazy Ana, I tell you, no matter how you feel about a parade, this is one you would be wise to avoid."

She gave him an intense look. "Would you let someone in your family go?"

"No more than I'd play poker with the Devil."

She stood up and offered him her hand. "Good enough for me. That settles it."

29

OFFICE OF MAYOR JAMES "SUNNY JIM" ROLPH

* July 21st, Simultaneously *

VIGNETTE SAT IN A CORNER CHAIR in the mayor's office, watching Sunny Jim pace from one window to another, checking each view as if it might hold some avenue of escape. He never seemed to find whatever he was looking for. His overall manner was that of a man who had just watched his life burn to the ground.

Sunny Jim found the calm face on the young woman sitting in the corner to be most helpful in keeping raw panic at bay. This Vignette Nightingale, Randall Blackburn's ward, showed a positive attitude which impressed him, yes, even Sunny Jim, a guy nicknamed for his glowing disposition. She told him the home she shared with Randall was blown up that afternoon, and yet the only visible impact on her was a grim set to her jaw and the vague smell of smoke.

Admiration for her equanimity was as far as inspiration could take him, though. This was all happening too fast. He had to find a way to slow it down.

Nothing came to mind. Sunny Jim had the weight of a seaport city on his shoulders, and yet for all the hoopla given to the transformation of the city government into a "strong mayor" structure, he now knew most of those tools of civic power were either unreliable or useless to him because none gave him any traction against terrorism.

It was a brand-new crime in San Francisco for a serious bomb to be employed against someone at a private residence. Not even the criminal elements had resorted to using them on each other's homes. It made the threats against the parade all the more credible.

He felt his innards tighten like two fighting snakes. He had theoretical command over the police, but who was supposed to carry out the orders? Whatever mix of bribery and extortion that was employed against so many key government workers had proved effective in the extreme. The corruption reached all the way up to his office and stopped barely outside his door, meaning it would point toward him as soon as it was discovered.

One of the most surprising things about this supposed "plot" was the fact that he was never approached to join it. Why was that? He wondered if it was his reputation for positivity that kept them away. Maybe they feared he might not just reject them but foil the entire conspiracy, ruin it all for them? Sunny Jim realized he might never know what the answers were to those questions, but the greater likelihood was they already owned so many converts, they simply had no fear of his expanded powers. After all, what is the power of an order if it won't be followed?

If his adjutant Saunders had still been alive, Sunny Jim would have been tempted to strangle him with his own hands. The man's greed and stupidity alone would have been enough for the mayor's administration to try to overcome, but that much would have been possible, at least. Even his odd choice of suicide might have been explained as some form of guilt over his exposure as a thief. But now with the murder of Mrs. Saunders, there could be no doubt that this thing was the tip of an iceberg and the scope of it went far beyond his administration.

The public would eventually find out about all of this. How could such a story be hidden? When the newspapers got wind of it, they would tear it all open. Unless he could find a way to stop the bombing and save the day, Sunny Jim knew his administration would take the blame.

That's when it hit him. Maybe his administration was going to take the blame because that was the intention all along? There was a term for that among the police. He first read in the *Oakland Tribune* a few years back: *fall guy.* He and anyone who was still loyal to him were supposed to endure a fall from grace in the public's eyes, one that was surely coming. Mayor Rolph and anyone too close to him had been set up to take the disaster on their shoulders to keep anyone from bothering to look outside the city.

"My own adjutant," he spoke out loud without meaning to, but continued out loud anyway. "That damned Saunders. Been with me for years. I've been to his home for dinner with him and his wife."

He shouted out his office door. "Name of Saunders's widow?"

His secretary's reply came back, "Felicity."

"Felicity."

Vignette shook her head in wonder. "I sure never saw any of the stolen objects when we had suffragette meetings there. They had to have hidden all of that loot every time they had a guest over."

"What a chore."

"Well, yes, what with the stuff scattered over every flat surface in the place. Especially upstairs."

"How did you know that?"

"Well. Detective work. You know." She cleared her throat. "But Mr. Mayor, who else can you trust around here without having to use up time in testing them?"

"There were the four men I sent to get the bombs. I could have sent my secretary as well, since I know she is loyal to me, but she has no skills for it."

"The ones you sent, that's everyone?"

Sunny Jim answered, "Present company excluded. Two are officers on my staff. I mean, we have to trust somebody. There's you and your, ah, Detective Blackburn."

He slapped Fickert's shoulder and laughed. "The truth is, Miss Nightingale, I brought our district attorney here to wait this out, but I don't know if it's even safe to have *him* around." Fickert made a weak attempt at laughing along with him.

Sunny Jim's smile disappeared. "I sent the entire City Council home until the day after tomorrow. If anything is being organized from this build-ing, I want that much stopped."

He gave her a quizzical look and ventured, "I realize it makes me sound like I'm not in my right head, but it's as if everyone around here is wearing a mask."

Vignette exhaled hard. "You are in the company of someone who has no trouble at all believing people can hide behind a mask. Hide all the time. Stand right in front of you as the beast they are, and be as convincing as anyone could want. All the while they are safe and sound underneath that mask. And then they drop it, and the monster comes out."

Sunny Jim regarded her with new eyes, as if she had somehow trans-formed in front of him. "Good Lord..."

The telephone bell interrupted them with a sharp trill. They both flinched at the sound. He gave her a wary look and said, "All right, let's see what they can tell us." He picked up the earpiece and placed it to the side of his head while he leaned toward the mouthpiece on the instrument. "Yes? Or hello, then?"

Vignette strained to hear. She could barely make out the caller's words.

"Jacob Prohaska calling in to report. Sir, the bombs aren't here! They're gone."

He let out a heavy sigh. "Are you sure?"

"No doubt, sir."

"Did you search the whole pier?"

"Yep, and we know they were here, because they left one bomb behind."

"Just one?"

"Somebody disarmed it. There are two wires torn out of place. I mean, they could have fixed it, I guess. Maybe it's a message."

"It's a message, all right. A taunt. So remove the explosive material, throw it in the bay, and send the rest of the device here to my office."

"Sir, I can't—"

"Do it now! You can accompany it yourself."

"Sir, we need more help down here. This dud bomb isn't the real problem."

"Why don't you tell me what the real problem is?"

"There's just me left here, sir."

"Nonsense. Call one of my staff to the line."

"They're gone, sir. Both of them."

"They left their post?"

"They're not just out for a smoke, sir. They sneaked away, if you don't mind my saying."

"What I 'mind' is hearing that my two staff members abandoned their duty and their post while I am in the middle of a civic crisis, and we have run out of people we can trust!"

"I'm sure there's lots of good cops ready to help us, sir."

"No doubt. As soon as you find out who they are, call me again. Because if you pick the wrong ones and they can anticipate our movements, any chance of stopping this is gone."

"You know, Mr. Mayor, I keep hearing the police chief telling the troops how these rumors of an attack are just gossip."

"I know. Like I said, we're running out of people we can trust."

"If you have anyone trustworthy up there, sir, I could sure use them down here."

Sunny Jim glanced at Vignette. "Listen to me: I'm going to send District Attorney Fickert down there to help you, along with a private investigator. This particular PI happens to be a woman, so don't get your girdle twisted over it. Her name is Vignette Nightingale, and she is partnered with Randall Blackburn on this."

"Blackburn, right. The legend! I've met his daughter, his partner, his ward, whatever the hell she—"

"The same." He gave her a look. "Here's hoping she's learned something from him. Search every empty pier down there. Talk to anybody you see and find out what they know. Even if you can't find the bombs, *somebody* down there has information we need!"

"Tell them both to hurry. We'll organize a pattern for search parties to follow as soon as they arrive."

"Good man." He turned to Vignette. "How soon can you get down to Pier 19?"

"Mr. Mayor, Randall explicitly told me not to leave here so he doesn't have to waste time looking for me."

"Miss Nightingale, Randall Blackburn is on this case for me, which means you are on this case for me. Right now, I need you down on the waterfront."

"Randall said—"

"I'll explain it to him. You'll be in the Embarcadero district. He'll find you if he needs you."

"*If* he needs me?"

"Now tell me, do I need to requisition a police car for you and Mr. Fickert, or do you have your own vehicle?"

His question drove the look of concern from her face. A broad smile replaced it. "All due respect, Mr. Fickert can ride with me. Your people don't have anything that could catch me if I felt like getting away."

Sunny Jim laughed out loud at that. "From your mouth to God's ears, young lady!"

Vignette turned to Fickert. "Have you ever ridden on the back of a motorbike?"

"Nope. Nor the front, neither."

She leaped to her feet, beaming. "First time for everything!" With that, she was at the door, waiting for Fickert. He shuffled toward her with obvious dread while she turned to the mayor and asked, "You'll explain this to Randall, though?"

"Yes! Yes! Go!"

She disappeared, and Fickert followed. A quick minute later, Sunny Jim heard the roar of a motorcycle engine being kicked to life not far below his open windows. He glanced outside and smiled. For the moment, at least, there was something reassuring to see out there.

30

VIGNETTE'S HARLEY AND CITY HALL

* Minutes Later and Early Evening*

VIGNETTE ONLY HAD ONE HELMET, since Randall kept his at home, which meant it was gone along with everything else in the explosion. Until they got the chance to sift through the ruins of the place, there was nothing available to them in the house. And there was no chance of getting back there before the parade was done.

It was strange in the extreme that their city services were already so compromised that the explosion and wreckage of their house failed to compel a major investigation. Of course without going back, there was no way to know for certain what the City's reaction was going to be.

She had to wonder, who *was* "the City" now, anyway? She and Randall were in cahoots with the mayor, but they were all avoiding the police.

At least there was no real chance any corrupted officer would know how to find her or Randall before the parade tomorrow, so long as they both kept their heads down. *One thing at a time.* Randall had drilled that one into her. *Facts, details, and evidence can build up and overwhelm you. What you do is sort one thing, then sort the next. Panic doesn't speed you up, it slows you down.* For now that was all that mattered.

She made D.A. Fickert wear her helmet, out of respect for the courage it took for him to accept this ride with her. He started to object, but she just stared at him. He took the helmet and put it on with his hands already shaking.

She climbed on the bike first to steady it for him while he got aboard. Exceptional circumstances were now unfolding in front of him, and he was game enough to be determined not to look like a coward in front of a girl. He took a deep breath and hopped on over the rear wheel, and she immediately jumped on the kick starter. The engine roared to life like a predator waking up hungry.

The Harley had no need for her to twist the throttle three times and send mechanical howls into the air, but it had a way of making her feel the need to do it for herself. She kicked in first gear, and they started out from City Hall, heading north on Van Ness for a block before taking a hard right onto Golden Gate Avenue. Six blocks later they took a soft left turn onto the wide expanse of Market Street, allowing her more room to maneuver through traffic while they dashed toward the piers of the Embarcadero district. Fickert tucked himself behind her with his arms wrapped around her waist, but his grip tightened a little more every time she swerved to dodge an obstacle.

She kept her right hand on the throttle while using her left to firmly pluck Fickert's hands from her, one at a time, and guide his fingers under the seat grip. Once his hold there was secure, she flexed her right wrist downward and the bike leaped ahead.

"Don't lean!" she hollered back at him.

"What?"

"Don't lean when we turn! Just sit straight or you throw our weight off! Let me balance the bike!"

"Yes, yes! Understood!"

She noticed a faint green pallor to his face and added, "Just sit still! Be dead weight!"

It was hardly in Fickert's nature to give up control to a younger female, especially where machinery was involved, but he was enough of a pragmatist to notice that she really was keeping the bike in balance by herself. *It would be nice to arrive in one piece. It would be great to actually do some good in this mess. She acts like she knows what she's doing. Pretend you believe it.*

He tightened his fingers on the bottom of the seat and held his body still while they powered down Market Street with the piers looming. Fickert didn't make so much as the slightest move. Dead weight.

———

The hour of five o'clock arrived while Sunny Jim kept his eyes on the open telephone line and attended to the hissing of the tap on the phone. Councilman Vincent Cinquevalli was known to be playing host for some strange reason to a certain visitor with a strong desire to destroy the host's way of life.

By way of the magic of the tapped phone, Cinquevalli's unsuspecting wife had just told the mayor that Galleani was leaving their home early in the morning. She claimed to have driven her husband to politely throw the man out, but she gave no indication why Galleani would agree as readily as her husband described. Was the man leaving their home, leaving the city, leaving the country?

Something nagged at him from the visual background, and he looked up to see Detective Blackburn standing framed in the doorway. Randall looked around the empty office, covered his eyes with one hand and slowly shook his head.

Sunny Jim jumped right in. "No, no, wait now, Detective. She wanted to stay here, told me how you asked her to wait here."

"I didn't ask. I *told* her to wait."

"All right, but she was good to her word. I simply overrode you and sent her to the Pier with D.A. Fickert. He's a good man, someone we can trust."

"Why would you send a young woman on a mission like that?"

"Because, Detective, we have a joke of a small force to put up against all this and no time to sort through the ranks to look for people who won't betray us."

Randall said nothing, but he exhaled hard. "All right, then. She's brilliant. Maybe she can cope with this."

"Your phone tap idea was splendid! We already know Galleani is leaving his hosts' home in the morning."

"Before the parade?"

"Yes."

"Not to return?"

"They offered to hold his baggage until the parade was done, but he wants to take everything when he goes." He patted the phone affectionately. "You know, in the future, police are going to use these phone taps all the time. Wait and see."

"Sir, my house was bombed today. Vignette and I got out in time, but the message is clear. They'll stop at nothing."

"She told me. Terrible thing. My sympathies, of course. That's why we can't go trolling for help. I am trying not to give in to despair here, Detective, but even the fact that we have this phone tap in place can't be allowed to get out. We can't give anything away."

"Exactly. Please stay on that phone tap, sir, it's already helped us."

"I mean, the police chief demanded to know what I'm doing up here, so I told him, but that hardly counts."

"No! Mr. Mayor, how do you know if he can be—"

"He's the police chief."

"Maybe, maybe not."

"He wears the rank. So I told him."

"His reaction?"

"He laughed and asked me if I'm dipping into the sauce on the job. I asked him what the hell he planned to do now that I, as his mayor, had informed him of this danger to the city. He insisted on leading a squad to the docks and searching every pier."

"Himself?"

"That's what I asked. He laughed some more and said, 'Mr. Mayor, if you're worried about who to trust, so am I. So I'll go myself.' I had to let him go."

"Sir. I passed the place on my way here. There was no police presence at all. On my word, Mr. Mayor. Nothing."

There was a flat gray pause while Sunny Jim stared at him with a perfectly blank expression. Finally he took a deep breath and nodded. "You'll be heading out to see to your ward, yes?"

"My daughter. And yes."

"Good luck to all of us, then."

He hurried off. The Waverley was double-parked out front with a street boy paid to keep anyone from trying to move it before Randall returned. He had given the boy fifty cents and promised more for a job well done. For that much, the boy would have gone after any potential car thief with a stick.

Blackburn burst through the doors of the building at a run, stretching his legs to reach the car. The exertion was barely enough to raise his pulse. "Young man!" he called out as he approached. "Good job!" He lobbed him a silver dollar, and the boy caught it like a pro.

He jumped into the silent car and rolled away.

31

HOME OF COUNCILMAN CINQUEVALLI

* July 21st, 5:06 p.m.—21 Hours Before the Attack *

LUIGI GALLEANI HELD HIS FACE in a placid expression while he fought to control his temper and keep his mouth shut. He could feel himself losing the battle. He had to wonder, how was it that this fool Mario Buda evaded law enforcement for so long? The man was a nervous mess. He seemed to be a genius with explosives and a moron with anything else. A shoe repairman, for crying out loud, calling himself "Bomb Maker Nonpareil."

And now with the City Council members dismissed, sent home by that simpering fool of a mayor, Galleani's hosts were right there in the house with him and his quivering visitor. No telling what they might accidentally overhear. Bad for the nerves.

He kept to himself but still noticed they were beginning to look vaguely nervous. He knew the signs from long experience; they were wondering what they had gotten themselves into by having him in their home.

Ah well, *c'est la vie*. One more night in that place and it wouldn't matter. He would disappear, and the hosts could seek out their own explanations for any questions that came their way.

The frightened lump sitting across from him was clearly suited for nothing else at the time. "Mario, we have less than a day left. You must prepare yourself mentally to deliver your weapon, while I check in with the men I sent to retrieve your creations."

"And I think it is you who must understand that the bomb I placed at the investigator's house was perfect for the job. It worked exactly as designed. He and his partner would be dead right now if they didn't go running out of there like that. They must have been tipped off."

Buda looked as if he could burst into tears. Any respect Galleani felt for him dissipated while the whining coward continued. "Somebody got word to them! They have a telephone. Somebody knew, Mr. Galleani. They knew I was coming, and they used that telephone to warn them."

"Well, they don't have a telephone anymore or a house to put one in. Our contacts at the phone company confirmed that Blackburn got a call from Chicago just before the explosion. We already knew he had a friend in that city, ex-partner or something, but we didn't realize he would go straight against a death threat and place that call."

"What happened to him?"

"It was no threat. Now listen, I have to go re-check with my remaining men. We're barely holding this operation together. Whoever sabotaged that one bomb down at the pier must have been interrupted or the bombs would have all been disabled or stolen. Do you understand how fragile this is? I can't sit here and hold your hand!"

"Mr. Galleani, if the authorities know anything at all, they will recognize my work. And if they found the bombs, they already suspect us."

"You. They suspect you."

"All right, they suspect me. But what about those private investigators who showed up at your rally? They weren't there to talk to me, they were there for you."

"And I made fools of them."

"I only question whether this one parade attack is worth all the risk. I just think if we look at the big picture, the most important thing we can do to keep America out of this war is stay out of prison. Behind bars, we can't do the cause any good."

"Brilliant. Give up the mission because it may be dangerous for us. Do you have anything else to offer here?"

"I don't mean 'give up,' but—"

"Mario. What you will do is be at the Clock Tower before sunrise tomorrow. While it is still dark, go to the little sausage stand that will be parked across from it. Deliver the devices and hide with them inside. It will provide cover for you."

"What if the stand isn't open?"

"It will be open, and it will be large enough to hold you and each man's explosive package."

"When I took this job, you said nothing about street duty."

"We *all* sacrifice as needed, Mario! You want to go back to the land of spaghetti and meatballs and get another job making shoes? Find a nice fat girl to stomp on grapes and make babies for you to feed with your capitalist wages?"

"No, I do not. But cobbling is an honorable—"

"Mario! The Clock Tower! The other men will arrive at one p.m., and just before they do, I will stop by to check on you."

Mario Buda sighed and shook his head. "What about the big bomb? At least can you tell me where you are going to use it now? It's my finest creation, sir. I would dearly love to see it in operation."

Galleani regarded him for a moment. No dice. He couldn't even tell him why he couldn't tell him. If the mad bomber found out he was being tricked, it wasn't too late for him to ruin everything by tipping off the cops. Time for a little deflection.

"All right, Mario. You did a splendid job in designing and building it, so I'll tell you. That particular bomb is going to decimate City Hall. Teach them a lesson they'll never forget."

With that, for the first time, Mario Buda relaxed into a smile. "Oh... Oh! City Hall, eh? Yes! I can see that. That's brilliant! Everybody will have their eyes on the parade."

"Correct. Everybody will have their eyes on the parade."

"So you must have placed it in the basement, yes? So the Munroe effect will cut right through the floors and collapse the place?"

"Mario Buda, you are too clever."

"Spare me the sarcasm. I was clever enough to pack enough explosive power into that bomb without triggering it, wasn't I? And you can be sure it will bring down a good portion of the building."

"Thank you for doing that." He lowered his voice to a whisper. "Now go. Go and let me finish preparations. You will continue building your reputation among our fighters by showing up tomorrow. We will see if this country actually has any stomach for war when it comes to greet them."

He opened the door to his guest room as if the place were his own, then stood aside, offering an unmistakable cue. Mario Buda walked out with a sigh and made his exit without looking at him.

Buda left the fancy house on Russian Hill feeling the need to burn off the tension gripping him, so he set out on foot. His fears of rotting away in prison tormented him with thoughts of being helpless in a tiny cell while he heard accounts of brave brothers and sisters in the anarchist cause, men and women committing their conscience-based crimes and teaching the world a sorely needed lesson. All of it would go by without him while he languished in captivity and left others to savor taking vengeance for all things.

Completely unacceptable, of course. He felt his faith in this Luigi Galleani character shaken to the foundations. He asked himself why he had revered a man who seemed to hold him in contempt. And if he felt the need to deride Mario's leather skills as if he were too good for physical work himself, then Mario had to wonder, in a come-to-think-of-it manner, what it was old Signore Galleani did to support himself, anyway? What had the much older man been doing in all the years of his considerable past?

He forgot his revulsion at shoe work. People liked to make condescending jokes about shoemakers, but of course that was only until something happened and they had no shoes at all. Things like international war, for example. And that was always when the light hit them. *Oh yes! Shoes!* The value of craft and capability became apparent to them. But only then. Shallow bastards.

At that moment, it struck Mario Buda that he had surely bought into a manufactured reputation with this Galleani fellow. Instead of using his head when they first met, he behaved like some idiotic Stage Door Johnny with a lump in his trousers waiting for the star of the show to emerge. Like the rest of Galleani's converts, he had allowed himself to be cowed.

A prickly cold sensation of foolishness ran through him. He had never once asked himself a serious question about Galleani's future intentions. *There he is, people, the voice of anarchy.* The man preached it, but he seemed to like living the good life and wielding authority like a boss.

Another boss.

Well, Buda's creations were far more effective voices than any printed pamphlet could ever be. And with that realization, what other conclusion could he draw? *Galleani is the one who ought to be nervous about living up to the expectations of the Bomb Maker Nonpareil, eh?*

Buda stomped away toward his Tenderloin district hotel room feeling grateful that the miserable little location would only be a necessary hiding place for one more night. Then at last he could be off to some other city, some more hospitable place where he could do his work without some self-appointed supervisor hovering over him.

The turmoil was so great under his flurry of thoughts, he took no notice of the shadowy male figure who picked up his tail the moment he left the Russian Hill home. The man slipped into Buda's wake and trailed half a block behind him, maintaining that discreet distance to escape notice while Mario Buda effectively led his tail all the way back to his hotel room.

32

HOME OF COUNCILMAN CINQUEVALLI

* July 21st, 5:30 p.m. *

THE KNOCK ON THE DOOR of Galleani's guest room was soft enough to show respect but firm enough to express resolve. It communicated what was coming to Galleani as effectively as Morse code. A world of meaning came through in that timid and yet determined knock: regret over breaking a promise tempered by a firm resolve to do precisely that.

And given the number of times he had felt his welcome wear out, he had no need of another hint. He sighed, *Let's be done with it*, then swung the door open to reveal his host, City Councilman Vincent Cinquevalli, privileged son of the famous European juggler. The fool would never know it, but Galleani picked him as his host because, being a student of irony, he loved the idea of the son of a juggler going into politics. Talk about continuation of a family line.

He greeted the councilman in Italian. "*Signore Cinquevalli. Buonasera. Come stai?*" The simple greeting was lost on his host, being why Galleani used it. The man was born in London and spoke no other language but his own.

Cinquevalli flashed a nervous smile. "Now, now, you know I don't speak the language. To my great regret, of course. My father never tired of reminding me of that."

"Ah."

There was an awkward pause Galleani also knew all too well. He waited it out.

His host cleared his throat. "Well. The missus and I are certainly glad you choose to spend time with us. Our friends are so envious."

"Mm."

"We were wondering how much longer your mission requires you to—"

"Leaving tomorrow."

"Oh. Oh, really? Tomorrow?"

"Yes. I was just coming down to thank you and let you know."

"Well, then! That's fine. That is just fine. Not that we...I mean, of course the missus and I..."

"I will be gone in the morning, and I thank you both for your kindness."

"Because we had no idea you were... While we knew there was a certain controversy around your name, we never..." He paused and let out a sigh. "Signore Galleani, I was visited by a private investigator yesterday. Full of questions about you."

This got Galleani's full attention. He controlled himself with effort. "I see. What sort of questions?"

"Well, nothing unusual, really. Just...you know, general..."

"Sir, do you realize your country is about to join in on the most horrible war you can imagine? Have you heard about the gasses they're using in the trenches of Verdun, right now, while we stand here today? Hundreds of men choking to death at the same time with nowhere to run."

"Of course! That's why we wanted to help—"

"You still don't see it, do you? President Wilson campaigned on staying out of the war, and that's why people voted him into office! But now he's lost control over this."

"You're saying our elected leaders aren't the ones who control the country?"

Galleani just stared at him for a few seconds, then let out a long breath and sat down on the bed with his head in his hands. "Have you heard nothing I have said since we met?"

"Oh, I assure you, my wife and I have listened carefully to everything you've told us."

"Have you bought copies of the major papers to check their propaganda lines? Do you recall that just last year they were all against American involvement in the war? Well, the war only got worse, so what changed?"

"I'm sure I don't know."

"I'm sure you didn't listen. Your own father has had his career destroyed and can't get work now even though he is famous, because word got out about him. People in Europe who understand this evil looked into your family name. It's Braun, not Cinquevalli. Your father isn't Italian, he's German, and so are you."

Councilman Cinquevalli stared in disbelief. "After all our hospitality, this is how you treat us?"

"What, by speaking the truth? If that surprises you, you are only showing you never listened to me. You only pretended to!"

"We do understand about staying out of the war! And yes, we checked a number of the national newspapers, and they all changed course at the same time. However—and this is a big one—my wife and I think there is something you have overlooked, sir."

"Enlighten me."

"All right, Signore Galleani, these dark powers you describe as operating in the shadows, we agree. They are there. And perhaps they quietly took over our government in some kind of a soft coup. Maybe President Wilson really isn't running things anymore. And thus these shadowy people and their hidden organizations might truly have the power to override the will of the People."

"That is exactly what I have been telling you!"

"Yes. *However*, we strongly differ on the reason for it."

"The reason?"

"Yes. We believe your atheism has blinded you to the truth here. There *is* a worldwide power at work. There must be. There is too much to be coming from mere human hands. No, sir. We are convinced this is all God's Will."

Galleani stared in disbelief. Under no circumstance would he allow himself to be drawn into a religious debate at this moment. He pushed his brain to deliver something persuasive that didn't entail challenging another person's religious convictions.

"You...you realize this new thing, this so-called 'Federal Reserve Bank' is not federal, it holds no money in reserve, and it's not a bank. And yet your so-called anti-war president installed them. Why? Ask yourself that. Because they are going to finance this war and slaughter millions of people."

"Ahem... I am always pleasantly surprised your English is so good. But we do not seek to understand the Will of the Lord, sir, but we believe anyone can see His Will in operation within the shaping forces of history. And this war will undoubtedly be part of that."

For this one, Galleani just shook his head and resorted to an expression he never used. "Jesus Christ."

"It was my hope to support you, you know, as a fellow *Pisan*, but—"

"*I* am a *Pisan*. You are German, Herr Braun."

"...We do hope it is convenient for you to find other accommodations after the parade tomorrow."

"Yes, as I told you, I was coming down to let you know I'm leaving in the morning anyway."

"Well, then. You are welcome to pick up your things after the parade, if that is more convenient."

Galleani barked a laugh. "Signore Cinquevalli, or actually Herr Braun, that is so very generous of you. I'll be leaving early. As you see, I travel light, and my bags will go right along."

"Well, that's fine, then." There was a pause. "All to the good, then."

"Oh yes. And you should not let this dampen your spirits about attending the parade!"

"Why would it do that?"

"My point is, you should both attend! I recommend it!" Galleani gave the overly broad smile of a politician on a baby-kissing tour. The smile was so out of proportion to the rest of his features, it could have been cut from someone else's face and laid over his own.

The sight of it chilled Councilman Cinquevalli to the bone. Tomorrow morning would not arrive soon enough, he thought.

Inside himself, he could only shake his head over his own misjudgments on this. It had seemed like such an inspired idea to bring Galleani to stay in their home after witnessing his fiery performance. His foreignness made his ideas feel more exotic, less boring, more worthy. He and the missus practically fell into heat for him, wondering if they might gain a feel for the true pulse of the world through this man. Show the other social pretenders how shallow they were.

Instead, within a few days of his residency in their home, they found themselves experiencing a face full of condescending attitude, vague criticisms, and a tendency to point out everything done incorrectly by anyone, anytime, ever. The man didn't seem to fit in anyplace. As far as they could determine from his stories, he had never been a part of anything but the desire to rant and destroy.

His English was excellent, and Cinquevalli figured it was safe to assume his Italian and German were as well. This gave Galleani the extraordinary opportunity to be obnoxious to a myriad of people while he carried out his travels throughout Europe and her endlessly corrupt nation-states.

After leaving his guest and returning downstairs, Mr. Cinquevalli was astute enough in the domestic department that he did not mention his concerns to his wife. Ever the protector, he told her only that everything had been peacefully and pleasantly resolved, and their guest would be gone in the morning.

He decided a nice day trip to see the big parade might be just the thing, and both of them should go.

33

PIER 19 – EMBARCADERO DISTRICT

* July 21st, 6:00 p.m.—20 Hours and 4 Minutes Remaining *

INSIDE THE COVERED STRUCTURE of Pier 19, Mario Buda stood with his hands in the air like the victim of a robbery, even though no gun was pointed at him. He squinted into the faint light from the tiny windows at the top of the ceiling. A drop of sweat ran down his forehead and into his eyes. He blinked it back with effort while he kept his eyes focused on the three men facing him.

Mario was not a large man, and there were three of them, after all. Words would have to do it. "Before you jump to any conclusions, I walked in here nice and easy instead of sneaking in. I'm not here to do any harm."

"This party is by invitation, Mr. Buda."

"You know me, then?"

"Oh, all of us know you over at City Hall," Jacob Prohaska said with a confident sneer. "I've also seen you around the Galleani meetings."

Prohaska turned to the other two, code-named Fox and Fire. "He's trustworthy here because he made the bombs, but he did his part and it's done.

Nobody is supposed to be involved in any step of the process unless they've got to be there."

Buda waved his hands, keeping them over his head. "Gentlemen, my brothers. I am here as a *Pisan.* We are compatriots by spirit! We till the same fields and plant the seeds for tomorrow, yes?" He looked at each of them in turn and added, "I only come to check my creations. My creations. I have more hope for success than you."

"Very nice. But you still don't have any authority at this point—"

"Yes! But I only ask two things. One: let me disconnect the hot wire so they cannot be remotely detonated. By radio, you see? A new thing, very new. These things as they are now can explode because they receive a radio signal that tells them to. Any one of them could go off, right now, if Signore Galleani gets arrested and the radio transmitter falls into enemy hands."

"And your second thing?"

"Two: once we know the bombs can't blow up, help me get them out of here for the night!"

"Are you crazy? The specific orders are for these things to stay right here until Mr. Galleani comes in the morning."

"And we can send word to him. Or we can have someone meet him in the morning and bring him to us. My brothers, in Amsterdam I saw our men get stopped and my bombs get captured because the police found out ahead of time."

He looked around and saw lukewarm conviction. "I know Galleani himself would tell you: we don't have the entire police force. Pockets of resistance are all over, and if they are given the time, they will organize against us. We must get my creations somewhere safe. Then we watch to see when it is safe to come out tomorrow and distribute them."

He began to move slowly toward the line of radio-equipped suitcase bombs. Gently easing his right arm toward them, using his body language to ask for permission to move closer to them even as he did so. "We go together, friends. We guard the seeds...these seeds...until it is their time for planting."

He slowly picked up one suitcase. "Each of you, carry them with me, no? My friends! We all want success here, yes? Let me help you!"

Jacob Prohaska was a practical man in most things. He remained a practical man in that moment, every bit as practical as he had been upon meeting with Galleani and switching sides once he was granted a stunning look at his potential future—yes, him, meek and modest little Jacob Prohaska—if only he curried favor with the powers behind all this by directing all immigrant head tax receipts to them, under the heading of their brand-new government agency. All he had to do was follow orders and stay stupid.

"I suppose the 'Bomb Maker Nonpareil' has someplace safe for them? Where nobody will suspect?"

"My hotel room! A run-down hotel. A million such places and they cannot search them all. We go together, no tricks! We only must keep them scarce for this night! These few hours!"

Prohaska gave a reluctant nod of acceptance. "What about those two?" He glanced at Vignette and D.A. Fickert, both tied with thick ropes against the wall. Vignette's clothing was torn, but she appeared unhurt. Fickert had taken a beating to his face that would require weeks to heal. He lay without moving.

"How did this man get in this condition?"

"We just held him," said Fox, glancing at Fire, then at Prohaska. "It turns out Mr. Prohaska here fights like a ferret if you hold the guy down for him!" Both men laughed at that.

Prohaska sneered once more. "These two won't be any trouble. They can't get out of those ropes, and there's nobody to hear them if they call out."

Buda persisted, relentless as a lava flow. "We can walk it. Gentlemen!" He carefully picked up a suitcase, keeping his movements smooth, not aggressive at all. "And we take them to my hotel room! Together, eh? Private room! We stay with them."

When they hesitated, he rushed ahead, "The old plan is not enough! Now somebody is trying to stop us, we must change to make sure *the work gets done*. Eh?"

That last one hit like a well-struck gong. The men agreed without discussion and began to gather up the suitcase bombs.

Vignette stared down at the floor, as she would do in the presence of a pack of predators, observing with her peripheral vision but not confronting with a direct gaze. Although D.A. Fickert remained unconscious, she was fully aware beneath her passive demeanor.

As far as she could tell, it never occurred to the men to dispose of the intruders out of an abundance of caution, or even—say it—just for the fun of it. No, the plain fact was they all had other priorities, and the killing of helpless individuals who were already tied and powerless on the floor was something that never occurred to the two men, code-named Fox and Fire; nor to the formerly honest but now much less so Jacob Prohaska.

That frail distinction between murdering for profit or murdering for satisfaction offered just enough nuance to leave Vignette and District Attorney Fickert alive, for the time being. Without a word spoken, the men turned away and left them there, two pieces of irrelevant trash.

Their footsteps faded, and the space around Vignette went silent. She noticed the lapping of waves beneath the pier, even the distant drip of water coming in through a hole in the roof. Her velour walking suit protected her legs from the cool air, but she could feel the chilled breezes coming up through gaps in the decking, scented by decay from the rotting dock. The air smelled like a whale had belched just outside the walls.

She twisted her neck around to get a look at Fickert. The man was in a bad way, still unmoving. She had to take the next step alone. The best thing for him was to stay put until he could be transported to a hospital. His body needed time to absorb the shock of that beating. Scratch one potential helper.

There was a definite rush on getting Fickert in a doctor's care as soon as it could be managed. Certainly before morning. If they failed to find a way to break up this operation, the hospitals were going to be packed and Fickert would be less likely to get the help he needed. A lousy reward for risking his life to help.

She kept her breathing deep and slow, tamping down her dread of what she had to do. It wouldn't hurt so much right now, but it would give her pure hell in a day or two.

She had heard the term "double-jointed" but still had no idea it fit her. All she knew was she could stretch the muscles around her joints to make some of her joints, mostly the shoulders, move far beyond their usual range of motion.

She exhaled to empty her lungs and squeeze her chest to half its thickness, then visualized her muscles stretching. Pictured it clearly, as if it were moving in front of her. She saw her muscles slowly stretching, melting like warm taffy.

When the joint felt ready, she gradually twisted her shoulder muscles away from the joint far enough to allow her to wriggle her way out of the loops. It took another minute or so to shimmy out of the ropes and bring them down an inch, but it was enough to prove the mind trick worked.

In the time it took a smoker to burn two inches off a cigar, she was able to come halfway to her feet and drop her rope bindings to the floor. That done, she paused to breathe, unsteady on her legs.

It took her several more deep breaths before she managed to pull herself to her full height. She flexed her major muscles and shook herself. Body serviceable, mind sharp.

Maybe there was still time for her to pursue the men. She looked down at D.A. Fickert, then quickly untied his ropes. He opened his eyes and focused on her, but barely stirred. She waited another second or two, then nodded and bent to untie his boots and pull them off, then removed his outer clothing. He had no strength to stop her. She kept her own riding boots but took his pants, crammed her smaller boots through the legs, then adjusted the belt to fit her.

She covered him with her discarded clothing to keep him warm and whispered that she would be back as soon as possible, while she put on his jacket to finish the look. Then she picked up the helmet where Fickert had dropped it during the attack. Once it was on her head, she could leave her female self behind and blend in with the men on the street.

Outside the pier, she caught sight of her players less than two blocks away moving to the northwest out of the waterfront district toward a residential area. They were carrying the large suitcases, but they did not slump under the load.

These men were of ordinary size, indicating a bomb load of what, maybe twenty-five, thirty pounds? If half of that was explosive material, how much damage would that gunpowder or dynamite or TNT wreak upon flesh and bone at point-blank range? Considering the level of deception that brought her and Fickert to the pier, along with the sudden violence of the attack on them, the answer would have to be terrible.

She tailed them by silently pushing her motorbike on the side of the road fifty yards behind them. Her helmet stayed on, for whatever disguising effect it might have, and she kept her face pointed toward the ground while she walked the big bike along, doing her best impression of being a skinny guy who had merely run out of gas.

34

PIER 19 – EMBARCADERO DISTRICT

* July 21st, A Few Minutes Later *

RANDALL PULLED THE WAVERLEY to the curb outside the rough wire fence blocking the entrance gate at Pier 19. He stepped out to get a better look around the area, but Vignette's Harley was nowhere to be seen.

He could see why the closed pier was chosen as a hiding place. All piers to the north of the Ferry Building were given odd numbers, and Pier 17, the next one to the south, was a flat expanse of open deck stretching out into the water. But Pier 19 was fully covered. Who could tell what was inside? Why, with a properly bribed ship inspector, anything could be unloaded and disbursed out into the city, or loaded in secret and sailed away.

Randall loosened his revolver in the underarm holster. Throughout his career, he was only forced to shoot a perpetrator every now and then, mostly wounding them. It was fatal for a few, but they were righteous shootings. He could have easily died on those streets like so many of his fellow officers.

After another visual check in all directions, he ran on tiptoe to the gate and ducked through the hole in the fence strung across it. He kept it smooth and silent while he slipped into the moldy darkness beneath the covered pier, moving like a man wise enough to know fear and react with caution. During his early years pounding a beat in the Tenderloin district, back before graduating to the detective bureau, he frequently found himself chasing perpetrators into darkened spaces like this one. The sense of exposure and unpredictability was always fierce. He hated it back then and felt the same way now.

He hung back in place for half a minute to let his eyes adjust. Monochrome gray shapes gradually began to form. Tall stacks of something, wooden pallets, perhaps. All the shapes were geometric, nothing rounded or human.

Ambient light began to register in his vision, painting the picture for him. The place was empty but for the stacks of pallets and rolling ramps waiting for the next job. The pallets lined the wall while hand-pulled pallet loaders waited next to them.

Along the rickety wooden walls, coils of rope hung at regular intervals. He moved with light steps in the space between the pallet stacks and the long wall, easing his way toward the nearest rope coil. He slid forward just close enough to graze his fingertips across the surface: thick hemp rope, dry.

He put his nose next to it and inhaled. That was enough. There was such a thing as a "new rope smell," and it was hanging right there on the wall. The pier may have been falling apart. This rope was fresh and was surely reliable. Why was it there?

He began to move forward along the wall, feeling his way from one rope coil to the next. They all had the same smell and feel. The farther he went out onto the pier, the darker it became. Fewer holes and missing shingles back there. It turned out a lot of the roof damage was in the front near the gate.

He stopped and knelt next to the wall, straining his ears to the elements of sound there. The slow drip of rainwater; the lapping of seawater on the pillars below; a faraway gull screaming at the world. Everything he would expect in such a place.

Until a foreign sound struck a sour note. Faint amid the patchwork of shore noise, only apparent for being so out of place.

Scraping noises from somewhere down on floor. The slight creak of floorboards, perhaps? Somewhere further back in the blackness, something alive was producing those sounds.

In a flash the background noises all disappeared from his awareness. He homed in on the scratching sounds like an animal tracking prey in the deep darkness.

Closer, closer, until he realized it had to be right there, practically at his feet. He reached down and felt a man's leg, and the leg instantly recoiled. The man began to shout words made incoherent by some sort of gag over his mouth.

No female voice. Randall swung his free arm in a semicircle to check for Vignette's form, but there was nothing.

Touch and sound were not enough. He had to see. He had no choice but to light himself up and become an easy target.

He struck a wooden match. The amber glow instantly revealed everything for several feet in all directions. D.A. Fickert lay in front of him squirming to get out of the rope and be rid of his gag. Randall pulled it from his mouth and worked on the knots with his free hand while Fickert gasped and fought to regain his breath.

"Blackburn! Thank God!"

"Where's Vignette?"

"She got out after they jumped us. Sons of bitches! They knocked me out somehow or other, and when I came to, they were gone and I was here and she was standing over me. They had tied us both up, but she didn't look hurt."

Randall struck another match and held it higher up. The light ball expanded to include a set of discarded ropes on the floor a few feet away. He managed to emit a small laugh that somehow expressed acceptance, frustration, and relief all mixed together.

Fickert continued, "She told me they were moving the bombs, and I was hurt too bad to help her. True enough, but she left the gag on. Said sorry, she had to be sure I wouldn't attract attention and give away her escape." He winced under a jolt of pain in his back, stiffening, and moaned in pain.

Randall pulled the last of his bindings away. "Can you sit up?" He offered a hand. Fickert took it and gingerly pulled himself to a sitting position, but when he tried to get to his feet, he collapsed back to the floor.

"They were waiting for us, Blackburn! They tricked us here with a fake call to the mayor's office. Two of them are my men, treacherous bastards!"

"Your men?"

"Yes! On my staff, you understand? Winkle and Marsden! Part of whoever is behind all these threats. Bastards even have code names for each other, 'Fox' and 'Fire.' What the hell's the purpose? They used them in front of me like they were mocking me. Like using code names made them smart."

"Mr. Fickert, I need to know everything that happened. Here, I'll help you stand and walk you out. We can't stick around this place."

Fickert struggled to his feet and leaned on Randall for support. They moved ahead in shuffle-steps. "It was that Jacob Prohaska from downstairs!" He grunted and gasped in pain. "I got a few busted ribs, sure as hell. Can't hardly breathe."

"We can slow down. We're almost out."

"Two men on my damned staff! I trusted them. What must they have been offered?"

"Doesn't matter now. Tell me about Jacob Prohaska."

"What's to tell? Prohaska's one of them, plain enough."

"I don't understand that at all. He's the one who pulled us into this."

"A lot of people are dropping, showing their true colors."

"Makes sense to enlist him, I suppose. Someone in his position could be valuable."

Randall managed to walk Fickert off the pier and back toward the street. It took time, and he was aware of every minute of it, almost to the point that he could feel the hands on his pocket watch speeding up their motion while there was no way to speed up his own.

They shuffled off to the exit and at last made their way out. The air was fresher without the tinge of mold, and he took a deep breath. "Mr. Fickert, you need to be seen by a doctor right away."

"Wish I could argue with that."

"My vehicle is right over there. We can—"

The roar of Vignette's Harley broke through from the street ahead when she came flying around the corner. She headed straight for them and made no move to hit the brakes until the last moment. She skidded to a stop two feet from them.

"Randall! I thought you were still at the mayor's office, and I was on my way to use the public phone at the Clock Tower. I see you found Mr. Fickert. I'm sorry, sir, but as you see, you couldn't come along."

"Yeah, yeah," he muttered. He tried to take another breath and winced again.

Blackburn gazed up the street and noticed the approach of a large automobile. "Vignette, stand here with Mr. Fickert for a minute, will you, please?"

She put the bike on the kickstand and stepped over to take his place. Fickert grunted with a shock of pain caused by transferring his weight, but she got her arm under his and held him.

Randall stepped into the middle of the street and held up one hand high while he waved his PI badge with the other. The badge gave him no authority to stop traffic, but as long as he didn't let the motorist see it up close, he trusted the ruse to work.

The car was a large diesel with wide seats and no passengers, just the driver, who looked like one of the shipping magnates who liked to come down to check their inventories. And to the best of Blackburn's experience working down in this place, there was no such thing as a shipping magnate who had not been corrupted up to his armpits.

The automobile pulled to a respectful stop a few yards in front of him. Randall stepped to the driver's side and explained that this was a police emergency, they had the district attorney injured over there, and he had to receive medical help right away.

Within seconds, the car pulled next to Vignette and Fickert, and both Randall and the driver helped Fickert into the back seat. He insisted on being taken to St. Luke's Hospital, even though others were closer. The driver eagerly agreed, possibly calculating the size of the future political favor he was building for himself.

After Fickert was situated in the big car, he made a display of thanking Randall while excluding Vignette. She failed to notice, fired with the news she carried. She was on Randall the moment the car pulled away.

"Randall! Did Fickert tell you about Prohaska? His whole approach to us was fake!"

"He did. And he also told me Prohaska's secretary has abruptly left town. Now we can't confirm his alibi for Saunders. They must have found a way to turn him."

"He's more violent than he looks, too. He's the one who did most of the damage. We were so outnumbered. They had a couple of cops with them too, but those guys disappeared."

"I'd say the best news here is that the opposition is keeping it small, with as few people in the know as possible. It reduces the size of their force."

"I got out in time to follow them, Randall. They moved the suitcase bombs to some rathole flophouse called The Gloriosa, less than a mile from here. Four of them, now. Buda the bomber, Prohaska, and those two impostors on Fickert's staff. Buda's room is number eight."

"How do you know that?"

"Well, I inquired of the hotel desk clerk."

"Bribed?"

"Not too much. All I had was a fiver."

"Five bucks got Buda's room number? Nice work."

35

GLORIOSA HOTEL

* Minutes Later *

THE LARGE SIGN BEARING THE NAME "Gloriosa Hotel" was a crowning bit of irony atop a grotesquely oversized shack of three unstable stories. Truth in advertising would have named the place "The Gloriosa Hotel for the Down and Out." Their twenty-five-cent rooms did not include sheets or towels.

As an investigator, Blackburn felt a grudging admiration for Mario Buda's choice of hiding spots. The place was so miserable to look at, he doubted anyone would have searched for the bomber or his fancy products there.

There was no lobby, only a clerk's cage next to the entrance. The clerk was nowhere to be seen. Apparently once people paid for the day, the establishment lost interest. He and Vignette pushed on inside, and when they went unchallenged, they hiked up the rickety stairs to room number 8, which was the back room on the top floor. It was an ideal hole in the wall. He figured Buda must have specified the top floor as well as the room down at the end.

Now as they stood in the deserted hallway, he turned to whisper to Vignette. "All right, let's try it the polite way."

He gently knocked on the room door, careful not to bang hard enough to frighten anyone inside. They waited, no answer.

He tried again, harder this time. Still nothing. So much for the polite way.

He looked at Vignette, raised his eyebrows, and nodded. She smiled and reached for a hairpin...

Moments later, they stood in the room looking around at an unoccupied living space. The rumpled blanket on the bare mattress bed was the only sign that the room had been used at all. No people, absolutely no bombs.

"They panicked, Randall. They must have. They ran."

"You think somebody spotted you?"

"Hell, I don't see how. I tried to play it casual. But their side had more eyeballs."

"It's all right. They also had every reason to be far more watchful than usual."

Vignette looked crestfallen. "Oh, brother, did I make things worse, Randall?"

"Worse? Hell no. How could you have done that? Maybe they wouldn't have run if they didn't see you, but so what? If you didn't follow them, we'd have no idea where they were, anyway. It's a wash."

"He's still in the wind with the bombs. Maybe we could grab Galleani? Buda's still just his henchman."

"Except to arrest Galleani and hold onto him, you need reliable police. The mayor couldn't even get the chief to come here to do a search! The man just lied to him about it."

He spoke in a soft voice because he knew the words were hard. "We're still on our own, here. The first thing we have to do is not make this any worse."

"You know, if you want to just say to hell with all of it and go grab this guy, and I mean snatch him right off of the street and toss him in a basement somewhere, I'm all for it!"

"So am I. But we have to assume the event is set to go off without him. If we kidnap their figurehead, we just turn him into a martyr. More than anything else, we need those bombs."

She took a deep breath and nodded. "So now we go back up to tell the mayor, see what he wants done?"

"Maybe not. There's a public telephone at the Clock Tower building. I've only got folding money. You have any change?"

"Let's see: a couple of nickels, some pennies..."

"Pennies are no good. Nickels work."

"We've got four. Plus two dimes."

"A nickel's enough."

"Just the one?"

"So you really haven't used one of the coin-operated ones yet?"

"Been avoiding it."

"Why?"

"...No reason."

"Here we go, then. Good news is we keep the dimes. It's not a long-distance call."

36

SAN FRANCISCO DOCKSIDE
WATERFRONT

* July 22nd, 4:00 a.m.—False Dawn *

ON THE MORNING OF JULY 22nd, the waters of the great San Francisco Bay lay quiet, typical of the season, gently lapping at the piers of the great Embarcadero and at the seagoing ships tied fore and aft. Down where the Washington Street Pier met the waterfront, any noises from trucks or trolleys were muffled by early morning fog.

Beneath the pier, no moonlight or starlight penetrated the darkness. The air smelled as if this was where the sea met death and marinated in it before retreating. The thick fog swirled the docks in the form of cold smoke. Four men huddled in the deep chill, carefully cuddling five lethally odd suitcases, keeping them high and dry. Although the men had concealed themselves for the time being, they could speak in normal tones, knowing their voices would not penetrate the small space around them. With the temperature hovering at just over sixty degrees Fahrenheit, it was balmy enough to suffer out the endless wait for daybreak.

Jacob Prohaska kept a leery eye on Mario Buda but felt nothing but disgust for Winkle and Marsden, who appeared to have no idea of the evil they were mixed up in. They actually joked back and forth several times in excited whispers, using their code names, "Fox" and "Fire." Like children playing a game.

Now they were taking turns grousing about the conditions. "I still say we would have been a lot more comfortable in that flophouse," muttered Winkle.

Buda shook his head and replied in a low voice, "Never give a spy a chance to report you."

"Except we don't know he was a spy," said Marsden.

Buda's face took on an expression usually reserved for one's first step into an unclean outhouse. "A man with a motorcycle runs out of gas and just happens to be walking it back to the same location we are going to?"

"It could happen."

"So could getting caught!" Buda shouted. The others looked startled and quickly checked in all directions.

"Easy! Easy!" Prohaska said, raising both hands. "All right, so you think we had to change places to keep these things safe. But the guy kept going. I don't think we had to use the back alley to escape. My shoes are soaked."

"Mine too."

"Same here."

Buda was close to the point of getting physically sick over the constant bickering from those two. They seemed to feel no commitment, no purity of philosophy, just a couple of American shitheads out for a quick score. "I won't tell you again. Whether or not that man was following us is no question! Once we noticed him, we had a *duty* to react! To trust our instincts and avoid any threats. We had to leave. That's all."

He looked at each of the three others in turn. "Don't make me repeat this."

Jacob Prohaska spoke up. "All right, then. We're stuck here until sunrise, anyway."

"We'll be gone soon after first light," Buda said. "The sausage wagon is supposed to show up before sunrise, in time to snag a good spot. We'll move everything there as soon as they arrive."

Prohaska stood, stretching out his back. "I have to grab a trolley home and change clothes, then get to the office."

"Good," Buda agreed. "You can't afford to do anything unusual today."

"All I have to do is make it into the office. I can nap there. That's usually enough for me. What about you? Can you stay awake by yourself inside the stand?"

Buda sneered at the question. "These are my creations. I could do without sleep for a week."

Prohaska turned to Winkle and Marsden. "When was the last time we can acknowledge seeing each other?"

"Mayor's office, yesterday," said Winkle.

"Right," Marsden agreed. "Unless you want to mention being down here..." He grinned like a man who just made a brilliant joke.

Prohaska ignored him and tossed a quick "Good luck" over his shoulder while he mounted the crossbeams to climb back onto the pier. After having spent so many years flailing around out in the bureaucratic weeds, trying to do an impossible job for a government who didn't seem interested one way or the other, it felt wonderful to be on the winning team at last.

37

THE EMBARCADERO CLOCK TOWER

* Sunrise *

THE NICKEL WAS WELL INVESTED. A five-cent phone call saved them a lot of time.

"Go! Go!" Sunny Jim called into the receiver like a man hailing a ship. "I haven't heard anything but static on the radio receiver you left with me. Meanwhile my wife brought me a change of clothing! And some dinner! A whole case of that soda pop drink! It's good, but it'll make you piss like an old dog. Don't walk under my office window, ha-ha! Take care of yourselves!"

"Thank you, Mr. Mayor," Randall replied, resisting the urge to yell along with him. "We just need to take a little bit of time to rest and freshen up."

"Yes! Go home! Sorry, not home! Home's gone! Oh yes! Get a room at the Palace Hotel! The city will pay. Don't waste time running around at this hour. I'll call you as soon as we get something you can act on!"

"The Palace Hotel. We'll be there, sir," Randall replied. He hung up wondering what kind of luck he would have in billing the City for the room.

———

The head concierge at the Palace Hotel was a top-tier attendant to those with extraordinary needs and welcomed the opportunity to put his skills to work on behalf of Randall Blackburn and Vignette Nightingale. He had just been presented with an impressive business card for "Blackburn & Nightingales – Private Investigation" along with a compelling ten-dollar bill and the statement that they needed to redo their attire from the ground up. And by that they meant right then, at that moment, hours before the stores were to open.

This made them interesting enough to break up his long shift, but add to that a pair who were perhaps really a father and daughter, or perhaps not. They claimed to have been displaced because criminals blew up their home, but perhaps not. Perhaps instead they were being hunted by the older man's wife?

The head concierge was nobody's fool. He had long since lost count of the "father-daughter teams" who came in seeking a room.

There's never a mother-son team, though, is there? The thought made him chuckle because it was true. Still, you never know what tricks the general public will throw at you. To his confusion and consternation, they each requested their own room. That was an unforeseen twist.

Nevertheless, he only maintained his lucrative position by remaining unbreakably in character during every moment on the job. He was the "You-Boy" born to buttle, leaping forward with a lighted match for every unlit cigar. And so he escorted this purported father-daughter team who understood the power of a good tip to the hotel's sizeable Lost & Found Department. They were invited to take whatever items they needed.

———

By the time the earliest hints of light began to trace the sky, Mario Buda found the yammering of the two City Hall men to be testing every ounce of his restraint. He sat unmoving with the deathly stillness of an introvert festering with a problem, while those two—all this time later—were still trying to find ways to get one up on each other over who did the best job of snowing the district attorney, their fake boss.

Buda had never experienced such a strange form of competition, which seemed to consist of nothing more than an obsessive determination to stand over someone else. He had lost all appreciation for snide remarks hidden behind facetious compliments, drizzled with ironic observations of the shortcomings of others. Every time they spoke, their voices sandpapered his bones.

When the sounds of the arriving sausage wagon reached his ears, his sense of relief was explosive. Without a word, he signaled the other two to help him by picking up the first two suitcases himself. They each took only one for themselves and gave him a smirk while they passed him and climbed up topside. Leaving three more suitcases sitting there.

The headache toying behind Buda's eyes spun off an acidic burn in the pit of his stomach. He took several breaths before he could retrieve them all by carrying one at a time, clambering back down twice more for the others. The two City Hall men stood watching him while he worked, sneering as if they had just pulled off some ingenious trick on this man who was arrogant enough to advertise himself as the "Bomb Maker Nonpareil."

Buda never looked at either of them, fearing his own rage. He was not a large man, but neither were they.

No. These two were organization men. Weaklings at everything but deception. King's men. He felt such rage and contempt for them it was as if he could kill them both by breathing on them. As if a drop of his blood would poison them in their tracks.

He picked up a suitcase and tucked it under his arm while he took another in the same hand and picked up the third with his opposite hand. He took two steps toward the food wagon, then stopped, staring at the ground, letting them know he was waiting.

Marsden and Winkle snuffed their grins and walked past him toward the stand. He followed behind, for no other reason than to shepherd his creations to their next destination, but he could feel them thinking. He could tell they were interpreting his place behind them as some sort of acquiescence to them, the fools. He had no words capable of carrying the heat of his bitterness.

Thankfully for Buda, the six men who arrived with the sausage wagon were eager to be on their way back. He had seen them around Galleani's events and figured there was no reason to ask why it took so many of them to deliver the thing. He also did not challenge them when they disengaged the powerful team of work horses instead of leaving them with the wagon before they headed back into the city. This effectively trapped him in the unmovable wagon, and it was clearly no accident, but Buda shrugged it off. He didn't need their trust.

They were gone within two minutes, disappearing into low morning light and persistent fog. Sounds of their motion quickly blended into the collage of morning noise from the docks.

The men left without saying anything to Buda about why they were in a hurry, but it would have greatly interested him to know their single-minded goal was to return the two Percherons to the rest of their team back at the Yerba Buena Hauling Company on Mint Alley. These boys intended to make themselves scarce until zero hour, because they were among the Mint attack crew and had a plan with a fat payday.

They had each been faithful to their vow of silence to Galleani, but not out of fear, which in Galleani's experience never worked without leaking, but instead from great personal greed, which never failed. As for their approaching afternoon task, it would be hard but not complex. *Load the wagons, drive to Pier 19, offload to a waiting ship, join the crew and sail away.* Live easy and die rich.

To Buda, the departure of the men was just fine. One less potential problem. That left him alone at the sausage stand with the two City Hall men. He took a deep breath, raised his eyes, and ventured a glance at Winkle, or was it Marsden, and was relieved he still retained enough self-control that he didn't automatically grab the man by the throat.

"Did you know Hemo killed Shadow?" asked one of the pair.

"How would you know that?"

"He needed our help to distract him."

"Yeah, he died because he failed," said Marsden or maybe Winkle. "He lost heart. Because of him, there won't be any arson attacks after Blackburn scared off the first ones. But it doesn't matter why. He died because he failed."

The little pissant actually turned his well-used smirk onto Buda, then glanced at the suitcase bombs. He perceived the man's implied promise of disaster if Buda's bombs were duds.

The two little skin-bags thought they had one over on him.

Buda lowered his voice to a whisper. "Hemo's name was Byron Morrisey. I drove him to Randall Blackburn's house to set the bomb."

That one stunned them into silence. Now it was time for him to lord it over them for a change. "Before you go, I need you to wait over on the north side edge. Yes, over there. Only to act as lookouts! You don't have to do anything. You will see a two-man boat come gliding right up under the pier. I need to know the instant it arrives!"

Before they could begin a witty tirade of objections to his absurd story, he herded them to the side of the pier. It only took a few seconds of walking time.

Traces of light teased the sky. Fog swirled in every open space, ruining visibility and damping sound. Buda's two-shot derringer used .22-caliber short shells in each barrel. Winkle, or was it Marsden, went down first. Easy shot to the back of the head. Fully effective and instantaneous.

The second one, probably Winkle but possibly not, had just enough time to recoil and bring up an arm, giving Buda adequate room to fire under his arm and into his face. The victim may not have died right away, but they both hit the water with the same satisfying splat. Right out there in the refreshing salty mist of the early morning air.

Mario Buda practically floated back to the sausage stand, buoyed by a joyous sense of relief. *Son of a bitch, a little peace and quiet!* For one brief moment, he began to wonder if anyone would miss the two City Hall men, then realized he didn't care.

At the door of the stand, he put out a "Closed" sign and locked himself inside with his creations. Hours to wait. Safe enough to nap for a while.

38

THE PALACE HOTEL

* Parade Day, 10:00 a.m. *

VIGNETTE'S MOTORCYCLE OUTFIT WAS too dingy to sustain her for another day, but the only clothing in the Lost & Found that didn't swallow her thin frame was a blue velour jacket and matching floor-length skirt. There was no way her bike would be drivable in that, so she took a pair of men's pants to wear with the top half. She had enough fashion sense to be well aware of her appearance, but as far as she was concerned, people could stare all they wanted.

Randall's outfit was a threadbare suit that fit him well enough. It was an older style that would do nothing to elevate him in the eyes of others, but at least he could walk around in it without being challenged.

Now freshly bathed and wearing passable attire, they sat amid the empty breakfast dishes, both positioned with their backs to the room to avoid the stares. The head concierge had kept an eye on them and noted their tense condition. As soon as the telephone message came in, he walked directly to them, moving with an air of purpose.

"Detective?" he quietly addressed Randall, glanced at Vignette, and proceeded to ignore her.

"Yes?"

"A telephone call just came in from the office of the mayor."

"And?"

The head concierge lifted his nose a bit with the importance of his announcement. "He asked you to come to City Hall right away. Something very important."

"Thank you."

The pair leaped to their feet so quickly the head concierge had to take a step backward. He could only stare while Detective Blackburn tucked a fiver into his hand and strode away with the young woman who, he realized, was possibly the man's actual daughter.

39

OFFICE OF MAYOR JAMES "SUNNY JIM" ROLPH

* Parade Day, 10:30 a.m. *

RANDALL AND VIGNETTE SAT in awkward silence before Sunny Jim's massive desk, with the silent radio receiver waiting nearby. Besides the mayor, one other guest was there, attired in dirty clothing and reeking of alcohol and sweat. He seemed to know his own condition and kept a self-conscious gaze on the floor.

The silence sustained itself while the mayor's secretary wheeled in a silver coffee service cart and placed steaming cups before each of them. On her way out, she turned her head so only Vignette could see her and slid her a seductive smile. But her playful expression turned to confusion when Vignette recoiled. She hurried out with the cart, leaving Vignette to reach for her coffee and mutter under her breath, "People are dogs."

"All right," sighed Sunny Jim. "Before we were interrupted, I was explaining that it took most of the day for Mr. Mummery to find an officer who would listen to him and bring a message to me."

Mummery lifted his head at that. "My boy Will was a good boy. Good enough. Worked odd jobs because I ain't no damn good unless I'm drunk. But that's me. He didn't deserve to die."

"He certainly did not, Mr. Mummery. We were horrified by his killing. We will do our best to see to it someone pays."

"That gonna bring him back?"

Nobody had a response to that. After another moment, Sunny Jim reclined in his big desk chair with one hand on his stomach. He pointed at the remaining half-case of Coca-Cola. "I'm not having any more of those for a while."

"Bet you're still wide-awake, though."

"Yep to that. Wide-awake."

She set aside her coffee cup. "I'm too tired for coffee. I'll have another bottle of wakeup juice."

"You realize they claim to have removed all the cocaine from their recipe?"

"Yeah, when was that?"

"Not sure, exactly."

"Maybe this city got sent an old batch, been in a warehouse since before the recipe change."

"They would never knowingly do that."

"Of course. Would you pass me a bottle?"

"All right. Still warm, though. Not as good warm."

"Wakes you up the same."

"I'm awake enough." He sat up, looking troubled. "Stomach problems, though. You must excuse me." He stood and started for the door. "Two of you, get going. Any of the police who remain loyal will be overwhelmed with parade security. Route goes on for miles. Fingers crossed I can send you some help." He started out the door of the office.

"Should you maybe call Washington or the state capital?"

Sunny Jim stopped and turned back. "To what point, Detective? The parade starts this afternoon. Even if they could and would help us, what would we ask them to do?"

Mr. Mummery spoke with a sudden flare of emotion. "My boy delivered messages for Prohaska before! Right before they killed him, he told me about overhearing him talk about a robbery with this Galleani character.

Heard him use the name a coupla times. See, he only remembered because Prohaska called the man 'Signore.' Said it was a huge payday. Gigantic."

Vignette asked, "A payday stolen from where?"

"The words he heard were, 'cracking the Mint.'"

Sunny Jim scoffed. "Cracking the Mint? What, the San Francisco Mint? What's that got to do with a political bombing?"

"Who knows? Maybe it doesn't. And something about the Embarcadero. You're the detectives. I just know what my son told me. Why would he make up something like that? What good could it ever do him?"

Randall shook his head, leaned close to the mayor, and muttered, "A Mint robbery only makes sense if the parade bombings are a ruse. A distraction."

That one caused Sunny Jim to drop the sunny smile. "Using mayhem as a *distraction* from robbing the Mint? That is the most insane thing I've ever heard! The place is a fortress. Nobody could break in there without days of advance work on the locks and doors."

"What about a tunnel?"

"Oh, Jesus Christ! The place sits on a pad of, I don't know, something like five or six feet of reinforced concrete! A *tunnel*?"

"We have to think of everything. Explosives?"

"Of course! All they have to do is smuggle that new railway cannon the French have now, four hundred millimeters, dig a giant hole underneath the Mint, tilt the cannon straight up toward the base, and blast their way in! Or make an even more dramatic entrance and blast in the front door right in front of everybody!"

"I just meant—"

"We need to get you back on the street, so please. We learned from the telephone tap that Galleani has left the Cinquevalli home, bags and all. So go ahead and take a run down to the Mint and patrol the place silly. Once we confirm nothing's going on, we can get back to the parade route. The boy also mentioned the Embarcadero. At least that makes sense as a potential attack point."

To Vignette he said, "Maybe while he checks the Mint you can start patrolling the Embarcadero, top to bottom. Call in with anything that looks out of place."

"Sure thing. I can call you from the Clock Tower public telephone. Five cents. They'll take dimes, but they don't give change."

Sunny Jim looked at her as if he thought she would say more. Getting nothing, he turned to Randall. "Detective, I am going to get a message down to the desk sergeant on duty and tell him we need increased patrols around the Mint and in the Embarcadero. If they actually show up, it might provide some backup for you."

"Or it might provide people who want to get in the way and maybe leave us dead."

"Yes, it might." Sunny Jim nodded with an uncharacteristic sigh. "Which has begun to feel like an ordinary day around here. I'll keep monitoring the radio receiver, but it seems as though they made a change in plans and don't intend to communicate that way."

40

THE EMBARCADERO & THE SAN FRANCISCO MINT

* Parade Day, Noon *

VIGNETTE MANEUVERED THE HARLEY in and around the chaotic morning traffic in front of the Ferry Building while she ran a constant there-and-back circuit from the Embarcadero's northmost pier down to the southern end. The industrial traffic was light in response to the parade but replaced by a far greater pedestrian presence.

At least nobody tried to knock her off the bike. Still the strain of keeping up a vigilant watch was giving her a fierce headache and tightening the muscles in her shoulders. After an hour of this, she had seen nothing remotely strange or unusual, other than a horse-towed sausage stand somebody left in front of the Clock Tower at the Ferry Building. It was closed up and unhitched and appeared deserted at the moment.

She only gave it a moment's thought. Maybe it was closed for business right now because today was a light day on the docks, with many of the men failing to show for work.

But in the next moment a bicycle messenger cut in front of her, and she had to jam her left foot to the ground, throw the rear wheel to the right, and fan-stop to avoid hitting him. The engine stalled. She averted the collision, but after she restarted the bike, she drove away feeling irritated enough to forget the oddly parked sausage stand. She kept going toward the south end of the Embarcadero.

Randall Blackburn completed his third trip around the Mint building after finding nothing out of place and was just about to head down to the Embarcadero to meet up with Vignette, but when he turned the corner into Mint Alley at the back of the Mint, he immediately stopped the Waverley and thanked himself for buying an electric car. Three men stood quietly talking in the shadows of the alley and had not heard his approach. He already knew Yerba Buena Hauling Company was a commercial operation. But twenty years of walking a beat had sharpened his sense to malfeasance, and the men's body language had a furtive quality he didn't like. He parked the Waverley in the distance and stood watching them until they went back inside. Once they did, he left the car and hurried on foot to the big sliding door of the stable, then leaned close to listen.

Voices came from inside, rough men laughing and talking. However, after a moment, the sounds faded strangely and then disappeared altogether. After several moments of silence, he pulled the door back just enough to squeeze through, slipped inside, and slid the door back into place.

Despite the daylight outside, the stables were completely dark but for one small lantern glowing in the far corner. Something that looked like a flat black square lay on the floor, as wide across as a grown man. The top of a wooden ladder protruded upward from the square and reached just high enough for someone to grab and swing onto the ladder.

He stepped over to the black square and realized it was the top of a shaft dug straight down and penetrating a good twelve feet into the earth. Another lantern glowed at the bottom of the shaft, illuminating a tunnel that ran in the direction of the Mint.

Faint sounds of voices floated to his ears. The men were returning from the tunnel back to the vertical shaft. One of the men sounded upset with the others, deriding them in some way. After a few more seconds, they came close enough for Randall to hear the words. The angry man's voice was clearest while they gathered at the base of the ladder and prepared to climb up. Randall recognized the sneering condescension right away.

"And now with the sight-seeing finished, you have no more reason to doubt me. Back up inside! No smoking in the stables, and no more going outside to smoke."

One of the men complained, "That's gonna be hours from now."

"So what? Think of the amount of gold we are about to liberate from those evil governments and you won't *need* to smoke! Or eat! Or do anything else until we're done! What you will do, what *I* will do, is wait here until the parade begins!"

A bomb. It had to be a bomb. But a bomb under the Mint? It was common knowledge that the Mint sat on a specially poured foundation. How could a bomb do anything more than collapse the tunnel, which was many times softer than the foundation? He couldn't make sense of it, but there was no doubting their intention.

While the men climbed, he heard them chuckling and murmuring back and forth in appreciation for the thought of carrying away all the gold their wagons could hold. The voices grew closer, and he saw the bouncing light from a handheld lantern while the men ascended.

He backed into the darkness of the stables while they emerged from the shaft. There were plenty of dark shadows in the place, back amid the silent standing forms of large horses dozing in their stalls on each side of the building. A set of six wagons also lined up in the center and could offer him a bit more cover.

He needed to be gone, but there was no escape now, no way to let the mayor's office know about the planned attack on the Mint. But of course even then, who was the mayor supposed to send to stop it? Would corrupt officers simply show up to demand a cut of the action?

How does anyone employ a broken system to stop crime?

He faded further back into one of the stalls and slid behind the giant draft animal while it impatiently chewed on the wooden gate. At least any sounds he accidentally made would be covered by the horse. There was nothing to do now but wait for Galleani to make the next move.

He managed to keep himself hidden in the shadows, but once the six wagon drivers showed up and Galleani ordered them to begin hitching up the wagons, it became more difficult with every passing minute to stay out of sight. He slipped to the back of his stall when one of the men pulled the big Percheron in the next stall out to get harnessed. But the move put him directly behind the giant horse.

Larger work horses were generally calmer than smaller breeds, but any horse could be prone to startled reactions. When one of the men gave a good-natured slap to the side of the stall, Randall's temporary companion was startled enough to quickly back up until its rear end hit the wall, meaning it hit him first. His right knee twisted out of joint and sent a lightning bolt of pain through him. His involuntary grunt alerted the man and brought him back to the stall.

And as quickly as that, he was caught.

Two of the men rushed in to seize him, and one stomped on Blackburn's injured knee as a particularly amusing way to subdue the intruder. The two men hauled him out of the stall to show their leader. Blackburn's howls of pain were exceeded by Galleani's howl of outrage.

"That's him!" he screamed, drawing out the words. "That's him! The fake newsman! Who are you really, Mr. Newsman, eh? Mr. Big Shot Nothing?"

"What's he doin' here, anyway?" shouted one of the men back in the shadows.

"Stupid question!" Galleani shouted back at the man. "Poor thinking on your part!" He turned back to Randall and said to the men holding him, "Tie him up. Leave him there. As long as he can't stop us, he doesn't matter."

One of the men holding Randall replied, "We didn't sign up for killing anybody in cold blood. I mean, if cops shoot at us, that's one thing, but some guy…"

"You're not killing anybody, idiot! You leave him there helpless and we finish our job!"

But the men persisted. "Because your parade job is your business, you know? The people who get killed, we got no part in that!"

"Think again!" Randall shouted in spite of the pain racking him. "Your boss here is the same man who set up the parade to get bombed! That means you'll hang with him!"

"Nobody is hanging anybody!" Galleani countered. "We'll all be at sea with the gold before the authorities put their pants on."

"What, *that's* it?" Randall cried. "You think you can break into the Mint and just drive away? You men are fools following a madman!"

Galleani laughed at that. "A madman would take offense to being called mad, eh? Instead, I will merely show all of you this detonator. I will connect it to the wire running out of the shaft just before the parade launches at a minute from now. It will detonate a bomb so powerful, the floor of the Mint will collapse. The blast will kill or disable the skeleton crew working in the Mint today."

He stepped to Randall and kicked him in the leg, but the detective held his reaction to a hard gasp. "By the time anyone finds this intruder and releases him, you will all be too rich to touch!"

Randall tried to meet the eyes of each man to check for any uncertainty toward Galleani. Nothing. These men were all in. He collapsed back to the floor with a grunt.

But at the same moment, it struck him that there was something very important about the San Francisco Mint that Galleani obviously did not realize. A pretty little fact that changed everything.

He pointed up at the man with a grim smile and quietly said, "Poor research on your part..."

41

EMBARCADERO, OUTSIDE THE FERRY BUILDING

* 1:00 p.m.—1 Hour and 6 Minutes to Go *

MARIO BUDA RETURNED TO THE sausage stand after relieving himself at the side of the Clock Tower. The hours dragged for him while he waited alone with his creations, and he had done a lot of thinking in the sausage stand. There was nothing else to do in that empty little box, so his thoughts ran away with him.

Because the more Buda thought about Galleani's plan, the less sense it made to him. He was beginning to burn with shame over having been taken in with such little effort on Galleani's part. He could now see how much he had made excuses for Galleani, explaining away his inconsistencies and refusing to question his "wisdom."

So the great Signore Galleani intended to use the parade to make a giant political statement, but he couldn't be there for it? The story was that he had other things to lock down. But what? With the bombs here and the men coming to this spot to get them, with the destinations already written in the suitcase holding each bomb, what "supervision" did Galleani need to perform away from here?

In Buda's eyes, nothing about this plan was working. He never should have had to dispatch those two City Hall men, because they shouldn't have been a part of the operation in the first place. Questionable loyalty, both of them. Lack of personal commitment. The great Signore Galleani failed to enlist reliable men for this operation.

Even Morrisey—who had actually called himself "Hemo," for crying out loud—failed to get it right on a simple bomb-delivery mission. At least he didn't survive to be questioned by the police, since not all the cops were on board. That could have been trouble for everyone.

No, he saw it now. Luigi Galleani didn't bring the revolution to San Francisco; he brought a circus. Buda opened the door to the stand to enter, but left the "Closed" sign in place to keep away prospective customers. His mind was made up. He would commit blasphemy and break his word to Galleani, opening up the suitcases to read their destinations. He had to know what the hell was really going on.

Safely closed up inside, he opened the first suitcase with trembling hands. Tacked to the inside of the lid was a small piece of paper with an address on the 1000 block of Lombard Street. Buda squinted, puzzled. That location was over on Russian Hill. Far from the parade route.

Then he realized this was the address where Galleani stayed, the home of his hosts! What could that mean? Did they have a falling out? Even if they had, why would he stick a personal attack in a political operation?

Buda opened the next suitcase with hands that no longer shook. The same equipment was inside, but the paper fastened to the lid also listed a place not on the parade route. He didn't know who lived there but recognized the address as another mansion in another rich neighborhood.

Neither had anything to do with the Preparedness Day Parade and the planned bomb attacks upon it. He dove into the task of opening the rest of the cases in a frenzy of mounting rage. These all had addresses that put them on the parade route, proving there was at least some intent on Galleani's part to follow through. The private homes were clearly those of people who offended Galleani enough to earn a death sentence from him.

Why would he waste bombs on personal revenge? What about anarchy and a new world and a great opportunity for those who helped to usher in the new age?

Two words leaked out of Buda's mouth on an exhale, barely a whisper. "A hoax."

He felt so dizzy he might have fallen if he were standing up. He could practically hear the crashing sounds of his world collapsing around his ears.

It was all a godforsaken hoax, nothing more than some sort of personal revenge operation. Except Galleani's reprimands were supposed to come from Buda's creations. And once word got out that Buda had quit making political statements and was using his genius to help others take acts of personal revenge, no matter the reasons, his name would become a joke. He had already blown up the detective's house, which might be explained away. But several such explosions would tag him as a rampant murderer with no real political devotion. No longer would the title "Bomb Maker Nonpareil" indicate a noble mind working against the world's inequality, but merely a hired killer who helps evil people carry out personal wars. A man with no regard for any code of honor.

Impossible.

Slow minutes drizzled by while he sat fuming and stared unseeing at the wooden wall. Whatever was going on, it was all a trick and Buda had been the principal victim. That was the truth of it. The cold realization sent him into a frenzy of action. He reopened each suitcase, exposing the bombs once again, then pulled the wiring from every single one. He didn't just pull the detonator wire, which some clever fellow might reconnect. No, he tore out every single wire in each bomb, leaving whoever transported them the happy task of trying to wire up a bomb themselves without knowing what they were doing.

Of course word would get out that Buda's bombs had not exploded, but word would also get out that they had been sabotaged. Blame would fall on the operation, not the one who armed it. And this operation had the name Luigi Galleani stamped all over it.

By the time the men arrived to pick up their suitcases and go set the bombs, Buda had begun to smile for the first time all night. He opened up the sausage stand and issued a suitcase to each man, allowing them to open the lids and check out the addresses for each one. Normally this would make him nervous, since these men were the weakest links in the entire mission, but they would never recognize his sabotage.

Happily, it no longer mattered. It made no difference if they got cold feet or if they were heroes to the last man. Even if they followed orders to the letter, they would do no more than deliver duds to some wealthy people who would surely be upset to find them, but who would also sigh with relief that the bombs didn't work.

And the great Luigi Galleani could deal with the aftermath, the loss of esteem, the loss of support from the worldwide anarchist movement. Buda would go on to build more bombs for grateful buyers, the kind of people who never allowed personal grudges to overcome their vision for the future. Galleani's reputation would wane while Buda's rose ever higher, gathering esteem from visionaries everywhere.

And to further that glorious day, he kept the last bomb for himself, still wired for action. It took no more than a quick apology to the man scheduled to deliver it, telling him Galleani's plans changed and he wanted Buda to do that job, but that the man could keep his money. Buda noted with veiled contempt how relieved the man looked at being allowed to hurry away keeping his cash.

And then he was alone again. He picked up the remaining suitcase bomb, scheduled for delivery to somebody who lived even higher up on Lombard Street than Galleani's hosts. Perhaps another city councilman? It didn't matter. Nothing on the street was a parade address. Not even capitalists were so arrogant as to attempt to run marching bands up hills that steep.

All right, then. That was fine. Because Buda was about to re-task this bomb for another, far better purpose. City Hall was the place to make a statement. Just in case Galleani was also lying about the City Hall attack, Buda now had the power to make one happen there himself. Any of the ruling class who were not out watching the parade could die in their offices and make their contribution to the future by demonstrating the fragility of their society.

Even if the building was basically empty, the explosion would still reveal the vulnerability of the city's most important structures. He sat over the disabled bomb and reconnected all its wiring, double-checking his work as always.

As a small point of personal doubt, he asked himself what if a one-in-a-million failure took place because he was recognized and got himself arrested or killed? What would he want the authorities to see when they opened up the unexploded suitcase?

He pulled the stub of a pencil from his pocket and turned over the paper with the address on it, to write the name Luigi Galleani in capital letters. Because Mario was one of those people who, on one hand, might not fight back when humiliated, but on the other hand, never forgets. Not ever.

He picked up the suitcase and faced the door, but his eyes were already seeing through it and across the country, visualizing explosions in Chicago and even in the great New York City. He hungered for them. Never again would he entrust his future to one who could betray him as this miserable Galleani had done.

The plan for the wagon was just to abandon it and let the police take it away, so he glanced around to be certain there were no small bits of evidence. There was nothing. Mario never smoked, he had not eaten, and he left no trash.

All clear. Just him and his happy vacation suitcase.

To hell with Luigi Stinking Galleani and his massive betrayal, he thought. Let the man explain it away himself, somehow, to the rest of the anarchist movement. Let his great, golden tongue flap its way out of the suspicions that will surround him if this tale comes to the surface.

Buda felt history coursing through his veins once more. This was how he was meant to feel. Every schoolboy knows the only fit response to treachery is more of the same, and worse. He owned the title Bomb Maker Nonpareil, and nobody would take that away from him.

And so there was nothing left to do but proceed up to City Hall and pay a little visit to the mayor's office. Drop off his respects. He suffered no doubts that the cloaked device would function as designed, and yet even if the cruelest of Fates somehow spoiled his device, the message written inside would cause a different kind of explosion.

He stepped outside and set the suitcase on the ground. There was no practical reason to turn back and lock the wagon door, but his professionalism was such that every detail mattered.

Inside that sausage stand, the identity of the humble cobbler was left behind forever. It was good to be the Bomb Maker Nonpareil.

42

THE YERBA BUENA HAULING COMPANY

* Parade Day, 1:30 p.m.—36 Minutes Left *

LUIGI GALLEANI STOOD IN THE DOORWAY of the stables with his finger poised over the switch on the connected detonator. He stared in anticipation toward the city waterfront and the parade route.

His cohort gathered behind him reflecting a mixture of fear and anticipation. Every one of them expected to become far richer than any working man ever bothered to fantasize: beyond the need to ever work again, beyond the reach of laws meant for smaller people. They were about to carry away so much capital they would have no more need of capitalism at all.

Back in the shadows, Randall had his right hand on the knife he had slipped into his pocket from the escape kits Vignette brought home. The feel of the cool blade brought back the thought of their home, which in turn carried him back to the impact of the bomb, how close they came to dying, and how there had not yet been the chance to go back and sort through the remains of the place.

The feeling steeled him. He bit the blade into the rope around his wrist and backhanded it forward and back until the fibers gave. Hands free, he quickly cut away the ropes on his torso and ankles. The knife was razor sharp, making it easy to slice through the rope fibers; the real challenge was to keep quiet while pain sizzled through him. The slightest movement seemed to jostle his knee joint, and every move brought a harsh sensation.

"How accurate is your watch?" he heard Galleani ask one of the men. He couldn't hear the man's reply, but Galleani said, "Good! Any second now, then..."

Randall looked toward the stable door just as the distant explosion of cannon fire echoed throughout the waterfront and brought distant cheers from the crowded streets. The massive Preparedness Day Parade had begun, as scheduled, with cannon reports and a blazing fireworks display. Marchers were already grouped by the hundreds to form up and travel a route extending three and half miles through the city. Never in the history of this overgrown gold town had there been a parade this big.

Galleani waited a bit more, but that's all there was: a cannon firing blanks. Harmless fireworks. He held his breath for another few seconds, but no bomb explosions greeted his ears. Not one.

Galleani didn't move, but his face turned purple. His thoughts raced for a workable response to this disaster while his fingers shook over the detonator switch. An idea struck, and he immediately put it to work. He shouted to the sky as if there were someone up there to hear him.

"So it seems the great Mario Buda failed to execute his part of the mission! Something terrible must have surely happened to him. We are the only part of this operation that has not been cursed! And now it's up to us to succeed anyway, in his memory! Will we not?"

The men shuffled their feet and murmured in vague appreciation of succeeding anyway.

"Without the distraction of the bombs, any police officers we don't control will find their way up here sooner than we planned. So we will cut from six wagons to three and speed up our exit. Two men to each wagon now!" He lifted the detonator once again. "Cover your ears!"

Randall stayed on the ground without revealing he was free of his bonds while he called out, "Galleani, this plan can't possibly work!"

Luigi Galleani showed no more emotion than a smug smile. He kept his voice low and calm when he replied to Blackburn and looked around at each of his men. "You only say that because you don't understand the science behind this bomb. An entirely new kind of bomb. And if you really were a private investigator instead of just a retired man who used to walk a beat in this part of town, you would know that!" He beamed a delighted smile of triumph and pointed at Randall. "Poor research on your part!"

He pressed the detonator switch.

In the next instant, a deafening explosion sent a blast wave rocketing through the building and threw an artificial earthquake through the ground beneath them. Although the blast came from hundreds of feet away and twelve feet underground, the pressure wave still thumped each man deep in the chest and left them all with ringing ears.

Galleani whirled to Blackburn and shouted, "You see? 'We are too soon old and too late smart,' eh, Mister Detective?" He beamed while he shouted to his men, "Our bomb maker got this one right!"

The men were still having some trouble hearing their boss but were happy to get to work. It was when they collectively turned toward the shaft, preparing to assault the Mint, that they felt it coming. The realization hit them the same way such things tend to do. Water. Rushing water. A great quantity of rushing water. They felt its movement through the vibrations in the ground.

The men hovered at the top of the tunnel shaft, staring downward by lantern light. Its amber glow was just enough to bounce off the top of the water level, which had filled the horizontal tunnel and was now rising up the twelve-foot shaft. It finally stopped a few feet below ground level, which was as far as the underground pressure pushed it.

This left the tunnel impassable for all practical purposes. Outside the building there would be no indication of a flood, but even if the bomb had blasted a perfect hole in the floor of the Mint's inner garden and stunned the workers inside, nothing short of deep-sea diving equipment would allow anyone to navigate the distance.

As soon as the group of former soon-to-be-rich men took in what just happened and what all it meant for them, they dissolved back into the hardscrabble world. No excuses made, no farewells offered. Each one suddenly carried a fresh appreciation for non-union day work, something far better than anything they would get behind bars.

Blackburn pulled himself to his feet, one hand holding the wall to support his leg. "There's an artesian well under the slab! It's where they get the water for their fire sprinklers. What was that you said about research?"

He spread his arms out and managed a laugh in spite of the pain, then added, "They make you learn that before they let you walk a beat down here."

Galleani rushed outside and started to call out to any of the men who might be close enough to hear him, but he stopped himself. They were gone in barely more time than a wandering dog needed to water a bush.

In that moment, Luigi Galleani's heart became one with every general who ever stared in dismay while their recruits disappeared from the battlefield. Resignation hit him like a runaway caisson.

He turned to Blackburn and ran his gaze over the injured leg. The sight gave him confidence. Rage propelled him toward the rotten American bastard. His single-minded intention was to attack the injured leg until pain overcame the detective, then strangle the much larger man with his bare hands. First the torment. First the pain.

"That son of yours," he began with a leering grin. "Stumbled like a dumb bastard onto our plans and reported it to his watch commander. But the watch commander already worked for us."

Blackburn's voice came out in an enraged whisper. "You...you killed...?"

"Not *me*! No! Galleanists! Loyal believers! Truck drivers who know exactly how to cut off a motorcycle so it runs straight into them!"

Blackburn stared at Galleani in stunned disbelief. Hot rage filled him. His gaze burned into him like sunlight through a magnifying glass. Galleani was momentarily startled at the intensity of Blackburn's reaction, then laughed in delight at the detective's pain and continued to approach him.

He was nearly at arm's reach of his quarry when Randall swiped the blade before him, coming within a fraction of an inch from Galleani's face. It was impossible to fight standing on his feet, so he lunged at Galleani from the ground like an enraged sea lion. He attacked with all the ferocity he could muster, again and again, slashing the air in front of Galleani's face. The tip came nearly close enough to take off his nose.

For an instant both men paused, fighting for breath while they stared at one another. Blackburn's face twisted into a smile, but it had no trace of humor or good will. "There's nobody I can call to help me take you in, and I can't chase you down. But you can try to fight me."

He didn't have to add, *and I will kill you.* All he said was, "Best thing you can hope for now is to fight another day."

Galleani studied him just long enough to feel the strength of this detective's will. He took one step back.

He turned to look behind himself, saw nothing, turned back toward Blackburn. Then he took one more step backward.

Randall felt himself sinking with exhaustion and pain. For a moment his vision swam in front of his eyes, but he sucked in a deep inhale and shook his head, blinking hard, ordering himself to stay in the fight.

He pushed himself up onto his hands and one good knee, bracing for a blow...

Instead, hasty footsteps receded away. Then nothing. Silence. He was alone there now.

He felt a rush of gratitude not to have to keep fighting, then took three deep breaths, clenched his teeth, and rose to his feet. Carrying his weight on his good leg, he twisted his body left and right to look in all directions. Nobody was in the area at all.

He hopped back toward the stable, although he could only cover a few inches with each jump.

Thoughts of Vignette kept him going. *Where was she when that thing exploded? Where is she right now?*

43

EMBARCADERO DISTRICT

* 2:00 p.m.—6 Minutes Left *

THE PREPAREDNESS DAY PARADE began as scheduled at 1:30 p.m. and wound through the first half hour with no harm done. Vignette lost count of the number of times she powered the Harley up and down the frontage road along the Embarcadero piers and the Clock Tower.

She wove around the traffic of parade goers and among a sea of pedestrians, studying the faces. Then with a cold rush, Vignette realized she had kept the big engine at an idle for a very long time, accelerating and then braking according to breaks in the crowds, and now there was a new problem: her gas tank level. She lifted the cap on the tank, stared into it, and shifted the bike to the left and right. Almost no splash at all.

She would have to peel off the search for Mario Buda and instead look for a petrol refueling store that might be open on this day. She passed Market Street again on the return trip and this time took a right turn up the hill to seek out gasoline along upper Market Street.

She slowed to a quick walking pace while she passed through the remaining crowds. She was so focused on seeking gasoline, if not for the large suitcase carried by one man walking alone, she would not have noticed that particular person at all. But everyone else in the parade crowd carried nothing larger than random food items. *Who carries a suitcase to a parade?*

Ping! *Suitcase Man.*

She reminded herself, of course the man could be an innocent traveler looking for a hotel. But in that one vital second, Suitcase Man happened to turn in her direction, and she got a good look at his face. She watched him idly glancing around as if waiting for a friend, until the moment he noticed her motorcycle.

He casually raised his eyes to meet hers. In an instant, his were twice their normal size.

Mario Buda felt that same old sensation of ice water flushing his arteries. The awful feeling tormented him every time fear took hold. His embarrassment over this particular trait felt even worse than the cold shock. He had hated the trait, whatever caused it, all his life. But he had no control. It was just there.

In that instant, he clearly saw the wheels spinning in the American bitch's head. Too late to worry about being recognized. He whirled and hurried down the sidewalk, moving as fast as the heavy crowd would permit.

Unbelievable! Now? At this moment, now? The Dark Angel of Timing had abandoned him. There was no other way to look at it.

He realized his only option was to catch an F-Trolley up Market Street toward City Hall. If he could make it that far, then he could still accomplish what Galleani obviously failed to achieve. That much, anyway.

He struggled his way back down Market Street toward the waterfront to look for an approaching trolley, knocking parade goers aside while he made his clumsy escape. He knew better than to meet their eyes and perhaps draw them down like wolves.

In addition to recognizing the female on the motorcycle as that American bitch who traveled with the private eye, it was clear she was searching for him. What could that mean, other than she knew something about the mission? She had to. Why else seek him out?

The essence of this was evident to him. If she managed to stop him from reaching City Hall, or from at least detonating his bomb at some meaningful location, the entire mission would be stone dead.

So far in his career as a bomb maker, Mario Buda had never endured failure. And as much as he hated having his catchphrase thrown at him, it remained true. He would rather die than fail.

But now with the American bitch on his tail, he knew it. He had lost City Hall. She could call for hard men to jump him. He could never get that far.

Now to escape utter failure, he had to detonate someplace where a powerful impact was guaranteed. If only he could do that much, then although Galleani's so-called grand display had turned to farce, Buda would still claim lives and bring mayhem in a fashion his fellow travelers would appreciate.

He kept moving as fast as he could with his burden. On a less festive day, one or two of the people he knocked aside would have run him down and registered their protest with a sound beating. But his luck held. The celebratory mood of parade day padded their reactions, and the din of the crowd covered whatever was shouted after him.

And although the Dark Angel of Timing had abandoned him, his old friend the Dark Angel of Chaos was there to help. And Chaos was close, so close.

Just bring the chaos, he told himself. *Bring the chaos! Let it loose! Nobody knows what the plan is supposed to be. But they will all remember the chaos.*

Anywhere the device went off, provided it was well placed, it would make the same statement, no? The people who really mattered would recognize that statement as his. Nobody packed a pipe like Mario Buda.

And since he couldn't make it to his first choice of City Hall, a close second would logically be the Clock Tower. He turned to make his way in that direction.

It was only a couple of blocks to the Ferry Building and its great Clock Tower, probably loaded with sightseers on this parade day. But Market Street was impossible, packed. He struggled with exhaustion under his burden and from the difficult footwork of his escape. There was simply no way to make rapid progress.

The sound of his own gasping was so strong in his ears it even drowned out the approaching sound of the Harley-Davidson engine revving behind him. The distinctive rumble finally broke into his awareness when the rider nursed the bike in his direction. In seconds, the machine and its rider were floating toward him.

He didn't even turn around. He simply increased his pace to the fastest he could manage against the crowded sidewalk.

The Harley engine growled like a shrieking animal and leaped ahead, passing him and continuing on for ten yards, twenty. Then it turned. He still couldn't see it, but the mechanical growl began floating back in his direction. Herding him. Trying to push him away from the thick crowds.

Buda felt as if a giant fist was squeezing the life out of him. Everything had collapsed. The whole plan was going to hell in front of his eyes.

The sound of the motorcycle engine drifted closer in the crowd, relentless. As if nothing and no one stood in its way. He poured the last of his energy reserves into a frantic sprint toward the Ferry Building, but at that point the strength in his spindly legs played out. He could do no more than manage a slow stagger while the muscles burned and the joints screamed and the lungs begged for air.

It struck him that even this modified plan would have to be modified a second time; the Clock Tower was too far. If only he could breathe, get a few clear breaths of air, but it was too far. Too far. Waves of distracted parade goers impeded him while the damned growling motorcycle engine exercised its power to cut through endless crowds.

He took a right turn onto the oddly spelled Steuart Street, moving along the west side of Steuart just a block from the waterfront. And it was there that his very own Dark Angel of Timing revealed the perfect spot to him through the swirling mass of people.

A section of plain brick wall ran parallel to the sidewalk. A flimsy wooden newsstand was there. Everyone in the passing crowds had to pass close to the wall, and the concrete and brick surfaces would be perfect to reflect the contents of his well-packed pipe straight into the masses. Democracy for all, fair and square.

Final plan, then. Mario Buda, still in control.

He hustled to the little wooden newsstand along the wall and set the suitcase down as if it belonged there, slipped his hand inside and, operating strictly by touch and memory, set the timer to the lowest position at one minute.

He heard the big bike's engine revving again, still trying to herd him off the parade route. This time when the engine roared again, the last few human obstacles stepped out of the way, and the bike and its rider emerged before him.

Mario would have loved the luxury of a moment to meditate on whether it was chance, or perhaps the Dark Angel of Timing, secret of comedy and some say of life, which caused the motorcycle's big tough engine to chug...and then choke...and then quit.

Out of gas? *Out of gas!* He knew the sound! Who wouldn't? He would have dearly loved to scream, "Did you come all this way just to make me laugh?" But the Bomb Maker Nonpareil had better sense than to call additional attention to himself.

He sprinted south toward Mission Street. The strength returned to his legs as a second wind took over. He could feel the power to outrun her and knew that with his long lead she could not hope to catch him on foot. Now lightened of his burden, he pumped his legs forward and sprinted in hopes of escape.

It had only been seconds since he set the timer and walked away from the ticking bomb, and by then Buda knew he had already disappeared into the crowd. Now with every passing second on the clock, success was closer to his grasp. History had come through for him after all. It spared him from this fiasco by keeping him free and letting him live to fight another day.

And as for today, he still had the device to speak for him, did he not?

And any old time, now: *tick, tock, tick, tock, tick, tock...*

44

CORNER OF MARKET AND STEUART STREETS

* 2:05 p.m.—One Minute Before the Attack *

VIGNETTE PUSHED HER DEAD MOTORCYCLE into an alcove behind the brick building at the corner of Market and Steuart, near where she last spotted Mario Buda. He carried no suitcase anymore when she spotted him, but she missed the drop.

There was no way to know where the bomb was, but a burn of dread began in her belly and a tight sensation constricted her chest. It grew stronger.

At that moment a little girl on a bicycle came barreling along the sidewalk without paying much attention and had just enough awareness to skirt the fire hydrant on the street side of the sidewalk, which worked perfectly to avoid the hydrant but set her on a curving path closer to the brick wall and the newsstand.

She was looking back over her shoulder when she ran her bicycle head-long into a man buying a paper at the newsstand. They both fell on top of the suitcase along with the bike.

One second later came the sixty-second mark on the timer, and Mario

Buda's well-packed pipe detonated with a blast that ricocheted off of the brick and concrete, and—just as he predicted—sent both primary and secondary waves of shrapnel to filet everything softer than stone, brick, or steel. The brick wall and the concrete sidewalk reflected the power of the blast straight out into the crowd. Power to the People.

At the moment of detonation, the perturbed man who had been knocked over was still lying on and over the suitcase, although the girl had tumbled away. The blast killed him outright. His body somewhat shielded the girl from the shrapnel, and she was spared, in the sense that she survived with both legs blown off.

A few minutes earlier, Randall Blackburn had hobbled back to the Waverley using a board from the barn as a crutch. The throbbing in his knee was relentless, but he was glad to know the intended violence had somehow cancelled itself out. In return for his injuries: (1) no grand theft from the Mint; and (2) so far, no bombs in the parade.

But he was silently rolling toward the Embarcadero to look for Vignette when he heard the blast.

Vignette got knocked away from her bike by the shock wave, shielded by the corner of the wall just enough to escape the flying shrapnel. Red-hot metal flayed the front of the bike. Her body was protected by the angle of the blast, but she hit the street hard and her head bounced on the cobblestones.

A foghorn went off in her skull and continued to wail. She hovered on the borderline of awareness, taking in information with her eyes but unable to process it. She made it up to her hands and knees, head ringing while she stared around at the scene.

The newsstand had vanished and left carnage in its place. Torn bodies, trails of blood. Twisted things impossible to identify.

She fell back on her elbows and tried to steady her breathing while the foghorn rang inside her. A hellish scene presented so many bodies, she had no idea how many people were victims. Everywhere she looked was the same display of merciless slaughter.

Luigi Galleani walked at a brisk clip, projecting the image of being no more than a busy fellow with a lot on his mind. He knew this was the perfect pitch of attitude to project when he wanted to avoid conversations. The art was in appearing mildly tense but not too angry. Too much anger could imply a potential for violence, which would invite scrutiny.

Instead his trick was to give off the aura of being someone who was just mildly irritated but still unhappy. Maybe the kind of guy who would love to bend your ear and tell you all his problems.

As usual, it kept people away.

He had just turned up his collar and made for the train station when he heard the distant explosion. He held his breath. Yes, yes, it *could* have been a celebratory cannon blast somewhere along the parade route. But seconds later, while he gazed back toward the direction of the sound, he saw the unmistakable smoke trail.

A bomb. One bomb...

He checked his watch: six minutes after two o'clock. One stinking bomb. Nothing at all at the 1:30 starting time, and now this.

He felt as if he were drowning in a vat of vomit. His great attack had turned out to be *one bomb*, detonated thirty-six minutes late. And of course no fires at all. With the loss of the gold and his chance at financial freedom, he was going to be forced back on the journey of stump speeches and propaganda pamphlets. The contacts who had tipped him to the secret of the San Francisco gold apparently had no idea about the underground spring that drowned his grand plan. Poor research on their part.

He spat in the dust. Everyone had failed him. Every single one of them. It would have been far better to have done nothing at all.

Time to go, flee the city, flee the state. Never mind his personal bags abandoned back at the stables. He would have to travel light.

At least he had his wallet. His reputation might take some small hit but nothing he could not easily explain away. He was thankful for his own restraint in avoiding all promotion of this attack in his magazine. Some bit of good fortune had held his tongue. What was it, he wondered? Not Fate, of course. There could be no Fate, since the idea of Fate implied some form of Deity or Divine Will, did it not? One look at existence nullified that nonsense. He now felt certain in his next idle moments that he ought to spend time considering whether or not the Dark Angel of Timing, secret of comedy and some say of life, was merely the personification of dumb luck.

In which case there was nothing to do but put it up to dumb luck that he had remained silent about his great plan. Thus his failure would remain unknown. And wonderful dumb luck it was, that even as a single bomb attack, the greater fiasco would be lost in obscurity for his brothers in Europe. Those fighters had far more on their minds than a fizzled attack all the way over on the other side of the Atlantic and then on the other side of America. He assured himself distance was his friend in this.

As for the utter failure of the parade attack, and most of all the great Mint robbery, what was the hardest of the hard truths? He already knew the answer.

It was that he permitted himself to rely on empty skin-bags who passed themselves off as competent people but who predictably failed under pressure time and time again. Betrayal and more betrayal in every direction. What difference did it make whether they were driven by cowardice or greed? If everything broke down at the crucial hour, motives made no difference and the same failures were assured.

So it proved impossible to intimidate the detective into staying away. With a hint of resentful admiration, he realized the man showed himself to be the very sort of character Galleani's employers were concerned over. Stinking Americans who didn't know when to quit.

But no. The fatal flaw rested with Galleani himself, and he recognized that. His mistake lay in trusting them, honoring them with responsibilities they did not deserve. He had availed himself of mere club members, when what he needed were fanatics and their militant obedience, pre-fanned to a state of combustion.

The human race, casting infections with every exhale, held nothing else of value for him. Without his squad of fanatics, his mission would be to no purpose. The failure to confine his labor force to proven believers was a mistake to be corrected and never repeated. From now on, for admission to the Galleanists, they could each come back and apply *after* a successful kill mission on American soil carried out against populations, homes, or businesses. True fanatics were his ideal fighters. There was going to be solid work ahead for them.

Since the same people who tipped him to the gold were still in control of the banks, they would be bringing him more work opportunities. They had to. There were far too many things in this world requiring vengeance from Galleani and his partisans. Otherwise, he did not doubt that if he lacked followers, he was doomed to die long before he could take revenge on everyone who needed it.

Randall pulled the Waverley to the curb as close to the bomb site as he could get, which was a block and a half away. Chaos still reigned, with dying and injured people screaming for relief. He had only seen devastation on the streets like this years earlier, in the hours after the Great Earthquake. Now some small piece of all that loomed in front of him.

He called out to Vignette, bellowed in his strongest clear-the-bar voice, but sputtering clouds of noise distorted his words to nothing.

He possessed enough experience with lethal street challenges to reflexively stop his survival drive from overtaking him. Instead he relaxed into his body and consciously shrugged off panic. It took all his skill to make that happen.

He kept scanning through the drifting smoke trails until he spotted Vignette. A rush of relief washed over him. Vignette was well enough to be bending over an injured woman. He hurried closer and got close enough to see her tying off a tourniquet on the woman's shredded arm.

He called "Vignette!" loud enough to be certain she heard him over everything else. She glanced up, and a flash of glee crossed her face for just a moment while she realized they were both alive and on their feet.

But then she was immediately back to finishing off the tourniquet and shouting for her patient to understand she had to allow the tight bandage to remain in place because it was saving her from bleeding out.

The woman was so deeply stunned, Randall couldn't tell if she was even aware of having been harmed and that rescuers were trying to help her.

He knelt next to Vignette without a word and threw his arms around her. She turned around to meet his eyes and instantly combined her gasps for air with sobs. "Randall! Thank God! Oh my God! We were right here! I was, I mean, and those people who were over there by that newsstand, they took the blast, I think...but, but... They did it, didn't they? They did it after all! How many bombs went off? Will there...will there...be more?"

She paused to breathe. She finally allowed herself to slow down enough to connect with him eye-to-eye, at last. "...You're here."

"Yes."

"Thank God."

"Are you hurt?"

"No. But help me get another tourniquet on her. Can you tear off more fabric?" She indicated the hem of the injured woman's dress. Moments later, he had just removed a strip and was about to hand it over to Vignette when the police chief strode over with three hard men behind him.

The chief glared at them in a rage and pointed his men in their direction. "Blackburn! So it's you two again?"

The men arrived at their side, and with a nod from the chief, two snatched up Blackburn and one grabbed Vignette. "I'm told you were sniffing around down near the piers for their bombs, and now you're here! Unofficially involving yourselves."

Vignette glowered at him and fumed, "God, this is too horrible! We're here because this would have been ten times worse without us, and I saw the bomber himself! It was that Mario Buda."

"You know him?

"No, she doesn't know him, sir, and neither do I. But we both recognize him as a dangerous visitor to this city."

"...You know the man who made that bomb?"

"No, damn it! I was chasing the man who made the bomb and nearly caught up to him."

"So where is he? Where did he go?"

"I don't know that."

"You don't know that. We need to sort out what you two know from what you don't."

He then leaned close enough to Randall to whisper, "To think I'd find you here like this, Blackburn. Some kind of legend, are you? Mr. Righteous, the guy who can't be corrupted. Not so righteous now, are you?"

Vignette felt the pull of hysteria but managed to avoid crying out until after they took her away. Until then she held her eyes forward and kept her mouth shut, ignoring taunts and indecent questions hurled by the brutes among them.

There was a flurry of movement at the jailhouse, a second flurry to get her behind bars. Soon all rituals were exhausted and the flurry stampeded away from her and her little private cell. A heavy metal door clanged like one of Hell's Bells, striking her with silence like a fist.

There was nothing but her own heartbeat. It hit her then: The Thing. Solitude. A never-ending fall into a bottomless well. She knew the lesson it delivered, learned it in her early years well enough to absorb into her blood and carry it in her bones.

Back at St. Adrian's, it always started when she was grabbed up and hauled away and left to simmer in some private place to await punishment. She tried to recall whether it ever gave her any comfort to know others were also stuck in some other room, waiting.

An instant of shame flashed through her like a primer charge and set off a major convulsion. Her body bent itself forward at the waist regardless of her volition. The convulsion forced open her mouth and throat, and no matter that it felt as if she were drowning inside herself, it had her without her will.

Her convulsing body hurled the contents of her stomach out of her mouth with enough force to splatter a long trail outward on the floor. *Good. Let that greet them.*

She knew any moment now the door was going to get yanked open and rough hands would be on her. It had always been that way with the monks. She had learned it while still very small. This was how these things worked.

Mario Buda was several miles from downtown San Francisco at the Bayside Motor Carriage Company, where the salesman was glad to keep the doors open past the six o'clock closing time because he knew a mark when he saw one. Mario did his best imitation of a working man who simply wanted to treat himself to a used automobile. His story didn't fool the salesman for an instant. Experience told him this customer was in a bind and needed a motorcar right now. He wished all customers could be this way: desperate, in a rush, and ready to pay cash on the nail.

Large signs around the lot bragged about offering the best deals on the West Coast. They even dared to post a sign right outside, how their used cars were *"The Three R's! Refurbished, Refreshed, and Ready to serve you!"*

Buda specified to the eager dealer that whatever vehicle he chose to purchase had to get him all the way to New York City without a breakdown. At least as far as Chicago. No fancy electric garbage, no diesels, no steamers. He wanted a gasoline-powered road runner meant to move a person from point A to point B, and just that. That and a comfortable seat, since he expected to be behind that wheel for a good long time.

He gave up more cash than the salesman would have taken but got a workable transport out of the deal, with enough left over for gasoline stops and maybe even a few meals. He could hit union halls along the way and seek out fellow travelers. Men with the experience to appreciate that their lives were shit with nothing to look forward to beyond becoming old and infirm in a life that would still be shit when they died.

But history had indeed protected him on this day, had it not? Just as he had hoped! He was alive and free to fight another day. What difference did it make if he couldn't explain why? There was so much work to be done to bring the gift of anarchy to the world.

Because America had to fall.

45

CITY HALL

SUNNY JIM WAS WIDE-AWAKE AFTER his three-hour refresher nap and two more bottles of that new soft drink, cola something. His secretary watched him polish off the second bottle with a wary eye.

"I heard that stuff has stimulants in it and that's why it gives you energy."

"Used to."

"Some people say it still does."

"Maybe. I like it. Like the taste. Bubbly."

"Yes, but should I remove the rest of it from the office for a while?"

"Not until we get Blackburn and his daughter up here. They might want one. You can bet they're tired out by now."

"All right. The jail just sent word they're releasing them both on your orders."

"Full apology to them?"

"Oh yes." She leaned a bit closer. "It just killed the chief to do it, though. He's still determined to bring them in on the charges for some reason."

"Mm-hm. Nope. Not gonna be any charges against them at all. These people are of far too much use to the city for that nonsense." He grinned. "This new 'strong mayor' thing fits me like a glove, when it works."

The sound of footsteps in the outer office caused Sunny Jim and his secretary to look up in time to see Randall and Vignette escorted in by several large police officers. The pair's clothing was in shambles, and both looked exhausted.

"There we are!" enthused Sunny Jim. "Come in, come in, sit down if you like. Have a bottle of this remarkable tonic. Full apologies to you for the arrests. I had a man bring your car around from the police impound and bring it to the front. It's right outside."

"Mr. Mayor, Vignette and I were trying to help the wounded when we were dragged to jail and interrogated."

Vignette could barely wait for him to finish. "That's right! Those people needed us! How could the police take us—"

"Yes! Yes! Terrible! And I got you out of that jail as soon as I heard! Would have been sooner, but I was sleeping myself. They didn't want to wake me, I'm afraid. All my fault. Terrible day. Lots of confusion. Innocent dead and wounded people. A tragedy, to be sure."

His face lit up, and his bright smile returned. "But! Also a tragedy far smaller than what might have been without the two of you! The city owes you more than we can repay." He lowered his voice and continued, "Our chief seems to have been inspired by outside forces to arrest you and try to draw you into this. I've put a stop to that."

"Why would anyone do that?"

"Your reputation. Honesty and all, not taking bribes. They didn't want you sniffing around." He laughed out loud. "Called that one right, though, didn't they. Eh?"

"Sir," Blackburn began with visible control, "please, sir. Half an hour ago, I was told they suspected me in the death of young Will Mummery, and the bombing of the parade. Now here we are, and it seems as though there's no such problem. So you understand if I'm confused?"

Sunny Jim clapped his hands together in his best get-this-party-started style. "I do understand, Detective! We're all confused. Politics, local, state, national, international, war, peace, I mean, who isn't?"

"Sir. Jim. That's not what I—"

"Now *you* are a hero, Miss, ah, Detective Nightingale! And I would sincerely love to shout it to the world with the same fervor I used in..." He took time to give a meaningful stare at each of them, right into their eyes. "...Pulling you out of jail. I just hope you will understand me when I tell you we can't speak of any of this, now or later. We would only encourage more attacks. These crazy bastards are getting worse all the time."

Air escaped from Vignette's lungs so hard it made a sound like "*Bwuh!*" The warning glance Blackburn threw at her was hot enough to ignite wood.

Sunny Jim smiled at Vignette and looked into her eyes with respect. "But I know you sacrificed, and you prevented a disaster that would have been terrible news all over the world."

For once neither Blackburn nor Vignette had a word to say. It was like waiting for the gallows to drop. Sunny Jim continued, "It's why I am insisting the City absorb the full cost of rebuilding your home. Right there on your land. Same house plan. Same color, if you like."

Vignette whirled to Blackburn. "See?"

He glared at her. "Not now."

"We both know it's the right—"

"Not now!"

Sunny Jim economized the conversation. "You should also know, Detective Blackburn..." He took a deep breath. "We will also say nothing to the world about the Mint." He quickly held up the flat of his hand to deflect discussion. "Because nothing took place there. Naturally, the horses and wagons are already gone. Public won't notice wagonloads of landfill being brought around to the stables. Enough to fill a tunnel. The Yerba Buena Hauling Company will be restored to normal condition."

"Have you told the owner?"

"Why would I do that?"

"...Ah."

"Nothing took place there, Detective, because it is of utmost importance not to give the world an image of weakness in such a place as our very own San Francisco Mint. You see that?"

Vignette appeared to have thoughts of her own on that, so Blackburn jumped in, "Yes. We do, truth be told. Certain things, I guess, constitute information that could never do any good."

"Thank you for that. I know what you feel; it hurts to let go of it, doesn't it? But thank you. Thank you. It's beyond politics. Now, as to your freelance work for the City in the future—and there'll be plenty of it—on each assignment, we'll give you, well, not free rein, but let's say 'a wide latitude' in your methods."

"Is that even legal?" asked Vignette in a tone of mock innocence. Randall glared at her; she was having too much fun. But nonetheless, she threw in, "It sounds like perhaps not."

Sunny Jim chuckled an easy little laugh and replied, "Sometimes the law gets used against us, Miss Detective. Sometimes we do it in reverse."

"Detective Nightingale."

"Of course, my apologies."

She smiled and spoke gently, almost with fondness, "Detective Nightingale."

"Detective. Nightingale. Most of the time when the law gets used against us, that's simply unfortunate and there's nothing we can do. But once in a while, there are matters so egregious, so terrible they require a strong response, and yet ordinary methods will not work. And innocent people suffer for it."

Vignette smiled at that. "And when that sort of thing is what you're dealing with and you call us, our investigative techniques are left up to us? They are not a problem for you?"

Sunny Jim matched her smile. "I see you are a plain-spoken person, so you will appreciate me saying: not if nobody hears about it." He laughed out loud at that, then leaned close enough to finish in a soft voice, "So listen here: your guardian over here—"

"Partner. We're partners in the agency."

"Right, right. I was told your *partner* was down in the jail regaling my sergeant with tales of this so-called 'moving things around' work you do. Apparently, it had a lot to do with preventing things from being far worse. I am a practical man, and I see no reason to object if it gets used in stopping other terrible things."

Vignette spread her arms wide and grinned. "I love this town."

Sunny Jim kept going. "Glad to hear it, Detective Nightingale. So remember that when I tell you this: Warren Billings and Thomas Moody are still going to be charged with the bombing. The prosecutors have nothing on your Luigi Galleani or Mario Buda."

Vignette coughed hard. "*Our* Luigi and Buda?"

"Outside my authority," he hurried on. "Outside my authority, and furthermore there's no evidence against the two, I'm told. What can I say? District attorney is an appointed position serving at the pleasure of the state governor."

"The governor's in this, too?" Randall shook his head.

"Detective Blackburn, ten people were killed by that bomb today. Forty more injured, some maimed for life. Rest easy that Billings and Mooney will be tried, found guilty, and sentenced to die. They're already suspected of a long list of crimes we can't prove, but the D.A. is certain he can prove this."

Randall lowered his voice to a confidential level and said, "I don't know anything about those two men, Mr. Mayor, their names never came up for us. My concern is Jacob Prohaska. He'll face arrest for his involvement in the murder of young Will Mummery, won't he? Prohaska's all dirtied up in this somehow."

"Oh! Well. There'll be an investigation. Lots of hot air and papers blowing around. Problem being, however, Jacob Prohaska isn't local; he's an officer of United States Customs." Sunny Jim held up a telegram. "This little missive came over the wire this morning. We've been called off any investigation of him. Federal level, you realize. Washington, DC, and all."

"Mr. Mayor, that boy was only twelve—"

"Street urchin. You've seen hundreds of them, haven't you? Ne'er-do-well."

"Maybe so, but his father helped us—"

"Demon rum, Detective. Do you see this daddy around? Do you know where he is? Because I know. He's wherever the nearest bottle of hard stuff happens to be."

"Your adjutant, then. I think it's possible that Prohaska shot Harold Saunders under orders from his bosses. As opposed to the suicide theory."

"Detective, at a time like this with a mountain of tasks ahead of us, please don't add to the pile. Prohaska may have killed Saunders, which may or may not be a bad thing."

"Come again?"

"What do we get if we win, Detective? What if we prove Prohaska killed Saunders? Maybe we also get him on suspicion of killing the messenger boy. His trial will be here, in the midst of a city so broken we don't even know which police officers I can trust to do their jobs. So during the trial, the judge receives a directed verdict in the middle of the night, and the next day Prohaska goes home. I am like a carpenter trying to build a house with broken and rusted tools. Nothing works."

He straightened up tall and slapped Randall on the shoulder as if they were two men just back from battle.

"We just have to hunker down, Detective!"

"Hunker down, sir?"

"The key to longevity is peace among nations and all that. Jobs to protect! Hides to save!"

"There's a lot of unfinished business here, Mr. Mayor."

"Ha! Unfinished business is another name for politics, my friend."

"I have no idea what that means."

Sunny Jim gave him one of his sunniest smiles, the one that reliably worked on most of the people, most of the time.

"But that's just it, you see! The meaning *changes*. It's a shifting land-scape!" He dropped his voice to a confidential level. "Randall, can I call you Randall? You should forget it now. It's politics, Randall. That's all it is."

Vignette piloted the Waverley with enough skill to keep away from the draft wagons, the spewing trucks, and the worst of the horse piles that mined the road like embedded stink bombs. Her brain ran on overdrive while her body felt drained, as if she could sleep for days, or better yet, disappear in the mountains until spring, there to hibernate for months.

Live on my fat, she grinned while she thought it. *It might last half a day...*

Randall sat slumped into the passenger seat, holding onto his injured knee and looking distant and distracted. That was all right with her. It wasn't often she had the chance to be his caretaker.

It was a glaring contrast to the darkness of the thick wet blanket that fell over her the moment she learned of her brother's death. It had seemed like an uncurable condition. But this evening while she piloted the car to their hotel, she tried to guess at how much it would cost to reclaim the Harley from the police impound and have it repaired from the damage done by the bomb's shrapnel.

Because the freedom of the ride was a gift to her from Shane, and she was certainly going to get back on that motorbike. Someday. Just not now. Not today. She and Randall had to get back to their lives, had to rebuild their home.

46

THE "SILENT CITY" OF COLMA

* September 1st, 7:30 p.m. *

FIVE WEEKS LATER, RANDALL AND VIGNETTE made their way to the "silent city" of Colma, some dozen miles south of the San Francisco waterfront. Many generations of San Franciscans were buried there in the years since the limited graveyards in San Francisco filled up. Colma now had a population of the dead many times that of their living residents.

Shane rested there, in that city of graveyards. He lay with people from every station in life. The cemetery was a place good enough for Wyatt Earp and his family. The Masons had their own section, along with the Odd Fellows, the Italians, and a host of ethnic and professional categories of former folks.

On this day, the finished tombstone had finally arrived and was being installed while Vignette and Randall watched. The granite slab was large, but the inscription was simple. *Here lies S.F.P.D. Officer Shane Nightingale, 1894-1916. Beloved brother and son, gone too soon.*

Now while they stood together with only the stones surrounding them, Randall stood at attention with his face hard while Vignette cried without making any sound. Finally she spoke out. "Oh, God, he would have loved to be here to help us against those monsters. We could have done twice the patrols. We might have stopped that last bomb."

"No argument from me. This was just the kind of battle he relished. Probably part of his reason for joining the force."

Vignette smiled for the first time that day. She reached up to touch his cheek. "No, Randall, it wasn't. He wanted to be you. And if he couldn't be you, he wanted your respect."

His composure broke, and he had to turn away. After a few moments, he turned back to her with a sad smile. "He already was a great officer. He was a real one. We know that. He just wasn't granted enough time to prove it to the world."

Vignette exhaled hard. "Don't we have any way to persuade the police to go after Galleani for ordering Shane's murder? How much damage is this man going to be allowed to do?"

"They can't handle the caseload they have here in town, let alone go after some international criminal who is long gone by now." He stepped to her and embraced her without giving her time to retreat.

With his lips close to her ear, he whispered, "So many people are alive today because of you. Without your help, this could have been the worst thing since the Great Earthquake. You have to think about all the lives you helped to save. It's how people survive this line of work."

He left his arm over her shoulder while he turned toward the gravestone. "I know your brother would be so proud of you, Vignette. So proud."

"But at some point we *will* find a way to go after Galleani and his bomb maker, correct? Certainly if we can't make the authorities act, we can deliver some sort of justice ourselves, right? Somewhere else but here."

"In another city?"

"Of course."

"Another state?"

"Why not?"

"So a private manhunt, then?" Randall looked down at the ground. "Why, Vignette. That would be illegal." The corners of his mouth barely twitched. To Vignette this meant a mission to get justice for Shane was already written in large letters in his mind, just waiting until the day came when they could take action.

Later, so early in the morning as to be an obscene hour for anything but sleep, Randall sat in his hotel room and stared into the darkness outside the window. A copy of the *Chronicle* lay on the floor, peppered with news of shocking events overseas. Fortunes made on misery with the manufacture of machinery and materials of war, tales of more people getting away with more crimes than the mind could comprehend.

How were the victims supposed to prevail? It was as if the cloud of war was made of locusts, and all one could do was to stand back and watch them devour everything in their path.

He sat, seeing nothing. His thoughts boiled.

How were he and Vignette supposed to get on with their lives? He had paid for young Will's grave to spare the boy from eternity in some potter's field. And yes, the house would be rebuilt by the city. There was nothing stopping him and Vignette from continuing to function as a PI agency.

But he had no illusions that allowing the City to throw cases his way would be anything but a dangerous habit, forming a growing dependency upon the authorities. *No to that.* He and Vignette would have to survive on their own, free of any backroom deals.

The real obstacle for both of them was having had so little time together to mourn the loss of Shane before this case broke loose. Now with the home they shared with him having been destroyed, all they had left was their shrunken family and a mental image of how they wanted to live.

As for private detective work, it had to continue. He might be able to succeed at some other occupation, but Vignette was far too outspoken to be employable, and she was certainly not about to marry herself off to some man in return for being supported. He had noticed her tendency to refer to the general public as "normals." Her combination of personal quirks and inner turmoil placed her outside that group and belied any chance of a stable life in what others called polite society.

What they had left was this little family of two. After having Shane torn from them and getting their house blown out of existence, after hearing the gunshot that killed an old friend who tried to help them, all they had left was one another. He saw no choice but to make it a priority in his life to silently block any efforts on her part to pursue Mario Buda or Luigi Galleani on Shane's behalf. Such revenge would indeed be sweet, so much so the thought of it nearly buckled his knees. But he would move Heaven and Hell to give her a fair chance at life, and that did not include murderous revenge. Not for her, at least.

He saw himself as too damaged to worry over what such a mission would do to him. Shane would be avenged one day.

Faint light from outside let him know he had ruminated away the night. But in the next moment, his head snapped to attention like someone trying to stay awake—*wait!*

There was something. Something missing. Empty space. Something definitely missing, what is it? Something usually there...

It hit him. No scream.

Vignette's room was next to his. The walls were too thin to keep him from hearing her when she inevitably cried out in her sleep. But on this night, for the first time, the quiet had remained unbroken. No scream.

The night terrors only occurred during dark hours. She always slept easy once morning began to break. Yet she had been right there in the next room all night long and made no sounds of torment at all.

He wondered, had something fundamental shifted inside of her? He could only hope it was true. He already realized she was more confident in herself in the wake of this case, with a strengthened sense of her abilities. Now he dared to wonder if something had quieted her inside. Oh, that would be so fine.

Because he had never heard her sleep undisturbed through a single night, not one time since she arrived all those years ago as a traumatized runaway. And now it was morning without having heard a peep from her all night.

A full night gone by in peace.

One down, then...

In the world of sleep and of dreams that bring no anxieties, Vignette's persistent curse of nightly torment was thrust aside by sheer elation. In that moment, the agony of her brother's absence was gone. Instead she was soaking in joy.

Somehow her visit to his grave and the finality of the new stone had served to set her memories of Shane free. And since time and reality are not captive to dreams, for her it was not really deep in the night, nor was she alone beneath the blankets. Instead she was bathed in broad daylight and barreling through Golden Gate Park on the back of Shane's motorbike while both of them screamed with laughter.

Even though Shane always maintained full command of his bike, he loved to tease her by seeking out hills to attack and bumps to fly over. To Vignette it was the best amusement park ride in the world. He seemed to know exactly how far to go for thrills without putting her in any real fear.

She kept one hand on the back of her seat and the other on his shoulder while they roared down South Drive and blasted past the Arboretum. For Vignette, the most wonderful part of having a true and trusted friend was the feeling of experiencing something powerful together, understanding what the other person felt almost as clearly as you experienced it yourself.

And suddenly the road, all the roads, the entire park, became magically deserted. Empty and quiet. The world's greatest backyard now belonged to them. The dream's magic did not end with providing an empty park on a perfect day; it also lifted the laws of gravity. They took jumps coming off of hilltops, clearing forty feet at the crest, then a hundred.

Her eyes watered from the wind and this blurred her vision, but Shane wore goggles and saw clearly enough to steer them out of harm's way, which he did every few seconds.

Happily, he had always been good about accepting her refusal to wear goggles. Shane was the only person in the world who knew why she never allowed anything over her eyes.

Now he called back to her above the sound of the engine, "You ready to try it this time?"

"I don't know! I don't know about this!"

He guffawed at that. "Yes, you do!"

"No!" she shrieked in mock terror, which convinced him.

"You want to! You're dying to!" He twisted the throttle hard and made the bike leap for emphasis. Vignette rewarded him with a fake yelp of fear and then laughed.

He kept at it. "You already handle a bicycle! You've got balance! And you've watched me do this!" He twisted the throttle harder this time, raising the front wheel and holding it high.

The dream made a quick shift to the bottom of a hill. They stood next to the parked bike. Shane pointed at the driver's seat. "Hop on. I'll hold onto *you* this time!" They laughed at the joy of actually doing this dangerous thing, both climbing on a powerfully built motorbike with her driving for the first time.

And then they were both on the bike and her hands were on the handlebars and the engine was rumbling between her legs. There was no one else she would allow to sit directly behind her, pressing his chest into her back, holding one arm around her waist. With anyone else, male or female, the sense of danger would overwhelm her. But this was Shane, and it felt oh-so-fine to have such safe human closeness soaking into her from her brother.

When she hesitated before starting off, he leaned forward and whispered to her, "You're almost as strong as I am, little sister. We're a matched pair."

"I see, *almost*?"

"Twist that thing!" he screamed, laughing.

She accelerated so hard the rear wheel threw up a spray of dirt and grass behind them. She ignored the road and headed straight up the steep grassy hill rising before them. Shane matched her cries with his, and they whooped in sheer defiance of every danger in the world.

———

The next morning, Vignette awoke with a wide smile on her face. The smile stayed in place while she got dressed and ready for the day. The smile remained while she knocked on Randall's door and blithely informed him she would be out on an errand until lunchtime. The smile persisted while she took the long trolley ride to Dudley Perkins's motorcycle dealership over on South Van Ness Avenue.

An hour later, thanks to some generous dealer financing, she drove her shiny new Harley-Davidson back to their hotel. This one had a bigger engine—and a sidecar.

Gold in Peace, Iron in War
Book #4 in the Nightingale Detective series

A talented detective duo must unmask a sinister child smuggling ring and expose the corruption in a world rocked by war.

Four and a half years after the terrorist bombing plot of 1916, expert detective Randall Blackburn is ready to face his toughest case yet. When a San Francisco mayor recruits him and his adopted daughter Vignette Nightingale to bust a horrifying child smuggling ring, Randall plunges into a sinister investigation with roots far deeper than he could have ever imagined.

As they begin to peel back the layers of mystery behind the so-called "Orphan Trains," Randall and Vignette piece together the shocking truth behind an underground railroad with ties across the Atlantic. Determined to stop the ruthless practice and bring down the culprits, the detective duo must use all of their wits to expose the corruption that lurks in the shadows.

But there are powerful figures who would rather keep the Orphan Trains a secret... and Randall quickly finds himself locked in a deadly battle to unmask the shady people who have crept into the upper echelons of power.

Get your copy today at
severnriverbooks.com/series/the-last-nightingale

ACKNOWLEDGMENTS

My deepest thanks to Lindsay Guzzardo, fiction representative with Martin Literary Management, for being among this book's first readers and an enthusiastic representative of both it and the entire Blackburn-Nightingales series. Her insight was instrumental in the developmental stage of the manuscript. Every writer hopes for such support and I am grateful for it.

My thanks to Severn River Publishing for taking a chance on this series, a story of two broken people in a nonromantic relationship whose mutual love makes them a formidable pair.

And as always, I acknowledge Sharlene Martin's sense of story, setting, and character, in giving me a safe and reliable sounding board for ideas, no matter how off the mark they may be.

Worth so much more than mere gold and jewels.

ABOUT THE AUTHOR

Anthony Flacco is the New York Times and international bestselling author of *Impossible Odds: The Kidnapping of Jessica Buchanan and her Dramatic Rescue by SEAL Team Six,* which won the USA Book News Award for Best Autobiography of 2013. His *Tiny Dancer* was selected by Reader's Digest as their 2005 Editor's Choice for the magazine's commemorative 1000th Issue, and he received the 2009 USA Books News True Crime Award for *The Road Out of Hell: Sanford Clark and the True Story of the Wineville Murder.* Flacco's *The Last Nightingale*, book one of the Nightingale Detective series, was originally released to acclaimed reviews including a NYT rave, and was nominated by the International Thriller Writers (ITW) as one of the top five original paperback thrillers for 2007. Anthony resides in the beautiful Pacific Northwest.

anthonyflacco@severnriverbooks.com

Sign up for Anthony Flacco's reader list at
severnriverbooks.com/authors/anthony-flacco

Printed in the United States
by Baker & Taylor Publisher Services